THE DRAGON'S MANSERVANT

SORCERER OF BAD EXAMPLES
BOOK 1

BILL MCCURRY

BOOKS BY BILL MCCURRY

DEATH'S COLLECTOR SERIES

Novels

Death's Collector

Death's Baby Sister

Death's Collector: Sorcerers Dark and Light

Death's Collector: Void Walker

Death's Collector: Sword Hand

Death's Collector: Dark Lands

Novellas

Wee Piggies of Radiant Might

SORCERER OF BAD EXAMPLES COLLECTION

Novels

The Dragon's Manservant

The Assassin's Dragon (forthcoming)

Here is the sailor, home from the sea,
and the hunter home from the hill.

—Robert Louis Stevenson

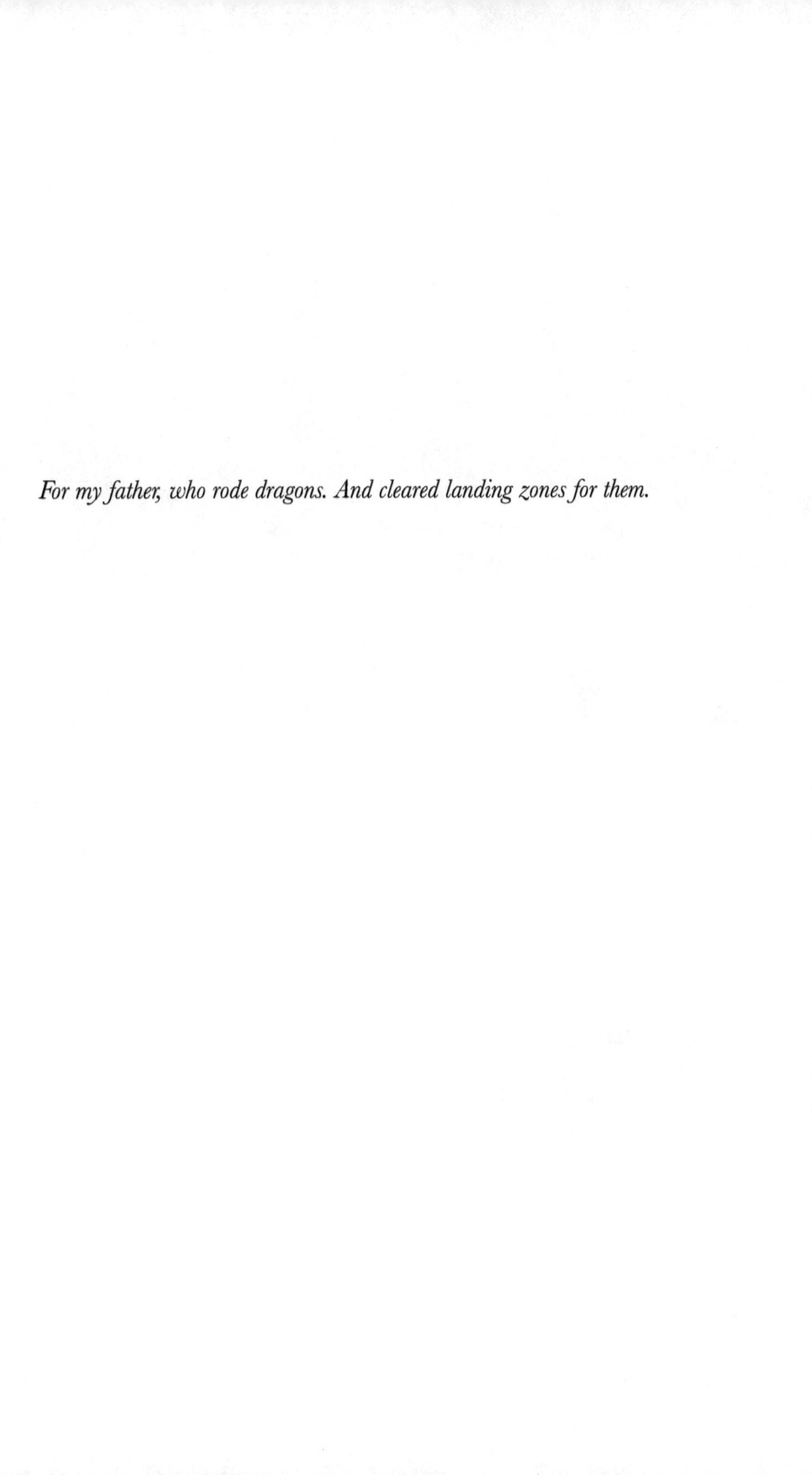

For my father, who rode dragons. And cleared landing zones for them.

ACKNOWLEDGMENTS

None of my books would be possible without the support of my wife, Kathleen, who is my alpha reader and has often warned me away from poor choices. She has also refrained from stabbing me in my sleep, even though I must have deserved it many times.

This book was made immeasurably better by the generous and sharp-eyed beta readers who often made suggestions that led to entirely new scenes (and that killed others). They are: J. Russell Bailey, Jean Beard, Diane Catanzaro, Morgan Chalut, Stephen Clingman, Michelle McLaren, Reed Richmond, and Bobbe Rose. They have my sincere thanks.

Although my father passed away before I published my first book, I want to acknowledge him and his support. He had a big heart and a deep knowledge of publishing. He told me that if I wanted to make a lot of money as a writer, I should write books about curing erectile dysfunction. That was more enlightening advice than it sounded at first.

I also want to thank my editor, Shaya Raquel. She has taught me a great deal and was the first person who said, "That's worth publishing."

The gods didn't send me to hell. I chose to live there. In fact, I went because the gods didn't want me there.

Nobody called it hell. They called it the Dark Lands, where gods can be killed, and I never aged, and both are less fun than they sound. I lived for seventy years in that terrible place, but to be honest, I was the most terrible thing there.

The only things worth a damn in the Dark Lands are death and love, and in that respect, they are about like any other place a person could live. Once I made the Dark Lands my home, I killed everyone who arrived there, as I had promised I would. I also lost everybody I loved. So, when I, Bib the sorcerer, call it hell, I am speaking with authority.

On my last day in the Dark Lands, I promised my wife I'd stop complaining about the cold and the enormous number of murders. Once in a while, she would gently point out that regular people didn't complain about the sun back in the places where regular people lived.

I had made her that promise many times before and broke it every time, but that didn't stop me from making it again. With the promise made, I gazed out over the mist-streaked, broken lowlands of this realm. A great deal of it was covered in soft but soggy black grass stretched like a nightmare carpet between gray trees so pale you almost expected to see through them.

For a while, I tried to whistle a song I remembered liking, although I had forgotten the tune thirty years ago. I wrung some water from my hat, noted the twenty-one people coming to kill me, and kicked a few rocks off the bridge. Almost by habit I muttered, "Nobody can atone in a place where gods have died."

My wife would laugh at me for being a grim whiner whenever I said such things. She'd say that atonement only seemed hard to me because I wasn't giving it proper effort. She was a cheery woman who poked fun at ominous sentiments, as if that could make them untrue.

I counted the slats beneath my feet on the misty Dark Lands bridge, even though I had counted them thousands of times before. The bridge was the truest and most substantial thing in the realm, one of those mystical bridges too profound and ancient to have a name. It would stand until the realm was destroyed, but it appeared so frail that a stern fart might demolish it.

Like many unworldly bridges, this one had not been built to reach from one place to another. It was meant to kill people who tried to cross it. No traveler was allowed to pass over this weed-draped, dripping wooden span unless he killed the Bridge Guardian.

In this realm, that was me.

The honor of bridge guardianship was why I was the person standing there on the bridge with water oozing into my boots. It's why I had a lot of time to think about things, probably too much time. It was why the former guardian had trained me to be as deadly as my personal limitations would allow.

My father had never expected this for me. He had expected me to catch fish, drink, have babies, argue with my neighbors, and drown in the ocean. I smiled at how disappointed in me he would have been, just as the twenty-one killers reached the hillside and started the damp, slippery climb toward the bridge.

Many of the travelers who reached the bridge wanted to talk for a while, asking who I was or what I wanted. Some asked me riddles, as if stumping me would make me surrender, or hurl myself off the bridge, or give them magic trousers. I couldn't give less of a crap about riddles. I told all those people the most fantastical lies I could think of, because my policy is to never tell a stranger something that might be true.

The twenty-one killers sounded as if they were progressing well, so I strolled sixty feet through the mist to the other end of the bridge. It wasn't spacious. Two people holding hands could reach out and touch the slick, wooden railings with their fingertips as they crossed.

I liked to let people advance onto the bridge so they might feel they were accomplishing something before they died. Well, that's a lie. I liked them to traipse onto the bridge unopposed so they'd be overconfident and easier to kill. I didn't care what they felt.

When I heard my twenty-one visitors reach the other end of the bridge, I stepped forward onto the slick, wooden slats. After three steps through murk that was becoming fog, I hesitated. Then with my sword drawn, I padded farther out onto the bridge.

I halted when a humanlike form showed through the dimness. The form then called out in a hollow voice, "Stop there!"

I answered, "I had already stopped, so you wasted that command, didn't you? Maybe you'd like to order me to do some other thing."

After a pause, the creature chuckled and the mist eddied, showing a tall, wide-shouldered figure that was fully cloaked. Although this realm was always chilly, fighting in a full cloak is a ridiculous pain in the ass, no matter how many fanciful drawings of assassins one may see. He grunted, "Now."

Two men and two women raced around him toward me, silent apart from boots slapping on the wet bridge. The closest held a sword behind him, nearly hidden but ready to strike. At almost the same time, a man wearing a collection of gray cloth held together by mats of dirt charged me on the other side, swinging a two-headed axe.

The swordsman intended to feint at my eyes and then slash my legs. I felt sure of it since a few hundred others had attacked me in just that way over the years. My slice was so small and quick that I probably seemed to do almost nothing while he ran his arm onto my blade. I twisted and sliced his neck just deep enough to kill as I was turning toward his axe-swinging friend.

I didn't recognize specifically what this man intended to do with his axe, but the general movement was clear. I shifted right to avoid the swing while at the same moment thrusting into him below the left arm. It was a killing blow that collapsed him. He and his companion tumbled together onto the slats.

A brown-haired woman had followed just behind these men, her hair held back by a white hat, and now she stalked me while swinging two curved swords. She kept her eyes on me and didn't glance at her friend, a tall, pale woman, who sprinted past holding her sword low. I stepped in, knocked the pale woman's sword aside, and cut her leg deeply enough to kill.

That put me halfway to the other woman, so with the same swing I cut one of her swords in two, close to the hilt. I had destroyed her three companions in a few seconds. She backed away, blinking. I lunged and thrust into her shoulder before withdrawing. She cried out as she staggered against the bridge railing, still alive.

The cloaked creature glanced back and forth between the dying and wounded. "Well, crap." Then he threw off his cloak.

I paused. "Kremm! The God of Death's most boring son! I haven't had a demigod show up in forever. I think most of the gods don't know that you exist, Kremm, but I heard a couple say that you're brave. They also said you're as dumb as a goat's scrotum."

Kremm raised his sickle that burned with blue fire, and he boomed like a drum, "Who took your arm, you dog?" He pointed at the stump of my left arm.

I stepped back and raised my eyebrows. "Dog? Hold on, give me a second to pick up what's left of my ego."

"Trust you to say something sarcastic when we should be fighting." Kremm laughed with astounding beauty. Most demigods were breathtaking. This one's clean-shaven face with its soft blue eyes and heroic chin was a smidge away from perfection. He took a powerful stance, dressed in a long burgundy coat over a silver shirt and trousers almost too bright to look at.

Kremm wore a golden helmet that might have been the most ignorant-looking headgear I had ever seen. It was fashioned like a wave as wide as his shoulders and just as high. Sharks, whales, lobsters, walruses, and all manner of sea life had been worked into it, with an octopus at the crown flinging five tentacles up in the air.

Compared to some demigods, Kremm was a modest dresser.

Shrugging, I pointed my sword at his left eye and, with great deliberation, lowered it to point at his crotch.

Kremm bellowed, "Swarm him!"

I saw soldiers clustered behind him. None of them moved.

"I said pile onto him!" Kremm's spit flew.

Three brave ones edged forward. I whipped my sword to drive them back behind Kremm, although I knew I should kill them instead. I brought my sword point back in line with Kremm's body and accidentally swung my arm straight through his burning sickle. Then I watched my right arm up to just above the elbow fall bloody onto the slick bridge. I couldn't imagine why I hadn't seen his weapon.

Kremm pointed down at my former arm. "Did you plan on using that?" he asked before giggling.

I shouted a few fetid names at Kremm as I backed away bleeding. A glance at the stump told me I probably wouldn't bleed to death. The demigoddess Parrifar, Kremm's walking rat's nest of a cousin, had whacked my left arm off when I killed her years ago. Without arms, I was forced to ignore this wound and just bleed.

Staggering back across the bridge, my back bumped against a pyramid of skulls. I tried to smile at Kremm with dash and defiance, but that failed when a dozen skulls tumbled down the wall to smack my shoulders and head.

Over the years, I had stacked the heads of my victims in great pyramids throughout the realm, and I concentrated them around the bridge. I didn't know whether they scared anybody away, but if I showed up in this dim, dank realm to fight a semi-mythical guardian, those heads would scare the hell out of me. Not that I wanted to scare them just to scare them. I really wished folks would stay home, drink too much, and cheat with their neighbors' spouses like regular people.

Hell, right now I wished I could do that too.

While I shrugged off skulls and Kremm laughed, his surviving soldiers shook their weapons, cheered, and insulted me.

"Murderer." Kremm addressed me by the stupid name the gods had given me. "You have been a worthy foe these many years." He spoke in polite, precise tones.

"You mean I've mashed your kind under my thumb like bugs." I managed a decent smile this time and took a couple of deep breaths.

He dipped his head. "All of that has ended, has it not? An era has closed, and I have closed it." He waved at his soldiers and called out, "Grab him!" The men shied away from him but began organizing themselves. Kremm puffed up like a quail. "I'll take him home to Father Krak as a prize." He flourished his weapon.

I said, "I'll bet the Father of the Gods likes me better than he likes you."

"Hah!"

"Are you angling to become God of Death? Krak already offered me the job, and I turned him down." I winked.

"Hah!" Kremm said with less fervor.

Four men trotted toward me, one carrying a rope. Twenty seconds of trips, kicks, and stomps later, two of them lay with broken necks, one was crawling away fast, and the fourth had dropped the rope to run.

"Kremm, I've killed more men with my feet than you've found women who could bear to sleep with you." That was an awful lie, but it sounded good. Sweat was running into my eyes and off my chin, and I felt light-headed. I shook my head to throw off the sweat.

"Cowards!" Kremm stretched out and whacked the running

soldier, knocking him over the bridge railing into the gorge. "You puling filth!" he screamed at the others. "Shoot him with arrows!"

A soldier cowered. "We weren't ordered to bring bows, Your Magnificence."

Kremm stared at his feet and then sighed. "Very well. At least find my father's sword. But don't touch it!"

After a silence, the same soldier asked, "What sword do you mean, Your Magnificence?"

"The God of Death's sword, snot brain! It's famous!"

Soldiers scattered around the bridge and even peered over the railing into the gorge. "We don't see a sword, Your Magnificence."

Kremm yelled as he joined the search, "All you bouncing turds must be blind. It's white with black smoke floating off the blade. The Murderer wouldn't leave it unguarded."

I slid down to sit with my back against the wall of skulls, trying not to go into shock. "Look past that slick place on the plains over there, Kremm," I called out, resting my chin on my knees. "That's where your father last saw that sword while I was killing him with it."

Kremm would never find that sword, even if he searched until the Gods' Realm crumbled. I kept it hidden by magic in a tiny space between the realms, outside normal places. I had put my mark on the space, and nobody could find the sword there but me. So far, at least.

I could call the sword to me at any moment I wanted, but since I had no hands, it would fall straight onto the ground. If I called it now to kill Kremm, the best I could hope for was him tripping over it and choking to death on a loose jawbone.

Even without hands, I could fling the sword by magic a few pathetic, unaimed feet from its hidden space. I might be able to strike Kremm if he walked slowly up to me and stood still for a few seconds to admire my wretchedness.

Well, it was my best chance to kill the bastard who had just killed me.

I had long ago given up the ability to heal by sorcery. It had seemed a wise choice at the time, the price for ending a war between the atrocious gods and their arrogant, realm-crossing enemies. Now I glanced at my stump and wondered whether I had been all that wise. Maybe I had mistaken my normal conceit and stubbornness for wisdom.

Kremm was still snarling and screeching at his soldiers. I shouted, "Hey, Krak said you would never be God of Death. Maybe God of Oozing Diseases."

"Quiet!" he yelled, not even a little polite anymore.

I saw that, like most demigods, Kremm had a phenomenal ego and was easy to bait. "I admire your hat," I said. "So redolent of the seas and appropriate since your mother was a dirty-toed fishmonger who couldn't read and gaped when she walked."

Kremm spun toward me. "Shut up! Shut up, or I'll cut you to pieces!"

"Now, what did the God of War say about you?" I went on: "I believe he said you're a floppy-crotched, snotty, empty helmet unfit to carry a scrub brush into battle. I didn't say that, mind you." I nodded. "But I agree with it."

With a sound like a half dozen charging boars, Kremm ran toward me, his flaming sickle raised.

I nearly mistimed it. Kremm swung his weapon, and I jerked aside just as I flung the sword into his chest. The sickle sliced a deep cut along my jaw. The God of Death's sword poked into Kremm's chest, not deep enough for a regular sword to kill. But the demigod's chest withered around the wound and then outward, puckering and desiccating his whole body in a second. Kremm's husk smacked into me as I sat there.

The soldiers stared as I clambered to my feet. I couldn't hold my jaw wound, so my neck and shoulder must have looked like somebody had cut off my head. Well, it would just make me more terrifying.

I faced the soldiers. "Tell Krak and the rest that I can still slaughter the nastiest they send. I have ghost arms wielding ghost weapons!" I wasn't sure what that meant, but it sounded appalling. "Normally, I'd kill you all, but you may flee if you carry my message!" I might as well let them flee, because if I chased them, I'd pass out.

When the soldiers had taken just a few steps, I shouted, "Wait! This conflict has marred the symmetry of my fine pyramid of skulls. Some of your friends are probably in that pile, so I know you must want to tidy it up before you go."

The soldiers scrambled to gather fallen skulls and replace them with care, if not with too much logic.

I gave them a profound nod. "You may go." The dismissal lost something without arm gestures, but everybody understood. They ran, leaving behind their dead friends and their dead friends' heads.

I grunted a little in amusement. I might as well laugh now since I'd be sad when I could never pick up anything again. When the next of Kremm's big-chested cousins came along, he or she probably wouldn't be as stupid as Kremm, and then I'd be killed.

The idea disturbed me more than I thought it would.

Panting, I trudged across the bridge to sit and gaze out at the realm beneath me. Properly speaking, I guarded the entire realm, and compared to most realms, it was tiny. During my first years in the Dark Lands, I had chased down every invader, which was a great amount of work. After a number of years, I realized that my predecessor hadn't bothered with this chasing nonsense. He had relaxed at the bridge. When I tried that out, I found that almost every visitor showed up there soon, as if the bridge were drawing them in.

It only took me thirty years to figure that out. My predecessor, Bixell, would have laughed his musical ass off at me.

Kremm's men were trotting away through the mist. Unless they did something fantastically dumb, they would survive to reach home. I thought of my wife and smiled. She hated killing.

Below me, the Dark Lands were as dim as evening twilight. That would have meant more if the concept of days had any meaning here. It was always gloomy, never bright and never dark, despite the name. I lost sight of the running soldiers in a blink, as if they had been swallowed by a fog patch.

A tall ridge stood way off to the left, and a black lake lay not as far away to my right. I noted the big, glassy circle a mile away where the God of Death had been destroyed. We might have thrown a party to celebrate if so many hadn't died along with him.

I sat on the wet, black grass for a while, gathering my breath and my thoughts. My stump was just dripping blood now, and that seemed to be slowing. I agreed with my earlier assessment that I wouldn't bleed to death, although the pain was climbing my arm and I felt no stronger than a piglet. At last, I heaved myself to my feet and left Kremm's papery remains behind me.

I trekked an hour toward the black lake, which lay in the middle of the realm and never rippled, although it condescended to allow an occasional mist across its surface. Like the bridge, nobody had ever named the lake. Anything sinking into it could never be found again—that was well known. Years ago, I had swum out of the lake by twisting my understanding of sorcery until it squealed. I was the last one to return from the lake, and it wasn't making that mistake again.

Trailing drops of blood, I shuffled along through pale trees that never swayed since no wind existed in the Dark Lands. When I finally arrived at the lake's curved, black shore, I lay down on the soggy beach beside a stone pile. I closed my eyes to shut out the awful mess of colored lights moving in the sky.

It wasn't possible for a human to sleep in the Dark Lands, even one like me who wasn't aging. But sometimes I stretched out and pretended to sleep. I remembered it as a regular thing that normal people in the real world did.

Resting there, I reached out to lay my hand on the stones of my wife's tomb. Then I stared at my new stump. If my wife had been there, she would have poked me and laughed at my foolishness, so I laughed for her.

I stopped laughing when I lowered my arm too fast and hit the sand. Pain jabbed deeper into my stump.

I hadn't been not-sleeping for long when I heard slow, splashing footsteps in the distance. I rolled to my feet and summoned the Death God's sword. Then I watched it splat onto the ground at my feet.

"Shit."

I willed the sword away and swaggered toward the noise anyhow. Sometimes confidence carries the day almost by itself.

"Bib!" called out a voice as dark and as thick as pitch. "Don't go turning me into a shriveled-up leather rug!"

"Hurd?" I yelled.

"It is me! Sound the horns and let the maidens dance!"

TWO

The squat, clay-colored creature named Hurd appeared from the dimness. He went where he wanted, even between realms, but I had never heard of him showing up someplace for a fight. He might run errands, carry messages, or even spy for warring factions if they were nice to him, but he was known not to give a bucket of dead pigeons who won as long as he was paid.

A fair but grimy young man with reddish-brown hair followed Hurd. He was strapped with so many packs, bags, and bundles that when he halted behind Hurd, he drooped and sighed like an old mule. An even younger man carrying just one pack walked far behind Hurd, more than one hundred feet distant, and stopped when Hurd stopped.

I had known Hurd since the first time I left the world of man to visit beings in other realms and get my ass kicked by them. He had served as my guide on my first trip to the Dark Lands. He was a lousy guide, but I guess he wasn't hopeless since I had lived through the experience.

I glared at Hurd. "You haven't visited in twenty years."

"Twenty-two. You have water dripping off your butt."

I had enough self-discipline not to try reaching for my backside, which was sopping from the wet ground. I also resolved not to mention my missing arms until Hurd did. "It is said that you only come when you're not called. If I call you now, will it force you to go away?"

Hurd acted as if he hadn't noticed that. Standing ten paces away, he squinted at me, shading his face with the blunt fingers of one hand, even though most of the sky was as black as his eyes. "Dang it, Bib, your face looks like something crows have been fighting over. You ought to learn how to duck."

I bit my lip, which was just as scarred as the rest of my face.

"You used to be so pretty." Hurd went on: "Now that you're carved up so, only a particularly open-minded girl would kiss you."

"With your bald head and ass like a bucket, I doubt any girl has ever kissed you."

Hurd laughed, showing square, chalky-white teeth. "Ain't you going to offer me a drink?"

"Sorry, I'm out."

"You drank it all? You greedy hippopotamus! But I guess you can't send out, eh?"

The boy standing far behind Hurd cleared his throat so loudly it must have hurt.

I had nothing to say to that or to Hurd. My wife had been able to go to the world of man and come back as she wished. Her trips were rare, but they supplied us with everything from beer to books to tools—anything the Dark Lands wouldn't provide. She had been dead more than a year, though.

Hurd said, "To tell it straight, I'm shocked to find you here. I didn't figure you could last four days without her." He walked toward me, holding out a hand to touch my shoulder.

"I don't feel like being comforted."

Hurd kept coming. "I know it hurts." When he reached me, he kicked me hard on the shin and then scurried away toward the young man loaded with packs. "That hurts too, right?"

I cursed and limped after him with no idea what I'd do if I caught him.

"I'm glad you didn't cut your throat," Hurd said. "Or maybe drown yourself, considering things."

Hurd was fast, and I'd had a difficult morning of dismemberment, so I gave up any idea of chasing him. I dropped straight down to sit, as graceless as a pineapple. When my wife died, I had supposed that a person in my situation might consider jumping from a high place or drowning in the lake. It had been a vague notion, though, as if I were thinking about somebody else.

Hurd patted my head like I was a puppy before sitting on the grass across from me. "Sorry about that kick, but I am old and wise, more than you, anyway. I have learned that when you're mad and want to kill somebody, you ain't likely to kill yourself first."

He reached back toward the young man, who shuffled up and handed Hurd a jug from a pack along with two wooden mugs. Hurd poured and then stared at the young fellow. "Don't make the man lap it like a deer in the forest! Can't you see the pathetic wretch is armless?"

The young fellow knelt beside me and lifted a mug to my lips. "Sure, I do notice that, and I guess I'm a fool, but it seems like a problem to me."

"Be respectful, you ignorant worm-squirt. Bib has had more murders than you've had breakfasts." Hurd glanced at me and said, "Well. Forty-seven years. In some places, four generations all added together don't stay married that long."

"There's no reason to talk about that," I said.

"Nice that you two was both ageless here, eh?"

"You saved me from death already, so stop talking about it."

"Well . . . do you know why she was out there on the lake?"

"Don't pretend that you know anything about it!" I snapped.

He nodded at the young man. "Vargo, slosh a little more in him, or we'll be here until the dang end of time. Bib, do you know why she was there?"

Swallowing, I shook my head. I had some ideas, but I didn't want to say any of them.

"So, you really ain't got any idea why she left and went out there? I didn't wander into these Dark Lands for the sun and the conversation, you know. Did she leave because you did something stupid?"

I shouted, "If she was going to leave because I did something stupid, she'd have left the second day she was here!"

The boy standing far behind Hurd flinched as if he'd been slapped.

Hurd cocked his head at me and then frowned. "Sorry to anger you there. Pil told me the same thing about you more than once. I thought the memory might cheer you more than dwelling on all your losses and failures here at the end of your life."

I stared at him.

"Stop it! You just stop!" the person far behind Hurd shouted, and I realized it was a young woman.

Vargo frowned. Hurd shouted back at the woman, "You hush back there! I am the one talking, as you agreed to, so shut up and let me talk."

The woman threw her pack on the ground and marched toward me. "You can stop being cruel to him this moment, or I'll twist something apart that you'd rather stayed together. Do you doubt me?"

The young man leaned toward Hurd and whispered, "Don't start doubting her about things, even crazy things."

The woman approached with an unsettling amount of determination, but I stayed sitting to show she didn't worry me.

I said, "Don't concern yourself, young woman. This may be harsh behavior for most creatures, but not for Hurd."

The woman stomped past Hurd and smiled at me.

I shivered and wished I had hands so I could rub my eyes. The woman favored Pil so strongly I could almost think this was her walking across the damp ground. But this woman looked about twenty years old. Pil's apparent age at her death was forty.

I rose to my knees, but with an easy hand, she pushed my shoulder back down until I sat on the grass.

"Who are you?" I asked.

She knelt and examined my raw stump before looking over her shoulder. "You've been talking to him, insulting him, and kicking him for minutes but ignoring the first thing we should do, which is bandage his wounds, you oafs! Vargo, give me some bandages!"

The young man started poking in a pouch. He grumbled, "You got your own pouch. Bandages don't weigh a thing. No excuse . . ." He trailed off.

"I'm Pala, Pil's granddaughter, and you wouldn't believe how much she told me about you. You might be embarrassed. That walking ham steak back there, Vargo, is my cousin. I'll say it right now, I apologize on behalf of my family for him and everything he might do, but he will never leave you in a hard spot."

I stared at her with my mouth open.

Pala patted my shoulder. "It's shocking, I know it is, for us to arrive here when you're probably about to leave, and you not having seen Pil in so long. Are you leaving here soon?"

"I hadn't thought about it."

"I hope you do, because from what Hurd says, if you don't, then you'll be cut into one hundred fifty pieces by tomorrow. People must know of your wounds. Heck, if we know, then all kinds of people and creatures know by now." She began bandaging my raw stump and was making a good start.

"I don't think I can just waddle out of here whenever I want," I said.

"When can you waddle out of here then?" Vargo asked.

"I can't imagine when."

Pala tapped the hilt of her sword with her palm. "Then we'll stay here and defend your life."

The anger on my face must have looked awfully amusing. She laughed like I'd given her a gift as she pulled the bandage tight. "I was joking. Although I can't imagine Granda's words if we did let you die."

"Granda?"

"Grandmother. Pil."

Vargo sloshed the mug. "More? Although I don't suppose you can be the terror of the Dark Lands, or not exactly, if you can't even defeat this beer mug." He said it the way he'd talk to a drunk or a sick person.

Pala frowned at Vargo. "I don't care about that. I must ask, why are you here, Bib? I've never exactly understood why you stay here guarding bridges of all things, and Granda couldn't explain it in a way that made sense to me. Mainly she talked about how stubborn you are."

"Not bridges. There's only one bridge here. Well, only one that's legendary," I said. "Hurd, did you let them come here entirely ignorant?"

"It ain't my job to educate children."

I scratched my chin against my shoulder. "I'll try to do this in as few words as possible. I was in the wrong place when things fell apart. There."

When I didn't say more, Pala's brows lowered. "We came a long way, so please give us a real answer."

I bowed my head for a moment. "I apologize. All right, first you need to understand something for anything else to make sense. The horrible gods and their wretched eternal enemies have waged war across the realms for eternity. Since they're all immortal, it hasn't really been war. It's been more of a hellacious, cross-dimensional pillow fight with lightning and volcanoes.

"Not long ago, the gods discovered this realm, the Dark Lands. It's a place where immortal creatures can be killed. That spiced up warfare for a while, but once each side had a few fatalities, war became less amusing."

Vargo asked, "Why would they come here just to be killed? Are they stupid?" He whipped his head to look around. "Are we stupid?"

"Maybe. You'd think that gods are smart to a godlike degree, and they are. But their egos are one hundred times as big as their minds, which makes them act foolishly. If you're ever talking to a god, remember that."

Vargo stretched open one of his eyes, managing to show both amazement and doubt.

I said, "The few gods with merely gargantuan egos warned that killing immortal beings like they were pigs on Sunday afternoon might wreck existence. Or maybe it would do nothing. Or maybe things would get a little better with fewer gods around. Nobody really knew, and nobody wanted to risk it.

"The gods and their enemies swore to stay out of the Dark Lands forever. Of course, their oaths weren't worth a crooked dog's knob. Immortal beings have all the willpower of a dandelion. If a thing can be done, they can't resist doing it. Otherwise, it will be tempting them forever."

"Who told you all this?" Pala asked. "I'm sorry, but it sounds like some bedtime story."

Hurd said, "Bib was around for the oath-taking part. I was too."

Pala asked, "Bib, how did you get here? That's the thing I don't understand most."

Hurd snorted. "I giggle just thinking about it."

I said, "Oh, let's not talk about who said what or who did which stupid thing that put me here enforcing the peace."

Hurd laughed. "No, let's talk about it! He came here like a fool, without being asked, to make up for doing a bunch of horrible stuff in his life!" He laughed again, harder.

"That's not true, and Hurd's an insane liar. Everybody knows it," I said. "The gods and their enemies considered me a meddling turd and sent their servants to kill me, and they have kept sending them. Did I leave anything out, Hurd?"

"You make lousy furniture."

I nodded. "Is that all you wanted to know? Because that's all I intend to say."

Hurd threw up a hand. "Wait! Before this conversation rolls away from us, I want to talk some philosophy. Bib, I know you have set great importance by the idea of atonement. Honestly, I can't understand a bit of that. You have been atoning as hard as you can for seventy years, and you've just about atoned yourself to pieces! How close are you to being done?" He pointed at my empty left eye and my stumps. "I could just declare you fully atoned while you've still got a few parts left."

"I don't think there's any measurement for atonement."

"If you can't measure it, what the hell good is it? And don't say you can't measure love or hope or some crap like that. I will sit here and argue with logical precision that neither love nor hope have as much real value as warm socks or a proper bowel movement."

"Nobody's going to believe that," Vargo murmured to Hurd.

"Quiet! Pull out another jug. My argument won't take more than two hours."

Vargo slipped another jug from a pack while staring at me with suffering eyes.

I rolled to my knees again, just about pushing Pala out of the way. "I'm not listening to two hours of Hurd logic."

"All right, if you lack the wit to endure the full discussion, tell me this: what are you atoning for? And tell me in three words or less. If you can't say it in three words, it's nothing but a fancy notion."

"Stealing people's lives," I said.

"Yes," Pala whispered.

"Fair enough," Hurd said. "And what have you done all these years to make up for that thievery of lives?"

"I kept everybody from making war in the Dark Lands, which protected my realm and others, including whatever realm of squatty thugs you come from."

"I might argue about cause and effect, but let's gallop onward," Hurd said. "How did you keep war out?"

"I killed everybody who came to the Dark Lands to make war."

"And you did that to atone for killing people?" Hurd gazed at me and waited.

"I admit the irony of it," I said. "But how else could I prevent war here? Bribe everybody? Hold festivals with jugglers? Build a gigantic whorehouse?"

"Breathe, you're turning burgundy. Let's look at this a different way. I don't know how many lives you stole before you came to the Dark Lands. Let's say it was a lot and that quite a few didn't entirely deserve it. You were in the red, so to speak." He paused, but I didn't say anything. "Now, I suppose that you have killed a lot more in the Dark Lands than you did before you got here."

I nodded.

"The people and demigods and monsters you killed here all arrived intending to do sketchy mischief. And you had warned everybody ahead of time not to show up if they didn't want to be killed. Slaying them was a service to every innocent being throughout existence!"

I grinned. "I see where you're headed. Go ahead and say it."

"Bib, your useful killings here have made up for your past dubious killings. Heck, you probably could have stopped atoning thirty years ago."

I stared for a few seconds and then sneered. "That's clever, Hurd. I don't guess anybody has ever thought about that before. You're a damn genius."

Pala put her hand on my shoulder and said in a quiet voice, "There's a problem with your logic, Hurd. A thousand justified killings don't bring back even one innocent person. It's not math."

"You're not helping!" Hurd snapped.

Pala turned toward me. "Am I helping?"

I sighed. "I don't know."

Hurd leaned toward me and whispered, "Let's just say you ain't atoned at all, you ass-thicket! But if you don't convince yourself I'm right, then you won't come with us. You'll sit here with no hands, and the next creature that comes along with at least one finger will poke you to death."

"Don't stay here," Pala said, her eyes large. Vargo paused and then nodded.

I considered it for a few seconds. "I don't know what I'd do if I went back. I can't imagine it."

Hurd said, "Do anything you want! Hunt rabbits. Bake bread. There are still sorcerers flitting around who can restore an arm or two."

"I don't care about anything back there." The words jumped out on their own and surprised me a little.

"That's where I'm a genius and all the rest are trash in the harbor!" Hurd said. "Pala and Vargo need your help and protection."

I laughed at them. "Hire some guards. Or buy a couple of big dogs."

Vargo looked as if I had stomped on his toe.

Pala held up a damp cloth as if she might clean blood off my face. Instead, she touched my forehead with her other hand and brushed her fingers across my scars. I shook my head to throw her off.

"I'm sorry," Pala said. "She told me about them, but I couldn't really imagine it." She cleared her throat. "Bib, it's a fierce war, and we don't know anything about fierce wars, and everybody all over is getting killed, and our whole family, Pil's family, will be killed too."

I said, "Wars are that way. I can't get involved in all the wars."

Vargo looked at Pala, who nodded. He reached into his shirt and pulled out something on a silver chain before holding it out to me.

I glanced at it and then back at him. "Do you want me to pick it up with my lips?"

He blushed but said, "I'd like to see that. Not now, though." The young man held the chain in front of my face. A black ring hung from it, and I had to admit it looked familiar. Pil's mark, a small knife, was worked into the ring. I said, "Anybody could have made that. Hurd, who's paying you to do all this?"

Vargo paused. "Granda said to bring this to you if we need help, and I've done that, but I can see that you're useless."

Pala slapped Vargo's arm, hard.

Vargo glanced at my stumps. "Well . . . Granda said that we should ask you to put on the ring as proof of our need, but I guess that's not happening, so . . ." He shrugged.

Thirty years ago, I had watched Pil carve and enchant two rings like this, one for herself and another for me. They kept the wearer warm in the cold and cool in the heat, among other things. She was a genius at making magical doodads, and some were fantastically powerful. I had lost my ring, and I thought she had lost hers too.

I sat back and stuck a foot up toward Hurd. "Take off my boot."

Vargo sighed, and Pala hugged my neck.

Hurd made a face but yanked off my left boot.

"Wait! How long ago did she hand you this ring?" I asked Vargo.

"She didn't hand it to me, not exactly. She sent me a note about where to go looking for it if we needed serious help."

"Huh. Did she say what she meant by 'serious help'?"

Pala nodded. "Serious help is when we don't mind if the person helping us destroys everything else in sight."

That sounded like something Pil would say, and Pala said it just the way Pil might. Hearing it hurt my chest. "Tell me, Vargo, in what deep, mystical vault did she say you'd find this ring?"

Vargo blushed yet again. "It was in a flour bin beside the stove in a whorehouse kitchen." He glanced at Pala. "I didn't linger."

I couldn't think of a single thing to say to that.

Pala looked straight at me. With a face as still and as smooth as the lake, she said, "Bib, come with us."

I stared back into her eyes. "Damn, aren't you even going to say please?"

"If you love us enough, you'll help. Saying please makes no difference."

"You lying, wheedling storm full of piss and thunder," I growled.

Smiling, Pala said, "That sounds like you're a loose thread away from saying yes."

If they wanted to talk me into something, they chose the right person when they sent Pala. I nodded for Hurd to put the ring on one of my smallest repulsive toes.

The Dark Lands were always chilly, but I warmed up right away. I hadn't needed to wait for warmth, though. The ring felt like Pil.

"What now?" I asked.

Hurd shrugged. "We got no other presents for you. No endless mug of beer. No trained elephant. Just say yes."

I couldn't say yes without one more stab of suspicion. "Why would you do this, Hurd? I know that you hate everybody and don't do favors."

"No, I don't as a rule. But I have a feeling down my backbone that it will be good to have you owe me a favor soon."

The ring was a trap, Vargo and Pala were stooges, and Hurd was tricking me somehow. There was no other sensible explanation.

Hurd leaned toward me with no trace of a grin. "Don't you owe it to Pil?" He asked it in a low, soft voice. It was the most suspicious thing he could have done.

Shaking my head, I opened my mouth to tell him to go to hell. "No. I don't trust you, Hurd, and I don't know those two."

Hurd crossed his arms. Pala and Vargo both babbled at me. Pala reached out to grab what was left of my arm but pulled back.

"Enough!" I shouted. "Maybe I'll die here, and maybe I won't. But you are definitely trying to fool me into something, and I won't stumble into it."

"Bib—" Pala started.

"Stop it. I'm done jabbering about it," I said. They all kept silent. "Hurd, put on my boot."

Hurd pointed at my foot and said, "Vargo, put on his boot."

I said, "Do you youngsters want to pay your respects to Pil? Her tomb is just down the shore."

They looked at me with blank faces.

"I'll walk with you. I go often."

"What tomb?" Pala asked.

"Well, I didn't recover her body from the lake, but I built the tomb anyway."

"What do you mean? She's not dead!" Vargo shouted, his eyes wide. "Or she wasn't two weeks ago." He went pale. "Did something happen to her?"

It was my turn to look blank. "I saw her drown over a year ago."

"No, you couldn't have seen that," Pala said. "I've seen her since then. Granda's alive and would certainly have come here for you herself if she could spare the time. We'd have hardly needed Hurd at all! But she was away on a task."

I backed away a few steps, not ready to think about this. "You're a bunch of lying bastards, and I know what lying bastards look like."

I turned and stalked up the beach toward Pil's tomb.

THREE

As I stared at Pil's tomb, part of me wanted to tear it down to see whether she was in there. Of course, she wasn't, and she never had been. Also, I couldn't tear down much with no hands.

I leaned against the tomb wall and wondered why I had such a strong pull to see her body now when everyone was saying she was still alive. I should have been overjoyed that she lived, and honestly, I would be if I thought it was true. But something about the idea of her survival bothered me.

If Pil was alive, why hadn't she come to me in the Dark Lands or found a way to send me a message? Since she hadn't, she was probably dead. But if she wasn't really dead, why had she let me think she was for all this time?

I couldn't answer that. I didn't even know how to think about it.

Pala caught up with me and stopped several paces away. "This is hard, isn't it? I didn't think it would be so hard for you. Granda told me how much you believe in love, but I didn't understand. I don't know anybody like that."

"Bullshit," I said without much fire.

"Stay here if you want to, or go somewhere else. I bet we can wheedle Hurd into bringing you to some other realm, someplace safe. Don't hurt yourself because you're angry."

I shook my head. It was still almost as if Pil were there talking to me, and it was starting to piss me off. "No. I won't know anything until I find out whether or not she's really alive. I'll come with you. If she's alive, maybe I'll even kill your enemies."

Pala grinned. "You'll destroy everything in sight?"

I stared at her with the gravest eye I could manage until she blushed and looked away.

"Don't feel bad, Pala. Pil is the one who put that idea about me in your head, and it's not her fault. If I help you, I'll destroy what needs to be destroyed and, if possible, no more."

She turned back to me, her face as serious as mine. "If I can help, I'll help."

Hurd and Vargo caught up. Vargo narrowed his eyes. "What's going on? You both look weird."

A deep voice sounded from some distance down the lakeshore. "Guardian! I want to speak with you!"

I hadn't noticed any intruders into the Dark Lands. Normally, I sensed almost everybody who arrived. I wondered whether this meant that the Dark Lands were rejecting me.

"Bridge Guardian! I will not fight unless you want to! Let us talk!"

I saw the speaker then, a tall, thin man with his hair tied in a long, black braid. His clothes were gray, even his boots, and he almost faded into the Dark Lands' murk. He carried a sword on his back and no other weapons I could see. I watched him approach.

The fellow waved at me. "Old man! Where is the Guardian? You, girl. Have you seen the Bridge Guardian hereabouts?"

I called back, "He's across the lake, picking mushrooms. It's an easy swim, and faster than walking all the way around."

The man stopped, and his eyes narrowed. "You wouldn't be attempting to send me into a fatal accident, would you? I have read about this lake."

"You caught me," I said. "I owe the Guardian a debt and serve by providing a little challenge for the unwary and the unready. I can't apologize for adhering to my oath, can I, you great, heaving bundle of tightly bound donkey members? I'm also charged with insulting the crap out of people to test their patience."

"I can see that you enjoy your work." The man halted fifteen paces from us. "Now that your oath is fulfilled, tell me where the Guardian is. I have taken an oath to vivisect all who impede me."

"I understand. I don't know his location, but he went that way." I pointed toward the breeding ground of some horrific predators that lay just below the surface of the ground.

The man drew his sword. "You are trying again to send me into an ambush. I am Alamore, greatest of the Five Heroes, and you cannot best me through deceit."

"Five Heroes?"

"Yes."

"Have they done anything I might have heard of?"

"We are sworn to serve Lossil," he said.

"Has Lossil done anything I might have heard of?"

"Don't presume to be flippant with me. Killing an annoying, arrogant cripple is an ignoble act, but I have on occasion told nobility to bite its own ass."

I bowed. "It's nice to meet you. I am Ungurdine, Servant of Shadows. I will check on the Guardian for you." I turned to Hurd and the others, whispering, "How do we get rid of him?"

"Hell, we thought you were working on it. What good are you?" Vargo whispered.

I whispered, "I am out here playing pants afire with the great lummox! My job is to distract him, your job is to make a plan. Casserak's moldy armpits!"

"Hero Alamore." I jerked my head toward Vargo. "This idiot eunuch will fetch the Guardian for you." I glared at Vargo, who glared back but ran in what I assumed was a random direction. "May I offer you refreshment?"

"No, I don't care for being poisoned. Call your idiot eunuch back here. I don't want him running for reinforcements."

I whistled and beckoned Vargo.

"Any ideas?" I whispered to Hurd and Pala.

Hurd whispered, "Well . . . we could teach him some songs."

"Shit!" I whispered. "You three scatter, then meet me at the bridge. I'll tell this horse apple some more lies and then run away to find you. We'll lead him on a chase until he's dragging his chin on the ground."

"No, I'll help!" Pala said. "I'm staying with you, and we'll stand together."

"Hush! When I call him a pudgy bunny, you run!"

Before I turned around, Pala pushed me and jumped out with her hand on her sword to proclaim, "I'm the Bridge Guardian. What do you want with me?"

Alamore bounded forward, drawing his sword. I threw my body at him, but he spun off me and thrust his sword into Pala below her breastbone. As he withdrew, a three-second blast of hurricane-force wind knocked us all down.

I rolled and staggered upright, but Alamore was nowhere in view. Vargo sprinted down the lakeshore. "Don't chase him!" I yelled.

Vargo stopped and ran back to us, screaming and pounding his legs with his fists.

I sat down by Pala. Vargo stared at me and then lay Pala's head in my lap. I guess maybe he thought I could save her. She mumbled, ". . . him . . ." She tried to say something else but couldn't quite make it. After a short time, blood trickled from her mouth. She clutched my sleeve with more strength than I would have expected, and she looked back and forth between Vargo and me. Tears began running from the corners of her eyes when her grip started to fail. At last, she stopped breathing.

I felt like I was watching Pil die again.

Vargo and Hurd built a tomb for Pala beside the empty one I had built for Pil. I spent some time at both, saying goodbye to Pala, whom I had hardly known, and saying goodbye to Pil in case she wasn't alive. Then I waved my stump at the distant cairns of my friends who had fought beside me and died in this realm.

I gazed uphill toward the bridge. "Is this Alamore one of the assholes trying to kill your family?"

Vargo said slowly, "I don't know. I've never heard of the asshole, but I know this Lossil is an evil knob. Maybe he's——"

Hurd slapped Vargo's shoulder. "Just say yes."

"Yes."

"That's good," I said. "When the time comes, stay away. I'll kill him. Hurd, let's discus terms."

"What do you mean terms?"

"I want your promise to restore at least one of my arms. And secure me some magical power." It was a ridiculous thing to demand in my position. But if a sorcerer can't be the most arrogant one in the room, he's not much of a sorcerer.

"No healing." Hurd looked a little sorry. "I can find you a small slice of magical power—half a square. I can't give you more."

I sighed. "I'm bringing some of the magic weapons I have collected here." In seven decades of killing conceited demigods, I had collected 271 magic weapons with a variety of effects. Two hundred seventy-two if you counted Kremm's.

"I ain't toting them for you," Hurd said.

"That's fine, as long I can load up Vargo."

"Wait, I——" Vargo said, but Hurd stuck a hand in his face.

Hurd's black eyes twinkled. "Done."

Hurd and Vargo followed me trekking back up to the bridge, which Hurd explained would be our path to the world of man.

"We're walking across the bridge to get home?" Vargo asked. "Isn't that kind of obvious? If that isn't too obvious a question to ask."

"We could drag our bare asses along the bottom of the gorge if you like," Hurd snapped. "You go see if it's safe. We'll wait here."

"I just thought we'd be open to traps or an ambush," Vargo grumbled. "If you die, this trip was like a picnic with nothing but ants."

"Don't worry. If you don't belong here, the bridge will just crush you to death," I lied.

Hurd retrieved my sword, which had fallen to the ground along with my arm when Kremm severed it. It carried a deceptively powerful enchantment.

Creating magical weapons requires power, and a truly potent weapon costs a lot of power. If a sorcerer wants to craft a sword that can cut iron, he'd better be ready to give up a horrible amount of power.

My sword had no such fantastic enchantment. Its one sad, magical quality was that it couldn't be dulled, which seemed like it might be a tiny bit useful. It certainly wouldn't have taken too much power to craft. But in fact, the enchantment meant that whenever somebody sharpened the sword, it remained just that sharp, until somebody with better sharpening skills came along. Over many years, the sword had been sharpened and resharpened by the heroes who carried it and then by the heroes who killed them. Now it was the sharpest blade I had ever seen, and cutting iron was dead easy. It would be even easier to cut Alamore into pieces.

Vargo strapped another sword onto my back. I intended to trade it to whichever sorcerer would restore my arms. I had given the young man a magic sword of his own, one that wanted to protect the person who held it. He thanked me with so much grave sincerity that I almost regretted poking fun at him earlier. I had no great hopes for his swordsmanship, but maybe this weapon would keep him alive a day or two in a land of fierce wars.

I selected a fourth sword, and Hurd strapped it to Vargo's back. I had no use in mind for it but took it anyway on the theory that you can't have too many magic swords.

When I offered Hurd a sword, he waved it away. "My job ain't to fight! My job's to have fun and look pretty! Are you done picking out your toys? Ready to go home?"

I nodded. "Lead us."

"You lead," Hurd said. "If we bump into something unhappy, it can chew off your head while I run."

I stepped onto the bridge, which led to the rocky highlands. Hundreds of men and other creatures had been in sight of those hills when I killed them.

"Oh, and don't stop," Hurd said.

Somebody punched me right in the mouth. It startled me more than it hurt, and I walked past an enormous, half-dressed, transparent, glowing man shouting profanity in my ear. I recognized him but couldn't say where from. Four or five more clammy, glowing people, I assumed dead, jumped up to pummel me no harder than a child but with great malice. Somebody grabbed me around the waist. I struggled but kept walking.

Halfway across the bridge, several dead people—ragged, transparent, and furious—flung themselves against my body all together. I stumbled. Others hit me the same way from behind, and I fell to my knees. I toddled my way forward on my knees so as not to stop moving while more of them piled onto my shoulders and head.

Realizing that these creatures weighed just about nothing, I turned and rolled to my feet, shedding them from my back to press on. Then a dozen or more pushed in, not touching me but screaming abuse right into my face and ears. I couldn't make out what any one of them said, and I was grateful for that.

I had almost crossed the bridge when the dead people rushed in again to grab my waist, legs, chest, and anything else they could reach. Since they had done this less than a minute before, I was ready. I glanced down and saw my dead daughter clinging to my right leg—wan, beautiful, and shouting to ask why I had murdered her. I wasn't ready for that, but I closed my eyes and kept walking until I was across.

Once over the bridge, I sat on the ground, sweating and panting.

"You took your time dragging your way across," Vargo said in a level voice. "And you fell down. Are you drunk? Or sick?" He paused and then said quietly, "Do you really want to go?"

I glared at him. "Son, remember this. Your magic sword means nothing. I could kill you three times while sitting here on my butt even without arms." I swallowed when I heard myself talk about killing the young man for no good reason at all.

Hurd slapped my shoulder. "He didn't see anything, Bib. One more step, and you'll be through, so don't wait around here."

I stood and took that step.

FOUR

Hurd had said he would bring me home, and he didn't lie. I found myself facing my childhood house, and it was a sour experience. I could imagine a thousand nicer things to look at, and I needn't exert myself to do so.

The unpainted house looked like it might sigh and collapse into a driftwood pile right there while I watched. But I had last seen the squatty shack 104 years ago, so in that light, it looked pretty damn good. Any honest person would judge that it had weathered those years better than I had.

Beside me, Hurd laughed like a creaking wagon wheel. "You lived here? Now I know why you liked hell better than home all these years." He poked me with a stout finger, and I felt my shoulder bruise.

"What is this place? Why are we here?" Vargo demanded.

"Village of Drup on the Island of Ir," Hurd said.

"That's the wrong question, Vargo." I kicked through some debris by the front door. "Where can we find Alamore?"

"Where the fighting is, I bet," Vargo said. "There's fighting near Sandell, where my family lives."

I nodded. "If we investigate every battle between here and

there, we'll find him."

Vargo scowled. "And do what to him? Call him bad names while our armless champion shows his butt? You can't even take down your own trousers!"

"And I couldn't save Pala, either, you're right," I said. "But we'll see who's alive next week. It won't be him. It might not be you."

Vargo walked away, kicking a rotten board.

I said, "Hurd, thank you for getting us here. Knowing your reputation, I might not be able to afford any more of your help. I politely ask that you either help me for free or go someplace and get drunk. No, just go get drunk and stay drunk until I need you."

Hurd wrinkled his flat nose. "You're welcome, and a four-day drunk sounds like the sweet afterlife that the gods promise us. But it would kill me dead if I missed all the ignorant stuff you're about to do. Who would tell my friends about it?" He mopped his face with a corner of his bloodred cloak, even though I was shivering in the stubborn sea wind.

I said, "To answer your question, I lived here as a baby but ran off as soon as I could steal a decent pair of boots. All right, the road to Sandell is over there . . ." I turned to gaze past the town before trailing off.

I had expected to see the dim, grubby fishing village from my boyhood. I was wrong about that. I would be wrong about a great parcel of things in the coming days, and this was the first one.

The ocean wind died off to a mere breath, so I felt like I might not freeze while I examined Drup. Dozens of buildings, three times as many as I remembered, pushed up against the gritty black paths. The grit had been ground down from black stones over hundreds of years by boots and bare feet. Some structures were lousy hovels like my father's house, but others stood straight and solid. Some had been painted white or green by people more industrious than any I grew up with. My folks had merely whitewashed the house each spring and let it fade until the next spring's whitewash.

People hustled along the paths, especially the one leading down to the dock at the rocky harbor, which held broad boats and even one fat-sided ship. No fish had ever been dropped gasping to die on those decks. Barrels, bundles, and crates were carried or rolled between big warehouses and ships while men and women loaded goods onto wagons.

I shook my head and gazed at the low clouds racing along just a shade lighter than the ocean. When I examined the horizon, I could hardly tell the difference between sea and sky. I hadn't often seen the wind blow so stiffly over the ocean while the air around the village fell still. Then the clouds opened over an expanse of sea, and sunlight turned the wavetops as bright as fire. I gazed at it for a minute.

"I guess these people have made use of the time I gave them," I said. "It's not the town I would have created. I can't see any taverns or gambling houses from here. But they didn't require my leave on what to build."

Hurd sniffed and stepped back. "Bib . . . don't kick me to bits while I make this helpful suggestion . . ."

I waved a stump at him. "Don't worry, I've already contemplated killing you six times today, and you're still alive."

He laughed at me, and the house blew apart. Damp timbers hurtled toward us.

Hurd was standing in the perfect spot to be smashed into jam. Three boards slammed into him and hurled him to the ground, but he was tough and I didn't overly worry. Vargo was standing behind me, farther away from the house, as if he could pull us magnetically away toward his hometown. I heard him yelp, but it didn't sound like a yelp of death.

I stood near the edge of the house, looking in toward the center of the lumber storm. I jumped back and twisted, just evading a stout splinter that would have pierced my left arm if I had one.

For an instant, I thought a great bear was charging through the house at us. It would have been the first bear with mustard-colored fur I had ever encountered. Then I saw that it ran on two long, muscular legs and leaned forward as it came, flailing lumber aside with sinewy arms. Its head sat huge on its hunched shoulders like a triangle pointing downward. Its slitted eyes lay near the top triangle points, which curved up in stubby horns. A slack, fanged maw lay at the bottom. It wore no clothing, and an unfortunate glance told me it would never procreate in any way that I could understand.

The monster gave out a great, grinding roar as it pushed through the collapsing wood. Then it stopped to peer at Hurd before cocking its head.

I called out, "I'm willing to discuss it all in a gentlemanly way, if you provide the refreshments."

Of course, I was just acting like an ass while I distracted the monster from Hurd. I didn't expect the beast to answer me, and strictly speaking, it didn't. It turned toward me and spouted three seconds of something between a wheeze and a howl. At the same time, I heard it speak in a tone that seemed tempered and even wise. "By the radiant butthole of Gek, don't make me chase you."

I didn't really speak the language of monsters. Pil, clever sorcerer that she had been, often went back and added effects to magical trinkets she had made, explaining that she was bored, there wasn't a damn thing to do in the Dark Lands, and I didn't dance. The effect she added to the onyx ring on my toe allowed me to understand much of what was spoken in other languages, even non-human tongues, although it wouldn't work with every language and wouldn't with the poetry of any language at all.

The mustard-colored monster followed up with, "Perhaps I can get them both." Then it ignored Hurd and leaped twenty feet at me. It would have smashed me to the ground if I hadn't jumped aside, tripped over the crawling Vargo, and sprawled across the grit.

I rolled to my feet and scrambled away, but the creature grabbed at my head with two well-formed hands. I ducked its exquisite, pearly talons and kept scrambling. It feinted a leap and then rushed to overwhelm me with its weight. I sidestepped away from that nonsense and kicked its knee. I may as well have kicked a millstone. My leg tingled to the hip.

Vargo jumped past me and slashed the creature's side, leaving a scratch that smoked. The monster swung its legs toward the boy. I expected to see him crushed, but he fell backward and took a glancing blow.

Since I didn't know this creature, logic might suggest that I retreat to draw it out and discover its weaknesses. The people who follow such logic soon die and remain unmourned by their comrades. When fighting monsters, a single blow can destroy you. Letting the beast have a few free swings so you may become intimate with its thinking is stupid.

Before I landed my next kick, the monster shrank to the size of a hunting hound. That astounded me so much that my kick just grazed it.

"How hard did you kick that thing?" Hurd yelled from behind me.

"Grab this sword off my back and kill it!" I shouted.

"Just this once!" Hurd stumbled toward me. "I ain't no stupid fighting man with a big shield and an itty-bitty sword!"

The monster tossed its head and shouted, *"Elibelb mur!"* It swelled back to horrifying bear size and grabbed at my head. Hurd pulled the spare sword from the scabbard on my back and gaped at the wave of green flames that trailed from the blade.

The beast bounded thirty feet to the side, away from Hurd's sword. When it touched the ground, it shrank again.

Hurd controlled himself and ran toward the beast. He swung hard and made a long, neat cut down the monster's side. "Scats!" Hurd shouted when the beast didn't even grunt.

"Elibelb mur!" yelled the monster, throwing its triangular head to the side, and it grew again.

Hurd withdrew and looked straight at me. "Ain't you a sorcerer? Magic the thing!"

I didn't have enough time or power to blast the monster with lightning or call every dog in town to come fight it while we ran away. I might bind it to my service, but only if I knew its real name. Well, I didn't know its name, and I doubted I could pull out any books to research it in the next few seconds.

But I had little magic and no arms, which left me few tactical options. Some lesser magical creatures had to conjure using their real names to perform extreme feats like flying, or changing shape, or breathing fire.

Of course, they wouldn't just spit out their name for everybody in creation to hear. They'd hide it in some way. So, if this monster was conjuring with its name, it sure as Krak's birthday ball wouldn't be *Elibelb mur*. It might be an anagram or a riddle.

I considered all this while I ran like mad away from the monster, sprawled on my face once, and scraped my chin bloody on a sharp rock.

The creature was conjuring an opposite transformation—changing from small to large. By dubious sorcery logic, its real name would be the exact opposite of *Elibelb mur*.

Rumblebile.

I ran through the logic and the probabilities in a second. Rumblebile wasn't certain to be the monster's name, of course. But the wisdom of all the sorcerers in history said that it was the highest probability and the best choice.

To me, that meant the monster's name would absolutely not be Rumblebile and could in fact be anything except Rumblebile. That name would be a trap for young and gullible sorcerers. As an old and jaded sorcerer, I now knew that I must gather more information by doing something stupid.

Still huge, the creature charged me, shouting, "Remain there!"

"Hit it now, Hurd!" I forced myself to stand still. When the beast was so close I could smell its breath, Hurd stabbed it from one side while Vargo slashed it again from the other. The monster jumped away.

I ran after the beast just fast enough not to trip this time and smash my skull. The monster landed, shrank, and turned to find me close enough for it to smell *my* breath. I didn't attack it. I stood motionless to take in every detail as it changed.

The monster hunched forward, dropped its hindquarters, glared at the sky, and shouted, *"Elibelb mur!"* Nothing happened for half a second. Then it tossed its head to the left and grew immediately. Then it knocked me down and stood on me.

Being crushed by a monster didn't keep me from reading the tiny word burned into its left shoulder. When the beast grabbed at my head, I squirmed so that it only came away with some of my hair.

I gasped, "Kruppin, I bind you."

The monster rolled off me and then rolled twice more as it shrank. It howled while I spent some power to magically place a glowing yellow band around its neck. Most sorcerers would create this sort of thing using their hands, but to escape the lake in the Dark Lands, I had taught myself to simply will magical effects into existence.

"You rank phallus!" the monster groaned.

"Kruppin, I bind you," I said louder. Two glowing orange bands appeared around the monster's wrists, bands that only I could see.

The monster gathered itself to leap at me but froze in mid-gather. It couldn't attack the sorcerer who was binding it. Kruppin whined, "This isn't right. It's not fair for some prancing sorcerer to do this to me."

"Kruppin, I bind you." Two more orange bands appeared, settling around Kruppin's ankles. That completed the binding.

A sorcerer could give a bound creature five commands, one for each band. After the fifth command, the creature would be free to go about its business. The first order of business would almost always be killing the sorcerer. Binding a creature was a ticklish affair.

"I didn't even plan to kill you or make you bleed much!" Kruppin huffed, now speaking my native language, the tongue of the west and the Island of Ir. "Just one ear would have satisfied me. You didn't have to turn yourself inside out and break wind about it."

"Why in the world would you want my ear?"

Kruppin looked up and opened its eyes wide. It looked almost innocent. In a casual tone, it asked, "Are you commanding me to tell you? You puny goiter of a sorcerer?"

I paused, examining Kruppin. "No, not yet. I won't waste a command to understand why you do things."

Vargo was examining the blade of his sword. "Well, I didn't help much."

I said, "You struck it twice and you're alive. I count that a victory."

He grunted. "I just think Granda might have expected better after all the time she spent teaching me."

I thought about that for a few seconds. Pil had trained with me for almost fifty years, and after that instruction, few fighters could match her. She never stayed at home long, so if she spent some of her limited time training Vargo, he must have been one of her favorites, although I couldn't imagine why.

I shrugged. "She expected better of me pretty often, so I'd say don't worry about that."

Hurd pointed past me, down the slope toward town. A couple dozen people were trotting up the hill. "Look, Bib. Some people you can turn into enemies. Take your dang sword back." Hurd resheathed it on my back.

"I should offer it to you," I said.

"Nah. If you tote swords around, that's like telling every fellow you see that you want to kill him. And it's sort of like wearing a dick on your belt. Unseemly."

The townspeople were rushing faster up the slope, and they were armed with a healthy variety of weapons. One woman carried a crossbow that looked older than me. They engaged in a fair amount of shouting, cursing, and pointing.

Hurd asked, "Stand here, or run?"

I scanned the crowd. "They look mad already. If we chat awhile, we probably can't make them hate us any worse." I turned to Kruppin. "Here is my first command to you. You will not speak in front of anyone except Hurd, Vargo, me, and anyone traveling with me. Instead, present yourself as my horrifying dog unless I say otherwise."

The orange band around Kruppin's left ankle, which only I could see, dissolved and floated away.

"Dog?" Kruppin sneered. He circled in place twice, sniffing the ground. Then from ten feet away, he lifted his leg and peed on my boots.

Showing his teeth, Kruppin nodded. "That's doglike, isn't it? A dog would do that very thing. I'll think about what other things a dog would do to you."

FIVE

I was more winded than I expected after fighting and binding this monster. I supposed that, outside the Dark Lands, some of my unnatural endurance would fade.

The townspeople had grown less sure about charging us and had slowed to creeping and muttering. I glanced at Hurd and then jerked my head toward Kruppin. "Hurd, did you have anything to do with this thing showing up?"

"Oh, you be still!" Hurd snapped. "This nasty creature almost crushed me. You should be happy I helped you at all. And, in fact, I probably saved your dang life. So, stop talking mean to me."

"I'm not a thing or a nasty creature." The hair on Kruppin's hackles rose.

"What are you then?" I asked.

Kruppin lifted its head. "The first of my brood to kill and eat a flim. Parent of thousands. And a very popular storyteller."

"And you're a monster," Hurd said.

"Of course. It's not an insult." It sniffed at Hurd. "You don't smell like a flimsy to me. You're a monster too. Accept it."

Hurd pretended he hadn't noticed.

"What in the name of my daddy's ass sack is a flimsy?" Vargo asked.

Kruppin snorted. "A flimsy is a man, like you." He reached out one paw-like hand, squeezing it into a paw-like fist. "Squishable, like a rotten apple."

Hurd pointed down the hill. "Your mob is almost here."

I smiled at the approaching townsfolk, and a few of them faltered. Most of my teeth had been broken off or smashed out over years of combat. I must have looked more appalling than Pil had let on.

I stopped smiling and called out, "Greetings! And you're welcome! We are happy to have chased that great, deadly monster off into the woods for you."

Kruppin's tail began wagging.

The people halted twenty feet from me in a semicircle. Now that they were within reasonable killing distance, none seemed anxious to use their weapons on an armless man, his short friend, their sour young hanger-on, and their disturbing dog. After some murmuring and shared significant looks, a tall, young woman stepped forward. She had red hair and light brown skin, like all the people of Ir— including me, although my hair was just about all gray now.

The woman kept her rough spear pointed at Hurd's throat. Almost everybody from Ir had red hair, and she tossed hers out of her face. I saw that she wasn't so much a young woman as she was a sweet-faced girl of sixteen or seventeen.

Hurd called out, "You folks make this child go out and talk to strangers for you? That says something about you."

The people muttered and glared.

"He means that it says you're all crawling cowards." Vargo squinted at them and curled his lip. "Except for you, young woman." He gave her a sharp nod.

I whispered to Vargo, "I hope you feel like fighting this whole town at once."

He lifted his chin as the people glared harder and muttered louder.

The wind had risen again since I bound Kruppin. It blew the

girl's hair into her face again. She shook it away once more, and the wind blew it right back. "Crap!" She pointed her spear with one hand to hold back her hair with the other. "Why have you three demons come here? And your . . . dog?"

"Demon? That's a nasty epithet," I said. "My name is Jimp the horse trainer. Do you have any horses that need training?"

"They're demons, all right!" shouted a tall, bald man to my left. "They just showed up, just appeared out of nothing, just came here like they were spit up out of the earth. I saw them do it!"

"Is that true, demon?" the girl demanded.

The man was correct. We had indeed appeared out of nothing, so I said, "No, that's ridiculous. Send that fellow back to bed. He has a fever or is drunk. Maybe kicked in the head."

Kruppin sniffed my leg and then threw himself away from me, whining.

An older woman just behind the girl yelled, "Stop kicking that dog, demon!"

Kruppin snorted.

The older woman went on: "I guess you came here with that big demon that ran off to plan how he's going to murder our children tonight. Demons lie with demons. It stands to reason."

I almost asked whether a lot of demons visited Drup, but that question might not be in our best interest. "I chased that terrifying monster away from your good and peaceful town. You ought to be thanking me. You ought to offer us drinks and food."

"Forget the food," Hurd said.

A tall man in the circle glanced at the older woman and muttered loud enough for me to hear, "He's got no arms, Jenny. How much harm can he do?"

Jenny took a step toward me and pointed. "Look at the swords! Two swords and no hands! He has demon arms that we can't see!" Most of them murmured at that.

The girl with the spear frowned at me. "I don't believe in arms you cannot see. You might be friends with that big demon and then trying to make fools of us. If you're real people, where were you yesterday?"

I jerked my chin to point behind me. "Havel. Just up the coast."

Some of the people grumbled, and a couple spit on the ground. No matter what else had changed in all these years, Havel and Drup still despised each other.

"What are those nasty Havelians doing?" asked a man I couldn't spot.

I said, "Sitting around, picking their thumbs, and farting like whales. Just like always."

I saw some nods, and everybody stood in silence for a few breaths. The girl spoke up. "There are bandits walking the roads lately, demon bandits. Maybe you can tell us something about that. I'll put questions to you later, so we won't kill you or run you off yet." She set her jaw in a way that said she might prefer to kill us. "I suppose a child and a one-eyed, old cripple cannot harm us."

That hurt more than it should, or at least more than I expected.

She nodded at Hurd. "And you're a mere squatty fellow."

Hurd grinned. "That ain't all I am."

"I'm Kenzie. I don't like it that you have all those swords. You've got four between you, which is two more than you can use."

"They're family heirlooms," I said.

She chewed her lip. "Well, lay those swords down by the road here. You, Squatty, you help your friend. Fingit shred it raw, I can't just call you Squatty! What's your name?"

"Hurd. Do you really think we're about to pitch all these swords on the dirt?"

Kenzie nodded and shook her spear.

I preferred not to harm these people, but I didn't intend to drop four magic weapons on the ground so that a bunch of porters and sailmakers could gamble them away in dice games. Hurd glanced at me and pretended to struggle with my sword belt.

I said to the young woman, "Tell me what you know about the dangers on the roads you mentioned. I guess we might have to face them unarmed."

Nobody offered me any knowledge. I feared that meant they didn't expect us to ever need weapons again. I prepared to plead with these folks to free us along with our weapons because I was so mangled and harmless. If that failed, I would start kicking them and not stop until most or all of them ran away. A single man will usually be overwhelmed by twenty enemies, but these people looked untrained and uncertain. They were definitely not expecting a brutal assault from a man with no arms.

A young, brown-haired fellow in a green jacket down by the harbor waved. In my mind, I named him Green Jacket. He bellowed, "Kenzie! They have come!" A few seconds later, a harsh bell sounded on the dockside.

Before I could ask what the bell meant, every person except Kenzie and Green Jacket scattered like mice. Most ran toward buildings uphill from the harbor. A few people near those buildings were already hurrying indoors.

Kenzie pointed at us. "You be good," she said, as if she couldn't imagine us doing anything else. "If you misbehave, I'll find you." Then she sprinted toward Green Jacket, who was beckoning her.

I followed right behind her. That wasn't good behavior on my part, and it might even have seemed foolish since I had no interest in Drup's conflicts. I might be risking harm or death on their behalf. I didn't know any details, and Vargo's family was unlikely to be waiting for me down at the dockside.

But following Kenzie was not foolish. I was hunting a stark, nasty, girl-murdering hero. I was also looking for sorcerers who could be bribed to restore my arms. Any unlikely or unexplained thing might be significant and had to be investigated. That included mysterious lights, talking animals, trees swaying against the wind, and people not behaving in a normally fearful way. To not explore such things would be irresponsible.

I ran hard, but Kenzie pulled ahead of me. I damned her for being young. Her fleetness was good luck for me, though. Black dirt hurled itself up right in front of her, making a steep mound twice her height. Although she staggered and glanced around, she didn't seem bothered about the earth squeezing a small hill up in her town.

Well, it bothered me. My understanding of the situation clarified. I had expected some kind of bandit raid or nautical disaster.

Instead, sorcerers were fighting. The people who ran to their houses looked pretty damn smart now.

I didn't know who or how many sorcerers were flinging magic around, what the argument was about, or what powers might be unleashed. None of those things mattered much to me since I had such a meager amount of power left after using some to bind Kruppin.

For many years in the Dark Lands, I had been filled with exactly as much sorcerous power as a dead toad. To survive, I had been obliged to burn every scrap I brought there with me in the first twenty years. The gods had been disinclined to help me acquire more, since I would just have used it to destroy their servants.

Hurd had found some magical power for me as he had promised. Before I had climbed the hill to the Dark Lands bridge for what I hoped was the last time, Hurd performed his ritual to give me a scant amount of power. He had Vargo empty a large leather sack and stick it over my head. Then Hurd required me to sing one of the songs of my homeland, one of the pretty ones. I figured none of that was necessary, but I was the one out of power. I did refuse to dance, no matter how many times he said I had to.

Kenzie didn't hesitate to scramble right over the dirt pile. I ran around it on the harbor side, keeping her in sight. Green Jacket, short and trim, stood to my left between us and the water. I was glancing his way when a broad, high wave leaped out of the harbor and knocked him skidding.

I heard a warbling call from Kenzie. From on top of the dirt pile she clapped one hand against her knee before rolling her head to the left. Then she pointed her right hand at a short, voluptuous woman who had come into view from around the corner of a large warehouse. The short woman clenched both fists at her sides and growled at Kenzie just before the front of the building collapsed. The rubble pinned the small woman up to the shoulders.

Dog-size Kruppin sat beside me panting. "This looks terrible. You might be slain in error. That would be unfortunate."

I cleared my throat. "It would."

"What is that hairy fellow over there doing? You could see more clearly if you stood closer."

I ignored him.

Green Jacket had struggled to his feet, wading in mud. He faced a muscular man with a vast amount of curly hair striding into town like the God of War entering the field of battle. I assumed this was the sorcerer who had used his vast, mystical skill to create that big muddy patch.

For some reason, Green Jacket burst out with mocking laughter and jabbed both hands toward Big Hair as if he were trying to poke holes through a plank wall. A sphere of flame flashed around Big Hair's head and died out just as fast, leaving the fellow staggering and holding his throat in a small cloud of wispy smoke. He was no longer Big Hair. Smoke wafted from the strands of hair he still had.

Even though Green Jacket could create fire, he couldn't burn a living creature directly. He had set the air afire for an instant to distract the man. It had done that, but it hadn't burned every bit of his hair away.

Kenzie ran up to the woman struggling under the timbers, who freed one hand and thrust it toward Kenzie with so much drama she could have been in a play. Kenzie tapped the butt of her spear against the woman's throat, and the dramatic hand fell limp. The tap couldn't have hurt a moderately large bug.

Kenzie yelled at Green Jacket, "I have her! Don't you play tricky with him!" She circled one hand in the air, palm up, while pointing at the ground and hooting.

Green Jacket shrugged without looking at her, and every bit of his enemy's clothing disappeared. Neither Kenzie nor Green Jacket seemed surprised by this development, and I wasn't either. The man probably shed his clothes himself, since nakedness is better than wearing trousers that might burst into flame around your crotch.

Hurd had walked up beside me to watch the fight. "Strangest dang thing I ever saw. What do you suppose is wrong with them?"

Kenzie cawed, and a seagull swooped to peck at the naked man's head. It flew on, but four more gulls pecked and pulled at the fellow's singed scalp as he flailed his hands at them. I almost felt bad about the shitty day he was having.

"Now!" Kenzie yelled. "Don't wait!"

The gull-bedeviled man sang a short bass note and swept both arms in front of him as if he were parting a big curtain. A great boom sounded from above him, and every seagull dropped to the ground, silent but still flapping hard.

Green Jacket had pulled a small object out of a pouch. He pitched it, howling and urging it on with both hands, as if that's what made it fly. I assumed it was a poor throw, since it struck the ground six feet to his foe's right. The object exploded there, flinging fire in all directions and hurling the poor man to the ground. He sat up and shook his head, but his skin was as red as a bad sunburn.

The scorched and naked fellow scrambled to his feet and waved both arms in the air. Green Jacket waved back, and the burned fellow trotted toward the collapsed warehouse.

Vargo said, "They don't mean any of this fighting, do they?"

"I don't understand none of this." Hurd crossed his arms.

I walked toward the warehouse. "I don't understand it, but I know what it is."

Kenzie had pulled lumber, none of it too large, off the trapped woman, and now Kenzie was rubbing the woman's ankle. They were chuckling. Green Jacket arrived, chatting with the naked man. Green Jacket pulled off that jacket, stripped off his shirt, and handed the shirt to him. "Cover yourself, Wallem, before you embarrass the women of this town. You would never be allowed to return, and who would I thrash then?"

Wallem grinned but didn't answer.

Green Jacket shrugged back into his jacket while saying, "This makes up for last week. Admit it."

Kenzie had called the small woman Pret after dropping the building on her. Now Pret grinned and said, "All right, Acton, it was fair—barely."

"Yeah," Wallem said.

"Shh. I'm concentrating." Kenzie was massaging Pret's ankle.

I looked around and saw no other townspeople. Hurd was

watching from the top of the dirt mound, elbows on his knees, and Vargo stood beside him.

"Destroying the air to drop the birds was clever," Acton said.

Pret sniffed. "But you'll see it coming next time."

"Yeah," Wallem said, rubbing his scalp.

"All done!" Kenzie helped up Pret.

Pret put her hands on her hips. "New moon next? You come to us?"

Everybody nodded and laughed. Pret and Wallem said farewell and walked away, waving behind them.

This kind of play-sorcery was something students in training did when they were twelve or thirteen years old, although using a fraction of the power. By the time students were sixteen, they would be bargaining with gods, healing diseased villages, killing their enemies, and often being killed. Magic was too grave and costly to play with.

I ran and caught up with Pret and Wallem. "Pardon me, I'm Jimp the horse trainer."

"What's wrong with your dog?" Pret asked.

"Runt of the litter. Are such fine contests common around here?"

They nodded, and Pret said, "We fight like this a few times each month. If you count up the sorcerers in all the towns and villages around, thirty or so fights happen from moon to moon."

"I see. I hope you're victorious next time. And remember me for any horse training."

I trotted back to the others. Kenzie was grasping Acton's upper arm as she said in a tight voice, "Worst of all, Acton, you hesitated in the first bits, and we lagged from there. We almost lost!"

Acton stood on his toes and stared after their departing opponents. "They will expect the same next time. They will not expect me to build a wall of fire in front of them so fast they can't move!"

"Can you do that?"

"No. But I'll figure out how before the new moon."

She patted his shoulder. "You basket of strategy and guile!" I realized she was probably a year or two older than him, or else he wasn't well grown.

"I'll want your thoughts on the problem. Will you help me?" he asked her.

"No, I trust you! And I have no sympathy with fire magic. It makes my teeth hurt."

Acton looked as if he'd been kicked.

Kenzie turned away and limped uphill. She had healed Pret, and for a while, she would now feel the pain of Pret's wound.

I wondered what this all said about the state of sorcery on the island. Maybe this area was a sad, isolated instance.

Kenzie looked over her shoulder. "Don't forget to thank Lutigan for victory in your prayers tonight!"

I stood unmoving and thought about that. No sorcerer who had bargained with a god could worship those cruel, random, self-glorifying creatures. That had been the case in my day, at least. But these two seemed to be worshipping and happy to do it. Was this behavior what my struggle and exile in the Dark Lands had bought?

I sneered at the ground. These children could play at sorcery and abase themselves if they cared to. The important thing was that Kenzie was a Caller, able to heal others. If she could ease a sore ankle, she could regrow two arms. It was a mere matter of degree.

I was about to become Kenzie's best friend.

SIX

Among my teachers at sorcery school, Master Oua taught the basics of magic and sorcerous feats to me and my thirteen-year-old ignorant hooligan classmates. Despite the title, Master Oua was a woman. A sorcerer who was generally acknowledged to be quite powerful, or knowledgeable, or deceptive might be awarded the title Master, whether male or female. Sometimes sorcerers just started calling themselves Master, and nobody much cared. Most sorcerers died by their early twenties, so who had time to get testy over all this master crap?

Master Oua wasn't just a woman; she was a woman of unutterable beauty. All of us yearned to raise mountains out of the sea and make the dead come to life (things no sorcerer could really do), yet we boys often found our attention drifting during her lectures. Whenever our devotion to her became so profound that she could no longer credibly ignore it, she required us to stand on one leg during her lecture until we collapsed, then switch to the other leg, then back to the first leg, and so on.

I was not a sharp or dedicated student, but I wanted to be. I wanted it so badly that I acted as if I were the best student of all, and I fought any suggestion that I wasn't both brilliant and hard-working. That led to odd behavior such as chopping wood by torch-light two hours before sunrise, which was where Master Oua found me one winter morning.

"Bib, do that later. You're keeping us all awake."

I bowed, and Master Oua signaled that I could rise. I said, "Master, if I chop wood now, everybody will have wood for their fire when they get up. I can't believe nobody has thought of this!"

"They have plenty of wood already. You aren't accomplishing anything."

"Well, maybe somebody has run low."

"You didn't chop this wood. You obliterated it." She eyed the piles of chips and slivers I had created all around the chopping block. "Maybe you're worried about something besides building fires."

I looked down and clenched my teeth.

"Maybe you're having a hard time with the mechanics of magic."

"It doesn't make any sense! Squares, and bands, and areas, and target areas!" The words bubbled out of me. "Just when I learn who the gods are, then I have to learn their histories, and what they like, and who they hate and why. I have to learn the name of some spirit in the desert that I won't run across in a million years! Can a Bender bend a whole pile of dirt, or just individual pieces of dirt? Is it better to call two wolves or a hundred chickens?" I bit back a frustrated scream.

Master Oua pointed at the chopping block. "Sit down."

I sat despite feeling that she might seize the axe and sweep off my useless head.

"Remember these things I'm about to tell you, Bib. You need power for magic, and you can only trade with the gods to get it. Gods will make you do awful things or have them done to you. You'll have to give up things and people you love, or lose memories, or learn things that you'll wish you didn't know. That's the simple part."

She held up a hand to stop the flow of ignorant questions from my mouth. "The gods want to screw you, they will screw you, and there's no way to prevent it unless you cut out this sorcery nonsense. Every sorcerer who rejects magic eventually goes back to it. There are no recorded exceptions. It's more insistent than any drug.

"Remember these things. They are the tree trunk. Hang every other bit of knowledge from that trunk. I want you to think about that for a month before you ask even one more question about magic. Now, smother that damn noise and go to bed."

That was the last time I spoke to Master Oua. She was killed soon after that, although I never heard how she died. She couldn't have been much older than twenty. Sorcery is a chancy business. Four of my early teachers were already dead when I turned sixteen, and the masters told me to go away, try to do something good, and not come back.

Kenzie and Acton were taking their sorcerous power—the kind that Master Oua had wielded to her death—and playing with it like little boys wrestling behind the house. I spit on the ground.

Hurd raised an eyebrow at me and spit too. "Maybe it all seems wrong because it ain't the way you like it."

I said, "Forget it, I have more important business than play-sorcery."

Kenzie called from behind me, "Wait!"

For only the second time today, I smiled.

She limped up the slope toward us. "Let me see your stump." She pointed at the right one.

If Kenzie wanted to heal even one arm, that was too much good fortune to contemplate. I let her examine it while I sighed and said, "Just leave it. I'll be hefting anvils tomorrow."

I had expected that would make her insist on healing me. I hadn't expected her to give my stump a vicious poke with her finger. I screamed like a child and turned away.

"Must be tiny anvils. Give it over." She removed the cloth Pala had bandaged me with in the Dark Lands. Kenzie said, "Maybe chipmunk anvils. I wonder what chipmunk armor would be like?"

"It would be a little bigger than a chipmunk," I said.

She laughed. "The people around this place wouldn't know a

sense of humor if it crawled up inside them and laid eggs. This looks bad."

Vargo said, "Oh! I thought his arm had been cut off in the good way."

"See? That was not at all funny. Push against my hand." She nodded. "All right, stop, you'll burst something you might want later. It's bad, the worst I've seen since school. But you'll live." She pointed at Vargo. "Find me some bandages."

That sapped my wind. "You don't think it—?"

"No." Her mouth set in a line as she sat back on her heels.

I couldn't blame her for not wanting to spend a lot of power for my new arm. I was nobody to her.

"I was admiring your sorcery earlier," I said. "Have you ever done something like restoring an arm?"

Kenzie hesitated. "No."

"I know a bit about sorcery. I could probably teach you some things about healing while you fixed my arms."

Laughing, Kenzie said, "Now that's humor! You're far too old to be a sorcerer! You're too old to be two sorcerers. You're even too old to be a horse trainer!"

I managed not to curse, not even under my breath.

At that moment, the town shocked me for the second time in an hour. Dozens of the residents had fled to hide in buildings during the sorcery fight. Most of those and probably more had now crept back outside to converge on an open space uphill from us. When a little crowd had gathered, they began shouting, scurrying, babbling, and passing objects to one another.

Kenzie trotted toward the open space without saying anything else.

"I can pay!" I called after her.

She ignored me.

"Are you having a party?" I shouted weakly.

Hurd yelled, "If you are, I'll come find you for a dance later. Wear something pretty!" He chuckled and said to me, "Aggravating her is about all the fun to be had in this place."

"Do you want me to haul her back here?" Vargo asked. "Politely, I mean."

"I think she's done with us," Hurd said.

Vargo dusted off his hands. "Why the heck are we still here then? It smells like the bad side of a goat, the people are ignorant, and my family lives someplace else."

I sighed. "Kruppin, I want you." Dog-size Kruppin raced up behind me, seized the cuff of my trousers, and shook it in a frenzy.

"Whenever you're finished . . ."

Kruppin sat with his tongue lolling.

"Kruppin, this is my second command to you. Tell me where Alamore the hero is." The orange band dissolved from Kruppin's ankle.

"I don't know, Sorcerer. I might not tell you if I did know. And you don't get that command back!"

"I understand." It had been worth the risk of wasting a command. "Well, let's go. Every hour we wait is an hour some crazy soldiers might spend cutting the throats of Vargo's people."

Vargo stared at me.

A man's voice behind us said, "You may as well leave." Acton had walked up and surprised me. "But you should wait until morning. The roads will be safer."

"I'll decide which way to walk and when," I said, peeved that he had sneaked up on me.

He nodded. "Kenzie has made up her mind about you. Changing her thoughts will be like towing that ship out of harbor with your . . . tongue."

"Have you ever changed her mind about something?" I asked.

Acton blinked. "Yes."

"How did you do it?"

He pursed his lips for a few seconds. "I threatened to burn her to death."

Without pausing, Vargo asked, "Did you offer to bash her senseless first? Or would you just let her scream?"

Acton swallowed, but his voice was steady. "I admit, I didn't specify."

"Either way, it sounds like a great deal of work," I said. "Do you think she'd change her mind if I threatened to kick her to death?" I tried not to grin at the pained look on Acton's face. "Come on, you were the one who raised the idea of killing her."

Acton stepped back and frowned. "Maybe she would heal you. But I don't think you'd like any arms she gave you under such conditions."

"I see. Young man, you've been far more helpful than I expected," I lied.

Acton shrugged and walked toward Kenzie and the open space, which I now saw was going to become a bonfire.

"Well done," Hurd said. "That was some prime negotiating."

"Bib, I hate to open myself to ridicule, but I've been thinking," Vargo said. "You're . . . well, you're not right, but you're less than all wrong. You'll be less useless with arms. If we can change that girl's mind about healing you, it will be time well spent. I don't believe that boy has tried every civilized way there is to convince her of things."

"All right. Let's walk up there to that crowd," I said. "Maybe a timber will fall off the pile onto Kenzie's head and make her forget who I am."

Near the wood pile we came upon seven men and women screaming at one another. Kenzie and Acton were watching, so I stood near Kenzie at a familiar but respectful distance. "What is this about?"

"The town elders are meeting again," Acton said.

I waited.

Kenzie added, "The hunched man and the plumpish woman want to rebuild the warehouse that I knocked down, and they want to use town money."

Acton nodded. "They're my favorite ones."

"Those twins with the veins popping out of their heads want me to pay to rebuild it." Kenzie crossed her arms. "The man with the big beard and the woman with the small mustache want to put me in shackles and make me personally rebuild the warehouse with my own hands."

Acton said, "And the man with the jowls like a mudslide wants to burn her on the bonfire."

"And everybody is blaming everybody else—and me—for everything that I've done wrong since I was born," Kenzie said through gritted teeth.

"Your odds sound poor," I told her. "Maybe you should run. We'll help."

"But the place I live is here." She almost whined it.

Vargo asked, "Do you mean that this place is your home?"

"Yes. At least for the next few minutes." Kenzie sighed.

Vargo asked, "Why the hell isn't your family here defending you?"

Kenzie ignored him.

Acton said, "They don't approve of sorcery."

Vargo stepped forward to flank Kenzie, holding his sword's hilt. He stayed close, but she wouldn't know he was there unless she turned her head his direction.

I appreciated that Acton and Kenzie were handling this perilous and ignorant situation with such calm. That lasted until Kruppin trotted up and sniffed Kenzie's crotch.

"Down! Back! Down!" she shouted, pushing him away while Acton grabbed the monster around the neck. "Stay away! Jimp, control your foul dog! We need none of your sort here, old man! You're mere reckless vagabonds with no home at all!" When she said *home*, tears began sliding down her cheeks, even though she stood straight and kept her face still. Acton put a hand on her shoulder, and she brushed him away.

Hurd walked into the middle of all that furor, pointed at me, and shouted, "Everybody! Everybody, listen! I can't bear there to be a misunderstanding. You all ought to stop calling this rank piece of leather Jimp. His real name is Bib."

I hated to be known by my regular name. It could cause complications, and little good ever came from it. Now as I scanned the gathered townspeople, I saw plenty of uncertain faces, but also some amused and a few angry.

Acton asked, "Your name is Bib?" People behind him murmured to one another.

I had been trying to avoid this. Years ago, Pil had spread around the story of my pre-Dark Lands exploits. I had hoped to duck any hero worship or celebrations, even though I had engaged in desperate combat to protect this realm since before most of these people had been born.

But it looked like I couldn't avoid being lauded at least a bit. "Yes, I'm Bib."

Kenzie giggled first, and a dozen others followed. Somebody laughed right out, and people picked that up quickly. Soon more than a hundred folks from my home village were laughing at me. Some were pointing too.

I took a step toward the biggest bunch of townspeople and shouted, "What? Did I say something funny? Is there something on my cheek?"

People laughed even harder. If I still had at least one arm . . . well, I doubt I'd have killed them, but they'd soon realize that laughing was a mistake. I stood there, simmered, and pretended I didn't care.

It hit me then. Despite my age, I had a juvenile dream about astounding everybody when I came home. It was as if they had treated me shabbily as a boy, but now I had come home in glory.

Now that I was admitting the dream, it seemed too foolish to bear. But the years I spent killing and being cut up in the Dark Lands didn't seem foolish at all.

"Why are you laughing?" I shouted again.

Acton wiped his eyes. "You know, it's the stories. Every child learns the Bib stories to understand what they shouldn't do."

Kenzie added, "Lying, cheating, murder, blasphemy, sloth, drunkenness, on and on. All the things Bib does in the stories. To say 'You're a Bib' is like saying 'You're a worthless ass.' When you make a mistake or break something, people say, 'You bibbed that, didn't you?' Don't you know this? Where are you from?"

Catching his breath, Acton asked me, "Why would you call yourself Bib?"

I wasn't sure what to say.

Acton chuckled. "The stories are famous on the mainland too. My grandmother told them to me when I was a little boy."

Kenzie murmured to Acton, "Don't be mean to him. Maybe he's so old he never heard the stories."

Acton pursed his lips. "Maybe he's so old that his parents named him Bib before it was a bad thing."

Kenzie walked over and laid her hand on my chest. "I'm so sorry for you. I understand why you changed your name to Jimp."

I cleared my throat and looked down. If I knew Pil, she had told the stories with marvelous accuracy, maybe even imitating my voice, so people had heard the straight tale. And I sure as hell had never been an example for anybody to follow. But for a full lifetime, I had fought, been maimed, and lived in hell for these people while they walked in the sunlight and mocked me.

When I looked up, Hurd was gone. Just about everybody else had gone back to building a bonfire and screaming at each other.

Vargo was standing beside me, and I waited for whatever insult he decided to toss. He cleared his throat. "Bib, don't pay them any attention. They're ignorant and cruel, but they didn't choose to be. It just happened that way."

I stared. "You said something nice. Who are you?"

He waved a hand. "They didn't choose to be stupider than hell, just like you wouldn't choose to kick them like they were dirt clods. It would just happen that way."

I grinned a little. "When it comes to defending myself and enforcing my will, I'm a broken dandelion of a man. A few hard kicks here and there don't change that."

"Bull! That's bad thinking. If you kick the first one so hard he curses Krak and screams for his mother, the rest will pay attention."

Pil might have said those exact words in that very way. I almost gaped at Vargo. Instead, I turned back to problems of self-defense.

I had bound Kruppin and could command him to fight for me. But if I did, he might be killed. Kruppin was beastly, but even monsters have families. If I threw his life away, he might have brothers who would want revenge. Hell, it seemed that in Kruppin's monster world, the young arrived in broods, and he could have hundreds of brothers.

Since Kenzie wasn't keen on giving me arms, I needed magical power to do nasty things to bandits and bullies. It was time to visit the gods and find out where the trading of power stood these days. It might have changed quite a bit in the seventy years since I had engaged in it.

I mentally lifted myself, feeling as if my being were stretching up through the top of my head. I called out silently to Fingit, the god who might hate me least. "Fingit, I come to trade. Or maybe to gossip."

For a second, every sensation ceased except a stab of nausea. Then I found myself standing in a hard rain on a muddy dirt patch. I saw a forest to my left, indistinct through the rain. To the right, I saw a field of white flowers covering the top of a slope that may have extended forever. I had never seen the end of it. In front of me stood a massive white marble gazebo. This was where the gods looked down on sorcerers and cracked them like bones for the marrow.

A nasal voice sounded from the shadows within the gazebo. Although I couldn't see the speaker through the heavy rain, the voice sounded nothing like Fingit. I had never heard a voice like it.

SEVEN

The nasal voice in the gazebo said, "Hello there, Murderer! I've been waiting for you to show up. You sure have a sense of the dramatic. So, let's talk. We haven't met, so we know almost nothing about each other, right? How do you like the rain? It sure washes things away, doesn't it?"

His words were fast, definite, and steeped in arrogance. I still couldn't see him, but I saw his outline striding toward the edge of the gazebo.

I said, "If we haven't met, then you ought to introduce yourself. I came into your home, and a polite creature wouldn't lurk there anonymously and talk about the weather."

"Oh! I assumed you had heard at least this much. I am Harik!"

I waited for the joke, but it didn't come. Harik, the miserable God of Death, had tormented me for years upon years. Pil and I had finally killed him, and my debts to him were paid. At last, I said, "Harik, you sound damn good for a shriveled corpse with a puckered hole in the middle of its chest."

"You're thinking of the Old Harik. I've taken over. I'm doing the job now. God of Death and everything. I have to say, this whole business has been pretty easy, so I'm hoping for you to stir the pot a little, if you know what I mean."

Even before I came to the Dark Lands, Krak had been looking for somebody to be the new God of Death. I guess this was the lucky fool. "Well, that's all as entertaining as hell. Who were you before you achieved godhood? One of Harik's horrible spawn? Never mind, I'm not really interested in the little doings that you gods engage in."

The new God of Death laughed, sounding as if he really thought that was funny. "Things may get more interesting for you as we go along."

I said, "I can't call you Harik. I couldn't look at you without getting queasy."

"But my name is Harik now. It is." The rain began to slack off. "You've got to call me something, and Harik is it. I have the job now."

"I'll compromise. I'll call you New Harik— No, wait! I'll call you Baby Harik. That's perfect."

After a pause, Baby Harik said, "I guess that'll do." He sat on the edge of the gazebo, dangling his feet, and finally I could see him in detail. He had the same black hair as Dead Harik, but there the resemblance failed.

Dead Harik had always appeared perfectly handsome and muscular, although I found his idea of perfection to be puerile. Baby Harik wasn't even handsome. His face was pale against his black hair and a bit lumpy in places. It wasn't freakish like my scarred face, but he looked as if he'd been in quite a few fistfights. His suit was an appropriate shade of black, but not nearly as black as Dead Harik's robe. Baby Harik's suit was not a robe. Instead, it looked like something a wealthy usurer might wear.

Baby Harik said, "I have to be honest, I've been waiting for this for years. Now that I have you here, insult me."

"What was that?"

"I want you to insult me. Fingit says it's part of the full God of Death experience. I don't want to miss out."

"Since you want it so much, I don't feel inclined to say nasty things to you." I felt a little creepy sensation up the back of my neck when I said that.

"Come on, come on! It will be easy for you. Let's start our relationship off the right way. You insult me, and . . . well, I'll show you in a minute what I'll say back to you."

I waited, but the bastard didn't say anything else. He just stared at me with a smarmy grin. I said, "Can't we just haggle? Cheat each other? That's the essence of the sorcerer-god relationship."

"All right, fine, if that's the way you want it. You won't insult me, that's your choice. I even respect it a little bit. You don't insult me, and I don't tell you where the Knife's family is now."

"Aren't they in Sandell?"

Baby Harik shrugged. "In war, refugees scatter to the strangest spots. So, do we deal? Or are we done here?"

The Knife was the gods' name for Pil, just like my name was the Murderer. I shook my head and sighed. "You crusty, pin-dick, whirling raccoon's ass!"

Baby Harik laughed and clapped his hands. "Oh, I know you can do better than that. But it's a good start. You want to know where the Knife's family is? Somewhere in the world of man."

"That's it?"

Baby Harik laughed again. "You've been gone too long, Murderer. You failed to state the degree of specificity with which I would provide the location. Too bad for you. But at least you didn't lose much."

"I will blister you with insults three times if you tell me exactly where the Knife's family is, within six feet," I said.

"Oh, no. I think we've played that game enough."

I took a deep breath and calmed myself. I had made a foolish error, but anger was the one thing that always led to regret in the gods' trading place. "That's fine, I can find them on my own. What I really want is Alamore the hero. I want to know where he is within the length of his stupid-ass pigtail."

Baby Harik made a face. "Alamore? Nasty. I'll give you this as a gift, Murderer. If you live, you'll see him. He'll fall right into your path, but he won't be alone."

"That's awfully cryptic."

"What do you mean? It's as simple as pudding. If you live, you'll look up and see him one day. He'll bring friends, or allies, or retainers. Or maybe he'll be going on a picnic or riding somewhere to trade horses. I guess you're right, that was pretty cryptic." Baby Harik chuckled.

"Sure. By the way, what the hell are sorcerers doing nowadays? Gargling, flapping their arms, and breaking wind to do magic? Praying to you? Will you have them sacrifice goats next?"

"We never suggested they do all that, although being prayed to is always nice. It's their idea. The goat thing's a nice touch. I'll mention it to Krak tonight."

I shrugged. "I can't say I care all that much. These sorcerers got themselves into this mess. I'm pretty sure they deserve it. Ir is all screwed up, and I say that as somebody who's spent time in the Empire."

Baby Harik lowered his voice. "Oh, the poor Empire. That never came back. Now it's a hundred fiefdoms owned by squabbling, inbred thieves stretched across a thousand miles. I never get tired of watching them stumble around."

"If you're not going to tell me where the Knife's family is, Baby Harik, perhaps we can trade for power. I extend to you the privilege of making the first offer."

"You do like gods to make the first offer, don't you? Do you really think it gives you an advantage? Never mind. In exchange for one square of power, you must murder both of those little sorcerers that are buzzing around you like flies."

That was typical of openings when the gods traded. They would require something outrageous, like burning ships full of innocent people, just to stake out a strong bargaining position.

I stuck out my lower lip as if I were considering the ridiculous proposition. "No, I won't do that. But for eight squares of power, I'll break the boy's foot."

Baby Harik grinned. "No. Two squares if you kill one of the little sorcerers. Take your pick."

I said, "Just to be objectionable, I'm not killing anybody."

"Really?" Baby Harik sat straighter. "Murderer, you're not objecting out of some sense of morality, are you? Could you be wasting my time? I'm the incomprehensible God of Death, so don't show up unless you're willing to deliver some death. And it better be some interesting death, not wiping out somebody who deserves it or a diseased peasant about to fall down anyway!"

"I see. How about this? For six squares, I will kill every chicken between here and the road out of town."

"Goodbye." Baby Harik flung me into my body, and I slammed onto my back. No time passes in the world of man while a sorcerer is trading with the gods. To the people around me, it must have looked as if I had thrown myself onto my back with no preparation or warning.

As soon as I looked up, Acton shouted, "Run!" Half a dozen men and women were grabbing for Kenzie, and she was backing away fast while swinging her spear. That pushed her enemies back, and she turned to flee uphill around the unlit bonfire. Vargo knocked down two men following her. Acton tripped another and ran straight out into the dusk instead of following Kenzie.

Hurd was nowhere around. "Come on!" I yelled at Vargo as I followed Acton. The young sorcerer didn't seem likely to murder a hundred people by fire, but I wanted to be safe if he tried. The safest place to be around a Burner was right beside him.

Yellow light flared to throw my shadow ahead of me. Then the bonfire's whoosh and crack slapped me, followed by the heat. I glanced back to see that Acton had kept the fire small so that it would no more than singe the screaming townspeople.

Acton ran toward the road at the top of the hill. Beyond him, I saw Kenzie pause for him before running away fast.

No, in my mind I didn't see Kenzie running away. I saw my two new arms running away.

EIGHT

I thought that Vargo and I would catch Kenzie and Acton in a couple of minutes. Vargo did a creditable job and had just about caught up to them while the bonfire was still in sight. I was fifty feet back and thinking bad thoughts about Vargo and his young legs. I would be pleased if he stepped in a hole and sprained his ankle.

That didn't happen before the two young sorcerers turned back toward us. Kenzie shouted, "Go away! Go away home, or I'll turn your stomachs into nests full of rats!"

That might have made me go home if I hadn't known how empty her threat was. No sorcerer could accomplish a feat like that. Well, a handful might, but they were peculiar and rarely seen.

I walked toward the youngsters and called out, "We just want to travel with you on these scary roads. That's safer for all of us, right?"

Acton yelled, "We do not need the companionship of a bib and his dense friend. This night will be challenging enough without that."

"As I said before, I can teach you some sorcery."

"Stop the lying!" Kenzie yelled. "You shouldn't talk about sorcery. Your legs will fall off just like your arms did."

"Challenge me on numbers," I said. All sorcerers excelled at basic math.

I was close enough now to hear Acton say, "He's wasting our time. He's probably slowing us down so the others can catch us."

"It will take not even a minute," Kenzie said and then called out, "What's 42 times 77 plus 903?"

"4,137," I said without pausing.

They stared at me. Acton said, "What's the square root of 121 times pi?"

"19.497."

"Ah! Is that the square root of 121 multiplied by pi? Or is it the square root of the number that results from multiplying 121 times pi?"

I said, "Just to entertain ourselves, the cube root of the first one is 3.257. The cube root of the other is 2.691. Maybe the bandits that come along in a minute will have harder questions."

Acton frowned and cleared his throat. "What's—"

"That's enough," Kenzie said. "Are you a sorcerer then, old Bib? Or are you trying to trick us somehow? That seems more likely."

"I used to be a sorcerer." I waggled my stumps. They didn't need to know that I could do magic without my hands.

"I don't trust strange sorcerers," Acton said. "You must want your arms restored, but you may simply kill us once Kenzie's finished."

It was a hell of a time to show he'd learned something useful like suspicion.

"You can hold my servant hostage against my good behavior." I nodded at Vargo.

He backed away a step. "The hell you will."

"And if I break my promise to be good, you can have my dog."

Kruppin howled from someplace in the woods.

"That poor dog. So ugly," Kenzie said. "But I don't want it."

It was time for the real prize. "And no matter how I behave, you can have this magic sword." I jerked my head toward the hilt over my shoulder.

Kenzie shook her head. "I don't like swords overmuch. The spear is better for me. I have long arms. Keep your magic sword."

Acton cleared his throat but didn't contradict her.

I felt like I'd been kicked in the stomach by a disgruntled mule. "What would you like in exchange for healing one of my arms?"

"I can't think of a single thing," Kenzie said. She grabbed Acton by the sleeve, and they trotted north up the road toward Sandell. At least they were headed in the right direction.

"That was a catastrophe, and don't argue. What are you going to do now?" Vargo asked as we ran after them.

"We'll stay close. They'll get into some sort of foolish trouble soon and need a kind, armless stranger to save them."

Layers of clouds had been sliding across the sky all afternoon. Soon they closed in, and it was as dark as anything I had ever seen except for a tomb. The moon wouldn't rise until late, and the clouds blocked the stars.

Kenzie and Acton slowed to a creeping pace, and we caught them by sound in just a few minutes. My eyesight was superior, but not enough to see in pure darkness.

The young sorcerers didn't try to chase us away, but they also refused to leave the road and wait for better light when I suggested it. They feared that their bloodthirsty friends and neighbors would overtake them, and no argument from me could sway them. They trotted up the road, lucky that it ran straight hereabouts, and well-nigh certain to blunder into any horror that might be waiting.

The road ran along the coast about a mile from the ocean. I made sure to stay on it by walking slowly and paying attention to how the ground felt under my boots. The salt smell overwhelmed every other scent. I had traveled this road a couple of times in my youth and remembered passing dense thickets of bare, flesh-tearing trees that covered the slope down to the beach. Steep hills of sharp, black rocks blocked the way inland."

I said casually, "Have care. The trees and brush just off the road here are harsh enough to tear your flesh bloody, to say nothing of your eyeballs and private areas. Do you see them?"

After a pause, Acton said in a wavery voice, "I do."

"That's good," I said. "My brother bumbled into those thickets, and what came out was more dead than alive."

Kenzie asked, "How far off the road would we find the thickets?"

I stopped. "You mean you can't see them? That could be a disaster. Well . . . the distance varies. Let's go."

After a few minutes of uncertain creeping along the road, everybody else fell back and let me lead, but they still refused to delay.

We traveled that way in the darkness for a couple of hours before Vargo stopped dead. "I hear something."

We all stopped to listen and heard footsteps coming toward us at a run.

"In the bushes!" I whispered. I pushed my way into the dense, scratchy undergrowth and settled to watch the road from hiding. I heard the young people doing the same.

Just a few seconds later, a hornet stung my arm. I heard Acton say "Scat!" as he slapped at something.

In a fierce whisper, I said, "Quiet! Be silent if you want to live!" That might have been an overly dramatic statement, but I needed to slam the idea into their heads.

Runners came closer, some carrying torches. A hornet buzzed, and Kenzie squeaked.

"Quiet, dammit!" I growled. "Those hornets are just protecting their nests. They deserve a home too, so hush!"

In the darkness, Kenzie stifled a whimper, and I wished I hadn't talked about homes in front of her.

I figured thirty or so runners passed us while we breathed deep and twitched every time a hornet stung us. Then the formation halted about one hundred feet down the road.

Out of breath, a woman's deep voice said, "Rest three minutes, not more than that."

A few men groaned.

"Shut it! You'd rather get hung and bled?"

The woman walked back up the road and stopped in front of us, along with a tall, stooped man.

"I thought they was nothing but stories," the tall man said in a sad voice.

"We need to stop all this ignorant thinking crap and just run away," the woman said.

The tall man answered, "Maybe they'll stop at every village and town. Maybe."

"Maybe, maybe, maybe!" the woman mimicked in a whine. "Maybe they'll sprint all the way to the southern end of the island."

"If they do, we might still get there first and steal some boats, may—" He coughed.

"Oh, of course, that sounds easy enough." She paused. "It's an idea, though. Although the seas will be rough. Let's charge right through these pissant towns. I bet those horrors will stop to kill everybody behind us. Probably the big, ganky ones."

I saw the tall man hang his head. "We're paying now for our cushy-pushy, feathery life. The gods are punishing us for our wickedness and theft."

The leader said, "Shut that! If the men hear that, we'll fall apart. Every flipping one of us will die. Time to march."

"March, my ass."

Within a minute, the formation ran away south toward Drup. We picked our way out of the thicket, rubbing our welts.

"My lips are huge," Kenzie mumbled. "Must have stung me just on the lips a hundred times."

"I can't see." Vargo hissed. "My cheeks and eyelids are too swollen."

"I will be pleased to tie a rope around your neck and lead you," Acton said.

Vargo grumbled, "Oh, that's funny. If you try, don't let me grab you first."

I said, "All of you just think, if you hadn't suffered and held your asses still, we'd be dead now. Well, maybe not me. But nobody is playing at combat out here. You'd better understand that quickly if you want to live. Of course, you'll probably die anyway, but at least you won't be toddling around about it like a five-year-old."

"What did she mean by saying, 'hung and bled'?" Kenzie asked. "And what are the ganky ones?"

"Don't know." I laughed. "Isn't this a fine adventure? From here, we head on north, have our adventure, and maybe die. Or we can strip off all our skin walking through these aggressive trees down to the coast. Or climb those nasty hills and die falling off. What's your pleasure?"

I didn't care what they said they wanted. I just wanted them to argue and beat on each other enough so they wouldn't argue with me. I intended to follow Kenzie and her healing hands even if she bled her way to the coast and wandered to Sandell picking up seashells.

They each wanted to do something different, and they defended their desires in passionate argument. I waited for them to run down, and I smiled when they chose to head north exactly as we had been doing already.

After another hour or so of marching, I spotted light ahead. "Maybe that's an inn, or a horse trader. They must have a lantern out."

I led us forward but slowed when I saw that the light was coming from the ground near the inn, which was dark.

I glanced back toward the others. "Stay here."

Vargo said, "I'll come too. Don't thank me. If a fight comes, I don't want to think about you slapping people with those stumps."

I didn't argue, and all four of us walked to the inn. Light shone from the ground in four irregular spots, each the size of a bedsheet. Although the soil in this part of Ir was black and grainy, the dirt in these lit areas was light brown, dry, and covered with scraggly, dark green grass.

Acton trotted around to the other three areas. "They're the same as this one."

"Holy Krak!" Kenzie yelped. "Something's there!"

I had seen it too. A small, gray creature had scurried into the light and run all the way across it. I couldn't see where it had gone, even when I knelt to look for a trace.

"There's another one here," Vargo said from another lit area. A gray creature was nosing around near the edge of the light. It looked like a squirrel with huge hindquarters. "Mine's better than yours, Kenzie. Meatier."

"Everybody be still," I said. "If it runs, try to mark where it goes." I walked toward the animal, staying out of its blotch of light. When I was two feet away from it, I stomped the ground. The creature didn't twitch. I jumped up and down. I shouted and whistled, but the big-butt squirrel just nosed the grass and chewed.

"Acton," I said. "Slowly extend just your fingers into that lit area, up at arm height."

Acton did so, and the big-butt squirrel seemed not to notice him. "Now snap your fingers."

When Acton snapped, the squirrel jumped and shot away.

"I don't see where it went," Kenzie said.

"Me either." Vargo was patting the ground where the animal should have been running.

"Vargo, hand me that rope out of your pack," I said.

Within a few minutes, the rope was tied around Kenzie's waist, and she held her spear in both hands. When she stepped into the lit area, her boot pushed in by about a foot and then bounced back as if she had stepped against a sail pulled taut. She tried twice more without success.

I glanced at Acton. "Not many more things to try."

Acton lifted an eyebrow at me. He picked up a black rock and tried to toss it over the lit area. The rock bounced off the empty air and back toward Acton's feet. Acton picked up the rock and examined it. "I wish we had a shovel."

"That would be fun," I said. "I don't think we can accomplish anything more now."

"Have we accomplished anything yet?" Vargo asked.

Acton said, "We can add it to the list of things we don't understand."

Vargo snorted. "Those spots look foreign to me. At least, they don't look like the rest of this garden spot."

"Maybe they are foreign," I said.

Everybody stared at the lit areas. "Do you mean they might be openings to a foreign realm?" Acton asked.

"I'm pretty sure I didn't mean that, but you have pointed out an interesting possibility." I scratched my beard. "Why would Lossil want them?"

Vargo said, "Maybe we've lost already. Maybe these spots will grow and cover the whole world. Make it . . . something full of squirrels with big butts."

I shook my head. In just a few seconds, Acton and Vargo had come up with clever ideas while I stood there gaping. "We can't rub them out right now, and we have other problems chasing us like wolves."

Kenzie walked back from the inn with an unlit lantern. "It's deserted. Everything's orderly, but there're no people about."

"I had thought we might sleep at the inn, but let's not," I said. "I'd rather not follow the missing innkeeper to wherever he went." Vargo started to strike a light for the lantern, but I stopped him.

"Every villain for two miles will see us, hide, and jump out to kill us," I said. "Better to flounder a bit in the darkness."

We resumed our march.

After midnight, the clouds slipped aside to show a gibbous moon. We moved at a better pace, and I hoped that moving faster would offset the risk of stumbling into something nasty.

When sunrise still lay a couple of hours off, I spotted something far down the road. I shooed Vargo and the others into another thicket. After a few seconds, we all relaxed when no hornets stung us.

A military formation twenty-five strong approached at a fast march. Each soldier was armed with a short spear and a sword that was improbably long since none of the soldiers looked to be taller than five feet. I could tell that they were broad men, and I saw no hair on their skulls or their faces.

When these soldiers had come within one hundred feet of us, I whispered, "Be still and quiet!"

Two of the soldiers pointed straight at me and said something in a language I didn't understand. Pil's language charm failed me. Six other soldiers peeled off the formation and trotted toward us.

"Thank you so much, Bib!" Kenzie whispered.

I whispered, "If they want to take you prisoner, let them, and don't show that you're sorcerers. You can escape later." I spent one second debating whether to use Kruppin's third command here and decided there was too much to lose if I didn't. "Kruppin, I want you."

Dog-size Kruppin pushed through the brush beside me. "Would you like your feet rubbed? Your butt wiped?"

"Take my swords and Vargo's. Keep them safe. Give them only to Hurd, Vargo, or me."

"Glad to," Kruppin said. An orange band dissolved and drifted away from Kruppin's wrist.

I heard Vargo shout in pain. Then a snap of pain tore through my waist and chest as Kruppin ripped the two sword belts off my body. A bound creature couldn't hurt or kill the binder. But if the binder was a moron and commanded the creature to do something that would hurt, making it hurt a lot was within the rules.

The soldiers hauled us out of the thicket—not gently, but without much brutality, either. They tied everybody's wrists behind them except for me. Three of them discussed the problem and finally decided to lead me by a rope around my neck. They goaded us south with their spears, and we headed back toward Drup.

We marched for only half an hour before we met a similar force herding about one hundred of Drup's residents and a few of the bandits we'd seen. Quite a few people were bloody. The townsfolk of Drup had stopped screaming at each other and had taken up crying and begging instead.

Then we stood around until dawn. These soldiers made it clear that talking was the worst crime a prisoner could commit, so we were left with our thoughts. I relaxed and considered ways to escape.

We might not all get away. In fact, it was likely somebody wouldn't, and I could take advantage of that. Vargo was Pil's kin, so I shouldn't betray him. I needed Kenzie, at least until she restored my arms. That left Acton available to sacrifice when it came time to escape, if I needed a diversion.

I blinked when I realized this might be the kind of thing people didn't like Bib doing in those stories.

NINE

At dawn, another formation of thirty soldiers marched in from the north herding about fifty people from other villages. These troops towered over the short, broad ones. They towered over me. The tiniest of them was a head taller than me, and most were wide in the shoulders.

The short soldiers were wearing furs, and at first, I thought these tall ones were as well. I soon realized that they were instead covered with their own fur. The colors ranged from medium gray to white and even blond. They wore leather loincloths, belts, and harnesses where they carried their long, barbed swords.

A deep voice from the rear, so relaxed it sounded sleepy, said, "Pull off any blindfolds, will you, please? They won't be killed by witnessing our beauty, will they?"

A few of the short soldiers around me chuckled. By his voice, the speaker struck me as lazy or shy. Every strong leader I had known had been definite and energetic, even domineering. This one probably couldn't get a damn thing done and should expect to be murdered by his own men soon.

The leader pushed his way forward. I held my breath when I saw him. I felt sure that he was a monster in the technical sense. For the most part, he looked like a great, brown cat about like a tiger in shape but more massive and far less striped. His claws glinted like crystal, and his fangs dripped with something that smoked as it fell.

He would have no discipline problems, even if he wriggled on the ground with his belly in the air.

The Not-Tiger's tail twitched. "Who would like to go back and chase stragglers?"

Several soldiers, both tall and short, shouted at the same time.

"Go on then, but mind that you come back soon. And for the sake of One, don't get wrapped up in killing people. Unless you have to. You know what I mean."

The half dozen soldiers trotted back toward Drup. One of them laughed that Drup's women smelled bad and broke too easily. As the others guffawed, I realized that when the tall and the short soldiers spoke to each other, they used my language—the tongue of the western kingdoms.

I put this quirk of language away to think about later. Now I had a moment to really look around. I saw a hundred or so people from Drup bound and standing in well-guarded clumps. Some were bloody, but most stood without help. The rest must have escaped or been murdered.

The Not-Tiger spoke up. "Some of you may not yet have heard, so I shall tell you about my deal. I am Burrud, and I wish to make you, the fine people of Ir, this offer. Some person arrived yesterday in an unusual manner. I wish to talk to this individual. If you point out this person for me, I will release everyone here to go unharmed, and I will give you each a piece of gold. Then I'll just go away. Wouldn't that be nice?"

Vargo and I were screwed. Nobody cared about us, and there must be thirty people who could point us out. I shouted, "It's that old woman there! The one with the blue skirt and the mean face!" I used my chin to point at the woman who had given me such grief when I was talking to Kenzie. Vargo joined in a few seconds later.

That did it. Two dozen people denounced me right away, but they couldn't point because their wrists were bound. Twenty or so took this opportunity to turn on other people present, probably neighbors or family members who had made them mad somehow. Some of those retaliated against their accusers or even turned against other townspeople. Then people from different towns threw out some hideous accusations about Drup and each other. The bandits stayed quiet and tried to make themselves small.

Within thirty seconds, half the people were shouting about how guilty somebody else was, sometimes denouncing two or three people at a time. Dozens were being accused of some vague but certainly bad thing, and I was just one among them.

Burrud growled twice, a sound that created a rumble deep in my belly. Then he roared, loud and long. It was a great creature promising that he wouldn't just kill me and wouldn't just eat me but would start eating and eat until I died. People cried out, leaned on one another, or collapsed to huddle on the ground. It was the rare sort of event that sorcerers like to examine because so much can be learned about people.

I jerked when I realized I was the only person standing and watching everything as if it were all a trained pony show. I cried out and dropped to the ground, trying to force my face into the dirt.

Burrud purred. "I see you."

He lay on his belly and stared at me. "If you don't find it inelegant for me to say, your disguise is shockingly good. Who did you trust enough to cut off your arms? I'd like to meet him."

I stood and rubbed my cheek against my shoulder, which may have put on more dirt than it took off. "I am Bib, the . . . bad example. If you don't let me go, within a week, your men will all be corrupted by willfulness and treachery."

Burrud peered at me, whiskers quivering around his eyes and cheeks. "You don't belong here. Well, you do belong here, which makes it even stranger that you don't belong here. Don't you agree?"

I shook my head with great emphasis. "I'm not this . . . whoever it is you're looking for. Just let me go. How dangerous can I be wandering the fields and beaches with no hands?"

"Oh, I intend to let you go, don't worry about that, as soon as I find out a few things. Trust me," Burrud said, purring again.

"How about this? Let me fight for my freedom against your best man."

Burrud's ears came up and his tail whipped. "You wouldn't be a sorcerer, would you?"

"Even if I was, I can't use my hands, so you're safe. And to make you safer, even if I was a sorcerer with hands, I promise not to use any sorcery. Which I can't do anyway, of course."

Burrud gave me a slow blink.

I shrugged. "I don't see how you can say no and keep any kind of self-respect."

"It's tempting," Burrud said. "But if you are defeated, you will be dead, which won't help me. If you win, I'll lose a good man, and we will be shamed because a person with no arms defeated us."

"We could fight until the first touch." By this point, I had no idea what I was doing. I was just saying things and hoping something smart came out of my mouth.

Kenzie may have seen that I was floundering. Her eyes flashed, and she drew a breath to commit suicide by cursing Burrud, telling him he was cruel and unfair, and maybe spitting on him. I saved her by saying, "Let me answer your questions, Burrud, so we can put that behind us."

He snorted. "Tell me something truthfully. Is this kingdom your home?"

"I suppose so."

"Do the people here love you?"

I laughed.

"Do they respect you? Tolerate you? Would they pull you out from under a falling granite block?"

"Probably that last one."

Burrud asked, "Do you have any family in this kingdom?"

"No, not anymore." Pil's family wasn't my kin.

"Where do you belong, then? I don't mean your home. Where do you really belong?"

I waited for a few seconds, trying to predict what he'd say next.

"Do you belong with these people?" He whipped his tail toward the mass of townspeople. "Or do you belong with heroes from across the realms, throwing magic that reshapes worlds? Performing unparalleled feats of arms?" He leaned closer so that his face almost touched mine. "Beer, wine, weapons, women, and horses—the finest in every realm."

I snorted. "You're overselling it. Nothing could be that good."

"You're right, it's better. We also have all the subterfuge and prevarication that a subtle person could desire. Join us for a month, or even a day. If you don't like it, you can go your way with no harsh feelings."

"Damn. Now I know it's too good to be true."

Burrud laughed. "I would say the same thing if I were you. But I would be wrong."

I sighed and jerked my head toward Vargo. "I'm here to save that young man's business. His family has a brothel with a gambling house overlooking the ocean. It's unique. I have to do that before I do anything else."

The big cat's whiskers twitched. "I cannot promise that you would be allowed to do that, and I won't lie to you. We can ask Lossil when we join him."

I managed to keep my face straight. Alamore had said he served Lossil. I raised my eyebrows and asked in a light tone, "So, Lossil is your boss?"

Burrud's tail twitched. "He is."

I examined Burrud down the length of his body and up from his claws to his teeth. "Lossil must be twenty feet tall with marble skin and an iron-plated dick."

Burrud's lips curled into something like a smile. "No, he's nothing like that." He paused. "He could easily kill me, but his penis would be irrelevant. Think about what I have said."

"I certainly will, Burrud. I'll think hard about it."

A short soldier hustled me away from Burrud, who started a little conference with a few troops of both sizes. The soldier stood me in place, picked up a rope, and stared at me while chewing his lip. Another laughed and pushed him aside. This one bound my upper body with the skill of a sailor.

Everything around looked as organized as a barrel of chickens to me, but when Burrud ordered us to march, the troops fell in right away. They shouted and shoved the prisoners northward. The farming town of Pith lay that direction, and the city of Sandell farther along.

I returned to watching for chances to escape. Maybe sacrificing Acton wasn't the right thing to do. I felt sure I'd do it anyway if necessary.

I listened to the short and tall soldiers chatter, complain, and throw insults. They discussed the miserable cold weather, their horrible officers, and petty slights that individuals of one race offered to beings of the other. Their talk wasn't always friendly, but it wasn't hostile, either. I put aside any ideas of pitting one race against the other.

These troops also talked in quiet tones about Lossil. I couldn't tell whether they just didn't know much about him or didn't dare gossip about him. They tended to look down or away when they said his name.

After two hours of hard marching, the six soldiers who had gone back for stragglers caught up with us. A tall, white one, maybe the leader, spoke to the short one who had been bossing the soldiers near me. "It's done."

"Anything interesting?" the short one asked.

"No, it went about as well as the others."

I looked hard at the tall one who was reporting in. He was heavily bloodstained, and the men in his detachment looked the same.

"Damn fine." The short one grunted. "You and your men fall in at the rear."

I had thought that Burrud's main task might be looking for somebody who had arrived from another realm and that he had captured some townspeople along the way. I'd been wrong, though. His main job was to terrorize and kill the people of Ir. I was just something to retrieve if the opportunity arose.

I called out to the short soldier who seemed to be in charge around me. "Hey, where are we going?"

"Be quiet and tame yourself."

"Tame myself?"

He sneered. "Be good. Orderly."

"I am well known for orderliness. Where are we going?"

He raised his club and grunted.

I said, "I'll assume the question hasn't been settled yet. Well, where are you fellows from?" Any bit of knowledge might help me if it came to another fight. "Your home must be a fine place but challenging."

"You're full of questions." He snorted. "That's a big way to talk."

"I really am curious."

We traveled at a march for a while. Then he blew out a breath and said, "We are reks. We come from Rek."

"That sounds simple."

"It's not. We came here to kill in this place without love." He stared me in the eyes with no love at all.

"What? Why?" I asked.

He muttered, "It's how things are done. We kill and go home. Maybe. So shut up."

"I didn't mean to poke a sore spot."

The rek whacked me with the club, but I bet he could have hit me a lot harder. He raised his voice. "It's not sore like a little cut. Reks don't kill, but I have. You creatures kill a lot, but reks don't."

"But you said you kill and go home."

The rek glared at me. "If we could stay in Rek, we wouldn't kill."

I was quiet for a few seconds. I couldn't bring myself to ask the obvious question: What would happen to him when he went home to his people who weren't killers, and how would they look at him? Instead, I asked, "Why did you even come here?"

He shrugged. "Somebody has to. Shut up," he said without much snap.

Hell, I understood that rek better than I had any human I'd met since I came home. "I'm called Bib. If you don't mind, I'd like to know your name."

"Ere. Knowing my name won't stop me from killing you."

I nodded.

I sympathized with Ere. But even if I could sing the songs of the rek people and cook like Ere's grandma, I needed to escape soon. I had no idea what things might convince Burrud to kill me or to free me. I bet the killing list would be a lot longer. I edged away as far as the lead rope allowed and let Ere march in peace while I contemplated mischief and freedom.

Clouds had begun gathering again by late afternoon when we reached the scraggly, after-harvest wheat and barley fields of Pith. The little town smelled of cold mud, pig shit, and woodsmoke. Farmers spotted us and rushed away toward the village. Burrud's column broke into a run, and we reached the village in good time.

About three dozen small buildings stood in the village, mostly daub and wattle structures with clay walls, thatched roofs, and small doors. People ran in all directions, and Burrud's troops began encircling the town.

With a powerful growl, Burrud ran and bounded atop a larger building, lifted his head in a magnificent pose, and fell straight down through the thatched roof when it collapsed. "Shit!" he yelled. "One burn it forever!" A young woman, her face stretched in terror, hurried out through the partly crushed doorway and scurried across the lane, bouncing off a startled rek.

Burrud's face appeared in the damaged doorway, and he pushed against it, but the space was too small for his head. His soldiers started laughing as he cursed some more and scrambled up out of the house like a cat struggling out of a rain barrel. He shook his head when he reached the ground and started laughing too.

I had moved away from the frivolity with a casual shuffle. I carried more than enough magical power to rot the rope binding me. When the tall guard watching me looked away, I would rot my ropes, snap them, and then grab Vargo to race across the fields to the inland woods.

I let my head fall forward as the pain in my stumps throbbed to remind me I didn't have any dang hands. Just what did I think I'd be doing all this snapping and grabbing with? Well, I could break wellrotted ropes with my remaining upper arms. Why did I need to grab

Vargo anyway? If he couldn't follow me on command, he was less useful than a dog. I couldn't leave Kenzie behind, but I could arrange her escape better from the freedom of the woods than from the middle of Burrud's troops.

My unimaginative scab of a guard was chuckling along with the others at Burrud but never looked away from me.

"What's so funny over there?" I asked. "I don't understand."

"Burrud is doing some silly thing to raise our spirits." He kept staring at me.

"Does Burrud's tail always do that weird thing?" I asked.

The guard's head turned a fraction but stopped to keep his eyes on me.

I raised my voice. "Krak's ass! What the hell is that?"

The guard grinned. "Burrud is laughing. Everybody's laughing. Stop trying to fool me. You look dumb when you try."

I tried to look calm, but it's hard when you're clenching your jaw. "Hey, when do we eat?" I wasn't accustomed to hunger, since my un-aging body hadn't required food in the Dark Lands. But now my stomach wanted food, and I hadn't eaten since I returned yesterday afternoon.

My guard did not explain the feeding schedule. Instead, he laughed and shoved me. That was probably a bad sign.

Burrud must not have wanted information from the people of Drup and Pith. Soon his soldiers gathered the families, some wailing and some stunned, in the fallow field west of town. The soldiers carrying clubs began bashing the heads of every adult and child as they ran screaming.

I had mostly resolved not to help the people of Ir, especially once they told me about the Bib stories. As I watched the butchery in that field, my resolution not to help shattered all to hell.

I could command Kruppin to fight for these people. He'd be killed in a couple of minutes, which would nicely prevent him from trying to kill me after his fifth command. I decided against it because I suspected he'd be useful in other ways I couldn't yet predict. Also, news about a sorcerer mistreating a bound being spreads remarkably fast among creatures he might bind in the future. I could end up longing for the days when the worst thing a bound creature did to me was pee on my boots.

The best help I could give the villagers was a better chance to run.

The air was moist from the sea wind, which helped. I summoned four white bands with just my thoughts, a trick I had years before discovered while trapped in the Dark Lands' black lake. I sent them in four directions. Within a few seconds, the air went almost still. I tossed three more white bands across the field full of begging and dying people.

I drew the air above the ground a bit colder. Then thick fog settled across the entire field and over part of the village.

"Ahh!" Burrud groaned. "By One's tippy-tips!" He bounded over and growled at me, his nose a hand's width from my face. "Stop that, sorcerer!"

I wiggled my stumps. "I couldn't do magic even if I was a sorcerer."

Burrud whipped around, leaving slobber on my face, and ran off into the fog. "Everybody, guard the edges of the field!"

"Edges? Which way is that?" a rek asked, but not too loud.

I turned to whistle at Vargo and flee around the south edge of the field. The tall soldier holding my rope yanked me onto my butt.

Within a few minutes, the screaming had fallen off to a remarkable degree, while I heard soldiers cursing. The wind was trying to rise again. I spent some more power to hold it down, but I reserved enough to break free. I shouted, "Everybody, run now if you're going to go!"

My guard kicked me on the side of the head, and I ended up lying on my side. I tried to sit up, but he pressed down on my neck with his boot. I coughed, but nothing felt broken.

Screams picked up again, but not many. I hoped that was because some people had escaped, not because most were dead. I debated spending the last of my power to freshen the fog. If I ran out of power, no ropes would be rotted in the service of my freedom, but I felt clever enough to escape in some other way.

The unnatural fog thickened before I could do it. Some weather-calling sorcerer was out there throwing bands of his or her own, and my first thought was Kenzie. As a Caller, she had the proper skill.

The screams faded and died away, leaving just the profane yelling of Burrud and his soldiers. The fog lifted a minute later as the wind picked up, and the guard dragged me to my feet.

Burrud showed me his dripping teeth. "You did this, didn't you?"

I glanced across the field. About two hundred people had been herded into it. Now 130 or so bodies lay on the ground. "How could I have done this, Burrud? I've got no hands, and when the fog got thicker, I was on the ground under that fellow's nasty boot."

Burrud produced a growl that seemed a lot longer than it probably was. Then he loped away toward the middle of the village.

Now I could wait until dark, break the rope when nobody was watching me, and disappear into the woods. I thought that was a fine, solid plan, but I was wrong.

Lossil arrived before sunset and ruined everybody's plans.

TEN

I was a loud, impatient boy when I lived in Drup, which I guessed was now a town full of corpses. My innate rowdiness made me a poor hunter and not much of a fisherman, either. I did learn that when all the birds stop singing, you have been spotted. Or something more frightening than you is wandering about.

Lossil made his soldiers act like birds. When the sun fell below the clouds and threw light like a knife across the world, the troops near me stopped talking. Silence reached me from the west and moved past. Every silent soldier began applying himself to his task with a nearly religious determination. All of them glanced to the west now and then, but nobody came right out and looked.

I ignored the soldiers, stood, and peered west, although I could hardly see through the brilliant sunlight. I regretted having no available hands to shade my eyes. Then I spotted Lossil, a tall, lean figure that blocked the sun for a moment as he strode toward town.

Lossil's eyes stood out, heavy-lidded but pale gray and bright. He leaned forward as he came. The bridge of his nose was so thick it ran straight onto his forehead without a dip. His jaw was thin, his skin olive, and his short hair white. He wore a long, woolly fur coat and carried a long, oddly curved sword in his belt.

Ten creatures fanned out behind Lossil, all wearing fur coats. They were similar to him in features and form, although shorter. I looked back at my guard, who was retying my bonds even though they were already plenty tight. I asked, "What is that next to—"

The guard hauled on the rope and almost dragged me to the ground. "Shut up! Look at the sky or something."

I looked at Lossil instead of the sky. A medium-size, unexceptional brown dog paced him on the left. On his right stomped some sort of monster that looked like a hornless rhino with a thick, flat, gem-studded ridge over its neck.

Burrud ran out to meet Lossil, and they spoke too softly for me to hear. By scale, I saw that Lossil must be well over seven feet tall.

Lossil and his companions perplexed me, so I delayed my plan to escape. Anything that I heard him say or saw him do might be valuable intelligence should I survive to find Alamore and help Pil's family.

After a minute, Burrud ran off toward his troops in the field. "We shall not be staying here! Bleed the bodies in a speedy fashion. Lossil will lead us to the next town in fifteen minutes."

I expected to hear grumbling and some soldierly curses just soft enough to pretend they hadn't been spoken. Instead, the soldiers worked faster without a word.

Lossil walked into the middle of town, not forty feet away from me. He glanced at the house Burrud had fallen into but didn't comment. His gem-ridged monster charged the house three times and left it a pile of sticks, grass, and broken clay.

Burrud spoke to Lossil in a language I had never heard, but the charm on Pil's ring allowed me to understand him. Burrud said, "The men need rest, sir. The reks especially are suffering from killing these helpless people. If they were armed enemies . . . Well, it's not easy for them."

"It's not easy for anybody. One expected us to be finished a week ago," Lossil said in a flat tone. "It'll be a long night. Keep them going till moonrise and then rest them. We'll clean out two more of these towns by then." Lossil paused. "Tell the reks they don't have to kill any more of these peasants today. The difar will do it." His eyes flicked toward one of the tall, pale soldiers. "They like to kill."

Lossil's dog sat scratching his ear. When he had scratched it enough, he trotted over to Lossil, sat again, and watched his master with unblinking adoration. The monster was now stomping the already-destroyed house into splinters and dust.

Burrud nodded toward me and said, "That man may be the foreigner that One told you about. It seems unlikely, I admit, but he has survived somehow even without arms." Burrud hesitated. "He seems to belong here and also not belong, if you know what I mean." He gave the feline version of a shrug.

"I'm not sure you know what you mean." Lossil didn't smile, but he sounded as if he might be amused. He marched over to me but looked at my guard instead of me. In a rumbling voice, he said, "Zutt, that's no way to tie ropes. Let me show you." Lossil spent the next two minutes explaining how to tie better knots, demonstrating them and watching Zutt tie them. "Good. Well, better at least. The ropes won't fall off the first time he shrugs."

Lossil turned to me, and Zutt watched him. I expected to see resentment or fear. Instead, the tall soldier watched Lossil wide-eyed, leaning forward as if waiting for something. If he'd had a tail, I think it would have wagged.

Lossil stared down at me and spoke in my language. "Did you show up here from a different realm yesterday?" He spoke in a rumbling bass.

"No, sir. I've been on a pilgrimage down the coast and haven't seen a person in three weeks. All this fighting is curious. What's it about? Who is hating whom this year? All this hating and fighting is why I went on a pilgrimage."

"How did you lose those arms?"

I wiggled my right stump. "For this one, I was caught stealing, I'm ashamed to say."

"And the other one?" he asked.

"It was crushed off between two boats. It hurt worse than my grandma's broom handle. Sir, I've seen my share of atrocities, but can you tell me why so many of these villagers need to die? Any reasonable person might think it excessive."

Lossil ignored my questions. "Why are you here?"

"I was tied up and led here." I glanced down at the rope and then pointed at it with my chin.

"Don't be a smartass." Lossil grunted. "I may give you to your gods. Or I may torture you before I feed you to some wild animals. What do you have to say about that?"

"I'm fairly devout, so I'd prefer that the gods have me. You mentioned One. Who is One, anyhow? Is it some god trying to be subtle? Maybe Trutch?" Trutch, the Goddess of Life, had been Dead Harik's wife, and I had felt uneasy for years about her interest in vengeance.

Lossil pushed on. "Are you a sorcerer?"

"Hell no! I hate sorcerers! Wait, are you a sorcerer? I hate all of them except for you, I mean. What's your dog's name?"

Without hesitating, he said with a mere shade of wistfulness, "Sestis." Then he clenched his teeth.

"Named after your daughter?" I guessed.

Lossil went still. "My son. Why did you say that?"

I did a foolish thing then. I said something that was true. "I haven't seen my children in a long time. You look the way I feel sometimes."

Lossil turned away from me and walked toward the center of the village. I hoped that I had been odd and interesting enough to grab his attention. It was clear that the only opinion that mattered around here was Lossil's.

Lossil yelled in a fine seagoing voice, "I know that everybody wants to rest. I want to rest too. But the sooner we get this nasty business done, the sooner we can go home."

Soldiers were carrying pots and basins full of blood from the field and dumping them on the town's streets.

Lossil pointed at me and said to Burrud in their language, "Kill him."

"He's not useful?" Burrud asked.

"He's too dangerous. Don't use his blood—it may be tainted."

I had not been odd and interesting enough.

Burrud nodded to my guard, who hefted a thick club.

Three things saved me. First, I understood Lossil's words, so I was ready when the guard picked up his club. Second, I possessed vast experience in the use of weapons. I saw how the guard hauled back his club, so I could tell about where he'd hit me. I leaned and turned my head at the last instant, so I received an awful but glancing blow to my skull.

Third, I was lucky as hell and always had been. Over the years, I had developed beer-soaked theories in various bars about my fine luck, debating the matter with many disreputable sorcerers, some of whom I later killed.

I avoided a skull crushing, but the blow still knocked me to the ground where I lay with no thought of moving since I was senseless.

I came to later with the inside of my head in turmoil, since my brain was fighting for space with a wildcat wearing armor made of spikes and poison. I had enough sense to lay still. Dusk hadn't yet become darkness, and I recognized the sounds of soldiers gathering their gear.

During the afternoon's gruesome killings, I had noticed that Burrud's troops had been lax about making sure their victims died from a single blow. Maybe that was understandable since their next act was to cut the victim open and bleed him. Their laziness and Lossil's order not to bleed me saved me from death while I was passed out.

Just as I silently celebrated that luck, somebody walking past kicked me in the face and moved on. I guess he did it without looking at me, otherwise he would have seen a moment of fury before I lay still again.

Now I had a broken nose and maybe a broken cheekbone. Between the bloody nose and the bloody club wound on my skull, a good part of my head must have been covered with gore. That helped sell the notion that I was dead when Lossil and his little army marched out of town. They left on a small road heading northwest.

When clubbed, I had landed on my side, which of course was better than having my face plowed into the dirt. I was able to see around me. After Lossil and his hooligans left, I had nothing to do but look about and wait.

Not long before sunset, I saw an object in the sky that seemed too large for a bird. The curious creature had dipped down from the low clouds. I blinked several times as the object dropped lower into the clear air. Then I whispered, "Harik's girlish braids!"

The shape of a dragon in flight was unmistakable, at least from the many etchings and carvings I had seen. No real dragon had been spotted in centuries. This dragon's broad wings stretched unflapping. The wingspan reached about twice the length of its lizard-like body.

Of course, I had just been hit in the head with a club, so I might be addled. I closed my eyes for a few seconds. When I opened them, the dragon was still there. Its tail was far longer than its neck, but the neck was still prominent. In the dimness, I couldn't tell what color the dragon might be. However, its wings held a soft shimmer, even with no sunlight.

If something happens only twice, it could well be a coincidence, or in this case, a delusion. I closed my eyes longer this time. When I opened them, the dragon was gone. So, it had never really been there. Probably.

With nothing else to do, I worried over the reality or unreality of that dragon until pure, black nighttime arrived, with the moon still hours away. I rolled to my feet and staggered west toward the woods.

As I entered the field of dead farmers, I saw big patches of ground all over the field that glowed as if they were windows into daylight. I crept up to one of the spots and saw clean, gray stone in it, lit from the side as if by sunrise.

Somebody in the dark whispered, "Hello, old Bib."

I crouched and waited.

"This is what happens when they bleed people," Acton said.

Close by in the darkness, Kenzie's strained voice said, "Acton, how did you know that he wasn't killed? To me he looked dead."

I murmured, "Children, let's leave this field of death before somebody comes along and plants us in it. Then we can talk about this horror while we crown Acton king of all knowledge and a robust lover to boot. Come on."

As the four of us crossed toward the forest, Vargo growled something I couldn't make out. Then Acton muttered, "Told you."

Once among the dense trees, my headache and I thumped down to sit.

Vargo said, "I waited for you to follow us. These disloyal piglets wanted to desert you."

"Stop it, I did not." Acton cut him off in a flat tone. "Why do those monsters want to kill everybody? To get the blood? Why does blood make these odd places on the ground . . . whatever they are?"

"I don't know what all this is. I really don't." I shrugged.

Kenzie said, "It's insane. They're insane."

Vargo murmured, "Bib, are they going to do that to my family?"

"Probably," Acton said. "Some of them are monsters. They must all be monsters."

"What must we do about the bodies in the field?" Kenzie asked.

"Nothing," Vargo said. "Do you want to be in the middle of burying them when the next monsters come along? Maybe build a great pyre to signal the monsters they should come back?"

No one argued against him.

I said, "We should wait here until Lossil has had a chance to get some distance away."

Acton said, "I see. Let us talk about the sorcerer, then. Who is she? Why did she help those people by raising fog?"

"And where is she now?" Kenzie said.

"Why are you saying *she*?" Vargo asked. "Did you see some *she* out there? What does she look like?"

"I didn't, but it's probably a she," Acton said. "I sensed it was a woman."

"You're right, Acton." I was interrupted by a short coughing fit. "She's out there. I'm protected by a mighty sorcerer who wields ghost arms and remains out of sight, so don't screw around with me."

Kenzie paused. "If that's so, she and her ghost arms are doing a black horse's ass of a job about it. You should be as dead as anybody back in that field. Let me feel your face." She shifted closer to me.

Acton sniffed. "I have never read nor heard of such a thing as ghost arms. I think you may be lying to us, old Bib."

"Son, I could take us on a discussion about truth and falsehood that would last for two days and still astound you on your deathbed."

Acton said, "I see. That means you are definitely lying to us."

I flinched when Kenzie pushed on my cheekbone, then I said, "I am not lying. I am describing reality in more poetic terms."

Vargo chuckled. "I wish it was light. I want to write that down."

"Did you three get away in the fog?" I asked.

"Yes," Kenzie said. "I think your cheek is unbroken."

"So, the sorcerer's not a woman, then?" Acton said in a low voice. "You're the sorcerer, aren't you, old Bib?"

Kenzie laughed. Vargo stayed silent.

I knew Acton was a smart fellow. I hadn't credited him with this much intuition. "Yes, I am, son."

"Hush, Acton!" Kenzie said. "Don't encourage him to go twisting our bits with that rubbish."

Acton asked, "How do you make it work, old Bib? Since you have no hands to speak of?"

"I have my own set of ghost arms! You can't see them, but they're deadly."

Vargo said, "Really? That would explain a lot." He turned a laugh into a cough.

"No, not really! He's still lying," Acton snapped. "If you pay attention to him, listen closely, you can tell that he's lying all the time."

I said, "Not true. And even if I don't have ghost arms, they do sound elegant, don't they?"

"We should leave," Kenzie said. "He's just a sad, old bib playing games with us."

I sure as hell didn't want Kenzie and her healing hands to get away. "Kenzie, here's a question. You do magic with your ten fingers, but what else do you have ten of?"

"Dissatisfied lovers?" Vargo asked.

Kenzie ignored him. "Toes . . ."

"Right, you can use your toes. It takes practice, though. I could show you how. It took me a whole year to learn, but I can show you in a few hours."

After some seconds of silence, Kenzie said, "You are lying to us! If toes could be used for magic, the masters would've told us."

"No, wait," Acton muttered. "I don't know whether he's lying about this."

"Son, you sound like you'd rather piss a horseshoe than admit you don't know something. That's a failing. You're better off assuming that you don't know a single thing." My stomach flipped, and I turned aside to vomit.

Kenzie said, "Oh crap! Bib, I'm going to feel your head. Don't move around! And stay awake!" She poked at my head, muttering, "Lies and toe magic! We're not so simple as that, are we, Acton?"

After a moment, Acton sighed. "Yes, you must be correct."

"I don't know anything about magic," Vargo said, "but I know this is boring the hell out of me. Bib, do some magic and shut them up. Turn that bush into a beer fountain."

I waited for Acton and Kenzie to object. Magical power wasn't to be wasted on making a point. But neither of them said a word, and I couldn't let Kenzie trot off without me. "Fine! I'll do one little feat. A tiny one. Acton, take off your hat."

"I lost it."

"Couldn't tell in the dark."

I summoned a yellow band and tossed it over the entire area around us. I didn't use my toes. Instead, I willed the magic to come, but I sure as hell wasn't going to teach that skill to these infants. I found two mice nearby and convinced them that a winter's worth of food lay on top of Acton's head.

"What's supposed to happen?" Acton asked.

Vargo said, "I need to pee. Is that the magic? Do I have magical pee?" He snorted.

I said, "Hold still, Acton, no matter what happens."

Acton yelped, but I didn't hear him move. "What is that? Is something nesting in my hair?"

"It's just a couple of mice making a point," I said. "Kenzie, you tell me when to let them go free."

I waited while Acton squirmed and muttered curses. I waited some more. "Acton, I think she's torturing you. Kenzie, can the mice go free?"

"All right."

I suggested to the mice that Acton's hair wasn't that much of a banquet and that better foraging could be found beneath a bush close by. He sighed as they ran down his body.

"You did that with your toes, I gather?" Acton said.

"I did it with just one toe," I lied.

"Bull crap!" Kenzie said. "You really are lying. There's another explanation."

Hell, maybe Kenzie was perceptive enough to sense my deceit. Before she and Acton could circle about infecting each other with doubt again, I raised my voice, "Young friends, I am Bib the sorcerer. Forget everything you think you know about the name Bib. A lot of it is true, but you had to be there to understand it. Let's talk magic swords."

Acton said, "What about them? Do you have some hidden hereabouts, like in a tree?"

"Or on top of a cloud?" Vargo added.

"A cloud?" Kenzie asked.

Vargo said, "Maybe. I'm not a sorcerer, but I'd have made a good one. Maybe one of the best."

"Of course you would," I told him, not meaning it one bit. "Kenzie, I am willing to trade one magic sword in exchange for some assistance."

"I told you I don't like swords."

"Whichever one of you carries the sword is up to you! Kenzie, I want you to heal and restore my arms."

"No!" Kenzie snapped.

At the same time, Acton said, "Let's talk about it."

"Wonderful." I smiled into the darkness. "There's already room for us to both get what we want."

Kenzie snapped, "No, I need some time to run this around in my head. I don't want to be cheated."

"Young woman, I want to get this done right away, but I'll trade fair. And I wouldn't resort to threatening you."

Kenzie dropped her voice. "Good."

"Threats take too much time. I'll just coerce you."

"What's the difference?" Acton asked, his voice hard.

I raised my voice again in tones suitable for a great sorcerer. "If you keep screwing around with me, you'll find out." Two seconds later I vomited again.

All three youngsters laughed at me. I couldn't think of a way to recover my dignity without violence, so I sighed and surrendered to my throbbing head.

ELEVEN

Acton took Kenzie aside, and I heard them whispering while I waited.

I murmured to Vargo, who was sitting nearby, "Just how many are in your clan? In case I have to steal a boat to carry you all away to some paradise."

"Almost thirty. That figure is all the information you need for boat-stealing purposes, right?"

"I do need more detail."

He hesitated.

"If there's something you don't want to tell me, then that's exactly the thing I need to know. Don't hold back. Picture the children's sad, starving faces. Tell me all about the clan."

He blew out a breath. "There's Grandma and Grandpa, who are my parents. Their kids have kids now, so it's easier to call them Grandma and Grandpa. Then there's Gamma, who's Grandma's mother—"

"You're right, that's way too much detail. Summarize."

He paused and then sighed. "Grandpa has four sons and daughters with spouses and a fine lot of children each."

"Which ones are yours?"

His voice was flat. "None."

I wanted to leave aside things he obviously didn't want to talk about, but I hadn't lied when I said I needed to know more. "That's hard. What happened?"

"I made a bad decision. I made my worst decision."

He didn't offer more.

"I made a bad decision with my family too. My wife died, and my little girl. It seems wrong that they had to suffer for my foolishness."

"I suppose that's true." Vargo spoke through gritted teeth. "My wife and boys . . ." He trailed off and then cleared his throat. "When Grandpa let me go search for you, I thought it was because nobody except Pala and I thought you existed. Now I think mainly it was because nobody would suffer if I never came home."

"Why did they let Pala go?"

"They didn't. She followed me. Who could stop her? She smiled and trotted along like a puppy that can walk straight through a mountain or anything else in her way. I bet her pa is still having a five-week-long heart attack about it. I hate that I have to tell him what happened."

I might have offered to tell Pala's father she was dead, but Vargo wasn't asking for help with it.

When Acton and Kenzie returned, she agreed in principle to heal me, but she couldn't just wave a stick at my stump and make an arm grow. She needed light to work, or moonlight at least.

While waiting for moonrise, Kenzie bargained with me like the determined sorcerer she was, demanding four magic swords in exchange for healing just my right arm. She pointed out that she might be my only chance to ever get anything healed. I countered that she would probably never see a magic weapon without me. In the end, I fooled her into believing the ridiculous idea that she and Acton would certainly die without a magic sword, while I could go on forever with no arms if I had to. After all, I had managed it so far.

The bargain we finally made was one sword for one arm. If that went well, we might move on to the other arm for another sword.

Kenzie was a Caller, like me, one of the five types of sorcerers. Only Callers could heal or perform magical feats on living things. Acton was a Burner and could set things—not living creatures—ablaze. Breakers could make things not exist, and Benders could make things change shape. Pil had been a Binder who could work magical properties into things.

If I hadn't given up the power to heal, I would have restored my own damn arms and cut a tidier figure when I returned home. But I had wisely let it be taken from me in the name of peace with the gods. I had since sworn off being wise, brokering peace, and being anything but nasty to gods.

Once we had bargained, Kenzie at last gave me permission to sleep. I slept for the first time in seventy years, and I don't recall dreaming.

When I opened my eyes, the moon still hadn't risen and the darkness was too pure for me to count my fingers if I had possessed any. I heard voices, so I lay still.

Kenzie said in a strained tone, "These monsters crawl up out of a big hole in the earth. That's the only explanation."

"No," Acton said. "There's no evidence of that. They are swimming here on the tides from the mystic southern islands."

"Where's your evidence for that, eh? In the seat of your trousers?"

Acton raised his voice. "Carcasses have been seen on beaches. And footprints as well."

"Crabs have been seen on the beaches! Do they come from the mystic southern islands too?"

A calm voice said, "I am not an expert on magic, but most creatures arrive in their own way for their own purposes. And they may not all be monsters."

My eyes popped open as I recognized Kruppin's measured, thoughtful voice coming from the darkness.

Acton said, "I'll bet that the people of Drup, Pog, and Pith thought they were attacked by monsters!"

"Maybe that's not what every one of them thinks," Kruppin said. "That's all I'm saying."

I sat up.

"Bib, you snore!" Kenzie said.

"Like two sharks in a cave," Kruppin added.

"What? What does that mean?" Kenzie asked.

I said, "Two sharks in a cave. Fractious and growly. It's a common saying in places I've traveled," I lied.

"Meet Kruppin," Acton said. "He's fleeing just like us."

"Hello, Bib," Kruppin grated. "Are you still alive? It does not seem likely, but sometimes rain falls upward."

"Do you know old Bib?" Kenzie asked.

Kruppin sniffed. "I know him. How much would I have to pay the two of you to—" He made a strangling noise.

I said, "The magic won't let you say it, eh?"

As moonlight edged up behind the clouds, Kruppin released a thundering fart that lasted eight seconds.

Acton broke the following silence. "Are you all right? I don't think I've ever heard a person sound like that."

"I haven't heard a person sound like that either," I said.

Kruppin sighed. "The truth you should observe, young sorcerers, is that you have a bad habit. You call beings monsters when you don't even know where they come from."

The moon rose high enough to push a bit of light through the thin clouds. Kruppin, grown to bear size, stood crushing a wide clump of bushes. He turned his triangle-shaped face back and forth to regard Kenzie and Acton.

Vargo broke out laughing.

Kenzie bounced to her feet and retreated, leveling her spear. Acton jumped up, stumbled on a bush, nearly fell, and leaped in front of Kenzie in the perfect spot for her to accidentally stab him in the back. They both started babbling to each other, to me, and at Kruppin.

"Stop!" I said. "Don't strangle yourselves on your own froth. You have already conversed with this very fine creature whose acquaintance I have made." I turned to Kruppin. "Creature? Monster?"

"I am a monster for certain."

"Greet this very fine monster who won't hurt you even a little bit. Not today, at least. So be nice to him. He's carrying your sword."

That calmed the young people a bit.

Kruppin shook his head and ambled away through the trees.

"Kenzie, are you ready to perform the most difficult sorcery of your young life and give me a pristine arm?"

She hesitated. "You promised you'd guide me through it, sure, but do you want to suffer the chance that I'll slip or hiccup? We could trot off to the sorcery school at Bleekhame. It's not far. They'll be glad to aid us, I know it."

I shook my head. "We made a bargain."

"It would be safer at Bleekhame. I don't want things to go wrong."

I stood silent for a couple of breaths. "I intend to have a working arm before sunrise. I don't intend to chase along for a day while you bump into every tree in these woods looking for this crap-named school you've only ever seen from the road! I don't intend to have some smug sorcery teacher no older than my boots stand over us and get every damn thing wrong! I'd end up having to show you how to do it all anyway, and the bastard would probably charge us!"

Acton said in a small voice, "We have only seen you charm two mice and be friends with a monster. That doesn't sound difficult. It's no proof that you know all you claim."

Kenzie added, "We won't ask for the sword until I'm done."

I turned on the two sorcerers like fury unchained. "Do you want to see some sorcery?" I breathed as if seeing sorcery could hurl them into the Void forever.

They backed up but nodded, their eyes wide.

I paused. I should probably have decided what sorcery to show them before I started swinging it around like I was a bull. "All right, here's something a sorcerer should know. When another sorcerer rises to bargain with the gods, you can grab on for a ride."

"That sounds awfully ridiculous," Kenzie said.

Acton narrowed his eyes and nodded slightly. "So . . . how do you do it?"

"You have to be close and pay attention. You can feel the other sorcerer rise like a draft in the chimney. When you feel that, imagine grabbing on with both hands."

"I believe I understand," Acton said.

"Good!" I turned to Kenzie. "What about you?"

She shook her head, shrugged, and then nodded. "Are we doing it now?"

"No, that would be reckless—" My spirit stretched up through the top of my head as some god hauled me out of my body. He or she must have been watching and maybe wanted to teach me not to take gods for granted.

Acton had joined me with a sure grip. Kenzie fumbled and then fell, but the god dragged her along anyway. I called out to Fingit, just in case he could take us away from whomever had claimed us.

After a spike of nausea, we arrived in the trading place. Acton and Kenzie stood on each side of me, and all three of us were placed on the brown dirt patch that the gods allowed sorcerers to befoul with their hideous, uncultured feet. Kenzie was facing me, while Acton faced the white gazebo. Neither of them could see or feel anything, and they could only hear what the gods allowed them to hear. This was a trading advantage that the gods had maintained over sorcerers for millennia.

I was able to see and hear whatever I wished in the trading place. Maybe all sorcerers would eventually develop that skill if they lived long enough. I was quite a lot older than any sorcerer I had heard of. An infinitesimal sliver of divinity in my heritage may have helped as well.

The golden sun was bright, warm, and every bit the opposite of the dank, chilly night we'd just left. In fact, the sun was immensely more comforting than any sun I had ever felt at home, so much so that I wanted to weep. Kenzie and Acton were crying, although they couldn't know why or even that it was happening.

The forest to my left and behind me was cheery green and budding with pink and yellow blossoms that smelled like honey. The field of blue flowers to my right waved in the breeze that slid across my skin like new silk.

"You've got to stop bothering Fingit." Baby Harik sat on the edge of the gazebo. "He's building some damn thing. I don't understand what it is, but he certainly doesn't want you bothering him. Murderer, I see you brought friends!"

I nodded. "Sorcerers, have you spoken before with Baby Harik, the God of Death?"

Neither Kenzie nor Acton said anything.

Baby Harik looked at Kenzie. "Go ahead, Feather." Then he made a gigantic show of grinning and pointing at Acton. "You too, Anvil. Say something if you want to." Baby Harik drummed his fingers against the floor of the gazebo.

Before I could warn them to keep their mouths closed, both of the young sorcerers started worshipping the god at the same time, spitting out devoted nonsense and claiming to be the most devout one in his neighborhood.

"Wait!" I shouted. "Let's hold on, before we break our backs kissing each other's asses. Youngsters, please pay attention." I turned to the god. "Baby Harik is a crass, lumpy, self-important echo of his wretched predecessor, who was looked upon with disgust by god and man alike."

Baby Harik chuckled.

"Bib . . ." Acton's voice wavered, but he pushed on. "Why hasn't the God of Death already killed us for what you just said?"

"Allow me to simplify, son," I said. "You have just witnessed the essence of the proper sorcerer-god relationship. If you respect these gods, they will screw you every time. If you don't respect them, they will still screw you every time, but maybe not as bad."

"That's an interesting take." Baby Harik brushed off his sleeve. "You kicked a few diamonds of knowledge into the gutter there. Have you thought about my earlier offer? Which one of these two floppy saplings are you going to kill for me?"

Acton and Kenzie flung themselves back toward their real bodies. Baby Harik snatched them both like they were the dimmest flies in the kitchen.

"Well, that wasn't very nice," Baby Harik said. "You don't leave my presence without my permission. Remember that. And I'll tell you this right now. Only two of you three are going to live too long when you get back."

"Bullshit!" I snapped. "None of us have made a deal like that with you."

Baby Harik stood and walked toward a marble bench. "You're right, Murderer. But couldn't you use a little power about now, with all the monsters and armies running around? If you deal with me, I'll help you find the Knife's family."

"I already know where they are. Sandell."

"Are they?" Baby Harik grinned. "Oh, don't worry. If you refuse to deal, I'll still help you find them. Parts of them, at least."

"I bet they're someplace in the world of man. Oh, I already fell for that." I grasped for the most ridiculous thing I could say to him. "Besides, I don't need your help. Lossil told me where they are."

Baby Harik narrowed his eyes. "Lossil tried to kill you."

"And he told me where they are so I'd suffer more before I died."

"Even if he did, don't listen to that scaly cretin." Baby Harik sat on the marble bench and crossed his legs. "He doesn't know where the Knife's people are any more than he knows where his dick is. But I know. Where the people are, I mean, not his dick."

I worked on a harsh and devastating reply. All I came up with was, "Wait. Just wait a second."

"I'm not going to wait or let you wait, either. You'll deal, or else the Knife's family dies. The only deal on the table is you murdering one of these two gaping idiots. You can choose which one, but I suggest you kill the Anvil." The god grinned at Acton. "He's so in love with the Feather here that he'll probably do some stupid romantic thing soon and get himself uselessly killed."

"What?" Kenzie yelped. "What did you say? Mi-Mighty Harik?"

Baby Harik grinned.

I said, "How about this deal? You tell me where Pil's family will be. When I reach them, I'll see that one of these young sorcerers is exiled from this island. And I want twelve squares of power too." That was an enormous amount, but I needed to be as aggressive as possible. I didn't have a decent sense of Baby Harik's weaknesses or what he wanted.

"That's a pathetic offer," Baby Harik said. "Did you lose all your guts in the Dark Lands? If you agree to my terms, I'll tell you where the Knife's people are. If not, they die, and they won't die clean." When I didn't answer, he raised his voice. "You've got to kill one of these two. I won't bend on that point. And because I'm a sweetheart, I'll throw in four squares."

"I won't kill either of them, but I'll get one imprisoned for years," I said. "A lot of years. Plus, tell me where Pil's family is and give me ten squares."

Still sitting, Baby Harik sighed and leaned forward, his elbows on his knees. "Let me make this clear. In any deal we make, any deal at all, you will kill one of these two. Just accept it. If you don't deal, the Knife's family will die. Slowly. With a lot of burning and shrieking. Not screaming. Shrieking. Even the children and babies and their pets. Do you understand?"

I nodded.

"Fantastic. If you don't want that, the only decision facing you is which one of these sorcerers to kill. If you kill one of them, I'll add six squares to grease the deal."

I wasn't going to let Pil's family be tortured to death. Neither Acton nor Kenzie was worth that. I looked them both over, deciding which one I'd destroy.

It was a sadly easy choice. Acton showed more potential as a sorcerer. Kenzie was sometimes an unthinking pain in the back parts but a quick learner. Sadly, she was likely to get herself killed. She was aggressive but didn't have the skill and knowledge to back it up.

Plus, Baby Harik had suggested I let Kenzie live. That by itself was a good reason to kill her.

However, she was the only person I had met who could restore my arms.

I decided to kill Acton as soon as I could do it out of everybody's sight. Then I'd blame it on something else.

I stiffened. Right there—this was how I did things. I was doing a bib. It could have been straight out of the stories.

Kenzie spoke up before I did, nervous and almost shouting. "I want to suggest another way, Mighty Harik."

Baby Harik raised his eyebrows at her. "Go ahead."

"Acton and I will overcome Bib and whack off one of his legs—but we'll not kill him! You keep Pil's family alive and point us to them so we can rescue them for Bib. And I want twelve squares each for Acton and me."

Baby Harik's head came up like a hound's. "Really?"

"No, Kenzie!" Acton said.

"Yes, really!" Kenzie shouted, then she cleared her throat. "Sorry for that."

Baby Harik began laughing, and he kept at it until his eyes teared. I didn't laugh. The whole idea appalled me.

I said, "Kenzie, give this up. It's a foolish path because you can't defeat me. We can find another way."

"Did your other way include killing me? Or Acton?" Kenzie snipped.

"All right. You're a full-grown sorcerer with your own special, secret sorcerer ring. I won't interfere."

"Good! Stay out of this, Bib." The way she said "Bib" made it a foul word for sure.

After he caught his breath, Baby Harik said, "That's not the worst deal anybody ever offered me, Feather. Of course, the Murderer will gut both of you as soon as you draw your weapons or wave your hands. There's no reason for you to know this, but he's probably killed more people than you've met in your young lives. Plus, two gods that I know of and enough demigods to sail a decent navy. I'm tempted to say yes to your offer, but let me suggest an improvement or two instead."

Acton broke in: "Kenzie, stop this—"

"Rude! I wasn't finished," Baby Harik said. "You be quiet, Anvil. I don't want to hear from you anymore."

From the way Acton appeared to be gulping air, the god had struck the boy mute, at least until he went home.

Baby Harik leaned back. "Instead of fooling around with the Murderer's leg, just kill him, or at least try. I won't kill the Knife's family, but I won't tell you exactly where they are. I'll put you in the vicinity. On top of all that, I'll give you and the Anvil eight squares each."

Kenzie didn't hesitate, and her voice didn't shake. "The same, except twelve squares each. There's not a deadline, but we'll keep trying to kill Bib until he dies, or we do."

Baby Harik rolled his eyes but then said, "Fine, with two changes. I'll give you, the Anvil, and the Murderer all three ten squares each. And if the Murderer kills you, somebody that you love will die too."

"But . . . wait," Kenzie said. "I want to go back to where we kill Bib and get eight squares each."

"Oh, that deal was offered and rejected. Pretend it never existed. There's only one bargain on the table now. Take it or walk away, but if you give up, I'll go right back to the Murderer and make him kill one of you. And I have a good idea now which one that would be."

Kenzie gave a sharp nod. "I . . ." She hesitated. "I'm not kicking this offer in the eye, but I think I must ask you something, Mighty Harik. Ten squares each is a great lot. Why so much?"

Baby Harik smiled at me. "Can you answer this, Murderer?"

I nodded. "If you get three squares, you'll use them constructively. If you get ten squares, you'll use three of them constructively and waste the others on things that can hurt people or kill you. To do otherwise takes great willpower."

"That is the failing of mankind right there, naked for us all to see," Baby Harik said.

After a few seconds, Kenzie said, "I agree."

Baby Harik smiled with what looked like genuine joy. "I like her, Murderer. When she tries to kill you, make her death creative and memorable."

"Where is Pil's family?" I demanded.

"Ebring, near the palace. At least they were there this morning." He flung all three of us out of the trading place and back into our bodies. We staggered but didn't fall.

Vargo stared at us. "Did you all trip over the same rock?"

I patted Acton's shoulder. "You're a smart boy, but not smart enough to see what's about to happen to you."

I wasn't smart enough to see what would happen, either. Both Acton and Kenzie turned and began shouting in my face.

Kenzie: "You lured us there, you spiteful old man!"

Acton: "What are we going to do now?"

Kenzie: "I'll bet you planned it, Bib. You and Harik planned the whole thing!"

Acton: "You should allow us to kill you, just to be fair."

Kenzie: "I will tell you this, Bib: you go ahead and sleep safe and deep tonight. Don't worry about anything, you pig's butt."

Acton: "What are we going to do now? I don't think—"

Kenzie turned on Acton and screamed, "Shut up! You shut up! Come here and explain yourself!" She seized Acton's arm and dragged him stumbling to stand under a moonlit tree. There she started their conversation by punching him on the chest, probably the least hurtful place she could hit him.

Vargo peered across the road at Acton and Kenzie, a deep crease between his brows. "What happened? I wasn't watching."

"Kenzie found out Acton's in love with her."

Vargo shook his head. "Just now? The boy has been just about throwing barrels of flowers at her since we got here. I thought sorcerers were smart."

I said, "Pay no attention to it, son." I didn't say that the reason he shouldn't pay attention was that Kenzie and Acton would try to kill me soon. Then I would sadly send them to join the many whose heads I had stacked.

TWELVE

"She's hardly hitting that boy at all," Hurd said from behind me, as if he had been with us the whole time. He pointed at Kenzie, whose head was down as she spit her fury at Acton. "When you play at smacking somebody that way, she loves him for sure. That bit of violence says every little thing that needs to be said."

Acton and Kenzie were making fierce gestures but talking too quietly for us hear. Hurd grinned. "The young fellow over there says, 'I'm sorry, I'm sorry, oh, please, please forgive me, I'm so stupid!'"

"It's amazing how accurate you are." Vargo grinned.

Hurd waved a hand. "Hush. Then the girl says, 'You're right, you're stupid, you're the stupidest pile of pig flop that ever lay in the dirt. Oh, I'm so mad at you I could spit.' And then he says, 'Please, please don't say that. You're the most beautiful woman who ever lived. I'll eat mud for you if you stop being mad at me.'"

Hurd went on: "And now she's saying, 'I should make you eat that mud! I would, except it would make everybody gossip.' And the kid says, 'Oh, don't tell them, I'll be so embarrassed, I'll run away and die.' Or something like that."

Kenzie leaned toward Acton until she was almost in his face and shouted, "So stop it!" Then she slapped him before stomping back toward us, leaving him rubbing his cheek and looking like he wished four or five trees would fall on him at once.

She yelled over her shoulder at Acton, "I mean it!"

Hurd grinned. "And she says, 'If you come near me again, I'll slap you twice as hard and tell you to go away a little closer.'"

"It's a shame," I said, hoping this wouldn't interfere with my arm getting healed.

Hurd nodded. "Young love never changes. It's always a stupid pain in the ass."

All three of the young people spun and froze as if they heard something.

"Young love is loud too," I whispered.

Reks rushed toward us amid shouts and the snapping of underbrush. I saw five, but there were more behind them.

Acton pulled his knife, backed away from a rek, and tripped over a bush to fall on his ass. Hurd punched that rek in the ribs, and the soldier crumpled. Kenzie and another rek were fighting with spears. A third rek jabbed at Vargo but couldn't get past his magic sword's guard.

I lost track of the others for a moment when a rek thrust his spear at my throat. Twisting aside, I kicked his knee, which popped louder than anything else in the battle so far. I knocked him over with my hip and jumped back as one of his friends tried to impale me. He ended up a bit out of range, so he rushed after me, leaning forward. I swept his front foot, and he tumbled. Then I dropped to crush his neck with my knee and popped back up.

Hurd, who was known for his strength, had slipped beside Kenzie's opponent, grabbed his arm, and wrenched it out of place. The rek shouted and writhed. Kenzie stepped back.

"Don't stand there with your thumb up your nose!" Hurd shouted at her. "Kill him!" He turned to help Vargo, who had killed a rek but was now being pressed by two more.

Acton was sitting on the ground, about to be impaled by a rek spear. He had grabbed the one whose knee I'd broken and was holding his knife to the rek's throat. "Stop! Or I'll kill him!"

That did not stop his attacker, who was a trained soldier. The smart move for me was to let Acton be killed. I felt bad, though, about just letting the boy die before he'd learned a bit about sorcery or anything else. That might have meant that I just plain didn't want to kill the boy. However, my decision to save him was mainly based on my concern that if I let him die, then Kenzie might refuse to ever heal me.

I ran two steps and bashed the rek with my body, almost bouncing off the short creature. He turned to grab me, which was a mistake. Three spinning steps knocked him free and sent him rolling across the ground. I followed and stomped to break his neck when he came to rest. I turned back to Acton, who was still holding the rek. I shouted, "Kill him! And stand up!"

Hurd was standing over two fallen reks, and Vargo had run to help Kenzie with three more. As Vargo cut one of them down, Kenzie was speared hard in the body, and she bent over the wound. I ran that direction, but something smashed the back of my head, which had already been smashed enough for one day.

From my viewpoint lying on the ground, Lossil's big, furry difar soldier looked as tall as a ship's mast. He raised his big, slow, barbed sword to cut me into at least two pieces. Lying on my back, I spun and kicked both his knees with all my strength. They didn't pop, but he howled and his swing lost its speed and force. I spun again and rolled into his shins. Since his ankles and knees each bent only one way, he fell on his butt. Ten seconds later, I had kicked him enough times with my heel that he had stopped moving.

I rolled up to run help Kenzie, but the fight was over. The last rek was staggering with Acton's knife in his chest. Acton was facing away, puking. Hurd stomped around the area, making sure that all our enemies were dead.

Kenzie lay moaning and rolling on the ground while Vargo knelt over her looking helpless. I knelt on her other side and examined the wound. It would kill her soon if we didn't do something.

I grabbed her hand. "Kenzie! Look at me! It's bad, but you can save yourself."

"No! You'll just fool me! Make me kill myself!" she groaned.

"No, if I wanted that, I'd sit under that tree and contemplate the beauty of my toes. I'll help you do the work. You just have to stay calm, pull the magic, shape it in place, and stay awake while you do it."

"So, I'm doing all the work . . . and you're doing nothing."

"That's right. You'll learn sorcery secrets like that when you're older."

Kenzie laughed, then cried for a few seconds, then laughed again.

Kenzie healed herself over the next hour or so. At one time, I could have done it twice as fast. Now I couldn't do it even if I had eternity, so I shouldn't criticize. I had talked her through it and kept her from making a couple of awkward mistakes, so I felt good about her chances. She fell asleep, which was a fine thing since she would still feel the pain of her wound for hours.

Ideally, we should move and keep moving. These dead reks must have friends somewhere who would miss them. Kenzie recovered only two hours later, an unbelievable gift of luck for us. We traveled several miles in the general direction of Sandell. We stayed off the road, but even walking along the edge of the brush was a struggle.

Late in the day, I called a halt. Nobody questioned my right to do that, so I figured I was now the leader.

"It's time for you to repair my arm," I said to Kenzie.

I saw a moment of fear on her face. I couldn't blame her for not wanting to go through such pain again. On the other hand, I needed my damn arm.

Kenzie cleared her throat. "I still think we should wait. It will be safer."

I took a step toward her. "We made a bargain."

Acton said, "She wouldn't have made that deal had she known we would be required to kill you. Now she would be foolish to give you an arm."

"I see. By that logic, you should just kill me now. I'll never have fewer arms than I have at this moment."

It might seem a poor idea to suggest such a thing, but in fact it taught me a lot. Acton's eyes popped open in surprise at the idea. But Kenzie's eyes didn't change at all. She had already been thinking about killing me now.

"I invite you to consider something. Acton, you're a Burner, the most dangerous of sorcerers. But in the fight earlier, you didn't even consider ways to use your power. You panicked. Kenzie, you fought bravely, but you were also just about killed. How many did I kill?"

They made noncommittal noises.

"That's right, a lot. With no weapons and no arms. Without even any magic. That should prove I can kill you whenever I want even with no arms. So, restoring my arm won't hurt you. Hell, you'll be making me happy and less likely to murder you in your sleep."

Vargo shook his head. "Why do you two have to kill him?"

"Just never mind why," Kenzie said. "We must slay him and do it soon. You need not help us if you don't care to, Vargo, but I invite you to. I hope you will." She smiled at him and brushed back her hair.

Vargo stared at her, then at Acton, and then at me.

I nodded. "She's telling the truth, son. They have to kill me. They'll fail and die, but until then, I imagine it'll be a party if you want to forget all about your family and join in."

Vargo shook his head. "I'd have been better off finding an angry goose to save us."

I asked, "Are we done trying to kill each other for now?"

Kenzie glowered at me as if I had just crawled out of a damp place. She seemed to have forgotten about how I had helped save her life, and that was the right way of thinking for a sorcerer. "Bib, I think you've done all and enough for today. But with or without an arm, you sleep well tonight, because you have nothing to fear from us this evening. Nothing at all." She sneered to punctuate that.

Acton's shoulders lifted and he stood straighter, staring at me as if I were a task, no more than a floor to be swept.

I could see fear in both of them, though. "Children, don't try to be sneaky—you don't have the sand for it, and you can't be sneakier than me. You two have been thinking that sorcery is all about little duels with other sorcerers. I admit that you're brave and skilled. But you've never faced the kind of desperate, all-out, bloody scrambling for life that a god has laid upon you—until now."

Kenzie opened her mouth, but I cut her off. "Kenzie, you showed damn fine courage and cleverness dealing with Baby Harik. You may feel that you achieved a poor outcome, but you're wrong. You salvaged the deal and did it about as well as I've ever seen."

She glanced down.

Acton nodded slowly. "We got a bad deal, but it is the best we could get, correct?"

"Right."

He drew out the next words. "Our challenge now is fulfilling it in a manner we can live with."

"That all three of us can live with," I said, hoping I sounded more optimistic than I felt.

Kenzie looked back up at me. After a few seconds, she almost smiled but pushed it back down.

"Don't pull out the beer and beef joints yet," I said. "If we don't get a good idea, and we may well not, then you won't be walking away from my corpse anytime soon. I'll kill you and anybody helping you." I glanced at Vargo.

"I understand," Acton said.

I knew that the boy didn't understand a single damn thing, but it wouldn't help him to say that. I snarled, "Now can I get my three-times-damned-to-Lutigan's-nasty-parts arm?"

"Wait!" Kenzie said.

I hung my head. "What?"

"Since you're not just a crazy old armless hermit, could you teach us more about sorcery?"

I stared at her. "I may not have heard you right. Did you say, 'Bib, aren't you going to sharpen a knife, put it in my hand, hold it against your own throat, and slide your neck side to side for me?' Because I think that's what I heard you say."

"You're right, that wasn't the bargain." Kenzie took a deep breath. "That was foolish of me."

"And you're wise to know it. Come on, come on." I kicked a bush. "Arm! I want to be able to shade my eyes with my fingers at sunrise."

Kenzie restored my right arm and hand with more skill than I expected. She had learned well with her own wound. I had to guide her through some difficult parts, but she had a fine touch for healing—gentle but strong. By sunrise, I had an entirely restored right arm. I picked up things, flexed my hand a lot, and excused myself to visit the privy.

Vargo called after me, "Too bad. I was hoping Hurd would come back before the next time you relieved yourself without hands. Somebody other than me needs to be mortified by wiping your ass."

Kenzie sat against a tree with her head down as Acton tied a sling for her right arm. She felt most of the pain I had felt in that arm when I lost it, and she would for some hours to come—maybe as long as a day.

As I walked back from behind the tree we had designated as the privy, Acton jumped up and asked, "How many swords do we have to choose from?"

"None. You don't get to choose. I'll choose for you."

Neither of them looked pleased about that.

"Stop looking like a hound with his balls caught in the door. How many of you have ever seen a magic sword? Neither of you, right? How would you choose the best sword for you? You couldn't. You might as well dump a bunch of them on the ground and take the one that lands on top.

"I, on the other hand, have fought with more magic weapons than you've had kisses. It's well known that I'm a liar and a son of a bitch, but I tell you this with the deepest sincerity. I will give you a fine weapon. Because all I have are fine weapons."

The sword I chose was the one Hurd had grabbed to fight Kruppin. I had offered it to Pil many years before. Its effects were inconsistent. When swung or thrust, it sometimes arrived a bit faster than it appeared to. The effect couldn't be controlled, but in a hard fight, it could be devastating. The sword also occasionally vibrated when it struck a blow, causing far greater harm to the enemy than expected.

In addition to all that, the blade burned with green fire. The flames had no effect at all and weren't even hot, but the appearance was astounding. When you drew that weapon, everybody knew that a magic sword had come to town. Of course, lots of folks would want to kill you and take the sword, but stylish magic was also dangerous magic.

Considered as a whole, it was a hell of a weapon.

When I took the scabbarded sword from Kruppin and handed it to Kenzie, the youngsters laughed like they were at a holiday festival. When she drew the sword to reveal the green fire, the two of them hooted as if they had won the festival grand prize.

I said, "Well done. It's a fine blade. Don't trip and cut your heads off with it. I'm headed to Ebring now to find Pil's family. You're welcome to come along so we can figure out how not to kill each other."

"Or if we can't figure it out, just kill each other," Acton said, grinning.

"Right!" I smiled and realized I truly felt like smiling for the first time since I'd come home. "All the violence and ambiguity make you really feel like a sorcerer, eh?"

They looked a bit shocked by that.

Kenzie perked up first. "The road to Ebring runs right past Bleekhame! We can reach it before sunset if we push. We can show them our magic sword."

"Will we find Alamore there?" I asked.

Vargo shrugged. "Hell, we may not even get there."

Acton chuckled. "I predict the masters will tell us everything about this blade, I'm sure they will. Bib's been a bit vague about the sword's details and provenance—not that we are offering complaints! We're glad to have you along!"

My smile blew away like dust. These young people weren't my friends and weren't at all like me. They were enthused and optimistic, ready to be enemies one minute and comrades the next. I had let myself think of them almost as friends for a bit, but I would likely end up killing them.

I muttered, "If I was just going to kill unlucky youngsters, I could have stayed in the Dark Lands."

Hurd's head came up and he stared at me, but he didn't comment.

THIRTEEN

E bring, the capital of Ir, sat on the northern coast of the main island. Sandell lay not far from Ebring on the northeast coast. The entire kingdom was properly called the Westering Islands of Ir, but its people would never call it that. They would just say Ir, or maybe the Island. It might be called the Island of Ir if somebody was being married, sued, or crowned king.

The kingdom contained one big island and forty-two tiny ones. Only three of the small ones could support more than ten families.

The people of Ir despised mainlanders. Big Islanders looked down on the Small Islanders, who resented the Big Islanders in return. The Small Islanders had no use for anybody living on a different, and therefore inferior, island.

Insults and fistfights were common, and knifings didn't surprise anybody.

Kenzie had healed my arm a few miles from the northeastern coast, near the Fine Old Road. Nobody knew where that ignorant name came from, but at least Ir-folk could lie to mainlanders about it and make them look foolish. I once told a traveling singer the road had been given such a pleasant name to lure strangers into the capital, where they'd be reduced to begging and then starvation.

The Fine Old Road was the shortest path for us to Sandell and then to Ebring. I now had an arm, so anybody standing on the road in my way should prepare to be run over or cut down.

I expected a bit of delay when we reached the sorcery school at Bleekhame. Acton and Kenzie would show off for their old teachers, play games with their former classmates, and generally fart around.

I didn't care if they visited for an hour, but I made it clear that if they dawdled, I would leave them behind. They had promised Baby Harik they would kill me, but I hadn't promised him anything. I didn't need to murder them or even hurt their feelings unless they tried to kill me. So, if they lagged and had to chase me to Ebring, that would teach them something.

We would reach Sandell more than a day before we got to Ebring. They both lay on the other side of the Craer River, which ran wide and fast year-round. The road crossed into Sandell over a modest bridge. I didn't trust anything Baby Harik said, but even if Pil's family had gone to Ebring, I would be searching for that wicked bastard Alamore in Sandell and everyplace else until he was dead.

Over the years, many travelers had discovered that the Fine Old Road was an excellent place to be ambushed. It followed a wonderfully flat, wide path that nature had provided right between a dense forest and a range of jagged, gray hills. Taking a different route or pushing through the forest could add a week or more to the trip north, and I didn't feel we could afford the delay.

Acton and Kenzie enjoyed the walk, chatting about Bleekhame, drawing the flaming sword over and over to admire it, and laughing about nothing at all. Vargo walked on the other side of the road from them, shaking his head from time to time. After reminding them to be quiet at least a dozen times, I gave up and just watched out for trouble. I glanced around for Hurd but never saw him. If he had disappeared, that probably meant trouble was close.

I felt no surprise when we rounded a gentle curve and saw five of Burrud's soldiers, three short and two tall, trotting down the road toward us. Burrud and Lossil had marched off in roughly that direction.

Acton drew his sword with fine speed, and its green fire blazed.

Burrud's troops stopped short, watching the fiery sword. One of them pointed at it.

"Acton, in the future, you might wait until you're closer to unveil the glory of your weapon," I said. "Otherwise, you'll spend your days chasing your enemies, or at least having to run into battle. It sounds tiring to me."

Acton nodded. "Should we charge now?" He was so excited he couldn't stand still. Killing the rek with his knife earlier had made him more confident. With the flaming magic sword in his hand, he seemed to think he was invincible.

"Not yet. Acton, you take the stragglers."

He scowled but didn't complain.

"If any of them run, make sure they don't get away. Kenzie, stay with Vargo and me. All of you, look at me now!"

They all looked.

"Nobody leaves the road for any reason! Right?"

They nodded.

I drew my utterly sharp sword. It was perfect for the world of man, where I might want to show mercy once in a while. The God of Death's sword was perfect for destroying monstrous beings in ghastly realms. Using it to kill one soldier would be like killing a bee by dropping a house on it.

"Stay behind me." I trotted down the road toward the enemy soldiers. I heard Acton's flaming sword *whoosh* as he swung it in the air like a flag.

Four of Burrud's troops charged us. The fifth, a rek, ran back down the road.

When I reached the enemy, my unfathomably sharp sword surprised me. In the Dark Lands, I had wielded it with a fine touch, but for some reason, here in the world of man, I had lost that sensitivity. I thrust into a rek's chest, intending to pierce his heart, but my sharp sword went all the way through him, putting two feet of my blade out his back.

His tall friend swung a thick mace overhand at my skull. I withdrew so fast I almost tripped, and the mace struck my sword's edge. The iron mace head split apart as if it were made of cheese. I twisted and cut him from side to side in the most emphatic way possible.

As the tall body fell in two directions, a flash made me wince. I thought at first it was lightning, but it wasn't bright enough. Eighty feet away, an elm tree leaning over the road had exploded. Yellow-and-blue flames engulfed it, and I felt the heat on my face. Flaming limbs and branches tumbled onto the soldier who was running away, driving him to the ground. He started screaming.

Acton had demonstrated extraordinary aim with his thoughtless attack.

On my left, Vargo had cut his enemy deep on the leg and then finished the rek as it stumbled away. On my right, Kenzie was fencing with a tall soldier whose reach was nearly a foot longer than hers. She had done well to stay alive this long.

I thrust up into that tall soldier's neck, flicking my sword as fast as a frog's tongue. A normal sword with the force I used would have made a shallow puncture. The same force drove this blade all the way through his neck. I withdrew, and he stumbled backward, whirling his arms for balance before flopping onto his back.

I turned to Acton and pointed down the road at the burning tree. I didn't quite shout, "What did I tell you to do?" The rek under the pile of branches had stopped screaming.

"Stop those who ran," Acton said slowly.

"Did I also tell you to create a great column of smoke that everybody within five miles can see?"

Acton turned red.

I pointed my sword at the black smoke rising from the burned tree. Then I sheathed it, thankful that the sheath was magical and designed for this weapon. "Speed is our only chance now!"

Kenzie ran northwest toward the fire.

"Not that way!" I yelled, glaring at her.

"But Sandell lies that direction!"

I lowered my sword and spoke as if I were teaching her how to lace her boots. "These fellows came from that way and probably have friends. So, out of every direction we could run, that's the only one where we can be pretty sure we'll find the enemy." I raised my eyebrows at her.

Kenzie nodded and ran southeast past me, looking at the ground.

Those children might not have been tactically aware, but they made up for it with speed and endurance. I was lagging them by thirty feet when they scraped to a stop.

A big group of Burrud's soldiers trotted down the road toward us. I can't say how big because there were too many to count.

The forest was as dense here as anywhere. I might slip away into it, but the young people would be caught in a minute. The idea of leaving them to die fluttered through my head. It would solve some problems, but it would also mean abandoning Pil's grandson.

I was still picking through ideas when I heard creatures rushing and crackling past us in the trees. They were cutting us off, and I knew then there was no escape for any of us in that direction.

I turned to the other side of the road and scrambled fifty paces up the closest hill. I sagged when I saw it end in a narrow gorge that dropped far enough to kill. A taller hill rose from the other side of the gorge. From the road, it appeared to be all one slope, which fooled me into thinking we could escape that way.

I took a deep breath and tried to display some confidence for the young people. "Let's put our backs to this drop-off so we can't be surrounded. Kenzie, have you been working the clouds?" I had sensed her doing just that.

"Yes, I have done. I need two minutes more for a storm bigger than spitting."

"We probably don't have that much time." I had tossed several yellow bands around the area while I was running and panting behind Kenzie and the boys. I hadn't found many creatures that could help us. Insects were a poor choice on this damp autumn day. I did find two dozen wild pigs and seven forest cats.

At least thirty of Burrud's soldiers were climbing the hill toward us, and more waited on the road. Some had bows. I saw Burrud himself behind them.

"Now, Acton," I said.

He unsheathed his sword and held the green-flaming thing up high. Everybody stopped, and soldiers began muttering to each other.

"Can you set them all afire?" I asked.

Acton swallowed. "No. Maybe half. No, probably less."

"Hold off for now, then."

"Wait there!" Burrud's deep, round voice echoed off the hill behind me. He trotted up and stared at me from thirty feet away. "Why aren't you dead? I'm not complaining, you see, but why aren't you dead?"

"I was hit a glancing blow just when I was saying a prayer and the stars of my birth were aligning with the moon. And I'm lucky."

"And is that also why you have an arm now?"

I hesitated. "Yes. That's exactly why."

Burrud blinked. "I did not care entirely for the idea of killing you."

"I think that was wise," I said.

"If you don't wish to be killed now, accompany me. You may talk to Lossil again."

"Sure. I feel there were things left unsaid."

I fell in beside Burrud, and we paced back down the hill, across the road, and into the woods. The young people trailed us, surrounded by soldiers. "Where are we going?" I asked.

"I regret that you and I have officially entered negotiations. Perhaps you might call it an interrogation. Regardless, I am bringing you to Lossil, not answering your questions."

"Are you here for any reason other than taking me to Lossil?" I asked because I had to say something. I didn't expect the answer I got.

He gave me a steady look. "Yes, I am."

I paused and didn't care for that look in his eye. "I don't think I want to know what that reason is. Are you my enemy?"

"You should ask me that again in an hour." The great cat made a sound between a purr and a grunt. "I have wondered something. Is it always so cold on this island?"

I glanced at the sky. "No. Sometimes it's a lot colder."

For the next half an hour, I traipsed along beside a giant, mystical, talking monster-cat and talked about the bloody weather.

Burrud led me down a narrow, hidden forest road that I couldn't have found if Krak had been holding me by the collar and pointing at it. We arrived in a clearing that seemed to be a camp.

I had glanced at the sky for a few seconds to explain something about storms. When I looked ahead again, I saw dozens of creatures among the trees carrying sacks, arranging weapons, cleaning things, and undertaking all the onerous tasks required by a fighting force. I saw no tents or structures of any sort. Some of the laborers were reks, but others had antlers, scaly arms, wiggly tails, or great, hanging jowls.

Several big creatures that I would describe as monsters stood around, not doing anything I could see. I guessed they were guards, or officers, or priests, or had some other job where they didn't have to work.

Burrud's ears lay back against his head. "Do please remain here. I state that with great emphasis." He walked away behind some trees. A minute later, he called out, "You may speak with Lossil now, Bib."

I said, "I sure hope that means you're not my enemy now."

Burrud growled and gave me his cat shrug again.

FOURTEEN

In Lossil's camp, three twisted trees marked an area the size of several large rooms. I saw no cot or tent, just an open chest full of what looked like curtains. Lossil stood in the center of the space. His dog lay between us, watching me. His gem-ridged rhinoceros monster lay on its back, snoring with its legs in the air.

"This is charming," I said. "So clean. When you're gone, nobody will ever know you were here."

Lossil bowed his head, and I caught a flash of a smile. "Nice arm. Think you can regrow it?"

"I already did."

"No. Regrow it if somebody cuts it off again."

I didn't answer him directly. "Since you're talking instead of cutting, I guess you think I'm something special—and of course I am, ask anybody—but why do you think it?"

Lossil stared at me. "Why do you have the presumptuous gall to ask me questions?"

When I opened my mouth, he said, "That had better not be a question. Think hard."

I smiled and inquired, "Why do you think I'm so special?"

Lossil was huge, but he caught me before I could move. He

struck like a snake as heavy as a beer barrel. His fist smashed my cheek, and I tumbled twice before ending up on my butt. It was the same cheek that I had earlier thought might be broken, and it hurt twice as much now. When I touched it, my hand came away bloody.

Before I could reach for my sword, Lossil flapped a hand like my grandmother when she burned the bread. "Oh, hell, that was impolite." He shook his head and offered me a hand up, which I took. He still hadn't disarmed me, which showed shocking confidence on his part.

I considered drawing my sword and killing him while he was standing so obligingly close. But I scanned the area first and saw that the surrounding thicket and trees were packed with his men watching us. If I could cut through them, I had plenty of thickets for getting lost or setting up ambushes. It was a far better situation than we'd had at the cliff.

Lossil blew out a breath. "Are you special? Maybe. And maybe I decided about you too fast. I didn't make a mistake, you understand. You did come here from a different place, right? Like us. You shouldn't fight us, you know. You should be our ally. What in the name of a dozen yaks do you owe the people who live here? I can't see anything you owe them."

"I don't owe them much, I admit that. But I'm not from a different place, I'm from a village down the road. And before I can decide about alliances and such, what the hell is going on here? Murders? Pouring blood on the ground? I'll bet you six horses and all the shit they can poop that you don't do this sort of thing back home."

"Of course we don't! I'm insulted that you asked that. What did you—"

"No, you still haven't answered my first question worth a flip, so I'll ask another. Are the five heroes hereabouts? It would be an honor to meet them, especially Alamore."

Lossil's nostrils flared, but his voice was calm. "You know about the heroes, huh? Two are in camp now, if you really want to meet them, Hask and Bethroti."

"Not Alamore? I've heard he's the greatest one."

"No, Alamore is away killing somebody. He's like a fever. Set him loose and watch the bodies fall. He's useful at the right times."

"Perhaps I could meet your heroes later."

"No, I'll call for them now." Lossil called to a rek on the other side of a tree, "Invite the heroes to drink with me."

I smiled and nodded to cover the fact that I was a dumbass who asked for some more deadly fighters to join us. While we waited, I asked, "When will Alamore be back?"

Lossil shrugged. "He covers a lot of countryside. It's hard to say when he'll be back. He's the most energetic hero."

I drew a big breath. "Lossil, have you already killed the people of Sandell? Or moved them? Do you know where they are? I guess that was three questions, but I'm truly interested."

"I see." Lossil stared at me, which made me uncomfortable. Then he smiled, which almost shocked me by how friendly it made him look. "That's a lucky thing for both of us, because I haven't killed them, and I know where they are. Most of them have run away from Sandell."

I waited, but he didn't say anything else. "Lossil, I'd love to get so excited that I pee myself over this, but I need a little more detail."

He didn't answer that. "Ah, the heroes are here. Bib the Bad Example, meet Hask of the Dead Empire and Bethroti of the Hill People."

Bethroti, dark brown and draped in furs, was one of the tallest Hill People I had ever seen, well over five and a half feet. She carried a black-shafted spear over her shoulder and wore her black hair straight. She didn't speak but examined me as if I would explode if she stepped the wrong way. That puzzled me; since the Hill People were the most dangerous fighters in the world, I imagine she felt entitled to look at me however she wanted.

Hask stood average height and wore her blond hair in braids that fell behind her thick shoulders. She was one of the few in the camp I had seen without furs, but she did wear a faded-blue padded jacket.

A few generations earlier, the Hill People had obliterated the Empire, which had been a thousand miles wide. That could have caused friction between these two, I supposed, but they seemed relaxed with one another.

Hask smiled and said, "Bib, eh? I've always thought those Bib stories were bullshit. You don't look all that stupid to me." Hask grinned at Bethroti. "Does he, Beth? He looks smart enough to pour piss out of a boot, right?"

Bethroti kept quiet, but she did stick out her lower lip in a way that said she might not murder me today.

A monster with flapping jowls brought us drinks in smallish, wooden mugs. I figured I should wait for Lossil to drink first, and the others waited too.

Lossil raised his mug and said, "To hell with glory."

We toasted, and I drank a gulp. It might have been pure alcohol with good thoughts dribbled in for flavor. Only the many years I had dedicated to drunkenness allowed me to keep it down.

With the mug still to my lips, I glanced around. All three were watching me from the corners of their eyes. They took another swallow, so I did too and managed not to cough the stuff through my nose. Tears were running from my eyes.

To demonstrate my stupidity, I rushed to take a third swallow before anybody else. None of them hesitated to go along. My ears were ringing, and I doubted I'd be able to taste anything for a month. A little liquor trickled from Hask's mouth as she smiled at me.

Three was the most favorable of all numbers, and I hoped to Krak's left ear that meant they would stop at three swallows. They did not. Lossil took a great gulp, and I felt I had to follow, as if we were tied together and he'd thrown himself down a well, dragging me along to destruction.

Bethroti lowered her mug then, so I felt I could lower mine without shame. I figured Hask would lower hers and let Lossil beat the rest of us, but Lossil lowered his mug too as he shook his head. I had met a number of men and women leading armies, and not many of them could stand to lose at anything. Lossil didn't seem concerned.

Hask was blond and pale, but now her face was the color of a radish. She took one more swallow, sighed, and smiled around at us.

"I must not burp. My teeth will explode," Bethroti said.

I said, "When I took that fourth swallow, I saw the gods."

Hask smiled at us all but didn't seem able to speak. She was swaying, or maybe she looked that way because I was swaying.

Lossil said, "Everybody sit down. This isn't the time to fall on the ground and break an arm."

For the next hour, we talked about our common interests: weapons, combat, the battles we'd been part of, and our many wounds. They knew little about sailing. When I mentioned horses, Lossil said, "Maybe again soon." Hask asked about my family. I shook my head, having no family to talk about, and the rest nodded as if they might not have any, either. Lossil changed the subject to bows.

I felt a good bit recovered by the time Hask and Bethroti left us. They laughed and threw a few entertaining insults. Hask even slapped me on the back. I laughed along with them, thought about it, and realized it was the first time I had really laughed since Pil died. Or since she seemed to die.

Lossil sighed and stopped smiling. "Bib, I can't tell you about Sandell unless you agree to something."

"I see." I rubbed my chin. "Lossil, I feel that we are in a delicate situation here. I have stated my desire, and you have said you can fulfill it. But you won't yet. I predict that next you will tell me what I must do to have my desire fulfilled." I raised my eyebrows at him.

"You predict well."

"Wonderful. I'm a reasonable fellow and understand bargaining. I am happy to bargain fairly. But if you try to make me do some impossible feat or kill some atrocious monster, I will not cooperate. In fact, I will kill every last son of a bitch in this camp. It may take me awhile, but it won't matter whether they're dead this afternoon or ten days from now. Do we have an understanding?"

Lossil stared, and I thought he might shout or hit me. His hesitation told me everything I needed to know about how honest he'd be with me. "I won't lie to you," he lied. "I'll ask a lot from you, maybe too much for anybody but a hero. I'm being honest so you'll stop killing my soldiers. I need them."

"That sure is honest," I said to the lying bastard. "You are a fine specimen of a leader. Where are the people of Sandell?"

Lossil didn't sag or slump, but his rigidity eased a bit. "I hate my orders sometimes," he said with what seemed like real feeling. "Do you hate yours?"

"Yes, I hate orders. I try not to take them."

"I'll tell you all I know about these people if you assassinate this island's king."

I stretched my neck. "That's an interesting proposal. How about this? If you told me where these people are, I would perform my task as well as you performed yours. That is, if what you told me is enough to find them, then I would kill the king all to hell."

Kenzie exclaimed something from far behind me.

I went on: "If what you told me gets me to the general area, then I would injure the king or put him in a bad way. And if your information gets me nothing, then the king would have no trouble from me."

Lossil paused. "I don't like this much. There's only one way for this kind of deal to work. I have to give you my information, then you'll search for these people. When you find them, or you don't find them, then you'll deal with the king."

"That sounds fair to me."

"It's the damned opposite of fair!" Lossil yelled. We stared at each other for a while before he hissed and said, "All right, I agree."

"Marvelous. Where are they?"

"Most of the Sandell folk have retreated to Ebring."

"Lossil, you're a clever hound. You wouldn't send me to Ebring and then play some damn trick that would force me to kill the king, would you? My people might not even be there, or within a thousand miles, but you would get what you want. I hate to believe you'd do that."

His eyes narrowed. "What are you saying? I'm not trying to cheat you."

"And that makes me feel good about you. I'd feel even better if you sent somebody with me. Somebody important who I could execute if you betray me."

Lossil's jaw clamped shut, and the muscles of his neck and shoulders stood out. "I can't spare anybody."

I waved my hand. "I don't see how we can reach an agreement, then."

Lossil's voice dropped even deeper. "I've given you the information already."

"That was poor bargaining on your part, wasn't it?"

Lossil yelled, "But we already agreed!"

"I heard you agree. Did you hear the words 'I agree' or 'I will' come out of my mouth?"

"You said you will kill the king," Lossil grated.

"No, I said I *would* kill him under certain conditions that may or may not come to pass, not that I *will* kill him. That's a big difference."

Someplace behind me, Acton burst out laughing before he was cut off.

Lossil took a deep breath, and I saw his body relax. "Well, that was a waste of time. Your help would have been useful, but . . ." He frowned and raised his voice: "Burrud, come over here! There's a problem!"

Burrud bounded to join us.

"Last chance," Lossil said.

I glanced back at Kenzie and the others. Their shaking hands were on their weapons, and they turned in place, probably trying to decide how to fight off the inhuman soldiers and monsters surrounding them.

Raising my hand, I said, "Hold on! Perhaps I was hasty. Let me give you the sort of answer you're looking for, the one that will bind me, and then we can get on with this business."

I had assumed that no fight in the world of man would justify employing the Death God's sword, but Lossil and his minions weren't from the world of man. I had killed creatures in the Dark Lands that made Lossil look like a wheezing toad. His soldiers resembled a handful of debauched sailors compared to the hundreds I had killed there. The monsters would be a challenge, but even they would be shocked by the carnage the sword could deliver.

Of course, that was in the Dark Lands when my body had been mighty and full of bridge-guardian goodness. Things might be different for me in the world of man. But I still knew everything I had learned in seventy years of fighting.

If a battle broke out, Acton and the others might not survive. In fact, they probably wouldn't, but they were two sorcerers and a decent fighter with a magic sword. Their lives were in their own hands, not mine.

Reaching into the tiny space that kept Death's weapon safe, I drew forth the sword to destroy my enemies just as I had destroyed the God of Death.

A chain of sausage links lay in my hand. They looked delicious but would prove damned awkward in lethal combat.

I glanced around. I had produced sausages out of nothing, and everybody I saw, including Lossil, Burrud, and the young trio, was staring at me as if I were spinning on my head and flinging drool.

I did the only thing I could do. Holding up the sausage links, I exclaimed, "In the manner of my people, I give you this gift to celebrate our agreement. By the way, I agree."

FIFTEEN

Lossil accepted my sausages with so much formality that he might have been mocking me. I found it hard to read his face. It seemed normal, although flat and heavy in the nose and brows, but I felt a little cold when he stared at me.

I put the feeling aside. After all, Lossil had been born in some crazy other realm. I waited while he described in artistic detail just how he wanted me to kill the king, instructing me to kill the king with his own knife and to make sure that the king's dogs, if he had any, watched the proceedings. Somewhere in there, I realized he wasn't blinking, or not much. I blinked about ten times for every one of his.

Lossil finished and I smiled, already forgetting everything he said about the regicide. I said, "We'd better rush to find our people and murder the sovereign ruler of this land. I feel snow coming."

Lossil swallowed and pulled his fur coat tighter, the first sign that he could be hurt by something.

"It'll probably sleet first for a day or so," I said. "The ice will cover everything caught outside, thick enough to break trees. I've seen it happen. I won't even mention how hard the wind will blow. A man could get frozen solid if he paused to lean against a fence."

Lossil stared at me unblinking for a little while before smiling. "And the wind will cover whole farms with snow. When it melts off, the dead will be so frozen you can break off their arms like twigs. Right?"

I nodded and turned away, but he caught my arm. He murmured, "Burrud says you belong here but don't belong. He may be wrong. Maybe you belong someplace else, just like us. It's hard to say. But this war will end sometime, and the winners will go home. That's why you ought to join us. If you do, I promise we'll help you get home."

Lossil might be a liar like me, but he seemed to mean what he was telling me. "Maybe. Once I find my people, we can talk about us all going home."

I turned and beckoned Acton and the others, chuckling at how foolish Lossil had turned out to be. I waved at him without looking back.

Thirty seconds later, I closed my eyes and stopped.

"What's the matter?" Kenzie asked.

I didn't answer her. I thought Lossil had turned out to be foolish. Maybe that's what he wanted me to think. Maybe he was really far cleverer than me and I had put us in some awful trap. I wished that Pil was here to laugh and remind me that I wasn't twice as smart as everybody else. And that it made me a challenge to love, but she struggled on.

Kenzie whispered, "I said, what is it? Is it an ambush ahead?"

"No ambush," I said, scanning ahead to make sure there really wasn't one. "Don't worry. It's nothing you'd understand."

I led us down the twisting path, well marked now that I knew what to look for. After a few minutes, I paused where two paths met. Acton pushed past me and strode down the right-hand path without pausing. I had no evidence to say he was wrong, so I followed. Kenzie walked behind me, and Vargo trailed us in silence.

When we reached the road, Acton faced me. "You are not going to try to kill the king. We will not allow it."

"He's not my king," I said.

"He's not my king, either," Acton said, "but it's still an evil thing to do."

"Well, he is my king!" Kenzie said. "Bib, would you dare to kill your own?"

I walked around Kenzie and on down the road. "I don't have a king."

"That's crazed. How can you not have a king?" From her tone, Kenzie might have been asking how I could not have a heart or a stomach.

"Leave him alone," Vargo said, stepping up to walk beside me.

Kenzie flinched away from Vargo, her eyes narrowed as if that had hurt her.

I said, "It's not hard to be kingless. Just stop bowing. It's none of your business anyway." Acton and Kenzie were working themselves into a fit, and I struggled not to laugh at them.

"It certainly is business of mine if you think to slay my king!" Kenzie snapped.

Vargo raised a hand. "Wait, stop a minute. Bib, there's got to be a king where you come from. Where does your family live?"

"No place. They're all dead."

Vargo's eyes opened wide. He breathed, "You're all alone?"

Acton stepped away from me and filled the silence. "Which is your patron god?"

"My what? You have patron gods?" I snorted.

"Of course! My patron is Fingit," Kenzie said.

I laughed. "Fingit is a fine choice. He keeps secrets well, and you wouldn't believe how much he can drink."

Kenzie shook her head and shouted, "You can't be much of a sorcerer if you don't have a patron god!"

I chuckled. "I don't need a patron god, and neither do you. I wish you could see how the gods laugh their asses off at you and me."

Kenzie was flushed, and Acton had grown pale as they yelled at me. I was simply the stupidest and most profane person who ever lived.

Vargo walked along with his shoulders hunched until he cut the sorcerers off by raising a hand and said slowly, "Bib, if nothing else, you have this land, where you were born. The island claimed you when you were born on it."

"I don't give a damn about this island, and I don't care much for its people, either." I thought about spitting on the road, but that might have driven them insane with rage.

"Of course!" Kenzie shot back. "You're a selfish, selfish man. Oh, sure, you're a killer, but would you twitch your nose to help a single person? Go back where you came from!"

The conversation had become less amusing in a hurry. I waved the offended sorcerers past me. "Go on and visit your fine sorcery school—it can't be too far now. I'll just follow at a polite distance so I don't desecrate the road in front of you with my unbelieving feet. Or maybe I'll go to Ebring some other way. Go on!"

From that spot, there was no other reasonable way to reach Ebring apart from the Fine Old Road, and I'm sure they knew it. They trotted past me without speaking, and Vargo hesitated before joining them. They started whispering among themselves. I hoped that didn't mean Kenzie and Acton were planning to ambush me just down the road.

Kenzie was smart, probably smarter than me, although she hid it. She was passionate about what mattered to her. Acton had admirable focus and insight, if not much judgment yet. Vargo was brave and usually a morose pain in the butt. I hadn't yet seen what qualities Pil had admired in him, but I allowed that they might emerge.

Half an hour up the road, I found Hurd walking beside me. I said, "We almost had the biggest slaughter since the Empire was overrun. I wish you'd been there."

"I was busy picking wildflowers."

"It's autumn. All the wildflowers are dead."

"I didn't say I was picking them here." He smirked.

I lowered my voice, even though nobody was nearby. "Hurd, something happened that concerns me."

"Just one thing? Looking at you, I can see seven things that ought to concern you."

I sighed. "When I tried to draw the God of Death's sword, I couldn't."

"I won't say that you failed to perform."

"Don't try to be funny," I said. "This may be something that fails to keep me alive or keep you alive."

"All right, fine then. Just what happened exactly when you gave it a try?"

"I pulled forth a string of linked sausages." I said it as fast as possible.

Hurd halted and stared at me. "How did they taste?"

"I didn't cook them!"

"I bet you didn't kill anybody with them, either!" Hurd cackled. "Sorry to poke fun, I know this is serious."

"What's happening to the sword?" I asked.

Hurd chewed his lip. "I don't know."

"Don't you have any ideas?"

"I have lots of ideas! I have a wagon full of ideas! I just don't know which of them are worth a pig's lip."

"Well, pull out the shiniest couple of them!" I glanced ahead but couldn't spot the trio. "Tell me about them!"

"Dang it, don't give yourself the runs over this! I think the problem is most likely you don't fit in this world too good anymore, and when you try to pull that sword out, it can't find you. Or maybe you can't find it, or something."

I felt a little sick. "I don't like that one. What else do you have?"

Hurd acted as if he were chewing something tough. "Maybe the gods put their hands in and screwed things up when I brought you here. They don't like you having that sword, right? This would be a dang good time to take it away from you."

"Shit," I whispered.

We walked on for a few minutes without talking. Then I spotted the merest smudge on the horizon. I pointed at it and said, "I've been away a long time. Is that the fine sorcery school Acton and Kenzie miss so much?"

Hurd shrugged.

I said, "If it is, then based on my extensive knowledge of catastrophe and destruction, the place is on fire."

"It is not! And I say that just to act contrary."

I said, "What is it, then? Maybe the world's greatest whale walked out of the ocean into these hills and is spouting a few hundred feet high?"

"Fine! That's the school, it's on fire, there's sorcery and sorcerers flying around everyplace." He paused. "Do you give so much as Weldt's manly man parts about those children?"

I gritted my teeth. "Kruppin, I want you."

Kruppin emerged from the trees in his dog size, dragging along with his head lowered. After ten seconds of waiting, I walked to meet him.

"Kruppin, do you know where Vargo, Acton, and Kenzie are?" It wasn't a command, but I hoped he might answer anyway.

He sat and stared me in the eye. "Yes."

"Do you know whether they're in danger?"

"I could tell you if you command it. Are you trying to make me do things without giving me commands? That is quite awful behavior, and you aren't even very skillful about it."

"I am the sorcerer here, not you." I stood taller. "Your place isn't to criticize me or anything else—it's to do my bidding. I think you didn't answer because you don't know whether they're in danger and you're embarrassed about it."

After a pause, he said, "Nice try." Then he peed on my boots.

"Hurd, let's go see the festival of destruction producing that smoke. We can join in, or at least search the place for treasure."

"Huh. You care no more for treasure than you do for blackberries, Bib."

I headed down the road at a fast trot with Hurd and his short legs running hard beside me.

SIXTEEN

The sorcery school of Bleekhame was set back in the hills a couple of miles from the Fine Old Road. Clouds began gathering before Hurd and I reached the rugged path that led up to the school. I suspected Kenzie was building the clouds, and solid rain began falling while we were still on the main road.

Lantern light appeared through the rain, followed by three figures coming toward us. I drew my sword, and Hurd shuffled over behind me. The figures stopped. I could tell that they were man-size and carrying weapons, but the rain hid any other details.

"Who are you?" a woman shouted.

I shouted back, "Travelers who don't want trouble."

"Let me look upon you, then!" she yelled.

I walked toward her and her two friends, who were men. She was tall and solid, with long, pale hair tied back and a longer sword in her hand. The man on her right was skinny and almost shriveled and carried the lantern. The man on her left wore a steel helmet and carried a double-bladed axe. His reddish-gray beard was as long as my forearm.

"Why are you walking on this road?" the woman asked in a voice that was soft and a bit musical now that she wasn't yelling.

"We are following some friends who went to visit the school."

The woman gazed around. "Sir, why are you saying 'we'?"

I glanced back to find Hurd missing. "My other friend seems to have run away. You must have terrified him."

She frowned, and I could see that her face was so delicate it hardly matched her solid form. "What are you called?"

"I'm Pudgore the turnip farmer."

The woman knelt, seized a small rock, and threw it at me, hitting me on the belly. "Stop that! I can see that you are not a farmer of turnips, so stop lying to us!"

I took a step toward her, and we locked eyes.

I had met a number of dedicated killers over the years, men and women for whom killing satisfies an appetite. They devote themselves to it. Lucky ones arrive at a way to kill that other people find useful, or at least understandable. Unlucky ones are despised and have a short life full of slaughter.

Some of them were lucky on one day and unlucky on the next, which made for an interesting life.

This woman's eyes, stance, and grip on her sword told me she was a serious killer. One who had just accused me of lying.

I said, "Telling you the truth would be awkward." The rain was beginning to slack off.

"This is a dangerous road upon which to tell lies." She nodded at the bearded man, then the two of them spread apart to come at me from two sides.

"I'm called Bib."

After a pause, she shrugged. "Another lie. Well, you have been told." She raised her sword.

"It really is! Why would I make that up?"

Lowering her sword, she stared at my face for several seconds. "Fine, you would not. But if you are lying, I will find out the reason. I am Evonne. These men are Kepp and Alber." She nodded at the skinny one and the bearded one in turn. "We saw the smoke over the school. If you are traveling to it, we will follow you. Do not try to walk behind us."

For the size of its population, Ir has always been bursting with sorcery schools. Three schools stood on the island when I had been a student, and a fourth had been built since then. I studied at Gallinn on the Mere, which was the school farthest south.

Bleekhame was farthest north and became the fourth sorcery school on the island. It had been built just forty years ago.

The schools didn't specialize in any official way, but over time, students shifted toward particular schools. Bleekhame catered to students with a scholarly bent. The oldest school, Poppling Knot, attracted students more interested in creating, while students drawn to destruction found more opportunities at Clefthall.

Students couldn't just decide to attend Gallinn on the Mere. One had to be invited by the masters. They had only one criterion. Gallinn was reserved for unruly students with a high opinion of their own intelligence and a low ability to follow directions.

The masters at Gallinn on the Mere kicked me out early for being an arrogant pain in their rarefied sorcerous asses. You could say that by their standards, I was the perfect student.

Kenzie had described Bleekhame to me in joyful detail when she discovered I was a sorcerer. That ended when she realized I was the most horrible man who ever lived. The school consisted of thirteen stone and timber buildings standing around a vast courtyard. As I tramped through the mud from the closest hill down into the courtyard, I counted seven pools and seventeen fountains.

There had been a big fire here, just as I suspected. I hadn't expected this level of destruction. The buildings weren't just burned. Several of them had been partly torn down.

Acton and Kenzie scrambled through the ruins, calling out names and digging through rubble with their hands. I didn't know who or what to look for, so I sat on the edge of a fountain.

"Aren't they your friends?" Evonne asked.

"Sure. They'll call out when they need me."

Kenzie screamed from inside one of the buildings.

I drew my sword and ran toward her. Hurd showed up and ran beside me. I didn't hear combat in any direction, which comforted me a bit.

The scream had come from within a tall, white stone building along the courtyard's north side. The structure must have impressed both visitors and students before it was cracked and blackened with soot. I slowed so as not to rush through the door and be slaughtered in an ambush.

The inside seemed to be a single, large room. Under the partly collapsed roof, tapestries and heavy furniture burned on the floor, throwing an unsettling, jumping light. I smelled cloth burning, dust, and blood.

Across the room, about three dozen bodies hung upside down from ropes. As I moved closer, I could tell that the people had been bled as if they were animals. Kenzie scrambled from one person to another, crying, saying people's names, and in some cases patting their arms or cheeks.

Acton met me halfway across the room, wiping at his tearing eyes. "I doubt anyone survived. There is a great mound of bodies behind the Highwhistle. Lossil's killers were thorough. May they eat firewood and shit hot coals."

I asked, "Is there a chance this was done by somebody else? Would there be a reason for some other enemy to do this?"

He shook his head. "It was Lossil and his army of monsters. It's monstrous enough."

Hurd said, "I haven't—" He sneezed so loudly the sound rang off the stone walls. "Krak-knackered smoke. I haven't found a thing that looks like it's worth anything. Just clothes and trinkets, nothing valuable or magical. Maybe those lousy nose-twisters did this to make us crazy for vengeance and charge off into some trap."

Evonne and her friends had followed me and were standing at the doorway. "We should leave here," she said. "This is a very bad place, and awful things happened here. We cannot make them not to have happened. We should leave."

"My future wife makes a lot of sense," Hurd said.

Evonne hissed. "Who are you, you terrible person?"

Hurd said, "Yes, I am terrible. But that's because I have lived through terrible things, and each one makes you a little more terrible."

Evonne said, "That is an excuse. There can be no excuse for you." She took a step toward Hurd, and he scurried behind me.

Vargo called from across the room, his voice strained, "Help us bring them down."

"Crap," I breathed. We couldn't tend the bodies no matter how dear they'd been to Kenzie and Acton.

"This is your festivity, Bib," Hurd murmured. "You have to tell them, not me."

As I walked across the room, I said, "There must be forty of them."

"Thirty-nine," Acton said with a knife in his hand. He sounded years older than fifteen now. He and Vargo had grasped a woman by the arms, and he was sawing at the rope that held her.

I said, "It's not uncommon for people who do this kind of wickedness to come back and view their work. To enjoy it, I mean. They may also find grieving people tending the dead and kill them too."

Kenzie faced me, and her shoulders fell. "What are you saying?"

As Acton and Vargo eased the body down, I said, "We can't stay to bury them or even cut them down. We can't stay at all."

Acton stood straight and yelled, "You damn monster! We're not going to leave these people hanging for the crows to eat!"

"I'm sorry, I know they were your friends. But I doubt they would want you caught and hung up alongside them."

"He's right. I hate him for it, but he is telling it right," Kenzie said, walking away from the bodies.

Acton shouted, "What? Stop! Come back here!"

Vargo was shaking his head as he walked away. It was hard to say with so much smoke around, but he might have been crying.

"Kenzie knows that I'm talking sense," I said. "It's a lousy kind of sense, but we don't get to control that."

Acton opened his mouth to say something foolish, but he clenched his teeth instead. Then he stared at me and nodded. "Fine, let's go." Acton followed Vargo to the door, kicking broken masonry on the way.

Once we had all reentered the courtyard, Acton turned back.

He swept one arm up, pointing at the clouds, and clenched a fist in front of his face. The clothing worn by all the corpses burst into white-hot flame. The fire lasted only a couple of seconds and wouldn't burn the bodies much, but I guess it was something.

As we crossed the courtyard, Acton walked beside me. "Aren't you about to chastise me for wasting power?"

"No."

After a few seconds, he asked, "Why not?"

"It's your power, not mine. If you ask for my opinion about power, I might offer it. I might even give you a piece of knowledge that could be useful. Kenzie! You should come and hear this as well."

Kenzie drifted over to walk on the other side of me, wiping her cheeks hard.

I said, "This can be a harsh lesson, but it's important. You are sorcerers."

"Really? I didn't know," Kenzie said through a stuffy nose.

"Hush. You don't know how much pain I'm about to save you. In most cases, only you know what you paid for your power. Only you are justified in deciding what to do with it. No one can judge you about your sorcery except you. People will try, but don't let them. If you do, it will end in your imprisonment or death. You may think that's an outrageous thing to say, but hundreds of sorcerers have found that it's true."

Acton said, "Our teachers never told us anything like that."

Kenzie gave me a half smile. "I thought maybe you were going to teach us something that would help us kill you. This is disappointing."

"Sorcery is full of disappointment. That's a true thing too."

Evonne and her men followed as we wended our way back to the Fine Old Road and headed north again. Earlier, clouds had lifted without Kenzie's magic to keep them together, but now they rolled down naturally from the high hills and even turned to fog. It became hard to see.

Evonne said that she and her friends were headed north, just like us. With no real agreement, they traveled with us but did not allow us to walk behind them.

The fog became even thicker toward sunset, and it was clear that travel would soon be impossible. We moved off the road and built a small camp with no fire to get a little sleep. Our provisions were meager, and so were Evonne's. By morning, our provisions were nonexistent.

The sun rose on the other side of the hills. I saw clouds bringing a stiff wind down from those hills, along with the season's first real cold snap. Evonne, Kepp, and Alber were dressed for it, but the rest of us were not. Soon, we all were shivering, except for Hurd. The colder it got, the better he liked it.

I estimated that we were a few hours away from the city of Sandell when everything went to hell. Men with swords climbed out of the brush that had replaced the forest on the ocean side. I glanced uphill and saw men with bows on the inland side above us. It was a sweet little ambush laid by somebody cleverer about ambushes than me.

"These are the bandits!" Kenzie cried.

"How can you tell?" Vargo sounded truly interested.

"Who else could they be?" Kenzie demanded.

"King's soldiers. Village militia. Some baron's retainers. Religious zealots. Sturdy drunkards." Vargo shrugged.

A lightly armored blond man, not tall but broad, pointed a lengthy sword at Kenzie. "You will now be quiet among yourselves, please."

Acton whispered, "I don't like how he talks."

The broad man cleared his throat. "I was only being polite. It was not a request, so be quiet. Who leads this band?"

When no one else spoke, I said, "I wouldn't call myself the leader. I'm more of a guide and spiritual advisor. But I think I can speak to you with some confidence. My name is Durar, the Wise and Old."

The broad man said, "I know some people who could benefit from that which you do. Put your weapons on the ground."

Evonne had fallen behind and now came into view. "Theo!" she shouted. "You may leave them to pass. They have come with me."

I was so grateful to Evonne in that moment that I wanted to give her a kitten. We were in a horrible tactical position.

However, Theo said, "I insist you lay down your weapons and then do as I say."

I looked over my shoulder at Evonne.

She said, "It will be easiest if you do what he says. Theogalt is a great insister of things."

I nodded. "I spiritually advise you, my friends, to put your weapons on the ground right now, and keep quiet while you do it."

Theogalt nodded. Soon all our weapons lay at our feet. He nodded to a nearby swordsman, who tapped a comrade. They began gathering our weapons. I caught Acton's eye and shook my head with a hard look. I didn't need him creating a massacre just because somebody touched his magic sword.

"Why are you on this road?" Theogalt asked.

"We have no ill intent," I said. "We're traveling to the city of Sandell for provisions and cloaks. As you can see, we're poorly dressed for winter."

He nodded. "Yes, I see that. You have not been a good advisor to your friends about that. I will now search you."

I expected his men to search us, but Theogalt had spoken literally. He himself walked up to me and, with both hands, began patting my head from the crown to my neck. It perplexed me so that I stood still and didn't comment.

Theogalt then gave my body the most precise and thorough search I had ever experienced. He smiled at me. "These are difficult times. I apologize."

He moved on to Hurd, who made no smart comments, but he did giggle throughout the whole procedure. I think it unsettled Theo, but he persevered.

Theogalt moved on to Acton and then Vargo. After the search, Theo seemed satisfied. If those boys had held back any weapons, they had hidden them in some profoundly sneaky places.

When Theogalt moved on to Kenzie, he said, "I apologize to the extreme, miss, and I regret this is necessary. You may refuse to forgive me later, if you like." Kenzie stood still and rigid, never making a sound as he searched her head.

"You must stop that!" Evonne said as Theo moved down past Kenzie's neck. "I will give my word for her."

Theogalt hesitated. "I have my orders. And you are not the one who gives me orders."

Evonne walked up to stand beside Kenzie. "At least wait until we can ask."

"I have not been told that I may wait or ask. This is my duty."

When Theo touched Kenzie's shoulders, Evonne slammed her shoulder into him. He stumbled backward an impressive distance but kept his feet.

Evonne drew her sword and pointed it at Theogalt's face. "If you try to touch her in that way, I will kill you. I will kill you with such force it will hurt people when they think about you."

Theogalt didn't appear angry at all. He walked back to Evonne until her sword was almost touching him. "I understand and respect what you are saying. Please respect that I must do this. I have no choice."

Evonne punched Theo in the throat with her left hand, and he staggered. I had rarely witnessed a faster strike. While he was gagging, she reached down and whipped his sword out of the scabbard. Now she held his sword in her left hand and her own sword in her right.

Back when this ambush was first sprung, I had begun pulling together the clouds. Conveniently, they were piled thick to start with. Warm air was scarce, but I guided enough off the ocean to create real storm clouds.

Once the storm had gathered above us, I had held it back from dropping any rain. When Evonne took Theogalt's sword, I released a furious deluge over the slope above us and the bowmen hiding in it. Within seconds, no archer in the world could draw a bow and hit anything through that rain.

I had plenty of rain left over to daze the soldiers in front of me and downhill from the road, and I raised enough wind to blow that rain past my companions and me so we weren't battered as much.

I turned toward Evonne and the others, shouting, "Run! Run!" This little storm was furious but would last only a short time. We needed to be out of sight when it dribbled away.

Evonne knocked Theogalt down and kicked him. Then she ran. Everybody else followed her except for Acton and me.

I had noted where Theogalt's men had taken our weapons. I scrambled through the rain toward the pile and ran my hand across the scabbards. When I found Acton's, I grabbed it and turned. He was standing right there and snatched it out of my hand. I reached back down and grabbed my sharp sword and Vargo's sword, then I turned to run.

Everybody was already sprinting away when I started running. I covered fifty steps or so while the rain eased. Then something huge appeared to my right, hurtling down the slope at me. I ducked and rolled, missing most of the blow, although something bashed me hard on the butt.

I came up weaponless and peered across the road. I had never seen this kind of creature before, but it looked monstrous enough.

It stood eight feet tall with what appeared to be spines sticking up another two feet. Its face was pink with patchy black hair and was roughly human, if the human had cheekbones sliding down and a tusk-filled jaw with a profound underbite. The broad, pink arms showed fine muscles and were double-jointed. The beast wore a faded black jacket open at the front with a yellow waistcoat underneath, as well as shiny green trousers. It also wore black boots, but the front of each had burst out, setting free greenish toes with curved claws.

I think the monster smiled at me. It was hard to be sure through that underbite. In some monster language, it said, "Got you! Rumblebile can eat my nuts!"

I decided this was a magnificent time to try drawing the Death God's sword again, and I extended my hand. I didn't exactly pray, but I did ask Krak nicely to help me out. I pulled forth my sword and instead found I was holding one end of a wet towel.

"Yeah . . ." I whispered.

The monster shouted, "I want a nose!" Then it jumped at me.

SEVENTEEN

I should have thanked Theogalt for groping us so thoroughly. He took his time, and time is the friend of the Caller. The moment he started to search us was the moment I began preparing the storm for some real fun.

A couple of minutes had passed since Evonne beat the shit out of Theo, and I had developed several tactical options that I felt would be useful against an inappropriately touchy bandit and his men. However, I hadn't expected to face a monster that wanted to tear off my nose.

All of that meant I dodged and ran like mad. Because the monster unknowingly warned me what he was after, I moved the instant I saw his muscles bunch, and I knew just where he intended to land his blow because that's where my nose would logically be.

This monster was not graceful. I had met sinuous monsters so supple they were mesmerizing, but this wasn't one of them. He landed with a thump and a skid, while I was already sprinting down the road away from him. I needed enough room so that I didn't kill myself.

As the monster turned to follow me, I wiggled a finger. The creature must have been a bit sensitive and felt what was happening in the ground. He jumped away from the danger, and the lightning bolt that flashed from the earth to the clouds just singed him.

That leap saved him, but it didn't save him for all time. I had figured he would jump when I saw his reaction to the buildup of lightning. I also figured he would keep chasing me both to get my nose and to whack me until I stopped throwing lightning bolts. I had seen how far he could leap, so the math was easy.

The monster jumped to catch me, and on the second bound, an eye-shredding, hair-lifting split of lightning ripped from the ground up to the storm, passing right through the monster. The creature bounced off the side of the road and slid down through the brush in a smoky wash of flopping arms and legs.

I didn't know much about this monster, which meant I didn't know whether he traveled with friends. Before I released the potential for lightning, I examined the world in all directions. Nothing looked threatening. Theo and his hooligans were running down the road toward me, but compared to the monster, they looked as threatening as a bunch of down pillows.

"Who did that?" Kenzie asked from behind me. "There's another sorcerer around here!"

"Bib did it," Acton said.

Kenzie jutted her chin at him. "It can't be. He didn't make a sound or move his hand."

Acton raised his voice. "He used his toes, or maybe one toe! He wasn't lying. Not about this."

"Toes? You're still babbling about toes?" Kenzie glared at him.

I laughed. "Kenzie's right, it wasn't me. My life is guarded by yet another sorcerer, this one an expert at remaining undetected. He might not like it when you try to kill me. I owe him several drinks."

Kenzie and Acton scanned both sides of the road, uphill and down, whispering and growling at each other. I was treating them with a shade of cruelty, but my tolerance for children who are certain they know everything was limited. I felt sure Acton would eventually convince Kenzie that sorcerers didn't need to wave their arms like they were shooing cattle.

Theogalt arrived and halted a respectful distance from us,

looking around at our group. "You defeated that great horror. There is a sorcerer among you. Is that correct?"

I said, "That is incorrect, my suspicious friend. We are all sorcerers, every damn one of us. We had intended to wait until you finished molesting us in the name of Krak knows what and then hit you with lightning and fire at the same time. But now that we've fought that horrendous, crushing monster, obliterating you seems too easy. We might fall asleep during the fight."

Theogalt clenched his teeth and looked past me at Evonne. "Why did you bring strange sorcerers here?"

"They are more polite and less literal than you."

Theogalt shook his head. "I can tell that the rest of you aren't monsters. I felt no tails, horns, or vile protuberances on you. I can't say that with certainty for you, miss." He nodded to Kenzie. "But I accept it as true. Those who kill monsters are our allies." His lips quirked as if trying not to smile. "We admire anyone who burns one of them black and throws it down a hill."

Theogalt's men had spread out behind him with their weapons ready. They may not have agreed that we were allies, and they sure as hell didn't look like they admired us.

Evonne said, "You may have your sword back when you rearm us."

Theogalt nodded to some men who scrambled to return our weapons. I had already snatched half of them when the rain started, including my sword and Acton's.

"What is happening here, Theo?" Evonne asked. "I have been gone just two days. Why are you now bothering innocents on the road who have their own business? It is uncivilized."

Theogalt raised his chin. "Foul beings haven't killed your children and destroyed your home. If they had, you would know that being civilized means little."

Evonne's outer jerkin had been torn in the fighting, and she pulled it closed, although it fell open again. "But why are you guarding the road in this manner? And do not lie." She flung up one hand as if she were grabbing a low branch and pointed at Theo with the other. "I am now a sorcerer too, and I will make unpleasant things happen with your lower parts." Her hands and voice were frivolous. Her face was not.

Theogalt took a step back and then nodded. "Our scouts spotted the enemy down this road. Who knows what shape they can take. If we want to drive the monsters into the ocean and drown them, we can't let them infiltrate our positions."

"Hope you have good luck with all that!" Hurd waved at Theogalt and muttered to me, "Let's go before anybody offers to go get killed on some brave and foolish mission."

I nodded and said, "Thank you, Theogalt, for helping us understand the situation even though you're terrified of us now. We are headed to Sandell, and if we rush, we might get there while it's still light." I walked straight toward Theogalt and would have knocked him down if he hadn't moved. Hurd and the rest followed me as we passed through the other men as if they were stalks of wheat. I couldn't hear any cursing under their breath, so I guess none of them wanted to be hit by lightning.

We came to a rude, wooden barricade just past Theogalt's position.

Acton sighed. "Must we go through all that nonsense again?"

"No, I think I can just run them off," I said.

A smiling, older woman stepped out from behind the barricade. "You can pass if you wish, and I will not stop you—not that I could, I guess." Although her short hair was gray and her face had fantastic wrinkles, she stood straight and carried a long knife in her belt. Like Theogalt and his men, she was dressed in a clash of plain but untidy clothes that hadn't been washed any time recently.

Vargo stepped forward and stuck out his chest. "Who are you, then? I know lots of people between here and Sandell, but you're a stranger. If you get in our way, we'll hit you with lightning too."

The woman kept smiling and raised an open hand. "I am Shura, from North Hynkrie. I am honored to help Theogalt and all his men and women find victory in this war."

Theogalt had followed us, stepping heavy and making noise. Now he ran up to stand to the side and just in front of the woman. "Shura is our leader." He puffed up and stared at me with his hand on his sword. I almost wanted to throw mud at her to see what he'd do.

"I've heard of North Hynkrie. But I never heard anything good." Vargo touched the hilt of his sheathed sword for a moment.

Kenzie put a hand on his arm. "No, please don't."

Shura said, "I will answer any question you want to ask about me or my town, but we should go to my camp where there are more warm fires and fewer monsters walking around."

It had grown windier and colder in the past couple of hours. Every one of us was shivering. All my traveling companions except for Hurd looked at the woman with some amount of eagerness.

I said, "As our group's spiritual advisor, I suggest we not follow you into the woods to be murdered and flung in a ditch. Goodbye." I moved to walk around the barricade.

Shura stopped smiling and met my eyes. "That is understandable and maybe wise, but we did not try to kill you. I want to tell you some things and ask you some questions. Before you say no again, I also want to give you food and some clothes warmer than an old sheet."

I didn't know whether Shura was a good leader, but she was good at convincing people to follow her back to camp.

The camp was far larger than I had expected. I couldn't see its full extent through the woods, but based on the activity around us, I estimated there might be as many as seven hundred fighters there, or even up to a thousand. Shura sat us around a big fire. Then three boys brought hot food and mugs of beer while two older men went around our circle handing us blankets.

Shura said, "We will find some coats for you before you leave us, and I would never send someone away with no food and water to carry. We have many provisions. That is not our big problem. I think we can even give you some beer to take."

Hurd said, "You're the best woman I've ever met! I'm looking around for a wife, you know, and you're in the lead."

The woman laughed. "I can't consider marrying again until all the monsters have been killed. But after that, I'll think about it."

A young shoeless boy came running toward us from deeper in the camp. "Shura! Shura! Shura! Shura!"

"What?" Shura snapped as she turned to the boy. I couldn't see her face, but she sounded the way my pa had when he was about to punch me.

The boy pulled up short and said in a small voice, "Bob said one of the Slangers stabbed one of the Free-Crags and to bring you now. And he said these two clans make more trouble than he can stand."

"Agh!" Shura yelled. "May they eat toads and toadstools! I should throw every one of the Slangers out into the cold winter!" She turned back to us, smiling again. "I will come right back to you in a few minutes." She followed the boy away at a trot.

That left a silence, but most of us were eating and didn't care. Evonne was standing nearby, and I realized she was watching us as likely troublemakers.

Kenzie saw me looking at Evonne and said to her, "When is the king coming?"

"Right," Acton said. "We should all join his army."

Evonne's voice was soft, but her jaw was tight. "He will probably not come."

"Why do you say that?" Kenzie demanded.

"Not unless he decides to change his mind about war," Evonne answered.

I asked, "How long has this war been going on? Maybe he's sitting on his ass still developing a strategy."

Evonne sighed. "Thirty-four days. The enemy has been killing only in villages and on farms. But the king and his generals defend only cities and the places of rich people."

"Has the king's army fought Lossil at all?" Acton asked.

"I think it has not. I did not see it happen or hear of it, and I was in Ebring."

"Why did you come here?" I asked.

Evonne smiled so that the skin around her eyes crinkled. "I am a deserter!"

"Wonderful! I have deserted many times." I raised my mug to her, and she nodded.

Shura strode back toward us, muttering.

With my mouth half-full, I asked, "Shura, what did you want to tell us?"

"I know where these damned monsters are coming from."

I stopped chewing. "You must think that monsters are my big problem and that I care where they're coming from."

"One of them tried to kill you."

"No, it didn't."

Shura laughed and even slapped her leg.

I said, "If you don't believe me, that's not my problem."

"Join us," Shura said. "It is a wise thing to do. You are old and still alive, like me."

"Old and still alive—you don't know how rightly you have spoken." I took another bite of rabbit. A boy handed Shura a jug, and she went around the circle pouring us beer.

I cleared my throat. "Do you know the five heroes? Alamore and the rest?"

"I've never seen them," Shura said. "They sound like trouble-makers. I mean, anybody who calls himself a hero isn't one."

"Have you heard where Alamore is?" I asked. Vargo had stopped eating and was staring at Shura like a hunting hound.

Shura said, "He'll probably be at the battle. I guess they all will."

"What battle?"

"We'll get to that in a minute."

"All right. What else do you want to tell me?" I asked.

"Are you really the spiritual advisor? Or are you the leader?" Shura put a hand on my shoulder as she poured my beer.

"First, we have no leader. If we did have a leader, it would be that young woman over there."

Kenzie sat up, her eyebrows raised.

"Second," I said, "I appreciate everything you're giving us. You are a cracking fine hostess. Third, I'm starting to hate you a little bit over how much you're trying to make me like you. I don't feel it is in your nature to fawn over people quite this much. So, why don't you sit your ass down on that log and cut out the fake sweetness?"

Shura did not laugh. Her eyes turned hard, and she handed the beer jug to the girl next to her so fast some of it sloshed out. Then she sat across the fire from me and stared.

I smiled at her. "I like you so much better now. Tell me what you want to tell me, and then I'll decide if I want to tell you anything."

Shura waited for ten seconds or so. Then she said, "I do not think you care about this country or its people. That's a little bit sad."

"I was expecting something more useful, or more interesting."

"Fine! I know where the monsters are coming from, and I know how to stop them. But they are too many and too strong for me and my men alone. You're a sorcerer. I remember how sorcerers did things years ago, and from the way in which you kill monsters, it looks like you do too."

I snorted. "Sorcerers do things the same now as they did before. Act like assholes, do stupid things, and die young."

"But you did not die young, which says something about you. I do not know what, but it says something."

I said, "I have a vital question. I'm searching for a family from Sandell. It's called . . . Vargo, what the hell is your family called?"

Vargo mumbled around a huge bite, "Pierce."

"The fine, forthright, and not-to-be-screwed-with Pierce family," I said.

Shura gave a sideways grin. "I want to lie to you and say yes, I've seen them, they are just over there where most of our enemies are waiting for us to kill them. Will you pretend I said that and not kill me when you find out that it's not true?"

I opened my mouth, but she interrupted me. "No, wait. It's fine if you kill me, as long as you destroy the monsters first."

I glared at her for a few seconds. "You're a nuisance."

"If we win and you let me live, then I will help you find your family."

"An enormous, reeking nuisance foul enough to smother pigs and babies."

She smiled. "My husband told me that sometimes. What did your woman call you?"

"None of your damn business."

Shura walked around the fire, sat between Acton and me, and leaned close to me, whispering, "I do not understand this kingdom or these people anymore. They've changed since I was young. I think that sometimes I hate them. But I help them because they need it."

I stared at the fire, taking a drink. Shura sat quietly.

Acton spoke up. "I have no answers to any of your questions, Shura, but I will fight."

Shura slapped the boy on his knee. "Good man! Do you have a sword?"

"Yes!"

I grabbed his wrist before he terrified everybody in the camp by drawing the sword of green fire.

Acton frowned and said, "I have a knife too." He drew a knife from his belt. It was well suited for cutting a loaf of bread.

"He doesn't know what to do with a sword or a knife," I said. "He'll fall down and stab himself through the face in ten minutes and take five of your soldiers with him."

Acton raised his voice: "I am a sorcerer! I can throw fire!" He glared at me. "I don't even need a sword."

I laughed.

Shura elbowed me. "Be nice!" She grabbed the back of Acton's neck and shook it in a companionly way. "You're worth fifty men with swords."

I glanced around the circle. Nobody else looked enthused. Vargo looked uncertain, and Kenzie gave Acton a weak smile.

Shura nodded around the circle. "Do you have more questions you are wanting to ask me?"

I appreciated that Shura and her people were desperate to save whatever homes and families they still had. I likely would have felt the same. But I was looking around their camp now, and earlier I had looked around Lossil's camp. I could predict the winner of any battle between them, and Shura wouldn't care for the outcome.

The Ir-men's desperation couldn't overcome two things that Lossil had: discipline and skill. Shura couldn't grow those things in a day, so she needed the next best thing: overwhelming numbers.

Lossil had said he was from another place. Moving from realm to realm always had limits, usually limits on how fast you could move people or things. So, the people of Ir probably still outnumbered him by more than a thousand to one.

Shura needed to fall back for a few weeks and gather fighters from all over the island. Then she could strike when winter was further along; Lossil's troops seemed to hate the cold. And desperation would be an advantage for Shura. Her people would sacrifice anything necessary to protect their homes and families.

I could tell Shura all that, but of course she wouldn't listen to a stranger like me. And even offering advice was almost the same as joining her doomed army of people I didn't care much about.

But if I could scare her into uncertainty, she might retreat while I traipsed along to Ebring. During a lull, I said, "Shura, do you think you'll have problems with the dragon?"

Everybody near enough to hear me fell silent.

"What dragon?" Shura asked.

"The dragon I saw yesterday. I guess it could easily kill everybody here."

The folks close by began a quiet chatter that spread outward from Shura's campfire. A few voices raised, and some people laughed. Diabolical, brutal dragons often appeared in the stories and songs of Ir. People heard them in their cribs and on their deathbeds.

For people fighting a horrible war, the chance to argue about a familiar but distant mystery like dragons was a gift. Even Shura turned to tell a short, bearded man he was a fool for thinking dragons had fewer than six horns.

Nobody was watching me as the noise grew. I stood up with a bag of provisions someone had laid beside me. I snatched Vargo's sleeve and nodded for him to grab his own bag. Then we strolled out of the camp to the sounds of laughter and speculation.

EIGHTEEN

I had learned several things since I returned to the world of man, but only two mattered. Alamore the murdering hero might be at this battle Shura was anticipating. However, traipsing through hundreds of recklessly swung swords did not appeal to me, so I needed to find him someplace else. Ebring was the capital. There would be somebody around there who could help me find Alamore.

Second, Pil's family was probably in the city of Ebring. Or, maybe they had been there once. Somebody in Ebring would know about them too.

So, there was one single place on the entire island of Ir that I knew I had to go to. Somebody else could go fight armies, monsters, and dragons.

When I reached the road, Vargo and I turned north and set a fine marching pace. I wanted to reach the city of Sandell before nightfall.

Soon, I heard running feet and saw Kenzie following us, her spear loose in her left hand. I kept walking up the road.

"Bib! You stop this very moment! You cannot leave!"

I shook my head and didn't answer such a foolish statement.

"You lied about the dragon, didn't you?" She paused, but I didn't answer. "There are no dragons, and you've told us all that you're a liar."

"I guess you're safe, then."

"If there were dragons in the world again, somebody would have said."

Kenzie had caught up, so I glanced over at her. She was about as tall as me. I stood straight and smiled at her. "I'm somebody. And I said."

"Whatever you wish, then. I'll pay no mind to this dragon talk. But please, please fight alongside us. I feel that without you, we'll die."

I stopped and raised an eyebrow.

She said, "Yes, I know that's poor incentive since we must kill you—"

"Horrible incentive. I'd be insane to help you live. If Lossil kills you, I should send him a present. Besides, I'm the most profane and awful man who ever lived. Is that who you want on your side?"

Kenzie set her jaw. "I was angry, and I take all that back. Bib, you're a sorcerer somehow. I don't know how, but Acton says you must be, and I believe him. I saw the lightning you threw down upon that monster. In battle, you must be worth ten of me. Twenty."

"Zero, because I won't be there."

Vargo laughed and slapped a knee.

Kenzie glared at him and yelled at me, "This is your homeland! Fight for it!"

"Kenzie, this is not my place anymore, so be still about it."

She lowered her voice. "Why? What happened?"

"Nothing happened. People changed, but I didn't."

"No, that isn't right. You changed. Come, which makes more sense? A whole kingdom full of people changes, or one single man changes?"

"Oh, how could I not see that, Kenzie? You're so old and wise, and you know everything." I walked faster.

Kenzie lowered her voice. "I've been thinking about the Bib stories, some of them."

I rolled my eyes and resolved not to lose my temper over whatever ridiculous thing she was about to accuse me of.

"And I have thought about them as differently as I may. It's been challenging. I mean, thinking as if every word was true and really happened to you, Bib, the person I'm looking at."

I walked even faster.

"Maybe nobody will say this, so I will. Thank you for whatever you did, whatever it was. I don't understand it, but look at how your body is all torn up and how sad you are. It was hardship, I'll bet."

I walked away and swallowed a couple of times. That was a thing I never expected I'd hear. I called back at her, "I'm still not fighting alongside you and Shura's dimwits."

"If you do, I'll heal your other arm."

That stopped me.

When Kenzie, Vargo, and I walked back into Shura's camp, I got a variety of welcomes. Theogalt smiled and nodded, which surprised me a bit. Evonne frowned and looked away. Acton welcomed me back with his words, but not with his eyes. I got the sense he had intended to ambush me with Kenzie sometime during the night, but I had ruined those plans. Hurd wasn't there. He had simply been gone when I looked for him around the campfire.

I had expected Shura to be happy that I returned, or at least not to throw dirt on me. I said, "Shura, I have reconsidered and will be pleased to assist your force in defending this land and its people."

Shura gazed at me with no expression. "That will be all right, if you stop talking about dragons that don't exist. I do not expect you to follow any orders because that is not in your nature. I do expect you to kill, and to kill a lot, because that is completely in your nature. Considering all this, I think you will help us more than you hurt us, at least until you decide to run away. That is in your nature too."

She walked toward the largest tent, then stopped and looked back at me. "Here is a thing you can do. I have sorcerers, and you brought two more of them with you. We have not much time, but I think if you trained them a little, it would help. They may not be killers like you, but teach them to pretend they are for a while."

Shura might have been put out with me, but she did order a young man to bring me a gray woolen coat. It had an unstylish number of holes, but it would keep me warm if Pil's ring failed or I lost it.

Once she turned away, I muttered, "I'd rather fight monsters than do this."

I asked a ragged fellow with farmer's hands to bring me a bucket and then gather the sorcerers under a big oak tree. After I had filled the bucket, I told the sorcerers to line up in front of me.

I pointed at Kenzie. "Make that dog lick his butt," I said, pointing at a floppy white hound under a tree.

Kenzie looked at me as if she had forgotten any ideas of thanking me for anything. "That's not a challenge. He probably wants to lick his butt already."

"You're probably right," I said. "Make him dig under that tree, then that tree, and then that tree."

"This is silly." Kenzie stuck out her chin. "I did harder things at Bleekhame . . ." She paused as her eyes sagged and her chin quivered. She shook her head. "I have done lots harder things than this."

"Do it!"

Kenzie clapped her hands, raised them, and pulled them apart as if she were opening a huge iron door. I felt her toss a yellow band toward the dog. The dog's head came up, and it stared at her.

To practice my manual dexterity, I spun one finger for half a second, then tossed a yellow band at the dog. Taking the dog's attention away from her was easy. Maybe she had never made a study of dogs, and it was showing.

When the dog resisted and listened to me instead, she got angry and tried to drag its attention back. I soothed the creature and convinced him that his bladder was full and that Kenzie looked like a wonderful tree. In fact, she looked like the best tree that had ever existed, or that's what I told the dog, anyway.

The dog bounded over to Kenzie and lifted his leg.

"Wait! Don't do that!" Kenzie backed away, shooing the dog with both hands.

I showed the dog the glory of a different tree across the camp from us. Once he ran that direction, I let him go, trusting that his last impression would continue to guide him.

"What happened?" I asked.

"I believe she did everything right." Acton glanced sideways at Kenzie. "Maybe she should have used her toes."

"Hush!" Kenzie's cheeks were tight, her fists clenched.

"You did do the right thing," I said. "It didn't work because somebody took the dog away from you."

Shura's five sorcerers all turned outward, examining the camp and the trees.

"Don't waste your time," I said. "I did it."

They may have wanted to cry out and object, but I was looking at them with my sternest, most forbidding, scarred-to-holy-hell, one-eyed face. They stared and waited.

"I want you to watch something. Everybody, gather around me. Acton, watch my hand, not my boots." I caught the dog's attention again using the merest twitch of my third finger. The dog raced back to us and began snuffling and licking one of Acton's boots.

"Watch this." I punched the air hard, spun my hand around three times, and gargled before slapping my knee. "This bullshit is unnecessary and dangerous. You may think you need two hands, a shout, and a big flag, but you can do the same thing with a finger or two."

Now they all talked at once. I let them tire themselves out asking each other foolish questions before I quieted them down. "You have to practice, but it's a lot easier than you think. The main thing is dexterity. And that brings us to my favorite part of the lesson. Line up again."

I had covered the bucket with a cloth. Now I knelt beside it and reached in to grab the first thing my hand touched. "Catch this!" I said to the oldest of the group, a time-tested boy of nineteen. I threw a horseshoe at his face, and he failed to catch it.

"Ow!" He rubbed the red welt under his left eye. "Why did you do that?"

"You need nimble hands. Everybody, catch whatever I throw at you." I reached into the bucket again.

"You're throwing other things?" Acton asked.

An instant later, I threw a chunk of wood at his mouth. Acton couldn't catch it, but he did slap it hard enough so that it only grazed his ear. By that time, I had thrown a boot heel at a girl younger than Kenzie, a dead mouse at another girl, and yet another horseshoe at a boy. By the time I reached Kenzie, my hand touched a live snake. I hurled it without hesitating.

Kenzie reached out and grabbed the snake out of the air, looking as if she wished she could convince the little snake to eat me. I didn't care. I probably wasn't saving their lives in any battle that would come up soon, but it might help a bit. Then I hurled a piece of cheese, a small cookpot, a boiled egg, and two linked sausages. Most of the young sorcerers got hit in the face.

I ran out of things to throw. "All right, gather everything and bring it back to me. Just dump it in the bucket." When they had done that, I told them, "Line up again."

The oldest boy snarled, "We're sorcerers. We don't have to suffer this—"

I threw the horseshoe at him with particular speed, and it bounced off his forehead. He fell backward like a cut tree. Before he hit the ground, I had thrown the cheese and the snake at two other dignified sorcerers.

This went on for most of an hour. By the time we stopped, all of them were tolerably proficient at snatching things out of the air.

"Good job." I held my face in an expression that said they had not in any way done a good job and that they should be ground up and fed to hogs. I tried to recall some of my sternest teachers. "Now you'll practice pulling and throwing bands with the fewest fingers you can. Let me warn you to also use the smallest amount of power possible so that you don't end up selling your entire future to the gods this afternoon."

"This is eye-opening," said Sveta, a young girl with Breaker powers. "And I am going to practice it right away, except, well . . . if I'm in a battle, I may find myself attacked by someone, or some monster, and not have enough time for magic. How do we defend ourselves?"

"A fine question. This is likely to happen, and it's happened to me many times. Here's how you defend yourself. Find two or three stout fighting men to stand in front of you and tell them you will buy the drinks and pay for the whores if they can keep you alive through the battle."

Several of the sorcerers chuckled.

"That is not a joke. If you survive this battle, you should learn to kill your enemies with steel in the most practical fashion possible. In a single day, there is no way you can learn to do anything with a sword except hurt yourself. Kenzie may have a chance since the spear is a fine choice of weapon and can be brought to a respectable level of proficiency quickly. But it helps her only because she has already used it in combat. None of the rest of you will have any hope if you try it today or tomorrow."

That shut them up.

Between that point and sunset, I guided the sorcerers, berated them, encouraged them, and berated them some more. In fact, I berated them a lot so they would train hard and have a chance to survive.

As Kenzie walked past me, she said, "I hate you. Thank you again."

Without meaning to, I saw an image of her bleeding to death on the ground in front of me. "Come back here! You too, Acton."

They stood in front of me. Kenzie fidgeted, but Acton stood like a tree.

I said, "I have just sharpened your knife and put it against my throat. You still owe Baby Harik my life, but I have been thinking about how to work it so that the two of you will be alive at the end."

Acton said, "Kenzie doesn't trust you. She thinks everything you say and do is a lie or a trap."

Kenzie reached out and shoved Acton, but not hard enough to

hurt him. "I can say what I think without your help. And I don't totally think that anymore."

I said, "I will be honest with you." I paused and thought of all the young men and women I had killed, some no older than these two.

"Well?" Acton said. "What are you being honest about?"

I shook my head. "As Kenzie has reminded me lately, I am a liar, and my word can rarely be relied upon. I understand that it means nothing to you when I say I'm being truthful. Regardless, I don't want to kill you. In fact, I think it might be the thing I least want to do."

Neither of them spoke or looked impressed.

"But my desires can burn to ash if that's what it takes to survive. If you want to continue being sorcerers, I encourage you to adopt the same philosophy."

Kenzie stared me in the eye and nodded. Acton just bit his lip.

"All right," I said. "Go get something to eat and go to bed."

They had been gone for two minutes before I realized I was talking to them as if they were my own children.

NINETEEN

Word was passed around the camp that we would attack tomorrow. No one shared the particulars with me, so I predicted them. Shura would split her force, mounting a diversion while the true attack came elsewhere. Theogalt would lead the diversionary force, and Shura would command the main assault. The sorcerers would be split between the two forces.

After the evening meal was served out, but before we lay down to sleep, Shura called me to her tent. It was a torn, leaky thing and one of only three in the camp. She said, "You are the sort of man who won't take orders, so I will not give them to you. Instead, I will tell you what is happening so that you understand it. Then you can give yourself orders."

I held up my hand. "Let me save time. Theogalt leads the diversion, you lead the main attack, you split the sorcerers."

Shura's eyes went wide.

I said, "Sing your death songs and pray to your favorite god, Shura. If I can figure this out, so can Lossil."

She breathed, "It is too late to change the plan. Theogalt and his men have gone." She lay her head in her hand.

"Call them back. Send somebody fast. Do you have any horses?

It's better to look like a damn moron than to send hundreds of men to their deaths."

"I have no one fast and no horses," she said. "All of our fastest people and the horses went with Theogalt. He has to march farther."

"You didn't keep anybody to carry messages?"

"Should I have done that?" Shura asked.

I stared at the ground and tried to think of a smart plan. Before I found one, shouting came from outside the tent. Shura and I ran out and found a cloth like a curtain hanging from a tree limb. Lossil's image showed in wonderful detail through the cloth.

Shura walked up to the cloth and touched it with both hands. It swung, but Lossil's image didn't shift. She said, "You are the one I will kill soon."

"I don't think that's going to happen," Lossil said. "I'll tell you what. You can go back south unhurt if you lay down your weapons and swear not to fight anymore."

"Hah! That is funny. I never knew how funny monsters are."

Lossil shrugged. "Then we'll kill you. I know where you are. My soldier hung this cloth on a tree not twenty feet from your tent, and you never heard him. There's not a single thing you can do that will surprise me."

"Oh?" Shura raised her eyebrows. "You will be surprised when we show you how wrong you are about that." She made a foul gesture toward Lossil's image. "This seeing-far cloth is a very fine thing. It must have a limit, though. Maybe you are so close now I can find you and stab you in your heart."

Lossil sighed. "We're too different to have peace. Come on and attack us. Wait!" Lossil craned his head as if it were sticking through the cloth and he could see to the side. "Is that Bib?"

Everybody laughed. Shura said, "There are no bibs here. I can't believe how funny you are."

"He might have told you another name. He's gray and scarred with only one eye. Oh, there he is! Bib, you agreed to do something for me. It's bad manners to visit with people who want me dead. Go! Go on!" Lossil shooed me with one hand.

Nobody moved.

Lossil whispered loud enough for us all to hear, "That means it's time for you to run."

I spun, ducked the arms of one soldier, kicked a shin, and slammed into a big man, who looked shocked as he fell to the ground. Only two more men stood between me and the camp's edge. I drew my sword as I ran, blocked one attack by cutting the sword in half, then dodged the last man.

Behind me, Shura shouted, "Let him go! He is filth! Just filth."

I reached the road and ran toward Sandell for ten minutes. Then I realized I couldn't trust that Shura was letting me go like she said. If she thought I was Lossil's spy and knew all her secrets, she might have sent two hundred fighters and sorcerers after me.

I turned off the road and picked my way down a long, brush-covered, rocky slope that led to the ocean three miles away. Ebring didn't lie quite in that direction, but now the terrain between the road and the coast was open enough to cross without getting lost in trees or torn to bits by great hedges.

In Ir, people sail as readily as they walk. If I stole a boat, I could travel faster by sea than I could on any road.

When I arrived at the beach, I jogged northwest along it. The night was clear and cold, and when the half-moon rose over the inland hills, it lit a broad, smooth beach with rolling surf. I didn't see any boats, but I'd find one soon if I followed the coastline.

I had traveled no more than ten minutes when somebody stepped out from the rocks along the beach. I drew my sword but then realized that Acton was walking toward me.

"We should never be surprised to find a sorcerer where we don't think he'll be," I said, "but I admit I didn't predict you'd be here. Have you come to capture me?"

I could see his teeth in the moonlight as he smiled. "No, I'm aware of what really took place between you and Lossil. He is merely poisoning Shura against you."

"She didn't like me that much to start with. So, you figured you could find me here?"

Acton gazed at the surf. "The road would be dangerous to

travel, and I knew you were going to Ebring. The easiest way to get there is by sea. So, I ran straight to this spot to get ahead of you. To be honest, I counted on running faster than a mature fellow such as yourself."

"Huh. Why did you bother?"

"Come back and fight with us," he said. "I will vouch for your innocence."

"You have great confidence in your vouching skills. No, I won't come. You should have brought Kenzie and Vargo so you all three could avoid this impossible battle."

"I will return to them soon," he said. "I won't leave them to fight without me. If you won't come back with me, can I at least walk along for a bit? You won't be alone."

I started to tell the boy that I was born to be alone and could do it better than any man alive. The words wouldn't quite come out. Acton was less aggravating than Kenzie anyway, and he'd be far better company than Hurd, who was an avalanche of aggravation.

"Fine," I said. "I guess I'd have to break your leg to stop you."

We walked without speaking for a while until Acton cleared his throat and said, "At your age, I suppose you know rather a lot about love."

I scraped to a stop. "Damn! Krak burn it, Fingit eat it, and Lutigan shit it out! Rolling piles of fury and damnation!"

Acton had backed away with enormous eyes.

"Don't worry, I can't stab you now, son. You're in love, which is all the suffering you can bear." I shook my head. "You ambushed me! If you had brought a bow instead of a yearning heart, I'd be as dead as my grandma right now."

"I didn't say I was in love!"

"Good! Then we don't have to talk about it anymore."

We walked for another minute or so before Acton said, "But if I ever was in love, how would I stop?"

"You can't."

"You just can't?"

I nodded. "I think the surf is higher. I may have a little challenge launching the boat."

He said, "Can you make—"

"No, you can't just make somebody fall in love with you, either."

Acton raised his voice. "What can you do, then?"

"I have never figured that out."

Acton sighed. "I have no idea what to do."

"I suggest not acting like an asshole."

"Does that work?"

"It works better than acting like an asshole. Listen, son, you are talking to the wrong man. I have lived with a lot of women, and all but three have run away from me within a week. Some of them stabbed me first."

Acton stopped. "This is pointless. I'm returning to camp. Good luck."

I nodded. "That's a smart decision. Grab the others, and wherever the battle is, go the other way."

Somebody shouted from way behind us, "Hallo!" Vargo was chasing us and soon caught up, hands on his knees and panting.

"I knew you'd find me, son," I said.

Vargo laughed through his panting and gave me a nasty gesture. Acton stepped back out of the way.

I said, "Acton and I have been pausing until you got here to discuss love." We walked along the beach at a quick march.

Acton dragged along, staring at his feet as he fell behind.

I said, "Don't pout! Love is wonderful sometimes. Just remember that you can never control it and it just about always ends painfully."

Vargo looked past me at the ocean.

"What manner of advice is that?" Acton asked.

"Foolish, but it's the best I have."

"What about you, Vargo? You're old." Acton raised his eyebrows. "What about love?"

Vargo was twenty-five or a little younger. Since he had lost his wife and children, I was interested in what he'd say.

"None of us deserves love."

Acton said some words that would have turned my ma purple. "What does that mean?"

Vargo shrugged and walked off toward the water.

We walked along in silence for several minutes before Acton said, "Bib, you say you're foolish about love. Perhaps you are also foolish about running away. This is your homeland, after all."

I laughed. "Don't bother me with the flag of patriotism. Kenzie already waved it at me."

"Since you mention her . . ."

I stopped, knowing exactly what he was going to say.

He went on: "She never had time to heal your other arm, but she promises to do it after the battle. If you happen to be somewhere around."

I worked my jaw and considered it. I supposed I could help with this doomed venture in exchange for an arm, although I would run like a squirrel when things turned against us.

Acton said, "Also, if you wish to have your new arm, Kenzie must survive the battle."

I snorted. "I can't travel with Shura's troops. They'll try to capture me or kill me."

"I know where the battle will take place, or approximately where," Acton said. "In the hills west of Sandell."

I plotted the course and distances in my head.

Vargo stopped. "Bib, I don't think you're doing this to save my family or anybody else. You're just taking time to get an arm, even if my family suffers!"

"No, we'll be going to Sandell anyway, and if you think I'm imposing with one arm, wait until you see me with two. This is our best strategy. We can sail to the Craeder River and . . ." I closed my eyes and felt the air. "Sail on upriver to reach Sandell by morning."

Acton jumped up and down like an eight-year-old boy. After three jumps, he stopped and turned away from me, clearing his throat. In a sober voice, he said, "I've never stolen a boat before. It should be educational." When he faced us again, he was struggling to hide a smile.

TWENTY

Vargo, Acton, and I found a tiny, unattended sailboat not far past the next rock outcropping, tied up to a crappy dock beside a dilapidated house. Nobody was around, so I didn't have to threaten or thrash anyone to accomplish this larceny.

The breeze lay on our starboard quarter, and we made excellent time up the coast. Since Vargo had grown up on Ir, he sailed almost without thinking about it. Acton showed himself not to be a hazard aboard, but he was a mainlander to be pitied for having no sailing skills. Once we tacked into the broad Craeder River, the wind lay on our port quarter. We pushed upriver against the strong current. Although it hurt our speed, we still made headway.

Toward morning, the wind faded and the river began pushing us backward. I spun a white band into the sky and raised a strong wind just behind us. It pushed us on up the river at a fairly small cost of magical power since I kept the effect limited.

We reached Sandell after dawn and tied up the sailboat at a small warehouse on the southwest bank, just across from the city. Between the three of us, our fortune consisted of two copper coins and one shiny black rock, so we immediately stole three horses. I was forced to threaten one man and shove another until they agreed that the horses looked better with us sitting on them. Acton proved to be a better horseman than he was a sailor. He had grown up around his father's stables until he showed signs of sorcery and was sent away.

We found the battle by midday, but it had already begun. We viewed the battlefield from a shallow hill and saw the fighting spread across the valley and up the next slope. Based on the number of dead and wounded on the ground, about 700 women and men remained out of Shura's 800. It appeared that Lossil had fielded 600 roughly manlike beings along with several assorted monsters. Maybe 500 could still fight.

A group of Lossil's soldiers burst into flames. Some ran screaming, and others fell unmoving. The soldiers near them fired a volley of arrows into Shura's fighters. Nothing more caught fire. Maybe the young Burner I had trained yesterday ran instead of being killed. I hadn't seen anybody flinging their arms around before the burning started. If the sorcerers kept things small and didn't stand out, they might survive.

I shouted at Acton and Vargo, "Right flank? Left flank? Right in the middle?"

Vargo's face grew pale, and he pointed. "It had better be right flank."

"Son of a bitch!" I said. A new formation of Lossil's men was marching around the hill across the valley to our right. They appeared and kept appearing until three hundred of them began racing toward Shura's right flank. Acton and I galloped toward them. I didn't reach for the Death God's sword because I didn't trust it. I couldn't slay many soldiers with a petrified walrus phallus or something similar in my hand.

Acton dropped back when I reached Lossil's personal guard. They looked similar to Lossil, tall and strong with heavy shoulders. They wore no coats or even shirts, and I saw what might be scales across their shoulders and chests. The scales did not deflect sword blades, and I killed or wounded three during my charge. Lossil's men tried to drag me out of the saddle, but I attacked both sides with considerable fury and a surpassingly sharp sword. I awkwardly wheeled my horse, who was bred to be ridden around the farm, not into battle.

I broke free of the formation and rode back toward Shura's lines, cutting down a few more soldiers on the way. A sizable cluster of white-hot flames burst among the soldiers behind me. Another followed two seconds later, and a third came right after that. If Acton was causing this slaughter, he wasn't hesitating to kill no matter what the Bib stories taught him.

Lossil's soldiers nearest me fell back from the fires in shouting disarray. However, the rest of his troops crashed into Shura's fighters from the right. Shura's force had been pushing their enemy back, but this assault shocked them into retreating.

Acton flung two exploding lead balls but couldn't throw them far enough to reach Lossil's entire assault. He kicked his horse to ride closer, but I grabbed the bridle.

"Don't ride down in there! Somebody will put an arrow in your eye or cut off your leg. Your place is distant from the enemy."

Shura's fighters were shaken but falling back in decent order. That changed when two of the monsters attacked them. One resembled a twelve-foot-long roundish frog. The other scrambled on five legs while tossing a head with three curved horns. Neither wore anything but skin or fur, things Acton couldn't set ablaze. Once the monsters were among Shura's men and women, fire wasn't a useful weapon, anyway. Neither was lightning, even though someone had already been calling clouds together, probably Kenzie.

I couldn't see Vargo. "Stay here!" I yelled to Acton as I kicked my horse into a gallop.

By the time I reached the lines, Shura's fighters had been routed by the monsters, and they fled with as much desperation as I had ever seen. I charged the frog from behind, as it had paused to eat one fighter and then another. I rode past and guessed at a good place to thrust my sword. The back of its head must have been a good place, since the beast jerked sideways, flopped on its side, and quivered.

I wheeled toward the other monster, which proved to be a bad decision. It swung its horns at me, smacking my horse in the head. I jumped from the saddle as the horse fell, hoping I could get far enough away so that the horse wouldn't break my leg or kill me as it rolled.

The five-legged monster reached me while I was on one knee. I twisted and sliced one of its legs, cutting it halfway through. The thing was fast, even with just four legs, and I didn't want to turn away from it. I backed off.

The monster charged, and I prepared to dodge again. A great hole appeared in the ground between us, and the monster fell into it, chittering on the way down. Sveta, the Breaker I trained yesterday, must have created that pit.

Earlier in my life, people would sometimes swear that I could sense an attack in some mystical way. That was ridiculous, of course. While fighting, I would listen carefully, watch shadows, and note reactions almost without thinking about it, so I generally knew everything that was happening around me. That proved handy when Bethroti the hero thrust her spear at my heart from the side.

I twisted and bent, leaving Bethroti's spear to make a bloody gouge across my chest. I staggered away as she followed up with three thrusts, two of which would have killed me. The third just missed pinning my foot to the ground, and I thought about our drinking game yesterday.

I sliced off Bethroti's spearhead while blocking, then I stepped in and cut the shaft two inches from her fingers. She skipped away backward, drawing a long knife. I closed with her, and she hurled the knife at my face. I cut it in half on the fly, but the blade whirled on to leave my left ear dangling. When she turned to run, I crippled her leg from behind.

I could have let Bethroti run, but I killed her instead. She would have understood why. If I let her escape, she would kill more of Shura's soldiers. Maybe she would catch Kenzie and kill her or catch Vargo. I couldn't know, so I couldn't let her run.

I turned to see a whole damn wall of Lossil's soldiers edging toward me. Two of them jumped forward to attack. Ten seconds later, they lay bleeding on the torn-up grass. None of the others seemed eager to run up and swing a weapon at me. Maybe they had watched me fight monsters and Bethroti.

Damn, I was tired. If I didn't retreat soon, the enemy would overwhelm me as I trudged head down across the battlefield. I feinted at the enemy, hoping to make these soldiers hesitate while I turned and ran. Before I could flee, white explosions began appearing among Lossil's men.

Reks and difar ran in all directions. They may as well have been bugs in a jar that Acton was shaking. He saw me running and galloped over in complete defiance of my firm suggestion to stay put. He was a sorcerer, and I wasn't qualified to give him orders.

Acton helped me swing up behind him, and we galloped back up the hill away from Shura's shattered army and Lossil's regrouping soldiers. Vargo arrived from someplace and fell in beside us, his left arm bloody. Besides my ear and chest, I had suffered several small wounds that I hadn't even noticed until now.

We rode uphill toward Vargo just as Lossil's soldiers fired forty arrows at him. In less than a second, I flung forty blue bands out to catch the arrows and rot the wooden shafts. The arrows fell apart, tumbling and losing force. Two struck Acton, but neither one drove itself into his body.

"You might want to put away that damn sword!" I yelled at him. "Every enemy on the battlefield will be firing arrows, hurling rocks, and throwing shit at you."

I examined the field. In my professional opinion, this battle was lost, so it was time for me to run. I could save some of my allies as I left the field. But if escape looked chancy and only one of us could escape, then the right person to save was me, of course.

I yelled at Vargo, "Give me your horse!"

He dismounted without even a questioning look.

As I mounted, I yelled, "Acton, follow me! We'll attack their rear and kill Lossil!" I intended no such thing, but I didn't have time to convince the boy to become a deserter. I cantered my horse away.

When I looked back a few seconds later, Acton wasn't following me. He had sheathed his sword and begun flinging lead balls to roll down the hill, where he could ignite them amid the enemy. Vargo stood near him, ready to defend Acton from enemies who came too close.

Well, I had abandoned men and women who were braver and better companions than these two. I kicked my horse to ride north, away from the battle and away from Sandell.

Ebring lay to the north. I could kill Alamore later even if I fled now. I could find that damned Lossil later and kill him too. If Pil's family was in Sandell and Lossil took the city, unfortunately I'd have to give up on helping them survive, just like I was leaving Vargo to die. Really, it would be sort of the way I had let Pala be killed. Not exactly, but I had been responsible.

I slowed my horse. I was riding away from death and killing in this battle, but hell, I was riding toward just as much killing. I wouldn't be staying to fight for my home and family the way most of Shura's people were. For me, there was no home and family to ride toward, anyway.

Somebody yelled, "Arrows!"

I turned in the saddle, spun a bucketful of blue bands, and took the arrows apart while they were in the air. Most of them, anyway.

I rode back to join Acton and Vargo at the hilltop, and I dismounted. "I changed my mind. It was a stupid plan."

Neither of them seemed to pay attention to me. Acton said, "I don't know what to do now."

I said, "We'll spend five minutes gathering the sorcerers who are still alive. Then we'll pull back and guard our people as they withdraw toward the city."

"Oh." Acton grinned. "That's exactly what I would've suggested." We trotted over the hill and down toward the city, trying to stay between the enemy and our terrified, fleeing soldiers.

The battlefield lay about three miles from the bridge across the Craeder River. Most of Shura's fighters retreated toward the bridge. Some ran south toward the camp, but we were pulled too thin to protect both them and the main force. Acton rode over, halted behind them, and drew his flaming sword. The enemy troops hesitated for a few minutes, giving some of Shura's men a chance to retreat.

My goal was to remain just behind our retreating fighters. I couldn't exactly call them an army. They had no form, so formation was inappropriate. But if we stayed just behind them, we could defend them against Lossil's advancing troops.

My job was easy for the first mile. Lossil's army had been regrouping when I retreated, and that required time. I found Shura and Kenzie. Shura apologized for doubting me and thanked me for my efforts. I told her to eat a cluster of bugs and then tell me what was at the bottom of the ocean.

She tried again. "I am sorry, Bib. We should not have treated you so."

"Don't apologize to me. Apologize to your men who were wounded or killed because a four-year-old could have predicted your battle plan."

That shut her up for a while.

Kenzie hugged Acton. Then she demanded to know where he had gone, what had happened to him, why he'd been away so long, and where he got that horse. He pointed out that there would be plenty of time to talk later in the city, and if they were killed, then they wouldn't have to worry about it.

"Have you seen Evonne?" I asked Vargo.

He shook his head. "No, we got separated. I think this sword saved my life at least ten times!"

We stopped some of our fleeing men and tasked them with helping their wounded comrades retreat. Some refused. They changed their minds when I offered to wound them too so they could enjoy being helped.

Lossil's army had come within half a mile of us by the time we had ushered all the retreating men toward the proper direction. From that point, we fell back exactly as fast as the slowest wounded man. The pace was glacial, since some of them had enormous leg wounds.

Acton couldn't throw a lead ball half a mile. He could set one man's clothes or weapon afire from that distance, but that was a lazy, inefficient use of power. Attacking Lossil's men fell to Kenzie and me. We brought lightning down on them at judicious times, which slowed them for a moment, but they never stopped.

Sveta began creating big pits in random places within the enemy formations. Not many of them fell in, but it hurt their enthusiasm and made a charge much less likely.

By the time we'd come within a mile of the bridge, Lossil's forces stood only a quarter mile away from us. From horseback, Acton said, "We're not going to reach the bridge before they get to us, are we?"

Evonne had joined us, having been separated from the main body of troops at some point. She must've found someone to fight, because she was spattered with blood from her hair to her boots. She said, "We must kill them without pause. We will die, but we can save some of these people."

"To hell with dying," I snapped. "Kenzie, get ready to flood the river and tear down that bridge. Vargo, run across the bridge first and rally as many men as you can to defend the city. Acton, you, Sveta, and I will slow the enemy down. Evonne, it's your job to take care of any monsters that attack us."

Evonne paled but nodded. "I will."

She looked so calm and determined, even knowing she would probably die, that I couldn't stand it. "Here, Evonne. Give me your sword and take mine. Beware, this sword is enchanted to be sharp. It is vastly sharper than you can imagine. I am not exaggerating."

Evonne smiled and took the sword, then faced the oncoming troops.

Nobody had argued with my ignorant, poorly thought-out orders. I had no right to give them. I just felt that somebody ought to be giving some, and nobody else was volunteering.

We backed away, slowing the enemy with lightning and pits, and soon with exploding lead balls. Lossil's soldiers began firing arrows at us in heavy volleys. I managed to rot many of the arrow shafts before they reached us, leaving the arrowheads to spin away. However, dealing with the arrows interrupted my lightning attacks.

After a few volleys, the arrows stopped coming, but an arrow had pierced Sveta's shoulder. No one could spare time to deal with her wound. Although she insisted that she could still fight, her eyes were rolling in her head as she said it. I put her on the horse and sent her across the bridge into the city.

I turned around from aiding Sveta and saw that Theogalt had arrived. He had been delayed on the enemy's right flank, where his diversion had struck and finally fallen apart. I assigned him to help Evonne. I heard them saying nasty things to each other, but that meant nothing when lightning and monsters graced the field.

Before Lossil's soldiers closed with us, three monsters bounded ahead of them. Evonne, Theogalt, and I met them. By the time we killed them, Theogalt lay smashed to death on the grass and Evonne was limping like an ostrich with one foot.

Now Evonne was wounded, and Kenzie had fallen back to work on flooding the river. That left Acton and me as the only defenders without serious wounds. We were outnumbered several hundred to two.

I wondered what the hell we'd do in a few minutes when Lossil's soldiers reached us. We were still more than two hundred paces from the bridge. At that moment, the enemy charged.

We sprinted toward the bridge, and I hoped we could make a stand there. We left a few wounded soldiers behind. Acton helped Evonne flee, but they weren't fast enough to reach the bridge ahead of Lossil's troops.

Evonne shouted "Here! Here!" as she held out the sharp sword to me. I skipped over and grabbed it.

From across the river, Kenzie brought lightning down to kill and slow some of them, but the rest never hesitated. If you can get used to lightning cooking your friends, I guess you can get used to anything.

I stopped and faced the charging enemy, leaving Acton and Evonne behind me to struggle on toward the bridge. Drawing a deep breath, I sheathed my sword. Then I reached into the realm holding the Death God's sword and pulled out a live chicken, which I was holding by the neck.

TWENTY-ONE

This business with the Death God's sword was foolishness. It had never behaved this way in the Dark Lands.

I lifted myself up through the top of my head, knowing that as long as I was in the trading place, no time would pass in the world of man. Lossil's soldiers would not be able to cut me into dozens of fascinating shapes while I was in some trance.

"Fingit! I come to trade! Hear me! It's better than smelling me!" Fingit had a sense of humor once in a while.

I arrived in the trading place, standing on the sorcerer's patch of dirt. Crazily, I wondered whether I should plant some gladioli the next time I was here.

The sky was dark gray. Not cloudy, but a smooth, dark gray shade as if I were under a big pot. The air felt full of potential, but I couldn't say potential for what. The forest to my left lay motionless, but all the trees bent toward me. On my right, the field of flowers contained no flowers at all, merely dusty gray soil. I smelled sulfur and oil.

Once again, Fingit was not standing in the gazebo. Baby Harik greeted me with a little wave, leaning against one of the columns. "Hi there, Murderer. You're in one rumbling bitch of a spot, aren't you? I can't see how more power's going to help you. Are you ready to die?"

"Baby Harik, O runty god which still has the foul digestive processes of lower beings, I might be ready. It depends on what sort of deal we can strike." If Baby Harik liked to be insulted, this was the time to satisfy that desire.

"Murderer, I see that you're having a little problem with my predecessor's sword. Maybe I can help you out with that."

I put on the most respectful face I could manage. "It's a little inconvenient. I'm sure I can work it out, though."

"I bet you can't." He raised his eyebrows twice.

So, he had done this to the sword, or to the realm it was in. He had probably asked Krak to bar any other god from dealing with me too. I said, "Are you willing to consider working this out for me?"

"Maybe yes, maybe no."

"I choose to interpret that as an initial offer in our bargaining. In exchange for resolving any issues with the death sword, I will kill at least one hundred of the enemies I'm facing."

"You mean the reks and difar? Nasty, greasy creatures," Baby Harik said with a flip of his hand. "And your offer sucks. You'd probably kill them anyway. However, I'll deal with your sword issue, if you use it once and then give it to me."

Now it made sense. I took the sword from the former God of Death when I killed him. Baby Harik, the new God of Death, would want that sword. In fact, the other gods might be mocking him for not having it, and Fingit likely wouldn't waste even one drop of divine sweat to make a new one.

"Baby Harik, I think your sense of humor is even better than Old Harik's, which still makes you sour and not funny at all. If you return the sword to me, I will betray the king once I meet him."

"Who cares about the king? You must think I have the brains of a dandelion. You could just stay away from the king and then never have to betray him or even listen to his boring stories. I'm tempted to fling you to your death. I stand by my offer. I'll fix the sword, and you'll give it to me after you use it once."

I squinted at Baby Harik. "You're a god. Why don't you just take it?"

"I could if I wanted, but it would be unartistic." His left eye twitched once.

"Oh, of course. How about you fix the sword, or else the last thing I do before I die will be to close the realm it's in. Then you can never get it."

He flinched.

"Aha! That's it! Control your face, Baby Harik."

Baby Harik snarled. It was the first time I had seen him angry. "Give me the sword after one use, or else die. I'd rather see it destroyed than anybody else have it."

That sounded like a true statement. My threat to send the sword into oblivion would only push him so far. "How about this? You return to me the power of drawing the sword, and in exchange, I will give you the sword in twenty years. But if I die before twenty years has passed, then the sword will be lost. So, you'd better keep me alive."

"That's foolish. How did you survive so long being so dumb?"

"People enjoy my personality. Baby Harik, you are an immortal god. How could it matter whether you get the sword in ten minutes, or ten years, or ten thousand years?"

In an echoing voice, he said, "The ways of the gods are beyond your understanding."

I thought about Baby Harik's likely problems. "You're right. I can't understand how Trutch, the Goddess of Life, who is now your spouse, is stripping off your hide every day about your—and this is not my word—impotence because you lack Dead Harik's powerful sword."

Baby Harik turned red in a snap. "No!" he bellowed. "You don't know anything! And my marriage is none of your business!"

"I am truly sorry that you're suffering," I told him with big eyes. "I mean that, sincerely. Becoming God of Death is a great honor, but gaining Trutch for a wife might make oblivion preferable." I bowed my head and took a deep breath.

"Give me the sword now, or die!" Baby Harik shouted.

I said in mild tones, "Fix the sword and let me have it for twenty years, or suffer the scorn of Trutch for eternity."

Baby Harik sighed and unclenched his fists. "You may have it for a month."

"Nine years."

"Two months." Baby Harik glared at me.

"Ten years." I managed not to smile. If I smiled, he might say to hell with it and let me die.

"All right, you pimply grease spot, six months!" Baby Harik shouted.

I squared my shoulders and looked Baby Harik in the eye. "I respect your bargaining enough to suggest that we stop all this bouncing around like baby goats. I have a proposal."

"All right, let me hear it."

"Two years," I said. "You fix the sword, and after two years, you take possession."

Baby Harik took a turn around the gazebo with his hands clasped behind his back. "I'd make one tiny change. Well, two. Right before you die, with your last impulse, you'll urge the sword into my possession. You can be sure that I'll know if you try to cheat, and you can't get away from my punishment. I am the God of Death, after all."

"What is your second tiny change?"

"I'm sure this sausage-and-chicken business has made you laugh. I know I've laughed until my butt hurt. Going forward, when you call the sword, something else will answer *sometimes*. Never anything that can directly hurt you, but it sure would keep you alert. It would happen randomly one time in five."

I stared at him and couldn't say now whether or not my mouth was open.

Harik smiled. "This is it. Either say yes or die. I can manage eternal existence without the sword. The weapon doesn't mean much stacked against the pleasures of immortality."

I said, "Let me clarify. You fix the sword, but one time in five, I'll pull some harmless thing out. Two years from this moment, I will give you the sword, or you'll get it when I die—as long as you don't cause my death. If you cause my death, you never get the sword."

Baby Harik clenched his teeth. He had probably intended to kill me in some fashion immediately upon my return, or soon after. He said, "I agree."

I said, "I also agree, you ripe puddle of congealing fluids."

Baby Harik shifted his jaw. "Not bad."

He wafted me back into my body. Maybe he feared that if he hurled me and knocked me down to be slaughtered, that would be him causing my death.

Acton and Evonne were between me and the bridge, struggling toward it. I heard Kenzie's thunderous deluge upstream. Soon, the river would be high and fast enough to wash away anybody, even a monster.

I let the charging soldiers come to me as I reached into the sword's realm and pulled it out. The blade was on the longish side but unexceptional, apart from the fact that it was pure white and produced wisps of black smoke that rose and disappeared a few feet above my head.

The first of Lossil's soldiers rushed to overrun me. I swept the sword in a great arc, and it cut three of them. None of the wounds would have been fatal if it had been a normal sword. As it was, everyone it touched shriveled as if they had aged two centuries in a second.

I backed up and slashed the next four reks who pressed me. They died the same way as the first three. By then, reks and difar were pressing me on both sides, trying to surround me. I turned and slashed left, then spun and slashed right, leaving five more withered corpses as I ran back ten steps toward Acton and Evonne before facing the enemy again.

The soldiers closest to my slaughter faltered. However, the mass behind them pushed ahead. I saw some shoved aside and others trampled. When the next wave reached me, I began slashing. When I retreated again, I left more than twenty dead behind.

Acton and Evonne reached the bridge a minute later and began to cross. I had killed and then fallen back three more times by then, leaving dozens dead.

I backed onto the bridge, which was wide enough for two carts to pass. That was a bit too wide for a serious choke point, so I had to hustle to make it work. I backed away one cut at a time until I reached the middle of the bridge. Then I held my ground.

The hero Hask, with her blond hair flying, pushed her way through the reks and difar, who fell back to make space for her. She pointed her sword at me and shouted, "This is not a little drinking game, you barbarian. Come face me!"

I lay the sword over my shoulder and walked to Hask at the end of the bridge as if I were walking out to the privy. She faked a swing and thrust at my throat. I parried and put my sword blade in her heart. As her corpse shriveled, the troops around us quieted. Laying my sword on my shoulder again, I backed away to the middle of the bridge before I nodded at the waiting soldiers.

They were slow to move, but soon they rushed me like a wave.

By the time Kenzie yelled that she was ready to rot the bridge supports, shriveled reks and difar were piled in front of me, and the ones behind refused to climb over the pile to reach me.

One of the reks, however, scrambled over the pile. I thought I recognized him as the fellow from the march to Pith, the one who just wanted to finish fighting and go back home. I turned to draw him in and whack his head with my sword's hilt rather than kill him. Even though he came at me with fury, I might have knocked him senseless if I'd had both arms. As it was, he rushed me swinging two swords, and I killed him to save my life.

When I was younger, I kept a careful tally of the people I killed, often remembering their faces. Now I didn't try to guess how many I had killed. In the Dark Lands, I had slain so many that I didn't just lose count, I lost the desire to ever know the number.

I ran across the bridge into the city and felt empty.

Kenzie destroyed the bridge right behind me, and Lossil's soldiers began to withdraw. My legs shook as I slid down with my back against the wall of some wooden building. Sitting on wet paving stones and pulling up my knees, I looked around to see who had survived.

I expected a sort of hesitancy from my allies and even fear. My sword was terrifying, and I guess I was too. But I didn't see a single person apart from two dirty, weaponless fighters. They came around a corner, saw me, and ran. I heard the unwounded survivors helping the wounded as they cried out, but they did it out of my sight.

None of the people I saved would stand where I could see them, let alone talk to me. I dismissed the sword and then scratched my head with my only hand while I tried to catch my breath.

TWENTY-TWO

I trudged down the riverbank in Sandell, not looking for anyone or anything in particular. I did spot four city residents who froze when they saw me and then scurried away like nicely dressed bunnies.

"I bet you feel all tired out," Hurd said from behind me. "That was a stout round of killing."

"Hello, Hurd," I said, without looking back. "Are you here to give me advice I don't want?"

"Let me take you home."

"Where is that?"

"You know what I mean."

I did know. When he said home, he meant the Dark Lands, and I decided not to be a blazing thorn in the ass over the point. "Not until I help Pil's people and kill that frothing dog Alamore."

"If you just get the heck out of here, I'll go do all that for you."

I tried to laugh but had to shake my head. "I don't trust you."

His laugh sounded like a wheeze. "Is that your only objection? We can find a way around that."

I kept walking. "Why do you care if I stay here, or go back, or sink into the earth?"

"The folks around here don't appreciate you. They don't deserve you."

"Even if that was true, it doesn't answer my question. Why do you care?"

With a straight face, Hurd said, "I hate to see you suffer like this."

This time, I did laugh and faced him. "Hurd, you don't care for anybody but yourself. It's well known across more than one realm."

His eyes narrowed, and he almost sneered. "Maybe I'll just send you back for your own good."

I thought about summoning the sword, but the notion made me queasy. "I don't think I can kill you, Hurd."

He grinned, but his eyes didn't. "You can't. If you call that cursed sword, I'll disappear. Maybe you can execute every other fool you see, but I'm different."

I smiled back. "Yes, you are, but you're not unkillable." Then I did something I had been dreading. "Limnad, I want you." Those words would summon a spirit that might want to kill me. I felt a wispy sense of relief at the thought, but it floated away. To hell with giving up.

I hoped that because of our past friendly acquaintance, the river spirit would tear Hurd apart before she did the same for me.

Limnad rose out of the swift river and rushed onto the bank, close enough for me to feel her breath. She was entirely blue, fitting for the spirit of the Blue River, and presented in the form of a perfectly beautiful, unclothed woman. She shouted with such great power that I couldn't hear for a moment, but I could see her lips move.

She was saying, "You left Desh to die!" By her face, she was shouting it, or maybe shrieking it.

It was not true that I had left Desh, my friend, to die, not in the strictest sense of reality, but it made perfect sense according to spirit logic. Desh had been her lover. He and I had left her behind to go fight gods. The gods had killed him for it, and I had come back without him. It must have been simple in her eyes.

Spirits were mostly a whirlwind of thoughts and feelings. As a person, it wasn't possible for me to understand how deeply she mourned him.

I said, "Yes, I did that, and I grieve for him too. I couldn't save him, and I couldn't bring him home since I never came home until now."

Limnad grabbed me by the shoulders, and I thought I would die before my next breath. She threw me thirty feet instead of killing me. I skidded across the paving stones and slammed into a wooden building. My left arm would have been broken if I had one. As it was, my shoulder and hip took a lot of the punishment. Before I could even twitch, Limnad was kneeling on my chest clutching my chin so hard I thought she might crush it.

Since I couldn't form words, I made the sounds, "I ought oo uh-hing."

She eased her grip on my jaw just enough for me to talk. "I know it doesn't make a damn bit of difference, but I brought you something. It's wrapped in silk in my pouch."

With her other hand, the spirit tore the pouch off my belt and yanked it open. When she unwrapped the silk, an appalling necklace fell out. It was made of small bones threaded on woven hair. The hair was Desh's. The bones were what remained of his fingers.

After a moment full of murderous potential, Limnad rolled off me, clutched the necklace to her breast, and lay on her side weeping. I had seen plenty of grief before, but I had never witnessed such profound, hopeless longing.

I had believed that this gift would touch Limnad. I had not expected how much. As I sat up, I rolled the problem in my head and realized that these were the fingers Desh had touched her with, the fingers fundamental to the work he loved, and the fingers he used to create every intimate thing he ever gave her.

"You didn't bring her here to kill me, did you?" Hurd asked in a shaky voice.

"Of course not," I said, wondering whether I should say anything to Limnad. "I brought her here to make her cry and then to kill you."

When Hurd didn't say anything, I looked around. He was gone.

Limnad wept for a good long time. Then she sat up and put on the necklace. She cried for a while longer before she bounded to the river and slipped into the water more easily than a seal.

I sat up, breathed with care, and waited until the sun had almost disappeared, but she didn't return.

I stomped around the city in the dark, windy, thickly clouded night. Sandell was a small place as cities go, with about one hundred weathered wooden buildings. None was more than two stories high, and few looked like they would hold more than a dozen people. After sunset, an occasional lantern hung in front of some establishment or other, throwing enough light for me not to bump into things.

People must not have recognized me in the darkness, because they passed like I was anybody else.

A couple of hours after full dark, I turned the corner and almost bashed into Vargo. He backed away. His eyes glinted huge in the lantern light, and he said with a slight tremor, "Bib! Where have you been? I thought you might have been killed and your body lost, but Acton looked at me as if I was stupid to say that." He drew a loud breath.

I had nothing to say to this boy. I started to walk around him.

"Kenzie is out looking for you, and Acton too." He cleared his throat. "Come eat something and rest. You had a brutal . . . I mean, a difficult day. I'll take you there."

Vargo possessed faults as a fighter, a grandson, and I guess a human being. But he reached out and grasped my arm before leading me toward camp on the other side of town. That took some courage.

At the camp, I sat beside a fire. Everybody there moved to sit at other fires. Some people nearby got up and walked away into the darkness. Those who stayed muttered and glanced at me.

After a while, Evonne limped into sight, carrying two mugs of beer, some hard bread, and half a joint of greasy mutton. After she set down the food on a bench, she didn't hesitate to pat me on the shoulder and sit at the fire near me. Glancing around the camp, she said in her soft voice, "You know why they don't like us.

But if we wished to be liked, we would sing songs and buy drinks."

I nodded a little.

Lit by the campfire, her face looked relaxed, but she wasn't smiling. "Thank you for saving my life. I will not insult you by offering to pay you for that. But if it will make you happier, I will sleep with you."

My eyes opened wider. "That's a kind offer, it is. But I'm searching for my wife's family." I coughed. "I fear I would be rudely distracted."

Evonne smiled. "Drink the beer. I think it is horrible, but you may not think so."

The beer was horrible.

After considering things for a while, I said, "Evonne, I would ask you to do a favor for me."

She gave a little smile. "I might."

I pointed at my left ear, which had been mostly cut off by Bethroti.

She asked, "Would you like me to bandage it for you? I understand that would be difficult for you, since it is on the side of your head, and you have only one hand."

"No, I want you to finish removing it."

Evonne was silent for a bit. "And yet you don't want to sleep with me. I think I should be insulted."

"Please."

Evonne starting chuckling and kept at it until she put my left ear in my hand. Then she shook her head and kept drinking bad beer.

Sometime later, Acton and Kenzie appeared and sat at the fire, as far away from me as they could. They said hello, glanced at the ear in my hand, and smiled at me so much it grew awkward. They also murmured to one another.

Without planning to, I jumped up and trotted away into the night, angling toward the riverbank northwest of the city. I ignored the young people calling out behind me.

In the darkness east of the river, I said, "Kruppin, I want you."

Bear-size Kruppin ambled out of the darkness. "You should thank me for what I'm not doing to your leg right now."

"Thank you. Kruppin, I want to make you an offer, not a command. I will give you my ear." I held it up. "I know you want it. You're not obligated to do anything for me. It's a gift. I hope you'll tell me why you want it, but that's your choice."

Kruppin snatched my ear when I held it out. He said, "To be entirely forthcoming, when you returned to this realm, the great Void Walker Gek set a bounty on you, open to monsters throughout the Void. None is allowed to kill you, but we will be rewarded for bringing pieces of you to Gek."

"That makes an appalling kind of sense," I said. I had done Gek a good turn in the past, but I had also aggravated him to an extreme degree. Gratitude didn't exist among the great powers like Gek, anyway.

Kruppin said, "I can now be the first to return with a prize. Give me the fifth command now so that I'll be free."

"Just a minute. If this bounty is such a big thing, why don't I have dozens of monsters attacking me?"

"Oh." Kruppin briefly lifted his head as if he might howl. "You have something of a reputation. Most monsters have decided that a prize from Gek isn't worth being slaughtered by you."

I drew my sharp sword and stepped back from the monster. "Kruppin, I unbind you." The yellow band around his neck dissolved.

"Well, you didn't have to do that," Kruppin said. "You are almost well mannered considering you are a hideous buffoon of a man."

"I'm glad you're not trying to kill me. I knew it was a possibility."

Kruppin made a noise like a wild boar gargling. I assumed he was laughing. "You are very amusing to think I would attack you. I just watched you slay one hundred forty-three men." Kruppin leaped away into the night.

The clouds had blown away, leaving a cold night with a lively wind. Something was moving on the other side of the river. I held my sword ready in case Lossil had figured out a way to take us by surprise.

"Bib!" A brief roar sounded, and I recognized the cat-monster, Burrud. "I have learned how awful the eyesight of a human is. I am invisible to you, I'm sure. We congratulate you on your victory, although it is puzzling how you won."

I couldn't think of anything useful to say.

Lossil's voice boomed across the river, echoing off the riverbank at my feet and then echoing back at me from the far bank. "You carried a weapon full of magic, and I've never seen one like it. Of course, you won't tell me about it. You can't kill every one of us, though, even with ten swords like that."

I shouted, "You state that with great confidence, Lossil. I have never seen great confidence lead to anything but defeat and suffering."

"Maybe. But maybe you're wrong. Just in case, I'm offering you a truce."

I yelled, "These people might be interested in your offer. I am interested in cutting out your heart and feeding it to some widow's pigs."

He may have laughed at that, but it was hard to tell. "I'm offering you a deal, not them. You can leave, and I won't try to stop you or chase you. You can sail to a place where not as many people want to kill you." He waited for a few seconds. "I have to kill the others."

"The others? Everybody on the whole island? You wouldn't be satisfied with half? It wouldn't even need to be the nasty half."

"It's got to be everybody, or near to it. Thanks to you, it will take a lot longer than I planned. I don't have a choice about them, but I can choose to let you go."

"You are one generous son of a bitch," I shouted. "I think I'll kill everybody on your side and offer to let you go. If that's so damn generous, you ought to take it yourself."

Lossil called, "I see that you won't abandon your friends."

I bellowed, "To hell with these people! I don't have a friend among them. They can all fall down dead and get eaten by rats. I don't care."

After a pause, Lossil yelled, "Why are you risking your life fighting for them?"

"I'm not fighting for them. I'm fighting to kill you. There's a difference, and if you don't understand it, then you're in the wrong business. Go home and grow cabbages, you pathetic son-of-a-rat-puke coward."

Lossil didn't answer. Burrud yelled, "Perhaps you are not the hero we believed you to be."

I made my laughter hard and loud. "I am not. But your heroes are sad little things."

Burrud shouted something else, but I had turned away and was strolling back to camp. I didn't like this feeling as much as I had when I was younger, but it was better than feeling empty.

TWENTY-THREE

After my sweet conversation with Lossil and Burrud, I found an isolated tree on the north side of the city and lay down. I had no trouble falling asleep or sleeping well. But sometime during the night, voices woke me.

I recognized Acton and Kenzie calling my name.

"Bib! Don't kill us!" Acton said. "We want to help!"

I sat up. "I'm here! Why are you bothering me? I was having beautiful dreams."

"You were?" Kenzie sounded shocked.

"What do you want?"

"Both of us made a bargain with you," Kenzie said. "I've come here to restore your arm."

"Although it does make it easier for you to kill us," Acton said. "However, an arm hardly matters. You could kill us with your toe."

I took a couple of deep breaths. "Kenzie, I will guide you again. After we're done, you'll know even more about healing. Acton, I promise to never kill you with my toe."

A few hours later, I had my left arm once more. It had no calluses and no blemishes. It had never been touched by the sun.

That wouldn't last, though, because we were half an hour away from dawn.

Kenzie leaned on Acton so hard he was almost carrying her away as she moaned and held her left arm.

The stunned and battered remnants of Shura's force dragged through the act of breaking camp. It was a struggle, but everything was packed and ready for travel by midmorning. I had convinced her to retreat south and recruit an enormous army, and to leave the battle planning to people who had planned at least one or two battles. If she gathered a lot of people, she was likely to collect some ex-soldiers.

Of course, I would be traveling in the opposite direction to Ebring.

Vargo took me aside after breakfast. "I asked around the city. Nobody knows a ding-dong damn thing about Alamore. My family's gone, just like we heard. They took everything with them, livestock and furniture too. My ma has family in Ebring."

"Why'd they leave? After all, you went to find me to save them."

"First, they don't think you exist. Second, Grandma has a little bit of the sight." He pointed across the river at the battlefield. "Maybe she saw that."

"Grandma? Do you mean Pil?"

"No, she's Granda—my father's mother."

"Don't explain it again, I'll get dizzy."

Shura was hurrying around providing for the badly wounded men to stay in Sandell when twelve horsemen rode into the city and halted in front of us. Everybody around me bowed, so I figured I'd bow too. Pissing off richly dressed people wouldn't speed me along to Ebring.

A tall, thin man in his prime wore the fanciest uniform of the lot. He leaned forward in the saddle and examined us as if we were cattle. In a nasally voice, he said, "Yesterday was unfortunate, but you damaged the enemy. For an irregular group of peasants, that was decent work. The trade-off in lives will ultimately serve our cause."

I wanted to argue with the snotty, handsome dog, but everything he said was objectively true.

He went on: "Now that you have been so ravaged, I shall take you under my command. You are part of my army. We will leave here soon, so be prepared and do not delay us."

The leader pulled out a small folio and began consulting it. The other eleven horsemen gazed around at the trees or at the gathered peasants. One bit off something in his hand and started chewing. They probably didn't expect anyone to object.

I leaned toward Evonne and found she was gone. I turned to Shura and muttered, "Who the hell is he?"

One of the horsemen pointed at me, so I suppose I had been louder than I thought. I wondered whether I had forgotten how to be quiet in the Dark Lands and resolved to pay better attention. The leader glared at me and sat taller. "I am Jon, Earl of Sunderhame. I am in command here."

He said it with such disdain that I couldn't be quiet like a good peasant. "And I am Bib, Duke of the Rattling Donkeys. My lord."

That created a nice period of silence. Shura looked sideways at me and said, "Shh!" She smiled at Jon.

One of the horsemen said, "This is the man I was telling you about, my lord."

"Your name is Bib?" Jon asked. "How outlandish. But you did well holding the bridge until everyone crossed."

"Not everybody crossed," I said.

Jon waved a hand. "Nearly everybody. I shall give you a warning, and listen well. Do not show me disrespect again. Should you do so, you'll remain in this city at the end of a rope."

It could be easier to get things done in Ebring if I were seen arriving with Jon, Earl of Scatterbrain. "I apologize, my lord. Something hit me on the head during the fight, and I still see double."

"Better. Prepare yourselves to march." Jon turned his horse as if he had already forgotten that we existed.

Under his breath, Acton asked Shura and me, "Will we ignore that man and go find reinforcements?"

I said, "I'm traveling to Ebring. You heroes can do what you want."

Most people started talking and milling around, but Shura touched my arm. "Bib, please stay here for a moment. I said before that I know how these creatures are appearing."

"Right, you did say that. I thought you were just lying to convince me to join you."

Shura smiled and looked down. "Maybe a bit, but I have heard about this from a man who said he saw it."

"Let's go talk to him."

She sighed. "He is dead."

"That's bad luck. Why tell me?"

"I think maybe you can do something about it."

I lowered my brow. "That sounds ominous and probably not true."

"I did not understand it all until yesterday. There is a monument, or perhaps a marker, or something significant in a mystical way. Maybe it is a pit. It could even be a holy tree."

"Or a door in the back of a tavern."

She nodded. "Maybe so. That is how these monsters get here."

"Where is it?" I asked.

"I don't know."

"How does it work?"

"I don't know that, either." She shrugged. "Sorry."

"Not that I intend to do anything about it, but knowledge is always good to have. How do you make it stop doing whatever it's doing?"

"Destroy it?" Shura shrugged again.

"Hell, do you know anything at all about it?"

"I was told a thing, but I didn't know then what it meant. It is your fault."

I raised my voice. "What?"

"You did something to make it happen. Maybe you can do something to make it stop." She smiled with remarkably straight white teeth.

I said, "Somebody has been lying to you. I just got here three days ago. Lossil and his scratchy army have been here a lot longer than that."

"Maybe that doesn't matter. The man I talked to said time works in strange ways from place to place."

I couldn't say much to that because it was the truest thing I had heard her say so far.

She went on: "He gave me a holy scroll, and this knowledge was inside. It fell in the mud and was stepped on a lot during a march, but I also saw the words carved on a tree that may have been holy. I am not sure how holy it was. I heard it in a dream, and then I saw it in a simmering pot of beans too. You cannot be more certain than that."

"Crap. Nothing but crap. Stop thinking the gods will guide you. Get a hobby instead. I recommend building furniture."

I walked away from her, but my stomach was flipping.

Sir Jon and his officers rode near the front of the column, preceded by two dozen armored horsemen. Another sixty horsemen followed right behind him. Some five hundred soldiers with swords, pikes, and crossbows marched along next.

One might think that was Jon's entire column, but the dozens of laborers and artisans required to keep a fighting force well fed and armed came after that, along with sixteen wagons pulled by mules. Spare mules and spare mounts followed.

We tramped along at the very end. Everybody stayed clear of me in a nice, ten-foot-wide empty circle.

Evonne had reappeared wearing a cloak with the hood pulled up. She limped along beside me, close enough to converse without shouting. "Bib, I need you to help me."

"Come over and let's talk about it."

She shifted to walk a more companionable distance from me. "I learned from a drover that we can cross back over the river ahead. The ford is not well known, and we can surprise Lossil."

"That's some stirring news! I'll order all these men and their creatures to hurry across the river and then wait around for Lossil to march by."

"You are not funny."

"That's true."

Evonne snapped, "We will surprise Lossil! His men are hurt and tired. We have fresh soldiers!"

"That is also true."

"You will help me? If we don't stop him, he will kill us all in the end. And it would be a great slaughter."

Her assessment wasn't quite true. Lossil would win if the king and his army let Lossil reinforce as I suspected he would. That would mean death for the people of Ir. But Lossil wouldn't kill me because I intended that Pil's family and I be gone the hell away from Ir before long. After I cut Alamore's head off.

I didn't tell Evonne any of that. I said, "What do you imagine I can do about it?"

"Tell Lord Jon about these things. Convince him."

"You convince him!"

"I cannot. I was . . . I was his bodyguard and deserted, so he will kill me if he sees me."

I didn't need to ask why she deserted the arrogant, ass-dragging oaf. I asked, "Do you want me to do it now, or tonight when he invites me to have supper with him in his tent?"

She grinned and glanced down. "You held off the enemy. You are the hero. He will listen to you. He will listen to you more than to anyone else."

"I doubt that."

"Perhaps he will not listen. But if he does not, we can kill him. His lieutenants will listen to you, then." Evonne met my eyes hard enough to say she wasn't joking. "They do not want their kingdom to die."

I held back my laughter. "I admire your plan, but it will fail. We'll end up killing Jon, which I admit is a worthy thing. But we'll also end up killing a lot of good soldiers just because they had the bad luck to serve a boob. By that kind of thinking, we'd have to kill half the soldiers in the world."

"This is not a joke!"

"No, it is not a joke. But after we kill all those poor men, their comrades would turn around and kill us. Lossil would have an easier time winning, not harder."

Evonne growled, "Your logic cannot be not sound! Everyone

says you are a deceiver. Do not lie to me."

I closed my eyes for a few seconds. "Yes, I am a liar, Evonne, but I am not lying this time."

The entire column halted for a short time at midday. Maybe some folks were fed, but the failed army of Shura had nothing to eat unless they carried it themselves.

Ten minutes after we resumed march, I found Evonne unconscious beside the road. Her left arm was broken, and her wheezing told me that some ribs had been broken too. Her face was bloody from a broken nose, two split lips, and some gouges that, in my experience, had been made with the toe of a boot.

When I knelt beside Evonne, I found that she might or might not die. It depended on how many times she'd been kicked in the head.

Kenzie pushed me out of the way and probed Evonne's wounds with her right hand. She must not have recovered from healing my arm, because her left arm trembled and collapsed when she tried to raise it. Kenzie shook her head and muttered at first, then she spit out fouler and fouler profanity. After a minute, she looked around at Acton, Vargo, and me. "How great is the need for us to reach the palace today?"

I started to say it was damned great to me. Pil's family might be suffering and dying that minute. But I looked at Evonne's smashed face and shook my head. Vargo hesitated and then shrugged. I guess neither of us could suggest we load Evonne into one of the wagons for a jolting ride that would probably kill her before dark.

Kenzie raised her voice. "Boys, lay her over there under that short tree, and for the sake of Krak's all-conquering phallus, have care!" As Acton and Vargo lifted Evonne, Kenzie muttered, "This is bad, this is bad . . ."

I fell in beside her as she walked toward the tree. "I can help you."

Kenzie stuck out her jaw. "How can you help me? With more advice?" She sucked in a breath. "Sorry, I'm not angry at you. You can assist if you help me with another thing. Come with me to kill the Earl of Sunderhame."

TWENTY-FOUR

Kenzie possessed the knowledge and skill to heal Evonne's wounds, but she did not have the endurance. The head wounds were the gravest, but if Kenzie healed them first, she would fall senseless if she was lucky. If unlucky, she would remain awake while the pain from Evonne's horrible wounds crashed around in her head for an hour, or ten hours, or a day.

The gods must giggle when sorcerers heal.

Kenzie dealt with the most serious wounds to Evonne's body, limbs, and face. Then she healed the worst head wounds, the ones that might be fatal.

When she was done, Kenzie lay sweating on her back, taking shallow breaths while Acton held her hand. Evonne had been kicked more than I had thought, and Kenzie had never healed anybody in such dire shape. After a few experiences like this one, some Callers became less eager to heal, or stopped healing at all.

Evonne had woken and sat up against a tree. Vargo brought her water and cleaned her remaining wounds.

Acton shifted over to sit close enough to talk with me. "I have never seen Kenzie so distressed. Will she recover?"

I nodded and almost smiled. "I've healed hacked-off legs and a hundred poisoned people at once. It didn't end up hurting me." I was walking on the edge of untruth, but I hadn't flopped all the way over.

Acton did look at me hard, but he didn't comment. Instead, he asked, "Do you intend to kill that earl?"

"Yes."

"No," Evonne said at the same time as she limped from tree to tree. "That would not win the war. I see that now. His men don't hate him enough." She limped faster. "After the war is won, then we can kill him."

"Why didn't he have you hanged today for deserting?" I asked.

"I was hooded, and when I began explaining the plan, five of his men threw me to the ground. Then the kicking and hitting started. I do not think the earl ever looked at my face."

Vargo said, "Maybe Lossil will kill him for us. If he does, I'll send Lossil a nice, fat sheep and some preserves."

I said, "That sounded almost hopeful. Well, let's set this all aside for now. We'll camp here and catch the rascal tomorrow. We're not many hours' walk from Ebring." I glanced at the sun as it drifted below the clouds. In the afternoon, we had turned west to march away from the ocean.

"Jon will stay at Ebring, or he will stay close," Evonne said.

"Why?" Acton asked. "The enemy isn't there."

Evonne laughed but didn't sound amused. "He defends the people he thinks are important. Since this war began, it has been the king's strategy to defend the important ones. Everyone else must defend themselves."

"Maybe we should kill the king too," Vargo said through clenched teeth. "I never knew he was such a bastard."

Kenzie pulled away from Acton's hand. She panted. "You hush! Killing kings is blasphemy. Noblemen are different." She groaned. "Kill them all!"

For a span of seconds, the only sounds were Kenzie's breathing and Evonne's limping footsteps. Then Kenzie blinked at Acton. "I don't mean all of them, not really. Not you."

Acton glanced at the ground. "I just happened to get it. I didn't do anything or try."

"Ah, you're noble and all, eh?" Vargo asked. "With horses and servants and buckets of gold?"

"Be still!" Kenzie smacked the ground with one fist and then winced. "If you keep arguing—" She screamed for three seconds and grabbed at Acton's hand again. After some deep breaths, she said, "Don't make me beat you both. You're good boys, but that wouldn't stop me." She started groaning.

Vargo leaned toward me. "Can't you do anything to help her?"

"I could hit her on the head with a stick. As healing goes, it's not one of the best options. She's suffering, but not hurt. She just has to weather it." I raised my voice. "Everybody, sleep as much as you can. There's plenty of time to comfort one another and be in love tomorrow."

Vargo walked off into the dusk.

I rolled to my feet, and my hip made an alarming pop. I had been sore and cut up with minor wounds since the fight on the bridge. "I'll stand first watch. But Acton, before you sleep, tell me something. You have killed a lot of the invaders, these reks and difar, in the past days. What do your Bib stories say about that? Is it a right thing?"

He looked around for Vargo, who was gone. He glanced at Evonne, who stared at him blank-faced. Finally, he said, "It's not terribly right. Normally, it wouldn't be right at all. But these are monsters, not people."

"So that makes a difference?" I asked. "You're awfully damn keen on killing Jon, and he's a person, mostly. Does that make a difference?"

Kenzie mumbled something.

I added, "Killing is exactly the kind of thing that story-Bib would do, right?"

It was almost dark, but I saw Evonne grin.

"It would not be right," Acton said slowly, "but it would be required."

I smiled. "I guess it would be. All of you go on to sleep. I'll watch for bandits and bears."

Nobody objected. Evonne began breathing deeply within a few minutes, and Vargo showed up to sleep just after that. Kenzie lay panting as Acton held her hand. If they didn't need sleep, I didn't care.

No bears visited us that night.

By sunrise, every smidge of Kenzie's pain was gone, and she bounced around like a girl, which I guess she technically was. We hiked up the road through shallow hills until we reached a great expanse of flat, grassy land. During the march, the young people gradually became less shy of walking near me.

By midafternoon, the walled city of Ebring came into sight along with the dark blue sea beyond it. By many kingdoms' standards, it was a puny capital, but several dozen stone buildings and three hundred wooden structures filled it. Dozens of buildings and farms surrounded the city.

Today, the city was under siege.

Lossil's besieging army numbered about six hundred, so the siege was mighty thin in places. He had concentrated it at the main gate and the side gate. The harbor gate was a weak point too, but he had ignored it.

The side gate was a foolish architectural feature. The builders must have envisioned a mass of defending soldiers riding out of it with pennons and frothing horses to sweep away the besieging army. In reality, the city had been taken numerous times, and in every case, the enemy breached the side gate. It made the place as defensible as a bowl of soup.

It took a horrible mass of soldiers to defend both gates and the harbor. The kings of Ir had never been able to field more than a regular mass of soldiers. I doubted that this king had gathered more than a routine mass of soldiers, either.

"What are we going to do about this crap?" asked Vargo, grimacing toward the city. "I mean, I'm not leaving my family to be slaughtered in there." He glanced around, meeting our eyes. "Will you help me? Although I don't know how."

"Let's think about this," I said. "Our goal is to save the family. We can sneak in, grab them, and sneak out, probably by sea."

"I like that one," Acton said.

"Or we can sneak in and join Jon's defenders in breaking the siege," I said. "Or sneak in and lead a force to sally and chase away Lossil's army."

"The first one still sounds best," Kenzie said.

"Hm," I said. "How sneaky are you? Be honest. Can you climb a castle wall without being seen?" Everybody shook their heads. "Maybe ten years ago I could have," I said. "If we stand outside and ask Jon's men to help us into the city, do you feel confident they won't just shoot arrows at us until we're overwhelmed and die?"

Nobody said anything.

"Since we can't get inside the city," I said, "we'll just have to break the siege from out here."

Everybody laughed except Evonne.

Acton said, "That's crazy."

Evonne said, "We do not need to kill all of them, just enough so that they go away."

"Look at the soldiers besieging the gate," I said. "They're not dispersed like they were on the battlefield at Sandell. They're working in clumps. If we can bring terror down on them fast enough, we'll break and scatter those clumps."

"We require speed," Evonne said.

"Not stealing more horses!" Acton said.

Evonne reached into a pouch and pulled out a double handful of silver coins. She shrugged. "If I was going to be a deserter, I thought I should be a thief also."

We spent two hours trekking back to the closest town, where we purchased the four riding horses for sale along with saddles and tack. I rode double with Acton to the closest farm and purchased a cart horse to ride bareback. Kenzie did all of our trading and left the sellers glum.

By midafternoon, we stood on a gentle hill that looked down on Ebring. I was more skilled than Kenzie, being a million years older than her, so I began pulling a storm together. I grew it as high and as strong as I could over the next two hours, and I wished I could work on it for two more. But we were nearing dusk, and darkness would be against us in the sort of attack I was planning. I did not allow the storm to rain yet, which cost me a noticeable trickle of power.

We reviewed the plan, mounted, and rode down the hill toward Ebring at an easy canter. The besieging army wouldn't devote a shred of thought to five puny horsemen who weren't even riding fast.

We slowed down half a mile from the main gate, and I pointed out stacks and wagons of provisions, weapons, lumber, and building material among Lossil's troops. I had scanned for Lossil and Burrud down there earlier and found neither one. I looked again and saw that they hadn't shown up. Maybe they were rallying their troops after the battle at Sandell.

Kenzie sat her horse and watched for incoming arrows. Vargo and Evonne held position a bit away from the rest of us. They were tasked with protecting us sorcerers from anybody who tried to run up and stab us. I kept an eye on the overall situation.

I nodded at Acton. Using tiny hand movements, he turned a wagon load of lumber into a white-hot explosion. Flame and blazing wood hurtled in all directions. I was forced to imagine the screams of the burning, scrambling soldiers, because five seconds later, Acton did the same thing to what looked like a blacksmith's wagon. For the next minute, Acton created blazing horror every five seconds, as regular as a timepiece.

I waved him to stop. Turning to Kenzie, I said, "Do you see where the soldiers have clumped together to get away from the fires?"

"I see them."

"That's where you hit them with lightning. I'll take over watching for arrows."

Kenzie had called her fourth bolt of lightning before I realized she was doing it at five-second intervals too. I caught her smirking at Acton.

After another minute, I called to Kenzie, "You can stop now. Watch for arrows."

She nodded and began scanning the battlefield, which was

pocked by a dozen spreading fires.

I added, "Acton! Help Vargo and Evonne watch for threats."

Lossil's force had lost over half of their troops in two minutes. I was amazed to see the rest withdrawing from the field in reasonable order.

I couldn't help it, even though it meant setting the worst example possible. But it was so dramatic, I couldn't resist some gestures. I raised my right hand and brought down plum-size hail on the retreating soldiers, using up a large part of the storm's remaining energy.

The troops ran in panic, especially since I was able to shift the hailstorm to follow them. Even through this, some soldiers appeared to be organizing themselves. I raised my left hand and consumed the rest of the storm's power to throw a gale at the soldiers, flinging the hail almost sideways.

The soldiers ran and kept running. I figured the survivors numbered less than one hundred.

Kenzie was glaring at me. "You hypocritical turd! Why didn't you break a glass bell and kiss your horse too?"

I laughed. "You're right. You speak for all the sorcerers throughout history when you point out my folly. We just accomplished a devastating sorcerous victory at a relatively low cost in power. You're due the right to chastise me a bit."

"Enemy behind us!" Evonne shouted.

I turned and saw fifty or so reks and difar, probably from the side gate. They had circled and come in right behind us. Vargo and Evonne had ridden out to meet them, which was brave but a poor tactical move. Acton couldn't hit the closer soldiers with fire because he might kill Evonne and Vargo.

Acton didn't hesitate to begin combusting the clothing of enemies farther away. Some burned, and the rest shouted and ran. That left us facing about twenty.

I rode through the soldiers and cut down three on the way. Evonne was doing about the same to my left. Vargo was fighting to my right, but his horse reared and two soldiers pulled him out of the saddle.

By the time I reached Vargo and scattered his attackers, he had been stabbed at least twice. I carried him away, and Evonne guarded us until we joined Acton and Kenzie. Then we all galloped away from the soldiers. Once we gained enough of a lead, Acton used fire to convince them to keep running.

Kenzie and Evonne lay Vargo on the dead winter grass. Kenzie was shaking her head and muttering "No" over and over as she examined his wounds. My experience told me he'd be dead before long, maybe in a few minutes. She began to work with her teeth clenched.

I hadn't realized how much grief and worry Vargo carried on his face all the time. Now that he was dying, all of it had fallen away as the tension seeped out of him. It surprised me how much he favored Pil. Looking down at him now was like watching her die yet again.

Well, he wasn't Pil, and he wasn't dead yet. To hell with giving up.

Kenzie struggled to stay ahead of Vargo's wounds. Fighting them was like trying to hold more and more sand as it was poured into her hands. Her arms were covered with his blood far up her sleeves.

Vargo's death still appeared likely when eight soldiers in clean uniforms rode out to us from the city. I recognized some of them as Jon's boys. One of them rode close and looked down at me. "His Majesty and the Earl of Sunderhame thank you and invite you to wait upon them at your earliest convenience." By the way he talked, I felt sure that "earliest" meant "right the hell now."

I said, "I'm busy, and I don't know yet when my earliest convenience will be. Before midnight, I expect. Please send them my regrets and ask them to save some wine for me."

The man raised his voice. "One does not refuse an invitation from the king of Ir!"

I turned to look back at Vargo and Kenzie as I said, "I'm not refusing it. The king said at my earliest convenience, and I take the man at his word. Are you calling the king a liar?"

I heard him draw his sword. Mine was still in my hand, so I

spun and cut his weapon in half. "Listen, pin-dick. Did you see how we destroyed an army in ten minutes? Or were you hiding behind a privy like a terrified child?"

The man's face was red, and he threw what was left of his sword onto the ground.

"Get out of here, you rancid, tit-flopping wreckage of your father's dreams!" I shouted.

He and his cronies rode a hundred paces away, dismounted, and waited.

Evonne leaned toward me. "Tit-flopping? You may have made an enemy."

I almost said, "Good! I've killed most of mine and need to replenish the herd!" But Kenzie was panting hard, and I saw the sweat dripping off her onto Vargo's limp body. I lost the desire to make foolish remarks.

Well before midnight, Kenzie outpaced Vargo's wounds and she finished healing him fully within the next two hours. Now she lay on her back holding her body with both arms and weeping without pause like a child. Vargo sat holding her hand. Acton might have shoved him out of the way, but I grabbed him first.

"Come with me," I told Acton. "If the king is a malicious idiot like Jon, I'd like to have an ally. Or a witness. Or somebody to write a song about tonight's lies and carnage."

Acton and I rode to Jon's emissaries. Without dismounting, I said, "I'd be honored to attend the king right away. Acton and I shall proceed on our old nags, which have been broken by their service in saving the city. If the king is in the mood for handing out rewards, new mounts would not go amiss."

The leader scowled. "Just you."

"Acton is our chief strategist. We can't talk to the king without him."

"If he's the strategist, who are you?"

"I'm the one who kills people when they ask too many questions."

He scowled even deeper. "Come on, then." He trotted toward the main gate. His companions fell in place around us.

We passed into Ebring and rode to the palace by lantern light. Quite a lot of buildings hung lanterns outside, which told me how prosperous Ebring was in a country where people usually had little. We were not questioned or commented upon.

Soon, we dismounted and stood in front of the palace, a great, three-story gray stone building about five hundred feet wide. The front gates were two broad bronze doors ten feet high, and if the hinge corrosion was evidence, they may never have been closed in Acton's lifetime.

Once inside and moving down a hallway, Shura met us running and was almost knocked down by Jon's men. She said, "Why have you taken so long? Never mind, come and talk to the king with me. He's wonderful!"

Shura's fortunes had obviously changed. "Why are you here?" I asked her.

"It's too much to explain," she said. "I am planning the next battle along with King Elgus, and we can use your ideas." She clutched my arm.

"Slow down and listen," I said. "A family named Pierce—that's Vargo's family—is somewhere in the city. Do you know where?"

Shura shook her head. "I haven't heard of anybody like that. Ask the king when you see him. He knows everything about his kingdom."

Shura pulled me by the arm along the hallway, passing Jon's men, who cursed but didn't stop us. We ran almost tripping up a stairway and raced around three corners with no discussion.

Ignoring two men guarding a plain, wooden door, Shura flung it open before pulling me inside. Acton trotted in behind us. We entered a wood-paneled room large enough to host a big wedding. Four stone columns supported the high ceiling. As Shura led me across expensive rugs, I saw four large tables and ten times as many chairs placed around the room. Everything was hazily lit at the walls and the columns by lanterns stinking of impure oil.

Jon, Earl of Sunderhame, straightened from leaning over one of the tables and glared at us, sticking out his regal chin. I recognized the three men with him as more of his toadies. Six tall guards with spears and swords were scattered around the room, along with two teenagers I figured to be sorcerers.

Three older well-dressed men and two men in uniform glanced up from another table, along with a pretty teenage girl just about swallowed by a fur robe. Shura guided me to the older men and bowed. "Your Majesty, this is the hero who broke the siege! The one I was telling you about!"

The shortest and fattest of the older men smiled at her with crooked teeth. He was about fifty, and his red hair had gone mostly gray, just like mine. He said in a voice like a polished trumpet, "We are deeply indebted to you, to all of you, sir! I will settle on suitable rewards tomorrow. I understand your name is Bib." He coughed, covering up a laugh.

I didn't have time for this shit. "Yes, Your Majesty, I am Bib, from a family of Bibs. My father was Bib, and my mother was too, and we're Bibs going back ten generations. I was told the Pierce family from Sandell is here. Are they?"

He took a step back, his eyes wide, but then he smiled and glanced at the older man on his right. "The Pierces? Didn't someone named Pierce give me a gift, Gradel? The mother was a charming woman. She was a polite guest and smarter than most of my wise men. She threw dice like a demon too. Oh." His smile fell off. "I think maybe they left."

I took a few seconds to get a real breath. "When, Your Majesty? And where did they go?"

"A week ago? Maybe two, I think." He turned to the man on his left. "Or three?"

The man smiled weakly and nodded while shrugging.

"I'll say three." The king gave me a cheery smile. "I haven't an idea about where they went, though. Enough talk about traveling families. I want to talk about the war."

I ignored the king and started planning the fastest way to question every person in the city, starting at the palace.

Jon spoke up from across the room. "I beg pardon for the interruption, Your Majesty. I have knowledge of where the Pierce family went."

TWENTY-FIVE

I stared across the room at Jon. "Did you say you know where that family is?"

He smiled. It was a thin smile sitting on his thin, cultured face. "I do."

"Tremendous. Where are they?"

Jon said, "Just now, His Majesty wishes to talk about the war. You should remind me about this family business later."

"Don't worry, I won't let him forget," King Elgus said. "Not at all."

"Yes, Your Majesty," I said, as I ignored him and walked straight toward Jon, knocking a chair out of the way.

Jon grinned when a guard leveled his spear at me. Five seconds later, the guard bounced off one of the stone columns. I kept walking, and Jon's grin faded as he took a step back.

In the seconds I had taken to deal with the guard, Acton had sprinted ahead of me. He reached back to hold one palm in front of my chest as he faced Jon. I could have run Acton down, or thrown him aside, or cut off his hand, but instead I stopped.

Acton bowed to the king and gave Jon a little bow too. "Your Majesty, this information about the Pierce family and discussing the war are one and the same. The two are integral to one another, as I'm sure you will see better than any of us once all is laid upon the table."

The king grunted. "Fine."

"I beseech Your Majesty to see that this is not in any way fine!" Jon said. "This boy is starting to use logic upon us, and that is something I will not have."

Acton nodded to King Elgus. "The king knows what is logical and what is not. I do not presume to instruct him about such things."

Jon said, "I didn't hear anyone invite you into His Majesty's war room, boy."

The guards had placed themselves between the room's occupants and us. The sorcerers had fallen back to the corners of the room.

"Bib was invited, and I am his bodyguard and strategist. Therefore, the invitation was implied." Acton nodded to the king.

"Let me handle this," I growled to Acton. He ignored me.

Jon said, "I don't know why this ridiculous Bib was invited, either."

The king said, "Hold on, Jon, I asked you to—"

"In fact," Jon interrupted, "I cannot see how either of them will improve—"

Acton cut in next. "The king wasn't finished speaking, my lord."

The pretty girl in the fur robe smiled at Acton as if he had killed a lion for her with his teeth.

"Stop talking!" the king shouted. We all shut up and bowed with varying degrees of depth and deference.

I turned back toward Jon and drew my sword three inches out of the scabbard. I gave him a satisfied smile.

The king asked, "Where did those nice, generous people go, Jon?"

Jon pursed his lips. "In the context of our war plans, they are roughly at— if things haven't changed, of course, and these days what doesn't change?"

I roared, "Where the hell are they?"

"Impoliteness will avail you nothing," Jon said.

The king laughed. "If anybody should know about impoliteness, it would be you, Jon!"

The guards held their weapons tight and were shifting their weight to stay prepared. The sorcerers kept glancing at each other. Jon's three hangers-on had stepped in front of him so that I'd have to go through them if I wanted to kill him. The girl had scampered around the table, and I saw that she was holding the king's arm. She lifted her chin and stared at Jon, but her head was quivering.

I had a moment of horrible insight. "May I say one thing to clarify the situation, Your Majesty?"

"You may," the king said.

I nodded at the girl, who was clutching the king's arm with both hands. "Your Highness, you needn't feel compelled to marry anybody you don't want to." I glanced at Jon. "There are people skilled at resolving such problems."

The girl stared at me for a moment before her face relaxed into an enormous smile.

The king said something about punishing me, but I didn't pay much attention. Jon and his three dancing maidens were shouting death threats, and I wondered whether I could use that as a pretext for killing them one by one until somebody told me where the Pierces were. Four of the guards were shouting for us to leave the room, while the other two were yelling for us to stand still.

That situation proved to be placid compared to what happened next.

It started with faint rumbling beneath our feet. Acton stared at the floor right away, and so did the two sorcerers. It might have been instructive to note how much longer it took each person to feel the rumble. However, the deep tremble resolved into the crash and clatter of stone-floor paving being broken and thrown through the air.

An alert guard jumped in front of the king and stopped a head-size stone that would have smashed Elgus in the chest. The guard crumpled, probably dead. Another stone struck the girl on the shoulder and sent her spinning. Two more guards slipped and fell, all the king's friends thumped to the floor, and two of Jon's men dropped. Jon himself stood wide-eyed but otherwise unaffected. Shura had been standing by the door and ran out of the room, showing the fine survival instincts that had allowed her to reach her advanced age.

Acton had been peppered by small- and medium-size pieces of paving stones. A few hit his face, which bloomed with bloody little wounds. He staggered aside but had shielded me from most of the stones.

An enormous wolf's head with a crazily pointed jaw, definitely monstrous, pushed out of the hole into the room. Black fur, bristly like a broom, covered its four-foot-long legs and its narrow shoulders, with a stripe of red fur down its back and covering the tail. The entire beast must have been fifteen feet long from snout to tail tip.

The creature squinted around until it spotted me. Then it howled, and everybody in the room either staggered or curled up in a ball. With the help of Pil's ring, I understood that the howl meant, "I'm getting your hand and killing everybody else!"

I drew my sharp sword as I backed away. Part of the stone ceiling fell on top of the monster, certainly a gift from one of the sorcerers. However, the creature seemed not to notice. It gathered to jump at me, and I scrambled to put a stone column between us. Acton had run to the other side of the monster from me, but since he couldn't set fire to flesh, he was limited in how he could attack the thing. He drew his sword of green flame and swung at the monster but missed.

An insanely brave guard charged the creature, who knocked him down with one paw and then killed him with a single bite. People all around the room began struggling upright or shaking themselves out of a daze. I twisted around the column and thrust my sword into the creature's side, but it was moving away. I pierced it deeply, but it ignored that wound just like it had ignored the falling ceiling.

Nobody was charging in to help me now, showing that they were far wiser than I had believed. Acton was shuffling about to get a good view of the monster, but when he thrust his blade, it slipped off the monster's hide.

In the corner, Jon was shouting, "Kill it! Kill it!"

I ran to another stone column, weaving around a big table. The monster knocked the table across the room with one paw and then followed me around the column, snapping its jaws.

That gave me a preposterous idea. I bent down and grabbed a fallen guard's sword. Now I had a sword in each hand. "Acton! Get ready!"

"Get ready for what?" He didn't sound calm anymore.

I didn't bother answering. I thrust the guard's sword at the creature's face. Since it wanted my hand, I figured it wouldn't hesitate to eat my sword and the hand holding it. I let go and yanked back just before the monster's jaws snapped down on my flesh. Then I hurled myself backward as fast as I could.

"Now!" I shouted, but Acton was ahead of me. He ignited the sword so that it blazed white-hot inside the wolf's maw. The heat was harsh on my face ten feet away. The beast convulsed, howled, and shook its head as it crawled back into the hole, collapsing the tunnel behind it. I don't know whether we killed it, but it left behind a nasty smell of burnt hair and flesh.

I made a show of dusting myself off and strolling around the hole toward the king's table like I was wandering at a village fair. "Well, Your Majesty, I'd say that the war has come inside your city. I'm glad we were here to strike down your horrible enemy. You're welcome." I turned to Jon and lowered my voice until it was full of threat. "Where are they? I have another sword here, and it will fit perfectly in somebody else's mouth."

Jon swallowed and then gave me what might've been a smile. "They sailed north a week ago. As you know, there's nothing but small islands in that direction for a thousand miles."

That sort of made sense. If Pil's family wanted to escape the fighting, one way was to escape the main island.

Jon said, "There's nothing else to the north, but the enemy's camp is northwest. Possibly these Pierces are traitors."

"I'm going to let that go," I said. "I'll just ask them how kindly they want me to treat you later."

King Elgus stood up from where his daughter had fallen, and he helped her stand too. She looked pale but was lucky beyond reason if that stone hadn't hurt her badly.

"I suppose this works out. In a way, that is." Elgus wiped sweat off his chin. "The best approach to the enemy is by sea. Since we must destroy the enemy's main camp, we can keep watch for these Pierce people as we sail past. Not the perfect circumstance, but we could have worse."

"We are not yet prepared to invade, Your Majesty." Jon smiled but glanced at the smoking hole in the floor. "My spy tells me that the enemy will concentrate his forces, but that might change now that we have broken the siege. I don't have enough recent details."

Shura, who had returned at some point, spoke up: "We need to scout the area!"

"Yes, that's wise." The king smiled at me. "This may be perfect. The scout needs to sail north and then come around. It will make them seem more innocent. We need someone capable to handle this scouting business." He pointed at me. "That person should be you."

The plans had run out of the king's mouth like mud off a roof, and they were just as valuable. However, once I was at sea, I could ignore everything he'd said. "I'll scout." I almost added a dashing smile but remembered my teeth just in time.

"But Your Majesty," Jon said, "how can we trust this man with such an important mission? We know nothing of him."

The pretty girl stretched up and whispered something to the king.

The king nodded slowly. "Jon, you're correct, and that's very insightful. Somebody must keep an eye on him. You go with him."

Jon flinched. "But I would be far more useful here training and organizing the army, Your Majesty."

The king frowned. "Who do you suggest I send? Snip? The bishop? No, somebody of great skill and unswerving loyalty is required."

"But Your Majesty—"

The king raised his voice. "You will go! Do you understand?"

Jon nodded, looking down.

The girl looked hard into my eyes and then glanced toward Jon. I realized that she was urging me to murder Jon when we went scouting.

I gave her the tiniest of nods.

Her face opened in a tremendous smile. After a couple of seconds, she turned it entirely on Acton.

The king said, "That is excellent! Somebody, call a servant to fill in this hole before someone breaks a leg or we lose a dog."

I asked, "Your Majesty, where is the enemy's camp?"

"Krak Hill, south of Bearing Bone Point."

I cleared my throat. "Maybe I'm misremembering, but isn't that place considered impregnable?"

The king said, "That used to be true. You will travel there to determine why that reputation must be wrong."

TWENTY-SIX

Acton and I returned to our companions before dawn and found that Kenzie had recovered from healing Vargo. However, she was not as pleased as she could have been. She was shouting profanity at Vargo, who clung to her left wrist with both hands as if it were a pole that kept him from drowning. He didn't say a thing to answer her abuse, and he stared at the ground the whole time.

As I walked up, Kenzie pulled her knife and pressed it against Vargo's throat. "I will kill you and kill you again if you don't let me loose of your nasty, murdering hands right this moment!"

Vargo twitched but didn't release her or pull away from the knife.

Acton ran to grab Vargo around the waist. "Evonne, help me pull him free!"

Together, Acton, Evonne, and Kenzie pried Vargo's fingers loose and pulled him away.

Vargo thrashed and growled like an animal, smacking Evonne in the eye as he flailed. He pulled free and rushed back to Kenzie. She shifted, aimed, and kicked him hard in the crotch. He groaned but grabbed her ankle as she pulled away. Then he lay at her feet, motionless except for panting, with her ankle clamped in both his hands.

Kenzie gave a short scream of frustration. "Hand me something heavy! I'm going to pound him to pieces!"

I said, "Did you think to ask yourself why he's doing this?"

"We asked him why! He just played grabby hands!" Kenzie snapped.

"Oh, he can't answer you," I said. "Here's something else that your teachers forgot to teach you. When a Caller saves somebody on the edge of death, once in a great while, the almost-dead person becomes bound to the Caller."

Acton stared down at Vargo, who still hadn't moved. "Bound? What does that mean? I've never heard of it."

"Like I said, your masters didn't explain it, and there's not much chance that a sparrow will land on your shoulder now to chat about the nuances of sorcery."

Kenzie said, "What is it, then? And how do I pry him loose?"

"You can't, unless you kill him. He has come back to full life and, for reasons we don't understand, is terrified all the time. He feels the only thing keeping him alive is the Caller who healed him, and he's compelled to touch that person at all times."

Evonne whistled in amazement.

Acton said, "Lutigan's bloody knuckles."

Kenzie shook her foot as if she were kicking off dried mud. Vargo hung on and moved wherever the foot pushed him.

Kenzie said, "I don't want to kill him, but I can't live like this."

I laughed. Kenzie looked both hurt and offended. I said, "It's not permanent. It shouldn't last more than a couple of days, or maybe three, and it will gradually get better until it goes away. This is as bad as it will get."

Kenzie grimaced and straightened her shoulders. "All right. I'll try not to cut off his hands before then."

"That wouldn't help. He'd just cling to you with his arms, lay his face against your back, even clamp onto your clothes with his teeth. It's all been tried and is well documented." I didn't tell her about the few documented cases in which binding went on and on until one of the two died. "Don't be afraid to reason with him, or at least try to make him understand simple things. Just imagine that he's as terrified as a person can get without dying of fear. Because he is."

After I brushed my horse, I walked back and saw Kenzie whispering to Vargo as he moved his grip hand by hand from her ankle to her forearm. I had also failed to warn her that these bindings sometimes resulted in strong friendships, or more than friendships, that lasted until real death. For example, Pil and I bonded this way within an hour of the first time we met.

The next morning, Jon leaned toward me across a damp dockside barrel and snarled, "Damn your people, and damn you!"

"My people are never more dangerous than when we've been damned."

"What do you mean? To yourselves?" Dawn was skimming sunlight across the harbor, making half of Jon's face just about glow while the other half lay in near darkness.

He deserved a chuckle for that, and I gave it to him. "The king commanded us to travel together, and my people are coming along with me. You can't squeeze in more than four of your flunkies unless you want us to capsize and drown. Although I suppose you could find us a ship instead of a longboat."

"And triple the danger of being seen?" he sneered.

I gazed around the dockside, which stank of pitch and sea salt about like every other dock I had stood upon. Laborers were loading provisions into our longboat. We could pack it with more than twelve people if we wanted. But if the weather turned harsh during our two-day sail to the beach nearest Krak Hill and then the two-day sail back, we might well be swamped.

"All right," I said, "you go find another sneaky boat like ours to carry the rest of your regiment." It wasn't really a regiment. He just wanted to bring himself, ten of his most loyal throat-cutters, and me.

Jon stood and drew a hissing breath. "I refuse to be outnumbered by you and your criminals on this boat."

"Jon, you won't be!" I said, as if I were explaining how a wagon wheel works. "You'll have four men, I'll have four men and women, and we'll have two crewmen to get us there."

"And back! Do not think that you're going to kill me on the beach!"

That was exactly what I intended to do. But I didn't need an advantage in numbers to kill this bent twig of a man. I was just arguing to see him turn red. "How about this, Jon?"

"You shall address me as my lord!"

"How about this, Jon my lord? You're a true child of the island, so you can sail anything that's wet on only one side, right? We'll dismiss the crew. Then you and I will sail the boat, which gives you room for two more of your men."

"Very well." He said it as if he'd swept the battlefield, and I wondered what I had missed. He went on: "I find that to be acceptable if we are accompanied by two additional boats for the rest of my escort."

I nodded, reminding myself that when it came time to ignore our orders and go searching for Pil's family, we could deal with Jon's two boats then. Not many wooden vessels can withstand a few lightning strikes. Then once Kenzie called some fish to leap, fly, and stun Jon and his men, Vargo and I would end them with the sword.

Alamore wouldn't be sitting cozy in the kitchen with Pil's family, of course. But after I saw them safe, I would track Alamore down like he was a spindly stag.

I smiled at Jon and held out my hand, which he ignored. "Jon my lord, that is acceptable to me. I know you'll want to supervise the provisioning yourself, since you don't trust me worth a damn. I'll be in that alehouse if you want to yell at me about something."

I winked at Acton as I turned away. Jon and his men found me more aggravating than hot wax on the eyeballs, so Acton would observe the loading for us. Evonne intended to keep hidden and board the boat at the last moment. If Jon and his men discovered her and wanted to toss her overboard, we could defend her.

The young lady in fur from the night before turned out to be Princess Bannice, and she had sent word before dawn that she wanted to visit us this morning. She had arrived while Jon and I were chewing on each other's asses. Now she stood chatting with Acton, flanked by four guards.

I dipped my head to Bannice. "Welcome to what must be the nastiest part of your kingdom, Your Highness. We mean well, though."

"I believe you do." Her voice was strong and surprisingly deep for such a slight woman. I put her at about eighteen years old, more or less. Last night in the midst of threatening Jon and destroying giant wolves, I had thought her pretty, and indeed she would be one of the prettiest girls in any village. Of course, she had never worked in a field or chased pigs, so that stood to her advantage.

Bannice surprised me by reaching to put her hand on my arm. Her guards stiffened. "Bib, you and Acton saved many of our people, certainly my father, and possibly me."

I had also saved my hand from being bitten off, but I didn't say that. "You can't let monsters go around crushing and eating people, Your Highness. It encourages them to truly bad behavior."

"That is the case with some people as well, isn't it?" She glanced at the dock where Jon was kicking a laborer.

"Killing is a surprisingly easy way to address such things," I said. "I have employed it far more often than I should." I didn't know why I said such a thing to her. It had just leaped out of my mouth. "It often requires still more killing and then more, and maybe it creates problems worse than the first one. I wish I could embrace it less often."

I realized that Pil had said these sorts of things to me and had done it more than once. I had agreed with her every time. I had forgotten it all every time I drew my sword.

Bannice's mouth was open as she glanced back and forth between Jon and me.

I waved a hand. "It doesn't apply to vermin, though. Nobody misses vermin."

She smiled again and squeezed my forearm before turning to Acton. "I am sorry, sir, that you were wounded defending us."

Acton's brows drew together, and he pursed his lips until she gestured toward his face. "Oh, it wasn't much. I had already forgotten about it, Your Highness."

She reached back, and a guard placed a small porcelain pot in her hand. "This unguent will help you heal and relieve your pain. I mixed it myself."

Acton's cheeks reddened a bit, and he glanced down. He had walked with proud steps since the siege and our defeat of the wolf monster yesterday. All that confidence dried up now that he was facing the princess. He said, "Thank you, Your Highness, that's quite kind of you."

Bannice lifted the jar's lid, stepped close, and rubbed some of the clear-looking stuff on one of Acton's cuts. He couldn't have looked more mortified if he had flapped his privates for every woman in Ebring. The guards shuffled, and one cleared his throat. She ignored them.

"Does that feel better?" the princess asked, not looking away from Acton's eyes.

Acton nodded, which only enhanced Bannice's rubbing motion. "Yes, um, Your Highness."

As Bannice went on to the next cut, Kenzie walked into sight from around the corner of the alehouse, leading Vargo by her wrist. When she saw what was happening, she went so pale that her brown skin faded to washed-out tan. If possible, she looked more horrified than Acton. Her jaw quivered as she clenched her teeth. I didn't think we had to worry about regicide from her, but now that she was in sight, she couldn't just walk away without being dismissed. She was trapped with Bannice, Acton, Vargo, and her anger.

Well, Kenzie was a sorcerer. She didn't need my help to either shut the hell up or deal with the consequences.

When all the cuts had been salved, Bannice handed away the pot and wiped her hands on a lace handkerchief. "Thank you so much." She took both of Acton's hands in hers, which was a short hop away from a marriage proposal. "I shall pray for your safe return."

Bannice smiled at me again, then gave Kenzie an even bigger smile with a raised eyebrow before striding away with her guards.

"What just happened?" Acton asked.

"Did you not like it?" Kenzie smiled through gritted teeth. "I should have thought you would like it. You had your face mashed by a princess." She raised her eyebrows. "Just how nice was it?"

Acton whispered, "Is the princess a witch? Is my face cursed?"

"Unlikely," I said. "She's mighty clever, though. Acton, if we return with proof that you killed the earl, you can be king of Ir someday if you want."

"What crap!" Kenzie said, but her eyes were uncertain. "Acton, she is working to fool you and use you. She doesn't care about you."

"Well . . . why couldn't she care about me? Is there something wrong with me? I come from . . ." Acton faded off.

Kenzie grabbed Acton's arm so hard she shook Vargo, whose eyes were closed. "I'll explain some things to you. Come here!" She dragged Acton around the corner behind the alehouse.

I wandered along the waterside to the hut where Evonne was hiding. I knocked on the door and entered when she said I may.

The dim and nasty hut was empty, unless Evonne was hiding among the ceiling thatch or under the floor. A few seconds later, she appeared in the doorway behind me and said, "Ah, it is you. Look." She pulled aside a cloth that was hanging on the back wall, and a big hole behind it led outside. "When I tell you to come inside, I rush out and around behind you."

"Nicely done," I said. "Evonne, I want to hire you as my bodyguard."

"You need not do that. I already will protect you."

"I know, but I want to formalize it by giving you a token." I held up the fourth magic sword.

"That is an awfully big token. I think token usually means something small."

"That's true. Let's say that this is a sizable token. Before you agree, know that you may have to kill Kenzie and Acton."

She said slowly, "All right."

"I know they're our companions, but they have made a deal to kill me sometime."

"I understand." She sighed. "Do you want me to go kill them now? Now is sooner than sometime."

"No, it may end up not being necessary. I'd rather not kill them if we can avoid it."

"Bib, for me, a bodyguard exists to protect you from harm. One of the best ways to do that is to search for people who might hurt you someday and kill them first." She raised her eyebrows.

"Well . . ." I nearly said that Kenzie and Acton were almost like my children now, but then I'd end up having to admit that I had experience killing my children.

Evonne rubbed her cheek. "I could tie them up in here so we can depart without them. That would be safe for everyone, yes?"

I stared at her, and she stared back for several seconds before laughing. "I see that is not your favorite idea. As for your token, I already have a sword."

"This one is enchanted."

She stood up straight and scrutinized the blade in my hand. "Tell me of it!"

"It's a silent sword."

"You cannot hear it? That could be helpful."

"No, the sword isn't the thing that's silent. You are the one who has to be silent. If you don't speak, grunt, whisper, or even breathe when you strike, the sword is exceptionally accurate and strong. It will make terrible wounds. But if you make even a tiny sound, it will behave like a normal sword."

Evonne's eyes grew bright as she reached for the weapon, but she hesitated. "What is it called?"

"You want a name?" I scowled. "It's foolish to name a sword." When she didn't back down, I said, "It's called the Silent Sword of the Lowlands in the Dark Lands beneath the Ridge of Death. How's that?" I handed the sword to her.

"That is lovely. I will call it Silent Death."

"Wonderful. Be ready to sail at midday, and come aboard at the last minute," I said. "Please don't tie up anybody and leave them in this shack."

Before we pushed off at midday, I offered the tiller to Jon for voyage. Suspicion gathered like dust around him, and he demanded that instead he work the rigging once we stepped the mast. I wanted the tiller anyway, and I noted how easily the boob could be manipulated.

Kenzie arrived leading Vargo and walking beside Acton. Both of the sorcerers looked grim. When I left them earlier, I had thought they might settle things between them. Rosy smiles and hand-holding wouldn't have surprised me. Neither would have glares and bruised faces.

Their sober resignation puzzled me. Maybe they had decided on some noble, juvenile sacrifice to save everybody's honor and feelings. If so, they were about to face some unhappy times, because that shit never works.

Heavily cloaked, Evonne jumped aboard as we pushed off.

At last, we rowed out of the broad, deep harbor, raised the mast, and sailed northwest toward Krak Hill on the peninsula of Stinan. Another longboat like ours joined us a thousand feet to starboard, and a third paced us a thousand feet beyond that. A man in the closest boat waved, and Jon waved back, adding twenty seconds of arm signals that must have been packed with dire, secret code.

We had a fresh breeze blowing from aft with easy swells, so we made good speed. By midafternoon, I could see a green line on the horizon, which would be the far-off peninsula. I steered toward it. We had sailed at an angle away from land and now could see the rocky coast two miles to port. That eased my mind. If the wind swung around and blew hard toward land, we had room to escape being smashed to bits on the rocks.

Our boat carried two mainlanders, unaccustomed to sailing on deep water. Acton had weathered our boat voyage to Sandell with a steady stomach, but the ocean wind and swells defeated him. Soon, he and Evonne were performing a duet of vomiting over the side. Kenzie sat in front of me with her hair whipping, and Vargo sat leaning against her.

After sunset, we were thirty hours away from our destination with fair winds. Kenzie nudged my knee and pointed. Lightning was flickering far behind us. With the present wind, I judged that with the luck of Krak and all his children, we might reach land before the storm overtook us.

I leaned on those optimistic thoughts for a while until the wind jumped from a fresh breeze to a gale. Within a few minutes, the swells doubled in height. For a small vessel, stronger winds may not mean better speed. The boat was not a lengthy craft, so it rode up the fifteen-foot swells and then plunged down the face of them. Jon took in enough sail to keep us moving and undamaged. Whatever his repugnant qualities, he was a fine seaman. I steered to keep the swells coming from directly behind us so we wouldn't be struck from the side and capsize.

Soon, half of the people in the boat were seasick. The other half were bailing like mad. As the lightning came closer, Kenzie and I glanced at each other, knowing that this storm was far greater than anything we could hope to control. She stared aft, and I could feel her trying to calm the wind directly around and behind us. After a minute, the wind eased a bit, and so did the swells.

"Do you have enough power to keep this up?" I shouted.

She shrugged. "For how long?"

By the time Kenzie had struggled with the wind for nearly an hour, the bank of lightning had almost overtaken us. Lightning would almost certainly strike the mast and maybe set us afire. But if we lowered the mast, we would lose headway, be pushed crosswise with the swells, and capsize. To make things more festive, the wind had increased to a fresh gale, and the swells came at us over twenty feet high, almost as high as our mast. We nearly disappeared in the trough between each swell.

"Kenzie, take the tiller!" She had been holding both Acton and Evonne so that a roll didn't throw them overboard while Vargo clung to her leg. I grabbed them and struggled to keep them aboard as Kenzie shifted back to grasp the tiller.

Now my job was to sense when lightning was about to hit us, throw a band of power, and shift its strike point away from the boat. I had done this before often enough, but not while pitching on the ocean in a storm.

With no warning, the longboat farthest away from us was

consumed by fire in a few seconds. No lightning strike had done that. Fire smothered the entire vessel from bow to stern.

I leaned forward and grabbed Acton's shoulder. "Did you do that?"

"Do what?" He stared at me, his face sagging with as much awareness as a three-week-old corpse.

I felt lightning building in the sea just beneath us, so I summoned three white bands and pushed the strike point out to port. The bolt struck forty feet off the beam. It deafened and blinded me.

When my vision cleared, Kenzie still had the tiller. She was struggling with every swell but hadn't killed us.

"Lightning's strong, but not too strong!" I shouted at Kenzie. "You can push it!"

We swapped duties, and Kenzie crawled forward. She pulled Acton and then Evonne, who resisted as much as rag dolls, back to me and sat them in the bottom of the boat. I pinned each of them down with a foot.

Kenzie knelt in the bottom of the boat, seawater sloshing over her hips. She stared at the mast, waiting for the next lightning strike.

I bellowed at Acton and Evonne "Find something and bail!" just as eight-foot blue-white flames swarmed over the other longboat from stern to bow. Then lightning destroyed the darkness. Kenzie had shoved the bolt thirty feet away from the boat. I didn't know whether everybody else was stunned, but I sure was.

When I shook my head and could see again, I glanced aft at the center of the storm. A wall of blue-white fire erupted on the ocean's surface and raced after us. I had no magic that would affect a candle, let alone this.

The fire died away just short of our stern, but before I could embarrass myself by thanking the gods, the boat was pushed straight down into the water. It popped back up like a cork and listed forty degrees starboard. Seawater poured out over the gunwale.

With my left hand, I grabbed Evonne and kept her from sliding out of the boat. I saw at least two of Jon's men tumble over the side into the great swells, and there was no way they could have survived.

Acton slid toward the side like a wet sack of grain. Kenzie grabbed the closest thwart with one hand and Acton's collar with the other. Vargo clung to Kenzie's leg with the force of terror, which probably overcame any seasickness he might have had.

Before I could look around and assess things, the entire boat was righted and yanked straight up.

TWENTY-SEVEN

The longboat had stopped listing but swung fore and aft as if it were hanging in a harness. The night still held no moon and no stars and was almost entirely black. When I peeked over the side, I couldn't see the ocean swells. In fact, I couldn't see any hint of water or of land, either. The lightning was far behind us, and the gale had fallen off to a strong breeze.

Evonne had dragged herself up with a knife in her hand to crouch in front of me, guarding me from everybody else in the boat. Just past her, Kenzie and Acton knelt in the bottom, clinging to each other, while Vargo clung to her. When lightning flashed, I saw men still in the boat toward the bow, but I couldn't tell how many or who they were.

Looking up, Evonne yelled, "Shit shit shit shit shit!"

"What's wrong?" I asked her.

"What is *not* wrong? Look up!"

I stared straight up. "I don't see anything." It was getting colder, and I rubbed my arms.

"Look at the place where the mast used to be. Then say *shit* a lot."

I examined the sky and saw an intense nothing in the middle of all the slightly less black nothing. Distant lightning flashed again, showing for an instant something big. I glanced to the side at the next flash and saw a foot with great talons clamped onto the longboat's gunwale.

I knew what it was then, but I wasn't ready to admit it yet. I leaned close to Evonne's ear and said, "All right, shit a lot."

After a long pause, Evonne yelled over the wind, "Is this your dragon, or is it something else?"

"We could look at its forehead. History says that a real dragon has a significantly bumpy forehead."

"There are unreal dragons?" Evonne shouted. "What do they have on their foreheads?"

"Wrinkles of regret that they're not real dragons," I yelled.

We both went mildly insane and laughed until we wept.

Without warning, the longboat dropped to a sliding, grinding halt on the ground, where it listed twenty degrees to port. One sob burst out of Kenzie when the boat heeled over.

A woman's high, thin voice from outside the boat yelled, "Out! All out! Out, out, out! You want to be out of this before I burn this whole thing! Put that sword away, you bony little twerp, or you'll be wearing it up your ass!"

I jumped out of the boat, and I suppose everybody else did too. The moon broke through the clouds, and I saw this woman, tall and so skinny she might have been stretched. She poked me on the shoulder with the end of a long stick. "Line up over there!" She pointed with the stick to a spot thirty paces away from the boat.

For terrorized people who'd been nearly drowned, almost slain by lightning, and taken prisoner by a legendary creature, we lined up in an admirable fashion. Looking down the row, I saw that Jon and three of his men had survived, along with Acton, Kenzie, Evonne, Vargo, and me.

"Stay there in your bloody line," the thin woman snapped. "And mind you don't pee on yourself. Red finds that distasteful."

The dragon crawled over the empty longboat toward us with the sinewy grace of a viper. Every one of my muscles seemed to lock into place, as if my body had decided to make it easier for him to eat me. His lizard-like head stood twice my height above the ground. It was the size of a pony and rested at the end of a long neck. His body was taller than it was broad, and his forelegs were lean but muscular. I knew it must have wings, but I couldn't see them.

The lack of light prevented me from picking out more in the way of details. Once the dragon came near enough, I did see that some kind of crap was sticking out of its forehead.

When the dragon approached Jon at the other end of the line, I caught its scent: a combination of flowers, spoiled meat, and molten iron. Jon wavered on wobbly knees, but he steadied himself. The dragon stretched its neck to sniff the air above Jon's head. Then it spoke in a deep, ringing voice, "Not Food."

I wondered why it was speaking our human language.

The dragon moved down the line to Jon's three men, one of whom fell backward like a pushed-over sign. "Food. Food. Food," the dragon said as it passed the three.

At Acton, the dragon paused. "Not Food." When he reached Kenzie and Vargo, for both he said, "Not Food." He sniffed Evonne and said, "Food."

At first, the dragon didn't look down at me, but I looked at him. Many of his sharp upper teeth were longer than my hand, lapping down over his lower lip. His nostrils were great, dark ovals, and the underside of his neck was far lighter than the top. Then he sniffed me, turned his head to examine me with one eye, and said, "Food."

The dragon's wings snapped out from its sides where they had been folded like fans. Swirls and eddies of color that glowed brighter than moonlight shifted across the wings, but I could also make out the longboat through the wings themselves. I admired the allure of them while I considered ways to save Evonne and myself from being eaten.

The thin woman whacked me on the calves with her stick. "All you Food! Go over there to that cave! Now, Food!"

The dragon launched itself into the sky with a thunderclap of noise from its wings and a gust of wind that slammed us at storm strength. As we walked toward the cave, Evonne caught my eye and touched her scabbarded sword. I shook my head slightly. I didn't want to count on the dragon being careless. If he hadn't disarmed us, he may have contempt for our weapons. Maybe we could kill him with magic weapons. Maybe not.

I said to the tall woman, "I'm not sure I ought to be named Food. I have skills that might be useful. My name—"

She swung at me, and I struggled to stand still while she whacked my cheek with her stick. "Shut your jaws! Red should eat you first, you stringy clot, and I'll tell him so!"

If I could trust what this woman was saying, the dragon was male and named Red.

Once we had shuffled into the cave, the thin woman tied a small rope across the entrance. It couldn't have kept a crawling baby inside. Then she walked fifty feet away and stood guard with her back to the cave.

Jon's men whispered arguments in a spirited way for a couple of minutes. I overheard them saying, "Gut her . . ." and "Once his lordship starts . . ." One of them turned to us and said, "We're escaping while we can. I don't care what kind of nasty criminals you are, I won't leave you here to be eaten. Come."

This time, Evonne shook her head at me, and I agreed.

Jon's men slipped under the rope with swords drawn and crept out to murder the thin woman. When they reached halfway, the dragon leaped on them from someplace without warning—but with plenty of screams and bone cracking. I believe the dragon smashed each of them with a separate clawed foot, leaving his fourth foot artistically free.

The dragon then ate them. It was an appalling event, and we turned away until the horrific crunching and smacking ended.

TWENTY-EIGHT

Evonne and I stood in the back of our oblong cave, which was just ten paces wide by fifteen deep. We faced the moonlit doorway from the darkest part of the cave, our swords drawn and sure that nothing could save us if the dragon decided he still felt peckish.

I summoned a white band and tossed it out to explore. Our cave had been dug into the side of a flattish, roughly bowl-shaped area the size of a small village. It was set high on Mount Seppal, one of the tallest mountains on Ir, and the sides of the bowl ran from twenty to fifty feet high with no gaps. A few small trees and some hardy brush speckled the bowl's floor.

More rough caves had been dug into the walls of the bowl. I dared to peek out and saw Jon, Kenzie, and the others outside across the way, huddled together beside the wall. The thin woman and a man were just in view, sleeping beside a fire at the mouth of another cave. Besides the complement of vermin and birds normal for a high area, a stout pen with lots of goats and a few yaks stood across the clearing from us.

Nothing about this place seemed natural, and I concluded that somebody had excavated it all.

Ir is a cold land. High up in the mountains, it's as cold as hell—and sitting on a stone floor didn't make it any warmer. Evonne shivered hard enough to chip teeth, but Pil's ring kept me warm. When her hands and feet became numb, we began trading off wearing the ring and also clung together for warmth. Amorous thoughts were as unlikely as drinking beer at the bottom of the ocean.

I found nothing likely to help us escape. The trees and brush were pathetically flimsy. A combined goat-yak charge might distract the dragon for a few seconds if he had a sense of humor. Even with great determination, the entire vermin population might not be large enough to assault the dragon's throat and choke him to death.

The only reliable magic for me would be the weather. However, I hadn't yet puzzled out how wind, lightning, snow, or fog would get us over the wall and down the mountain safely.

Evonne said, "I can see that you are planning our escape."

"I've hit upon a few possibilities," I said. "To escape being eaten alive, we might kill each other. Or we could choke ourselves to death on some sharp and nasty brush. I think we could form a human ladder, pull each other to the top of the wall, and throw ourselves off the mountain. That one is my favorite so far, but only because it's stylish."

Evonne laughed. "I think I like you better than almost any other man I have met."

"I'm too old for you."

She slapped my shoulder. "Yes, and you're in love with someone. I am also in love with someone, and I soon will see him unless we can be quite clever." She set her jaw, and her voice became hard. "Can we trade something to this dragon? Something he cannot get unless he frees us?"

"That's worth exploring."

Over the next hour, we thought of things we might trade. Dragons were said to like gold, but we didn't have much. We had magic swords but were vague on how a dragon might use them and why he would want them. We didn't know enough about Jon to effectively betray him in exchange for our freedom. Maybe the dragon liked riddles or games and would free us if we won. I suggested that I could sing or recite poetry. Evonne laughed at me until her tears ran.

The difficulty in all this was that the dragon could just take any nice thing he wanted and then crunch us up when he felt like it.

One possibility that I didn't mention to Evonne was binding the dragon, just the way I had bound Kruppin. The big problem, of course, was finding out the dragon's real name, because it probably wasn't Red. The enormous problem was that I couldn't imagine a more fearsome creature to bind. The greatest problem of all was that maybe the dragon was simply impervious to binding, and I would end up standing there smiling with my metaphorical privates hanging out.

"I feel beaten like a lazy husband," I said. "I'm going to sleep so that I'm alert enough to escape or at least make the dragon kill me before he eats me."

Evonne agreed. She and I slept, pressed together and shivering. We woke to trade the ring from time to time. I told myself that yesterday morning I had been insulting Jon on the docks of Ebring, and that was infinitely more amusing than this.

Sunlight was angling in through the cave mouth when the thin woman woke me with, "Out! Out! Out, Food! Come!" I reached my feet, and she swung her stick at my head. I leaned back and let it pass, which didn't seem to bother her. In daylight, I saw that her face looked stretched too, although her eyes looked hard, and she had lovely, vibrant red hair.

Evonne and I walked into the sunlight, which felt better than drinking whiskey while wrapped up in blankets with a dog that loves you. Thin Woman herded us across the bowl to join Acton, Jon, Kenzie, and Vargo in a line. Acton and Kenzie stood as far apart as possible, looking away from each other.

Jon glared at Thin Woman and even bared his teeth. I had thought that dragon captivity might make him collapse in despair, but he just stood straighter than normal with clenched fists.

A balding man with a red beard and mustache limped over to face us, supporting himself with a cane. His worn shirt and trousers hung loose under belts crossed over his chest. Six knives hung in sheaths from the belts.

Leaning on his cane, he held back a yawn. "Morning, I'm Pink." He pointed at the woman. "She is Helline. You who are food, your name's now Food. Everybody else, your name's Not-Food. Do you understand? Nod or something."

His voice struggled along almost aimlessly, but it wasn't shaky. "Pay attention." He twisted left, pulled out a knife, and threw it in one motion. The knife struck a bent tree thirty feet away. A ball of both flame and lightning erupted from it with a bang that rattled my eyes, and the tree exploded, throwing splinters in all directions.

Pink shrugged while Helline retrieved his knife. "Some of you brought weapons. Just imagine that the tree had a sword and a crossbow. Your weapons will avail you no more than the tree's weapon did. And even were you to kill me, you'd be killed right after, so what would you have gained? You're all now servants of the dire and stupendous Red. Serve him well for one thousand days, and you'll go free with a big sack of treasure. Except for Food." He shrugged. "Sorry. You're being saved for later." He took a deep breath and seemed to sag. "Don't play the troupe of village idiots and make me kill you. It sort of hurts my feelings."

Helline shook her stick. "Bothers me not a bit! I prefer you dead."

Pink pointed at Acton and Evonne. "Go feed the goats." He pointed at Kenzie and Vargo. "You two. Go with Helline. You other two, come with me."

Jon and I followed Pink into one of the larger caves. He grabbed a lantern off a table and lit it from a brazier. "This day, you care for the hoards." Right away, I imagined an impossible mountain of gold and treasure.

We walked through the deep cave, passing several darkened doorways. Just after a left-hand turn, Pink stepped through a doorway.

"The hoard . . ." Jon whispered.

We walked into a chamber of modest size. The hoard was not as impressive as I had imagined. Lantern light showed the room crammed full of buckets, barrels, and tubs.

"Gods!" Jon said. "Are they full of gold?"

Pink laughed until he wheezed, then laughed some more. "They are the hoard, dimwit! One of the hoards, anyway."

I scanned the room. "History says that dragons collect gold."

"Oh, they do," Pink said. "They gather up darn near anything that catches their fancy. This is Red's Outdoor Things That Hold Water hoard. Awfully complete too. It's held in esteem."

I didn't know what to say, and I don't suppose Jon did, either.

"Grab those rags in that bucket and start polishing. When I come back, I don't want to see dust. And make that lantern light shine off the wood."

I picked up a soft square of cloth.

Pink said, "If you do a good job, tomorrow maybe I'll take you to Red's Skeletons of Animals That Get Eaten by Other Animals hoard." He left the room, leaving the lantern behind.

Jon and I stared at the collection, then at each other, then at the collection again. At last, he said, "I should employ this lantern to set everything ablaze and blame you. You are Food, and it will be perceived as an act of defiance from a doomed person. Pink would not believe that you're innocent."

"That's clever, except you'd never leave this room alive."

"If you wish to settle things in that fashion, meet me in the hallway and we shall duel properly." Jon drew his sword as he marched out of the room.

A guttering roar more profound than a lion's echoed from someplace toward the main cave mouth. Jon marched back into the room quite a bit faster than he left.

"Do you want to take the tubs or the buckets?" I asked.

After an hour or so of silent polishing, Jon asked, "Why are you such a repugnant traitor? It seems like a bad choice."

"Why are you such a cruel, grasping toad? That's not among the best choices I've seen.

"Toad? You impudent . . . I should kill you right here!"

"I'll hold this tub in front of me. What will the dragon say if you get blood on it?"

"You are not humorous in the least!"

"Believe me, I know that."

Jon snapped, "Yet you persist in playing the ass who strives to be mirthful!"

"If somebody stays around in spite of my poor humor, I know they love me."

Jon opened his mouth and closed it. "No one can love you when you hate your kingdom."

"I admit that my love for Ir has waned. I don't hate the kingdom, though. I fought pretty hard for it at Sandell."

"But you were undisciplined! We shall never save the kingdom with such a lack of discipline."

The bastard was right about that, so I ignored it. "War and politics are relatively unimportant pursuits."

"Barbarian. What of your family?"

"All dead."

"Including your wife?"

"None of your damn business."

"Ah, then she is."

I raised my voice. "Is your arranged marriage to the princess just naked ambition? I don't think she cares any more for you than she does a bunion."

Jon shouted, "Elgus is a weak king, and we are fighting a desperate war! Among all the nobility, only I am strong enough to lead the kingdom, and the princess is the path to the throne! You must be able to understand that."

"I understand. You'll use her because you're arrogant and think you're always right!"

He shouted back, "You abandon the kingdom because you're arrogant and think you're always right!"

"Damn right! We suck!" I yelled.

Jon laughed, but I didn't see much humor in all this. He cleared his throat. "My condolences on the loss of your wife. Once I am married, I will never again see the woman I love."

"That buys you no pity from me," I said.

"And none for you," he responded. "These confessions mean nothing. I shall still kill you one day."

"Not without a troop of horsemen and a catapult."

We turned away from each other and polished like mad while I rolled the conversation in my head. Maybe Jon and I were too much alike to be anything but enemies. The thought nauseated me, but that didn't make it false. Still, he was a cruel son of a bitch, and I had to hope that I wasn't that cruel.

Hours later, Pink returned with another lantern. Ours had burned dry a little while earlier. He looked around the room and wiped at various barrels and tubs, but he didn't seem too enthusiastic about it. Then he led us back out of the cave.

I stepped into the late afternoon light, which strained my eyes for a time. Then I saw the entire dragon, all one hundred feet of him standing thirty paces away.

His neck was twenty feet long and his tail forty feet. The body stood over ten feet high at the crown of his back. Several short, black ridges ran from head to tail. The skin looked tough and scaly, and four two-jointed legs ended in wide feet with four claws each.

The dragon's mouth contained prominent teeth the length of my hand. A black ridge ran across his skull above the eyes, and four black, flopped-over things like short tentacles protruded from the ridge.

The most surprising aspect of Red's appearance was that he was not red. He was bright blue at the nose, shading to medium blue at the shoulders and farther back. His entire self was shaded lighter below than on top, and his skin was sparsely spotted with irregular white blotches.

The dragon's eyes were quite a lot larger than an apple, and in the daylight, I could appreciate how they almost glowed orange. His eyes also looked right at me from eight feet high, since he had brought his head low enough to speak with Lossil, who was standing right the hell there in front of him.

I didn't dare gape at Lossil, lest this dragon think I was rude. But I didn't understand why Lossil was here, or how he'd gotten here so fast. Were he and the dragon allies? Did Lossil serve him? Or was Lossil the master who went places flying on a dragon?

Maybe none of that mattered, because if this dragon joined the war, the people of Ir would be lost.

Lossil pointed at me. In the same language he had spoken with Burrud, Lossil said, "That's him, Red. You should kill him immediately."

TWENTY-NINE

Like any person, I fear death. Death will come no matter which way we jump, and it will do things to us that we can't predict or know until death has overrun us. The gods try to bribe us with promises of an afterlife, but I doubt they can manage it. They can't even throw a party without half a dozen murders.

Maybe a being exists that created us and loves us. If so, I'm sure the gods have done everything they can to hide the existence of somebody like that.

For a person who carries around the God of Death's weapon, and who has killed in a prodigious fashion, I hardly know a thing about death—not the important things, anyway. I have often walked the edge of death, and I possess no particular qualities that have saved me other than sorcery and luck. I should have died three times before I was sixteen, and the fact that I lived past twenty is a slap in the face of probability.

At some point in my life, I decided that in any dangerous situation, I would assume that I was already dead. It let me push some of the fear out of my mind, making room for ideas that would help me survive until the next time I almost died.

When Lossil advised Red the dragon to kill me right away, Red fixed me with his malicious orange eyes. At that moment, all my fancy ideas about assuming I was dead crashed as if they had fallen off a cliff. Instead, I imagined the dragon's teeth tearing my flesh as the unmannered creature began eating, ignoring many other better-tasting meals. I peed a little, or maybe more than a little.

I kept enough willpower to control one thing: I held my face still. If I reacted to what Red and Lossil were saying, they would know that I understood them. I would lose my greatest, and probably my only, advantage. Fortunately, I had eavesdropped on the gods many times while pretending utter ignorance.

Red spoke in a language I began to think of as the dragon language, and the charm on Pil's ring let me understand it. When he wasn't making announcements, such as telling people they were Food, the dragon's voice was softer than I expected and rather musical. "Kill him? I planned to eat him, but you're going out of your way to say I should kill him. What's wrong with him?"

Lossil looked away and mouthed something, maybe a curse. "I admit he looks harmless, but he killed enough troops to stall our assault on Sandell."

Red flicked his black tongue. "Horror. How many did he kill?"

"One hundred forty-three."

Red lifted his head and peered down his snout at me.

From the far wall, Acton shouted in our language, "He's a dangerous sorcerer! Kill him, or you'll be dead by tomorrow!"

Kenzie nodded, although her face was downcast.

This was their strike against me. I glared at them but had to admire how they jumped on this opportunity to kill me for Baby Harik without risking themselves. They would be clever sorcerers if they survived. If I survived this, their odds of reaching age twenty plummeted. The laws of probability would be pleased.

Red turned his head to stare at Acton. The young sorcerer yelled again about how bad and nasty I was until Red made a chuffing sound and six feet of flame shot out of his nose. Everybody froze, including Lossil, Pink, and Helline.

"Are those two people enemies of this man?" Red twisted his tail over his back and pointed with it at Acton and Kenzie.

Lossil shook his head. "Two days ago, they all fought as comrades."

Red leaped toward me, and I cowered. He snatched me in the talons of one foot and launched us both into the air amid the thunder of his wings. The world whipped around below me in crazy circles as Red climbed a thousand feet or more in under a minute.

He landed on a steeply sloped clearing near the peak of the mountain, and there he released me. The two of us fit in the clearing together if we didn't mind breathing each other's air. If he decided to breathe fire now, I'd be immolated.

If I brought out the Death God's sword, I might be able to kill Red. But if it turned out to be another of those sausage-waving situations, he might eat me right here. Even if I did kill him, how would I get down from this mountaintop?

Red settled himself on his belly and curled his tail around. He extended one foot and stretched one claw at a time to show how he would deal with misbehavior. "Sit," he said in a relaxed tone, using my native language.

I sat and managed not to look like a baby bird falling out of the nest as I did it.

The dragon sniffed. "So, you kill a lot of people, do you?"

"I have."

"Me too. I cannot understand the likes of you, though. I would never kill another dragon."

"I guess people aren't dragons." I winced. It was a true statement but a stupid, pointless thing to say. I pulled in a deep breath. "These days, I regret killing more than I once did."

"Who do you most wish you hadn't killed?" Red opened his mouth a bit, and I felt his hot breath on my face.

I didn't hesitate. "My daughter."

The dragon pushed his nose almost into my face, sniffed, and raised his voice. "Your daughter? Goodness, what's wrong with you?"

I shrugged.

"That wasn't some sad, rhetorical question! What's wrong with you?" He turned his head to examine me with one eye.

"That's a hell of a question."

"If you're smart, you'll give me a hell of an answer. If you lie to me, I shall know it!"

A lie had almost come out of my mouth, but I reconsidered. There was no reason to agonize, though. I blurted out, "I'm afraid I wasted most of my life doing the wrong thing."

"Stop doing the wrong thing, then!" Red growled loud enough to hurt my ears. "If I don't eat you, that is."

Wind slammed me from the side as something gargantuan whipped past us. Another dragon soared up over the peak and began circling it. I craned my neck and blinked at it with my mouth open, trying to fit two dragons into my picture of the world when a few hours ago, it had none.

This dragon was rusty red and twenty or thirty feet longer than Red, who rose to his feet but didn't take to the air.

The new dragon shouted in a voice like a deep horn, "Red, I see you plotting against me there! You traitor, you! Making sneaky plans with this sneaky sorcerer. Oh, I can tell, don't you doubt it! Maybe you're the one who can't tell, but I'll not be fooled!"

Red yelled, "Roll that fat tongue back in your head, One! If I want to sneak, I will sneak, and damn you to snow and thunder. I'll sneak with whomever I wish!"

"Oh . . . let me have him, Red. Please," One wheedled. Then he flipped over and dove toward me.

Red leaped forward so that I was hidden under his belly. "No, you may not! Don't you dare try to take this one too! He's mine."

Dragon One pulled up and hovered above us, his wings flapping about once a second. I judged that to be physically impossible for such a heavy creature, but Red shouldn't have been able to carry away a longboat, either. Dragons must have been magical down to their bones.

Dragon One shouted, "Take him, then, just take him, and may you choke on him! If you bring him out, Forty-three will turn the little twaddy into a steaming puddle!" One nosed over and glided away toward the mountain to the south, Mount Vidare.

I scooted out from under Red on my back. "A friend?"

Red brought his head around almost into my face. Smoke wafted out of his nose, and I sneezed. "Are you worth anything at all as a sorcerer?"

"I've lived longer than a lot of sorcerers, if that's what you mean."

"One brags about his sorcerers continually, every day from dawn until the sad end of nighttime. Pink is a good servant, but he is not a sorcerer." Red blinked at me, long and slow. "I will allow you to be my servant."

"Well, however I can help. Do my one thousand days start now?"

"Hm?"

That told me everything about this one-thousand-days crap. "The one thousand days I serve until I go free. Do they start now?"

"Yes. I was considering your name, though."

"It's Bib."

Red literally rolled his eyes like a teenager. "I mean a proper name. You are now named Chartreuse. If you serve me well, I won't eat you. And you'll be free in one thousand days, of course."

"How many days has Pink served you?"

"A lot. Not yet one thousand."

I hesitated, but there would never be a better time to try saving Evonne. "Since you mention eating, please don't eat Evonne. The woman who is still named Food. Change her to Not-Food."

"Why? She looks delicious. Both tender and smart."

"We're married. Mated. If you eat her, I'll be sad and distracted. I might fail in my Chartreuse duties."

Red produced a low growl. "Fine! I won't eat her. I'll eat your enemies instead, the two who so badly wanted me to kill you."

If Red ate Acton and Kenzie, I could argue that it was justice. They tried to kill me. At some point, they'd have to try again. Even a five-year-old could understand and agree. But letting Red eat them put things too far out of my control. I could walk over and kill the young sorcerers any time I wanted or let them suffer waiting for my attack, but only if Red didn't get there ahead of me. "Please don't eat those two, either."

"Did you think I was waiting for your permission? I have decided to eat them, and I will eat them. Your opinion matters no more than a pine cone stuffed up a porcupine."

"But I—"

"No, Chartreuse! Do not engage in familiarity with me or presume to question me."

The only possible response was fake contrition. "I'm sorry. I won't do it again."

"You aren't sorry, so don't pretend that you are!" Red said, curling his upper lip to show his teeth. "Is that a magic sword? I bet it is. Answer me, and if you're dishonest, I will punish you. You can still be eaten, you know."

I smiled and then remembered my smashed teeth. Maybe Red would see that jagged smile as a threat, so I grinned instead. "Yes, it's a magic sword."

"Stab me with it." Red flicked a wing.

I drew the sword and waited. "How will I get down from here if I kill you?"

"Hah! Stab me. No, not in the shoulder! Someplace that will really hurt. No, not the heart. Could you be any less creative? Maybe you aren't aggressive enough to be Chartreuse. Listen to me. Put. The point of your sword. On. My. Eyeball."

This was the sharpest sword I had ever heard of. I placed the sword's point on Red's left eyeball and pushed.

Nothing happened. The sword may as well have been a stick and the eyeball a boulder.

Red cleared his throat.

I threw my body weight behind the sword, driving it toward Red's brain. Still, nothing happened.

"Now put that silly thing away." Red blinked his eye. "You can't harm me even with your deadliest weapons, so don't think about hurting me. Just do as you're told. For a human, it's true that one thousand is a lot of days to wait for a reward." Red flipped the black tentacle things on his forehead. "If you serve me very, very well, you may ask me one question every day. I might answer."

I nodded. "As Chartreuse, what will my duties be?"

"You'll find out in due time." Red grabbed me in his talons and dove off the mountaintop, plummeting straight down. He added, "And due time is tonight."

THIRTY

After he flipped over and dove, Red carried me back to the bowl-shaped clearing. I engaged in grim, not-quite-desperate planning. Everything lay tinted orange by the sunset, and I had no idea how to turn my Chartreuse responsibilities into freedom.

Red dropped me on the dusty ground and flew away without looking at me.

Lossil glared at me. "You cannot fool Red. He'll understand how dangerous you are soon enough." Lossil paused. "Did you stab him in the eyeball?"

I nodded.

"That makes an impression, doesn't it?"

I nodded again. "I don't intend to disobey. I plan to serve my term of 2.7379 years and be set free."

Lossil stared, nodding, for at least ten seconds. Then he turned and strode off into one of the caves.

Pink stumped over and examined my face. "Turquoise?"

"Chartreuse."

He closed his eyes and patted my shoulder. "Get a couple of Not-Foods and follow me."

I beckoned to Kenzie and Acton, smiling to show them my broken, sharklike teeth.

Kenzie shook her head and backed away, grabbing Acton's arm to pull him with her.

"Come on! I won't hurt you," I lied, looking over my shoulder.

They embraced for a second, and Acton murmured something to her. Acton followed me, and Kenzie's knees shook a bit as she took a step. Vargo had mostly gotten past holding on to her all the time, although he still grabbed for her at loud noises. Now he stood and refused to let her walk away, clinging to her arm and pulling away like a stubborn five-year-old.

Helline marched over and started smacking them both with her stick. Kenzie tried to fend off the blows with her free hand, and Vargo hunched over and lowered his head, but he wouldn't let go.

When Helline paused, Kenzie cradled Vargo's head in her arms and began whispering in his ear. He nodded before standing straight and holding just her hand as she led him to follow us. Pink had watched the entire scene without commenting.

The entire clearing dropped into evening shadow in the time it took us to walk to the cave mouth. When Pink reached the big cave that I had worked in earlier, he grabbed a lantern for himself and pointed out two more for the young sorcerers. He yawned before blinking at Kenzie and Acton. "Bring those wheelbarrows."

Kenzie whispered to Vargo again and shifted his hand to her upper arm before taking hold of the wheelbarrow. He didn't resist.

The lanterns swung, throwing our shadows on the walls beside us to shiver and pace along with us. I almost failed to spot the dark side cave when Pink stopped at it a few minutes later. I couldn't have failed to smell it, though.

"Yeah, dragon poop," Pink said. "Shovel it up and bring it outside. I'll show you where to put it." He glanced at me. "You're in charge. You might want to limit your leadership efforts to watching. You can make sure they don't screw up the shoveling. It's up to you, though." He tramped away, leaving us with two lanterns, two wheelbarrows, five shovels on the wall, and a mound of dragon poop as tall as my breastbone.

Vargo stared at the floor and spoke in a quiet, shaky voice. "Kenzie, I'm sorry. I don't know why I'm like this. I just can't stop. I have never been more embarrassed in my entire life."

"You should be!" Acton said. "This is infantile behavior. Ridiculous and appalling!"

Vargo nodded. "I'm sorry." His posture and face didn't say he was sorry or anything like it. They said that he would collapse and die if the wrong thing happened.

"We talked about this," Kenzie said to Acton in a low, firm voice. "It doesn't mean anything, and he can't help it. We shouldn't be mean to him, and we shouldn't be sorry for him. It's no worse than if he stubbed his toe." She patted Vargo's hand with her free one.

I knew for a fact that this was a lot worse than stubbing his toe, but Vargo's behavior didn't hurt me and might actually help me.

I said, "Before you embrace your task or embrace each other, the dragon told me he plans to eat you. He didn't say when. I guess he'll do it when he gets hungry."

"But we're not Food!" Kenzie said.

"He told us that. *You're* Food!" Acton clenched both his fists.

I shrugged. "You got ripe. I spoiled. It's the way of life." I nodded at the three of them. "You've created a mighty complicated and painful situation for yourselves, especially if you toss in the princess's unguents."

"We didn't create it," Acton said. "It happened. It couldn't be controlled."

"Sure. I know. Well, maybe it could be controlled better than this."

"You don't know anything about us," Kenzie quavered, obviously afraid that I knew everything about them.

"Children, your problems are not my problems. Deal with this mess however you like."

I took two shovels off the wall and held them out.

I heard arguments and apologies, and even romantic exclamations. Once it died away, I sighed and nearly gagged on the smell of dragon poop. "I hope you feel better. Be nice. This is a good time for me to kill you."

They backed toward the doorway and reached for their weapons.

"I should do it because you tried to convince a dragon to eat me. But I'm offering you a gift. If you don't want to be munched up in agony, I'll kill you now without much pain at all. What do you think?"

Kenzie said, "I think that's cruel! Harik is forcing us to kill you, or we otherwise wouldn't have sought your death."

"He forced you, eh? Who first suggested that you harm me? I think that was you."

She looked away.

Acton said, "You don't have to kill us. We failed. Now we can accept Harik's punishment, whatever that is."

"I guarantee that being eaten by a dragon will seem like wild-flowers and wedding cake compared to what Baby Harik will think up."

Kenzie clenched her fists. "How about—"

I cut her off in a hard, quiet voice. "No. This is sorcery. It's not playing at magic with your friends. It's not thanking the gods in your prayers when they screw you. It's bad deals, desperate decisions, repercussions, and death."

Maybe I should have added a few things, like how they might want to thank the sorcerers who came before them and died to show which dumb things not to do. Like not shitting on sorcerers who suffered so that Kenzie and Acton could play around with astounding forces.

None of that seemed so important at the moment. "If you want to take your chances with the dragon, I won't kill you now. But if you end up bitten to pieces, remember how nice I was to make this offer."

"We'll wait," Acton said, and Kenzie nodded.

I jerked my thumb over my shoulder. "I invite you to shovel."

I doubt I would have killed them, even if they asked me to. I hadn't given up on finding a way for us all to live through this.

Pink retrieved us after a few hours. We hadn't reduced the mound of dragon scat by much. Maybe we'd have to attack it again tomorrow, but I didn't have time to fritter away worrying about it.

I sat with Pink and Helline around their fire. The clouds had blown off, and every bit of heat rushed up into the starry winter sky. I said, "Pink, how long have you served this dragon?"

He worked his jaw as if he were chewing. "Seventy-three days."

He was so far away from one thousand days that I decided not to mention that. "Helline?"

"Seventy-two days."

I waited for a story or explanation, but none came.

"As servants, what do we do?" I asked.

"Keep the others damn well working," Helline said. "Polishing and cleaning."

"Taking messages and running errands," Pink added.

That captured my attention. If I took a message to somebody, that person would be outside this bowl of a prison. Escape would be possible.

Helline kept on talking. "The collections are a wretched lot of work. The Hoard of Dead Poets and Their Sad Poetry, the Hoard of Fruit Trees, the Hoard of Cats."

"The Hoard of Kidneys." Pink grunted.

Helline nodded. "The Hoard of the Stumps of Trees More than a Thousand Years Old."

"The Hoard of Gold."

"The Hoard of Paintings of Old Women Wearing Hats," Helline said.

"Wait, go back," I said. "What did you say about gold?"

"A dragon's got to have gold," Pink said. "It's all the gold that Red brought from the other side."

I blinked a few times. "The other side of what?"

"The wickets!" Helline said. "Damn wickets. Damned-to-Krak's-left-foot-up-his-own-ass wickets. I guess it's really just one wicket from what Red says, but damn it three times as much then."

I narrowed my eyes at her. "So, it's some kind of portal?"

"No, it's a wicket, dammit!" Helline said. "A wicket's a tiny doorway, not some big portal! It's small. They can't just shove ten thousand soldiers through it at once."

"Where does this wicket go?" I said it fast in case either of them changed their minds about talking.

"Wherever dragons come from." Pink reached over and punched me on the knee in a familiar way. "You don't have to act slick with us, Chartreuse. We'll tell you anything and everything." He put both hands over his mouth and yawned.

"It doesn't matter, and to hell with one thousand days." Helline scowled, which looked terrible in the jumping firelight. "We're all going to die right here."

I pulled bits of the story out of them over the next hour or so. Wherever the dragons lived was crowded, and a passage into this world had appeared in their realm like a gift. They sent three dragons across, along with all the soldiers they could push through the wicket. They intended to conquer as much of Ir as they needed for dragons to spread out in a comfy fashion. The amount they needed was assumed to be all of it.

Pink said, "And the dragons they sent were One, A, and Red. Of course, those are fake names. They wouldn't fling around their real names."

"Could they be bound with their real names?" I asked.

"Do we look like pissant damn sorcerers?" Helline snapped. "I don't know what you could do with them and don't care at all!"

"Every one of them's as touchy as a mashed-off finger," Pink said. "Can't stand to not be first, so they took those names."

"I can see One and A, but why Red?"

"Says it's the first of the colors. Maybe. I'm not arguing with a dragon about it."

I thought about it all for a minute. Pink and Helline lay down as close to the fire as they could without touching the flames.

I nudged Pink's leg. "Have they talked about how the war is going? What the army plans to do next, that sort of thing?"

"We're not soldiers." Pink rubbed his eyes but didn't look at me. "The army is going to . . . just enough to . . . heck, what do they say the army's going to do?"

Heline said, "Quench the land with the blood of their enemies. They got to do it. Or maybe they like to do it. It's probably a damn excuse to pull out the guts of everybody we love." I saw tears on her cheeks, and a few seconds later, she was sobbing. Pink sat up and rubbed her shoulder until she had cried herself out.

I sat back. "Do you speak the language of the dragons? Did you overhear all this?"

Pink blew a nasty noise with his mouth. "No, Red never speaks to us in anything but the language we use."

"How could you know all this?"

"Red likes to talk. He's got nobody to talk to but us. Did he say you could ask a question every day?"

I nodded, and Pink nodded back at me.

Helline said, "I think he only answers if the question is interesting enough. And if you haven't screwed something up."

"Pink, what's your real name?" I asked.

"Pink. And don't say anything about it being something else."

Helline said, "Red didn't give me a name 'cause I'm not strong. He did let me keep my own as long as I'm useful."

The man kept yawning, but he was still awake when I nodded off.

The next morning, we went back to the dragon poop cave and shoveled for a few hours. Then Pink came to retrieve me. He said, "You Not-Foods, keep working." Then he led me back out into the thin air of the harsh, cloudless day.

Red half walked, half slithered over to us and said, "It's time for a discussion." He grabbed each of us with a foot and leaped into the sky, his wings slapping the air.

Less than a minute later, Red landed on a ridge overlooking an open, square area about as large as his bowl-shaped clearing. Tall ridges pressed up against three sides of the area, and the fourth appeared to end in a drop-off.

Red said, "Chartreuse, stay here with me where you can see everything, but you stay hidden! Do you understand?"

I nodded.

Red chuffed at Pink, shooting a short flame from his nose.

Pink didn't speak, nod, or acknowledge the dragon, but he began walking down stone steps to the clearing. A short, heavy woman was already standing partway across the clearing from us. Pink reached the bottom and walked toward the middle until he stood sixty feet away from her, waiting for something.

Soon, a third person walked into the clearing from the third ridge. This short teenager trotted into the square and stopped when he was sixty feet from both Pink and the woman.

Flames shot up from behind the ridge to our right, and more flames rose from the ridge to our left. Red chuffed and breathed fire thirty feet into the air above him.

I had been suspecting that a fight would happen, but I hated to see it. I didn't despise fighting in particular, but this seemed to be violence only for the benefit of the dragons. It was a hell of a "discussion."

Pink wheeled and hurled a knife at the teenager, who was already patting his cheeks and pointing with his elbow. The knife smacked into a mound of dirt that rushed up from the ground in front of the boy.

The woman, holding a one-handed axe, charged toward Pink. She may not have realized the young man was a sorcerer because she ignored him.

Pink saw the woman coming, turned toward her, and hurled another knife. I don't know whether he was aiming for her throat, but that's what he hit. Fire and lightning flared. She fell face-first to the ground and didn't move.

The teenager used that time to peek around the little hill, beat his chest with both hands, cough, and punch toward the ground. The earth swirled under Pink, sucking him into a shallow hole. Thick layers of the displaced dirt swept over Pink and settled like a blanket mounded on a bed.

I assumed that Pink was dying, so I ran toward the steps. Red growled, "Stay here! Don't let anyone see you!"

"What about Pink?" I asked.

"You know the answer. He's not my first servant anymore. You are."

"Why isn't it Helline?"

"My first servant must be somebody strong enough to participate in discussions."

I gazed at the mound. I hoped that Pink had been struck senseless somehow, but I feared that he hadn't.

I supposed I would be down there fighting in the next "discussion" unless I escaped first. The entire fight had lasted about twenty seconds. If it had been held to celebrate the glory of the dragons, they must not have required too much glory.

All three dragons flew down into the arena, flapping their wings in an aggressive display, showing their teeth, and growling a lot. The young sorcerer retreated up the stone steps to his ridge.

The third dragon, A, was about the same size as Red, but he was pure gray, like smoke. Even his underside was the same shade as the top of his body. A row of black blobs grew from his forehead. I hadn't paid attention to One's forehead when he was terrorizing Red and me, but I saw now that it sported black horns that looked mighty sharp.

Red spoke up in Dragon language loud enough for everybody to hear. "This is foolish. It's a near random way to make decisions."

"You say that because you lost," said Dragon A. The victorious young sorcerer had fought for him.

"Shut it!" Dragon One yelled. "I don't want us tearing at each other's flesh when you two asses don't see the logic of my decisions!"

"Your decisions don't matter today," Dragon A said. "I decide. You can trust me."

Dragon One growled, "As much as I trust you to succor a goat in your mouth instead of eating it! I hate you!"

Red said, "That's because you're hateful."

"This arrangement has worked for us well enough," Dragon One said, suddenly sounding calm and thoughtful.

"I'll accept that as a working argument, subject to being disproved," A said.

"You sound like a wee-gon. I feel sad for you," One said.

Dragon A bellowed, "A wee-gon? Ceslik strike you with a black malady, you betrayer! Listen to him, O Beymarr. This one calls me a sad, little smooth-headed wee-gon, the nasty wretch!" Dragon A launched into the air with a clap like thunder, then flew circles around the clearing. "Bring Lossil to me so he can report!" The back of my skull hurt from the loudness of his voice, and rocks fell loose to tumble down the ridges.

Dragon One asked, "Who are you talking to? I don't intend to go get him. You don't give me orders. It is a good idea, though."

"I'll send my new servant." Red turned his head to gaze up at the rocks hiding me on the ridge. "I suspect he's worthless. He'll have this opportunity to prove it."

THIRTY-ONE

When Red told me to fetch Lossil, I had thought he would set me on some path down the mountain, a trail that would lead me to Lossil's army. I asked why Red couldn't just fly to wherever Lossil was, seize his ass, and fly him back into the mountains, which would leave me out of it.

Red had sniffed. "I could do that. It would be an excellent way to make our existence known to everyone by ferrying people as if dragons are flying carriages."

It was the sharpest bit of sarcasm I had heard from the dragon so far. I deserved it. Red intended to send me to Lossil by magic.

The fifteen minutes I spent preparing for the trip taught me a bit about dragon magic, and I inferred more. I concluded that dragon magic lies in how things appear. In Shura's camp, Lossil's image had appeared and spoken. Travel for me would be similar. Helline would hang a cloth in one of the caves and send me to a cloth near to Lossil.

Based on that sliver of knowledge, I suspected that dragons, apart from being innately magical, could cause things to look like something different for a while, or make things invisible. They might even be able to permanently change how something appeared in a particular person's mind, or at least change it for a long time. It would probably be easy to make things look like the opposite of what they really were.

Anything that reflected light, like a mirror or a pool of water, would be a feast of magic for dragons.

I was engaging in an embarrassing load of speculation about dragon magic.

We prepared for fifteen minutes, and the trip itself took less than one second. I peered out of a cloth hung from a tree limb. Lossil wasn't nearby. Nothing was around except for the cloth, a bunch of trees, and me.

Listening for a moment, I heard voices not far away. I turned and walked off through the trees in the opposite direction. I would never find a more perfect time to escape.

I stopped a few minutes later. I wouldn't mind abandoning Jon. If he died, people would celebrate with games and dancing. But I felt awkward about leaving the others. My decision not to run from the Sandell battle haunted me, and I wasn't sure I could just abandon my comrades and still sleep well.

I decided to find Lossil, bring him to the dragons as commanded, and convince Red I was a good servant. I was a servant who deserved trust, the kind of trust needed for me to escape along with all his other prisoners.

But I hoped to Fingit's greasy hammer that my ability to run away when defeat was near hadn't been permanently damaged.

I cursed and turned back toward Lossil. For the first fifty paces, I considered how I could give Red's urgent message to Lossil while also insulting him and implying that he wasn't worth my time.

Two of Lossil's tall difar soldiers appeared through the trees, and I called out, "Is Lossil around? I have a message for him. It's important because he may offer me a drink for bringing it to him."

Maybe they wished to protect their leader from any unpleasant messages, because they ran toward me with great ferocity and raised swords.

Drawing my sharp sword, I ducked one attack and slashed the attacker, leaving a horrific wound that would kill him in minutes.

His friend thrust at me using his advantage in reach. I blocked his thrust hard enough to cut his blade in two near the hilt. He backed away, grabbing a long knife from his belt. I shouted, "Lossil! Just take me to him!"

The soldier flung the knife at me and ran. I knocked the knife out of the air.

I had no interest in chasing this fellow to kill him. But it seemed likely he would lead me straight to Lossil, so I followed him at a trot.

He did not lead me to Lossil. He led me to three of his friends, one of whom loaned him a club. Overcoming these four would be a distracting fight, and I preferred to avoid it. I cut to my right to run past them, but five more of these soldiers came out of the trees toward me.

I considered running left to throw them off balance. I also considered just running the hell away. When I glanced back the way I had come, I saw more tall soldiers. There were at least seven back there, but I was too busy and frustrated to make an accurate count.

Killing these soldiers would serve no useful purpose, and the plain desire to kill had drained away over my years full of killing. I looked around for some distraction among the trees.

"Lossil!" I shouted while summoning four blue bands and tossing them out to cover the land all around us. "Take me to Lossil, you bloodthirsty bastards!" Once the blue bands were out, I pulled four white bands and tossed them into the sky.

It was late autumn on Ir, and many of the leaves still hadn't fallen. Enough remained that the soldiers had been hard to spot through the trees. I twisted the blue bands hard, and every leaf on every tree within three hundred paces dropped at the same moment. Then I eased the white bands to create a swift wind that would blow straight down for a short while.

All the soldiers disappeared from my sight as the leaves were whipped against the ground and back up again. I could hear them shouting in their own language. The shouts did not sound nice.

I couldn't see anything past ten or fifteen feet, but I had known what was about to happen and marked where my enemies were. I ran toward the spot I expected to be populated by the fewest tall, pissed-off soldiers.

As I ran, a difar appeared from among the cloud of fluttering leaves. I sliced his leg as I ran past. It wasn't an awful cut, although I heard him fall. He shouted a curse that attracted two of his friends. One came at me from the left, and the other from the right.

I rushed one of them, and he swung down to split my head and maybe my chest too. He looked awfully strong. I shifted to the side and thrust my blade into his heart. He staggered backward, tripped, and fell. My neck prickled, knowing that the other soldier was behind me, and I had no idea what he was doing. I rolled away from him, over the body of the one I had just killed, and came to my feet facing this next enemy.

This difar was sprinting toward me, swinging his sword low from side to side. I had time for one move, and I blocked him at the wrist instead of blocking his sword. My sharp sword passed through both of his wrists. His sword and his hands flew one direction, while he ran the other direction, hunched over his bleeding parts. It was a profound wound, but he'd live.

The leaves had begun to settle. I hoped I had run far enough to escape being surrounded. I rushed to a sizable tree and hid behind the trunk, listening to the difar argue in their own language. I didn't understand their words, but they sounded like the words you say about somebody you want to pull into five pieces and send to your five worst enemies.

The difar's positions became hard to place as they spread out to search for me. I tried not to make a face over the fact that Pil's ring didn't work with some languages. That included the difars' native language, and the reks' language too. The words that difars spoke among themselves were as mysterious to me as bear grunts.

I sneaked to the next tree away from them and hid again. Since I am about as stealthy as a bucket dragged down a cobblestone street, one of them spotted me right away and exclaimed with joy. That brought a pack of seven to chase me.

A smarter and subtler sorcerer than me might have employed more magic to hinder the soldiers, or even to drive them away. I had never been described as having that kind of subtlety. I preferred not to slay another forty of these difar on my way back to Lossil. Therefore, I needed something dramatic to warn them away.

I raced toward the enemy, angling for the one farthest to my right. The rest curved around to trap me. When my target swung at me with his heavy blade, I blocked and sheared it. That might have been a tiny bit impressive, but not dramatic enough to make a trained soldier stop and go some other direction. I swung my sword right back around and sliced the soldier's body right to left in the most profound way.

His top and his bottom fell in two different directions.

All of the soldier's friends must have thought that was dramatic, because those who didn't freeze in place backed away, dead silent. I spun to run around them but faced another group of five just loping into view.

I charged the closest difar. I could have wounded him or simply killed him, but I heard soldiers shouting from a third direction. Running seemed a chancy proposition. When the soldier raised his sword, I swung and cut him in two, just as I had his comrade. The next closest must not have cared, because he slashed at me. I blocked, which split his sword, and I came around to sever his top from his bottom as well.

All the soldiers in view had just seen their comrades slain in a horrible fashion. I ran on toward the cloth I had come through. Six of the remaining soldiers ran ahead of me. Others paced me on each side from a good distance away, shouting as they ran.

I bellowed "Lossil!" as I followed those soldiers, and I kept shouting it. I held my bloody sword in the air. More and more difar converged to pace me until four of them rushed in for the kill.

I treated them the same terrible way I had treated their friends, although I gained a long, ragged cut across my left shoulder.

I shouted, "This is what will happen to anybody who threatens me! Tell Lossil I have come!"

Nobody else rushed in to attack me. I had killed a few brutally, but that was the price for keeping the rest too shocked to attack, so I didn't have to kill them too. There was nothing good about the tactic or about any of this, but I hoped it would turn out less bad than it might have.

I knew precisely where the magic cloth was, and I walked straight toward it. The soldiers came along, keeping at least sixty feet away from me and talking to each other in frustrated tones.

Lossil marched out to meet me. I lowered my sword and waved at him with the other hand. It felt nice to have a left hand to wave with.

"You killed my men!" Lossil yelled. "Did you really have to mutilate them?"

I had come on a peaceful errand and had almost been killed, and I was too pissed off to deal with Lossil's high-and-mighty hero bullshit. "If they didn't want to get cut in half, they shouldn't have tried to kill me."

Lossil didn't seem to be armed, but he might have a weapon hidden. A four-inch knife could make me just as dead as a four-foot broadsword. He stopped to loom over me and lower his chin with his fists clenched at his sides, showing no concern that I might cut him in half. If his men didn't already think he was a brave son of a bitch, they sure would now. Lossil sneered, "Have you escaped? Come to assassinate me?"

"This would be a piss-poor assassination, wouldn't it? If I'd come to murder you, I should have killed you first. Then your men wouldn't have needed to die. I am not here to assassinate you, though. One, A, and Red have asked me to fetch you to them."

"That doesn't require all this blood and maiming."

I stared at him. "Do I really need to respond to that?"

Lossil hissed but didn't answer.

"Lead me back to your magical curtain, then," I said. "I need to make sure you don't get distracted or run off to play games on the way." At this point, I was just poking at Lossil for no good reason other than him being a courageous, honorable, and upright fellow who annoyed me more every time I saw him.

Lossil said, "I will tell them what you have done here. In fact, I will make up some things that are even worse and tell them again to kill you. One will listen. Red will not be able to save you this time."

THIRTY-TWO

I found all three dragons waiting when I followed Lossil from the cave out to the bowl-shaped clearing. Kenzie, Vargo, and Acton must have been feeding the goats in the pens when the other dragons arrived. The three of them had already seen one dragon, so two more shouldn't have made much difference. But the total quantity of dragons seemed to have shaken them, and they pressed themselves against the wall, staring at the great creatures and pitching hay at random near the livestock.

Red glanced up and down at the blood all over me. "Go away now. Eat something. You can tell Helline she may waste some food on you."

Helline must have overheard, because she trudged toward a cave I hadn't yet visited. I lingered as close to the dragons and Lossil as I dared. I felt confident they didn't know I could understand them when they spoke in dragon language.

Dragon One started with, "What in the tail-chasing, icy fires of our fathers is going on down there, Lossil?"

"Our forces are gathering," Lossil said. "We'll overrun their capital in four days. Most of them are lousy fighters. I'll need two more days to make sure everybody in the capital is dead."

"What about their army?" Red asked.

"They won't be much of a threat. I've sneaked through their defenses and listened to their soldiers. They lack confidence." Lossil nodded toward me. "That man could hurt us. You should kill him right now."

Dragon A said, "He doesn't look special, although his face has a nicer texture than you find on most humans. If he presented us with problems, you could send some of those tall arm-rippers to, well, rip off his arms, I suppose."

"Twenty of them tried to rip off his arms an hour ago. He's wearing their blood like a victory cloak. I think there's something wrong with him."

Dragon One turned toward me. "If he's not going to join our side, kill him. I'll kill the lumpy little cow." He chuffed the way Red had before he breathed fire.

Before I could flee in a futile manner, Red spread his wings. "No. He belongs to me, and I'm not ready to kill him yet."

Dragon One spread his wings too, wings that were quite a lot bigger than Red's. "How dare you?" he roared. "How dare you take the part of that smear of paste over us?"

Dragon A said, "Not over me. I care nothing about him."

"Take his part over me, then—that's just as bad! The hearts of our ancestors peel and crumble in shame! This is what we have come to!" Dragon One chuffed and blew fire at me. I'd have been roasted if Red hadn't stretched out a wing to save me.

"Now, are you finished hissing and crashing about like Ceslik?" Red asked in a voice almost as loud as One's. "You are not the leader!"

"And sadder it is for you! If we are driven to woe, it will not be me who drives us there!" Dragon One launched into the air with a blast of wind that blew dirt into my eyes, and he sailed away.

Ten seconds later, he flew back over the wall and hovered with slow-flapping wings. "What were we trying to decide?"

"What will we do about winter?" Lossil bowed his head.

"That damned-to-all-sixteen-toes winter! Damned!" Dragon One bellowed.

Dragon A chuffed and tossed the black bits on his forehead. "Oh yes, damned. Damned so much. Couldn't possibly be any more damned."

Dragon One showed his teeth and hissed. A did the same.

I looked around for a place to shelter from a dragon fight to the death.

One nodded. "Really? 'Couldn't possibly be any more damned'? Really?" He showed his teeth and hissed some more as Red joined in.

I let out a breath. Even if I died today, I had accomplished one thing: I was the only man in the world who knew how dragons laughed.

Before I could gather any more unique, lifesaving knowledge, Helline dragged me to a cave for a meal of goat stew, leeks, and yak milk.

I puzzled over what my question for Red should be. I didn't need to ask about winter. I knew what their problem with winter was. Winter was damn cold in Ir, colder than the dragons' army seemed to find comfy. I'd rather know what the dragons planned to do about winter, but I doubted Red would talk about such a thing.

All three dragons had flown off after their argument ended. I didn't see Red come back, and I realized that I had rarely seen him at night. Did he sleep someplace else? If so, these caves weren't much of a lair. I asked Helline, "Red doesn't sleep in the caves, does he?"

"Nope."

"Why is there an enormous pile of dragon poop in there?"

She whispered, "Fear and laziness."

"I need more explanation."

Helline growled but said, "The time that a dragon is most vulnerable is when he's squatted to do his business. I understand that he usually does it in some high place like a mountaintop. But when Red is wallowing in the glory of his hoards—like the Hoard of Things That Catch Fish—he doesn't want to interrupt his reverie to . . . you know. So, he uses that little cave."

I waited for something else, but it didn't come. "To be totally clear, Red doesn't sleep here, then?"

Helline threw a thin stick of firewood at me and barked, "No! I said that already!"

As the day came on to evening, I watched for Red. He slithered and walked out of the caves, and I ran to catch him before he flew off. "Red! Have I served well enough today to ask a question?"

The dragon might have sighed, but I couldn't be sure. "I suppose, but I hope you can ask a question that's not foolish or boring." Red blinked his great, orange eyes twice. Then he snatched me and flew up to the small clearing at the mountaintop.

Once there, I dipped my head. "What is it that made the greatest dragon great?"

After a pause, he said, "We keep goats in a pen."

I waited for a while before saying, "Yes, you do."

"Why?" Red sounded impatient.

"Well, so you know where they are." I was starting to feel as stupid as I'd been my first day at school.

Red stared at me as if I had stopped in the middle of a word.

I said, "So the goats don't run away before you can eat them. I don't think I understand."

Red fanned his wings. "Pay closer attention! Harik God of Death killed half the dragons in the second war."

That was a shocking bit of information. "It's nice that Harik is dead, eh? I killed him, you know."

"Do you want to be given a gift? A party? Almost all the survivors gathered in a safe, distant place. Do you see now?"

I didn't see a damn thing, but I figured it would be unwise to point that out. I needed some kind of answer. I threw back my shoulders and announced, "The survivors went to safety so that asshole Harik wouldn't kill them too."

Red shifted, reaching out to grab me.

"But the ones who didn't go were great . . . because they didn't want to be goats." Something had thrown that to me, and I said it without thinking.

Red growled, sniffed me, and grabbed me before shooting into the air. He deposited me back into the bowl-shaped clearing a minute later and flew away.

I considered where my last answer to Red had come from, and I didn't have to think hard. Whenever Old Harik had threatened to kill me, I would rather have died than creep away to some safe place. The survivor dragons made sense.

Late in the afternoon, Red snatched Acton and me, then flew off with us. Within minutes, he glided into the fighting arena and dropped us behind the ridge before landing.

"Chartreuse," Red growled, pointing at me with his tail. "You will fight for me today. If you win, I shall strike ten days off your period of servitude. If you do not win, it will be because you are dead. Not-Food, stay here and stay out of sight!"

Walking down the stone steps to the arena floor, I spun two yellow bands and found a charming variety of birds. A whole lot of them seemed to find this high altitude enjoyable. I spun two more bands and collected the attention of about three hundred birds.

The dragons would kindly give me a countdown by breathing fire three times. I could make my birds dive at count one and arrive at my enemy's head at count three, the very moment the fight started and before he had time to move. It was probably against the rules, but rules were for people who felt comfortable about dying in combat.

The young sorcerer who fought for A last time was already in place. The way he had buried Pink alive showed that he was a Bender who could manipulate the shape and placement of things.

I reached my spot sixty feet from the boy and waved my sword at him. He smiled and bowed to me—the old idiot who was using a sword to fight a sorcerer. I turned toward the third set of steps and waited for my other enemy. I needed to assess that person before I could refine my strategy.

The third fighter, who was serving One, was a dark-haired woman of average height and build, wearing simple clothes. She didn't seem to be armed, or if she was, it was subtle. Ten steps from the bottom, she stopped short.

My heart went from calm to racing in a few seconds. The

woman looked like Pil, just as she had on her last day in the Dark Lands. I breathed deep and reminded myself that dragon magic could probably make anybody look like anybody else. One knew about me. He could have learned about Pil and disguised his fighter as her to distract me. If he had, it was working marvelously. I examined my enemy even though it almost hurt to look at her.

Or maybe it really was her. I shook that idea away.

Not-Pil had resumed walking into the arena, never looking away from me. I wanted to wave, or call out, or throw dirt in the air—anything to cause her to answer and make her really be Pil. I didn't do any of those things, though.

The first dragon flame shot up, and I realized I had been ignoring my other opponent. I urged the birds to dive on him, but they flew in a ragged fashion. Before I could pull them together, an image like a thin curtain with something behind it swept before my eyes.

I reminded myself that such curtain images were among the dragons' tricks, and I couldn't trust this one.

An image of the black lake in the Dark Lands pushed toward me. I saw Pil far out on the lake with an overturned boat, swimming, struggling, and being dragged under the shivery water.

Another image mixed with the first one. I saw Pil paddle out onto the lake, wave back at me, and keep paddling until she was lost in twilight. The two images remained mixed and hard to understand until both faded.

The third spout of dragon breath shot up. I glanced at Not-Pil, but she had focused on the other sorcerer. I could sprint over and kill her. But if she really was Pil, she would subdue the young sorcerer, if possible, rather than kill him. I ran three steps toward her, stopped, and shifted my weight back and forth, undecided about my best move.

The sorcerer finished an elaborate kick and a whistle in my direction. Maybe-Pil snapped a stick with one hand, and the sorcerer was instantly engulfed by a cloud of steam. He shrieked, and I didn't see how he could survive such a thing. I didn't believe that the real Pil would have killed the boy so brutally.

Before the steam dissipated, I fell backward into a hole that hadn't been there a moment ago. Layers of dirt smacked down on me and covered my face. It was exactly what had happened to Pink. By the time the rumbling ended and the falling soil had packed down, I estimated that four feet of dirt lay on top of me.

THIRTY-THREE

I had been buried before. The most important thing was not to panic. I deliberately spun several white bands to find out what was in the area. I doubted any tree roots were close by, and I was correct. No large, powerful burrowing creatures were nearby to come loosen the soil. No small, plentiful burrowing creatures were around, either. Seven rats were not going to be digging me out of this mess.

Could I call a thousand birds to fly down and peck away the dirt covering me before I died? Unlikely.

I panicked a little then because the bird excavation seemed my best choice, and it was frankly ridiculous. I tossed out six yellow bands to smother the entire arena and tweaked the attention of every bird around.

A great crushing and grinding pushed against my side as the dirt compressed to squeeze all the air out of me. I would have cursed if I could have managed a single sound. The grinding paused but picked up again a moment later. Two more sessions of grinding and crushing happened in a few seconds before I felt air on my left arm. I promised I would thank whoever or whatever was digging, because if they had dug straight down instead of beside me, I'd have been cut into at least two pieces.

Something rough dragged the dirt away from my face. I sucked in a breath that turned out to have a fair amount of dirt in it, and I coughed hard.

A dragon grabbed me in its talons and flew away. When I craned my head to look back, I saw Red flying behind me and A standing where the fight had happened, apparently watching me. Maybe-Pil stood beside the sorcerer's body.

I knew of only three dragons. Logic said I was clamped in Dragon One's claws.

Dragon One dove almost to the rocky ground and swept a tight circle that clenched my stomach. He breathed a long spout of fire at Red, which didn't seem to hurt him but did stop him. Red bellowed, "That creature is mine!"

"My fighter defeated him!" Dragon One bellowed in dragon language, while shaking me with his taloned foot.

"If you wish to be precise, my fighter buried him," Dragon A called out.

"Maybe so, but mine cooked your pulpy fighter like he was some human's dinner, and then I dug this one out of the ground!" Dragon One shook me in his claw, and my stomach jerked toward my mouth. "By any law you might want to claim, this creature belongs to me!"

Dragon One flapped his wings and shot up one hundred feet in a couple of seconds. He grabbed my legs with one set of claws and my chest with another. I imagined myself as a wishbone.

"Oh, take him, then," Red said with a tiny chuff. He set down and looked away as if the rock wall were a hell of a lot more interesting than any of us.

Dragon One paused, hovering, and let me dangle from one claw. "What's wrong with him? Why don't you want him?"

"I wouldn't find having him to be a burden." Red flipped his head tentacles in a casual away, flapped his wings, and flew a wide arc.

"Can he do something special? Or is he a problem? Is he the squeaking bastard who showed up from another realm?"

Red set down in the arena. "Nothing, no, no. And almost certainly not." His forehead tentacles fell to the side.

"Almost?" Dragon One shouted. "*Almost* certainly not? That means you do think he's that bastard! We can squeeze victory out of him! Why have you been hiding that from us? Or has he fooled you?"

Dragon A had walked and slithered across the arena to join the conversation. "Don't leap to assumptions, One. Perhaps Red has more productive things to do than investigate the background of some squishy man."

Dragon One lowered his voice. "Like appreciate how pretty his hoards are? The Hoard of Things That Burn although They Are Not Supposed To? Really?"

Red and Dragon A stiffened. A said evenly, "Do not impugn the value of another's hoard."

Dragon One turned his head sideways and looked at the ground. In a voice that seemed like a whisper for him, he said, "I apologize."

Red and Dragon A both grumbled, but nobody flung themselves to rend anybody else apart.

Dragon One launched with me in his claws, skimmed over Dragon A's head, grabbed Maybe-Pil, and soared above the arena. He called down, "I'll investigate this suspected realm-hopper and report what I find!" He flapped twice and zoomed away from the arena.

Two minutes later, Dragon One descended into a rough, oblong area bigger than the arena. It lay not far below the highest peak on Ir. Steam wafted out of the ground in a dozen places, and the smell of sulfur almost overwhelmed me. The dragon dropped me onto the grainy soil from ten feet in the air, then flew across the open area clutching Maybe-Pil.

As I rolled to my feet, heat slapped me. It would feel good to somebody coming out of the chilly weather, but they would be sweating before long. With Pil's ring, I wouldn't have to worry about that.

Dragon One shouted, "Lossil! Is this the creature that crawled in from another realm?"

Lossil and about one hundred of his soldiers had gathered near one end of the clearing. He walked to Dragon One with long strides but didn't seem to hurry. He was the only creature I had seen so far who obeyed the dragons but didn't seem to fear them.

He said, "I didn't think he was at first. After he performed some unlikely feats, I began to change my mind, but I was still skeptical. Now that he's survived capture and imprisonment by dragons, so far that is, I believe the chance of him being a realm-crosser is eighty percent."

"Oh, thank you so very much for telling me about him before now," One grumbled.

"I apologize."

Dragon One jerked his head at me and then toward a somewhat secluded corner. As I followed, he looked back over his shoulder. "I have learned that particular human gesture—the one with the head. It means to follow me. Or to come over here. Or sometimes to look over there. I haven't mastered it yet."

"If you're killing all the people, why would you need to know something like that?"

Dragon One laughed. "Ceslik and Beymarr! We're not killing all the people. Just the ones on this island. That leaves a lot of people in the world who will need to be talked to."

"Why this island?"

"Unimportant. The important thing is that you should join up with us, but for some blackened reason, you don't like us, and you hate Lossil to tiny bits. It makes no sense. He is a small but acceptable being." One swung his head to face me. "After all these days, you're still alive, and we don't know as much about you as I'd like. You're sneaky and spring back from being smashed. That says to me that you're more like Lossil and his army than like any of those pale flimsies down there. Join us! Ride to victory with Lossil. Or walk, probably."

"But those are my people," I said.

"Really?" One's sharp, black ridges stood up on his forehead, and he stared at me with a look of shocking intelligence. I had been assuming that One was a bully and a fool. He said in a quiet, rumbling voice, "Your people? I have talked to you for two minutes and can tell that's a lie."

I clenched my teeth. "Maybe I want them to be my people."

"Others will never be what you want, even dragons. They'll be what they want."

"That's sounds pretty. It would make a great song."

Dragon One spread his wings with a bang and reared on his hind legs. "You puffy daub of crap! Don't you be familiar with me just because I let you say a word or two without biting off your top parts!"

I dipped my head and wondered where the hell all this was going.

Dragon One pulled in his wings and sat back on his haunches, reminding me of a gigantic dog. "We will make this island a fine and safe home for dragons, should we require two weeks or two years. Accept it! Join us, and you won't die. Victory. Glory! But if you reject us, you'll die with every other snuffling flimsy down there."

"That's a lot to think about," I said.

Dragon One pushed his face out until it was three feet from mine. He rumbled, "And think about this. Do not even whisper to yourself that you could fight a dragon and live."

"I won't," I said. But I thought, *I'll bet I could take one with me.*

"Aw, listen, don't get all crackly and start whining. Now here's a nice thing, a prize to toss some gold on the yak. This is Lossil's last campaign. He's a legendary warrior but not young for his kind. He wants to retire, and we will need a ripping great killer to replace him."

I stared with no expression.

Dragon One wiggled his sharp, black forehead ridges and cocked his head.

"No. That will never happen!" I took a breath. "If Krak and

Lutigan manifested right here and kicked me back and forth like a ball, I would still not agree to that."

One's ridges pulled back flat, and his voice dropped a shocking octave. "Ungrateful cluster of fungus! It's an offer that's been made to no human before you!"

"And oddly, it's not the best offer I've ever had."

He blew a short flame over my head and shouted, "Twenty, come here! Take this willful tongue scraper and put him on the wall! He has things to think about!"

Dragon One jumped into the air and flew away. A tall, heavy man with hair so red it was orange led three other men toward me. He said in a lazy voice, "Don't struggle, all right? If you do, we'll pound you, and if you defeat us, then all those soldiers will pound you, and if you defeat them, then how are you going to get off this mountain?"

"It's a strong argument," I said.

"Arguments were once my trade. I used to be the Baron of Kebbhaught's man of law and numbers, back before the world ended." We reached a stone wall facing the middle of the main area. "Off with all your clothes, every bit, and don't be shy. We've had priests, artists, and even the Viscount Hesh on this wall."

I pulled off everything, chatting with Twenty and taking my time. Twenty liked to talk but didn't reveal anything important. A man carried away my clothes, my sword, my knife, and Pil's ring. Twenty's helpers locked me in manacles and chains that were connected to the wall in a way that wouldn't quite let me sit down and wouldn't let me stand up straight.

Once I had been chained, Twenty stared at me for a while.

I asked, "Where did all the heat from the ground go? It's like a banker's heart here."

Twenty said, "We're in one of the cold spots. One doesn't want the condemned to be comfy while they meditate on their crimes. Sorry." He stomped away.

The sun set about an hour later. The chains and the cold made things mighty uncomfortable, but I spent my time thinking about escape. I couldn't advance my plans too far since I didn't know

Maybe-Pil's situation and whether she was Real-Pil. By now, I had become almost sure she was Pil. I wanted her to be, so of course she had to be.

The sun had been down long enough for deep darkness to cover the dragon's lair and all the open area in front of it. The only exceptions were the clear, cold starlight and the campfires of Lossil's soldiers. Bitter weather had moved in, blowing away the clouds, and it looked to be the first crushingly cold air of the season. I listened to steam hiss out of the ground, and it just made me feel colder.

A figure crept toward me from across the open area. I could only make it out because it blocked a campfire whenever it passed in front of one. The figure eased closer. I didn't say anything, and it didn't speak, either. It pressed a frigid hand to my bare chest, and I snarled, "Damn your sister's dog, that's cold!"

The figure chuckled, a sound I will remember until I die.

"Pil?"

She flung her arms around me. Although I was currently in no position to fling anything, I pushed against her so that there was no gap or space or distance. I bent my head to smell her hair. Even dirty and sweaty, it smelled like home.

Pil leaned back. "It's not the worst spot I've ever seen you in, but you must've screwed something up profoundly. Why are you here?"

"Why aren't you dead?"

She paused for a few seconds. "Why would you think I'm dead?"

"I saw . . ." I lowered my voice because I was on the edge of shouting. "I saw you die. I saw you drown in the lake!"

She shook her head. "Nothing like that ever happened."

"How did you get here? Why are you here and not at home?"

Pil said, "I did cross the lake to go to the cave gate and not come back, but I waved goodbye and didn't drown even a bit, so what's wrong with you? And dammit that cold, wet, nasty place is not my home!"

"So, you didn't die. And you didn't let me think you were dead. That leads to a small question and a big one. Who is screwing around with the way I see and remember things? That's the small question. The big question is, why did you leave? Oh, hell, maybe that's the only question."

She answered slowly. "I'm surprised to see you here, Bib. Not because you couldn't get here, but because you're too monumentally stubborn to leave the Dark Lands once you said you'd stay!" She picked up speed. "You lie about every damn thing that ever happens to you, so why did you need to be so loyal about staying? The gods wanted you to leave! They would've whipped you home as soon as you nodded yes. But you chose to remain there, even though it changed you and was changing you even more. And you were going to die soon, and I didn't want to see it."

I then said the stupidest thing I could possibly say. "I wasn't going to die."

"I'm surprised you're not already dead." Pil wiped her cheeks. A long strand of black hair shot with gray had escaped her braid. "I thought you might *accidentally* let somebody cut off your other arm so you'd be helpless and then killed, and don't you dare say you weren't going to die! You've been disappearing for years!" She grabbed my neck with one hand as if now she wanted to fight.

I decided not to tell her that I had indeed lost my other arm and almost died. "Disappearing? That's too foolish for me to waste my breath talking about it."

"I watched you do it these past years, ground down every time you killed somebody."

"Grinding? I'm not sure that makes sense."

Pil's voice lowered. "I begged you to come back with me. I begged every day."

I didn't remember any of this begging business. However, Pil was a generally truthful person, far more truthful than I had ever been.

She went on: "Bib, sometimes you're unhappy and sometimes you're a bastard, but you've always been a hopeful bastard until now. Some people live fine without much hope or even none, but without hope, Bib, you are a ghost, and I saw it. You're already dead. The knife just isn't in you yet."

I paused for a few breaths. "You know me better than anybody, so I guess I've got to agree with you. But now I've left the Dark Lands, and I've got hope coming out of my ass! You don't need to worry about me and this hope stuff. We can go off together for some hopeful frivolity. Assuming we don't get burned up by dragons."

She shook her head. "People don't change so fast. It took years for you to get this way."

I said, "I've changed. I'm changing!"

"No, you became something different in the Dark Lands, and you can't just tell something like that to go away."

I shook my head. "I don't think that's right. I have hope. I hope we can go off together."

Pil wiped her cheeks again. "What if I'm killed tomorrow? What will you hope for, then?"

I couldn't think of anything to say because I couldn't think of anything I really hoped for except her. Then I lifted my head. "I can hope to stop being a miserable no-hope bastard."

She laughed. "Maybe you can, and I wish that for you. Maybe you can start changing if you can avoid the kind of massacres you did in the Dark Lands."

I thought about my latest massacres, at the bridge in Sandell and at the gate in Ebring. Maybe I wouldn't tell her about those, either. "Pil, if you were trying to get away from me, why did you send Hurd to bring me here?"

She paused. "What?"

"He brought me that black ring you made for yourself."

"I thought I lost it. Hurd brought it to you?"

"Well, Vargo did."

She shouted, "Vargo was in the Dark Lands? Why?" She shushed herself.

My stomach turned over. "I don't think you lost that ring. Hurd stole it, swindled Vargo into bringing it to me, and lied about it all. May Krak burn him to ashes and feed the ashes to his fat, heavenly pigs."

"Hurd did visit a few months ago." Pil was close enough so that in the faint light, I saw her stare at the ground for a couple of seconds and then use both hands to push her hair back behind her ears. Dozens of years had taught me that whatever she said next would be something she meant and would fight for. After a silence long enough to be worrisome, she said, "I'm going to kill Hurd. I'm going to torture him to death. I'm going to erase him."

I didn't respond because I hoped she was just frustrated and exaggerating. But the grinding power of her voice concerned me.

Pil added, "How could you trust Hurd about anything? How could you be that foolish?"

"I wanted you to be alive. It made me stupid."

I had hoped she might soften a bit at that, but she went on in grim tones. "Maybe Hurd was working for the gods to get you out of the Dark Lands, or maybe he was fooling you for some other reason—it's hard to know. I do know one thing." Pil pulled back her shoulders. "Before I kill Hurd, I'm going to kiss him for getting you out of that awful place."

A spout of fire crashed through the night above our heads. Dragon One and five soldiers stared at us.

Dragon One shouted, "Damned conspirators! I should crush you both like spiders and have you thrown off my mountain!" He breathed fire at the wall above my head, and I shook my chains, trying to get away.

Pil sighed, and her shoulders slumped.

Twenty nodded at two of his flunkies, who grabbed Pil by the arms. Twenty began cutting off her clothes, showing no more passion than he might cutting a loaf of bread.

Half an hour later, Pil stood next to me, naked and bound by manacles and chains like mine.

"Contemplate the last few hours of your lousy existence, idiots!" Dragon One said. "Tomorrow when it's light, I will eat you and enjoy the terror on your faces as I do it." He flew away, and the soldiers trudged back toward their campfires.

When darkness had slammed down on us again, I said, "We really could have been quieter."

"Are you blaming this on me?" Pil snarled. "I'm not the one with a death sword that could have saved us."

"There's something funny I need to tell you about the sword."

"Will that funny thing keep us from being eaten? If not, it can wait."

I said, "I missed you so much I thought I was already dead. I love you."

"I love you too. Now let's figure out how not to be eaten."

As we muttered ideas and abandoned them, I realized that I now understood something that Pil didn't and probably shouldn't. I knew her as well as she knew me, and she didn't sound confident when she said I'd been changing in the Dark Lands. She wasn't afraid for me, either. She was afraid that she was the one changing. She wanted to leave, but she needed a good reason to go. I had been it.

THIRTY-FOUR

Pil had come to the Dark Lands to save me. I'd been there twenty years by then, and she expected that I had been spending all my time either killing things or sitting under a tree waiting to kill things.

She knew me well.

Pil brought a piece of magical junk with her that would let a single person leave the Dark Lands and return. She planned for me to use it and go home while she stayed a few months. Then I would come back so we could take turns in the Dark Lands standing watch.

That is trust. I could have agreed and then abandoned her there any time I wanted.

I didn't accept her proposal, mainly because I didn't want her standing on that bridge the next time two hundred screaming, frothing maniacs tried to overrun it. When I declined, I thought she would call me a few bad names and go home. Instead, she stayed.

I was as lovable as a dead rat dipped in acid. But Pil had offered to take my place in hell, and you only do that for someone you love. I discovered a thing. When Pil loves you, it's difficult not to love her too. It was difficult for me, at least, and forty-seven years passed before things fell apart.

Chained to that wall in the dragon's domain, freezing off all our parts, Pil said, "I didn't miss you all that much, you know. There were plenty of things to do that didn't involve watching you pound yourself into dust, and most of them were more fun, although I admit that sometimes when people dragged their butts and whimpered over what to do, I wished you were there to kick over a chair, walk outside, and start doing things, and to hell with the whiners. But I only felt that way two or three times a day."

"If you missed that, watch this." I whispered, "Kruppin, I want you."

I heard Kruppin, probably bear-size, grunting, heaving, and slobbering right in front of us.

Pil said with a smile in her voice, "Hello, Kruppin. It's a pleasure to meet you."

Kruppin stopped making monstrous noises. "Why aren't you even a little bit afraid when you have heard all my most terrifying sounds?"

"I have lived with Bib almost fifty years," she said. "Nothing can frighten me now."

"I could say that you have my sympathy, but I really don't care." I heard Kruppin pee on Pil's foot.

Pil snorted.

"Kruppin," I said, "I had hoped that you were waiting and might hear me. I think I know why you're still here. You have my ear and would like a matching set."

"I do desire that."

"If you do me a small service, I'll give it to you freely."

"Hah! In your current situation, I could simply pull the second one free without any permission from you."

"That's true. But in that case, I wouldn't place my name upon it."

"Interesting. But you are in a quite nasty spot, and I won't set you free." Kruppin made chewing sounds. "I want you to put your name on the ear I have and your true name with which you can be bound on the other. See how much you like it, you weasel's danglers."

I forced a laugh. "That's a great sacrifice and a great trust."

Making myself vulnerable to binding would be a risk. But I had been bound before. In fact, Pil had done it. Giving commands to a bound creature was tricky, and I knew how to creatively misinterpret just about any command.

"I know that you're an honorable monster," I said, "so here is what I propose. In exchange for a small service, I will place my common name on the right ear and my true name on the left ear. If anybody doubts that you have taken my ears, you can show them the right ear with my regular name. No one except you will see the left ear, and no one except you will know my true name."

"Bib, don't do this!" Pil said.

"I must wonder if you're fooling me in some way," Kruppin said.

"I'm not. It's a straight offer."

"I accept, then."

"Please bring me my sword and put it in my right hand, bring the black ring and put it on Pil's left hand, and put a sharp knife in your hand. I will give you the ear before morning."

Kruppin did those things within a few minutes.

I considered the open area in front of us. It was a rough rectangle about one thousand feet by six hundred. The mountain-side rose sheer on one of the rectangle's long sides, and we were chained in the middle of the mountainside wall.

"Thank you for the ring," Pil said to Kruppin. "I feel warmer already. Bib, what do you plan to do with that sword? Wave it around really fast to create heat?"

"No, I plan to cut our chains."

Pil breathed, "Is that the sharp sword?"

"Uh-huh."

"Wait! Even the sharp sword makes noise when you cut some-thing. The soldiers will run right over here."

"We'll run away before they get here," I said.

"What about the dragon?"

"If One is like Red, he doesn't sleep here in the lair."

Pil snapped, "All right then, how do we get off the mountain?"

"I started planning this only one minute ago! Didn't you say you missed the way I take action and do reckless things?"

"I don't think I said reckless."

"Well, pretend you did."

I prepared to swing the sword from my wrist in the starlight to cut the chain running against the wall on my right side. I adjusted my aim. I paused and adjusted my aim back to where it had been. I adjusted the other way and swung.

The sword made a ringing clang off the chain, and it left a deep scratch along my side just above the right hip bone. The air was so cold I could hardly feel it. My aim had been impaired by swinging in the starlight while crouching with my arm chained from the wrist up.

With the chain cut, I dragged my arms free, although my wrists were still bound. Two more cuts freed Pil. Then she cut the chains at my wrists and feet before I did the same for her.

Torches were bouncing along in the darkness toward us from the soldiers' camp.

"Hold out your hand!" I found Pil's hand by feeling around. "Take this sword, the sharp one! Kruppin, follow me and I'll make good on our deal! Pil, run left against the mountainside. I'll follow and slow them down."

"Without a weapon?"

The soldiers and torches were almost on top of us. I called the God of Death's sword, and I hoped to hell I wouldn't get something like a boiled cow tongue. Harik's sword appeared in my hand. I swung it toward three torches with more speed than skill, striking somebody each time. Two figures dropped, another screamed, and three torches fell to the ground.

"Run!" I yelled at Pil and Kruppin.

I made a slow retreat and slashed at soldiers as they reached me. Two tried to circle around me, so I ran by them and cut them on the way.

Soon, soldiers cried out as they realized how they'd been

maimed or saw what I had done to their comrades. Glancing back, I saw dim light appear one hundred feet away, moving away from the mountainside toward an open area of the rectangle. Pil must be holding up something that threw a noticeable light, although it was too weak for me to see Pil herself.

I stopped to kill a couple of soldiers and drive back the others. Then I turned to sprint toward Pil until I was out of the torchlight. Once I felt sure the soldiers couldn't see me, I turned and angled back to run along the mountainside away from the soldiers.

Pil's light went out with a far-off pop. I kept running, hoping that Pil would run to meet me at the mountainside and lose any soldiers in the starlit darkness.

Soon, I heard voices shouting around the place where Pil's light had gone out. Distracted, I almost plowed into Pil. Together we ran along the mountainside with Kruppin following until we reached the corner of the rectangle. The soldiers sounded like they were running around, looking for us in the big open area where Pil's light had disappeared.

Pil and I scrambled up eight feet to peer over the wall and found ourselves staring down the side of the mountain. "What now?" Pil panted.

I said, "Go back and ask those boys if we can borrow a ladder?"

"Why don't you give me your other ear now? And make your sign on them both?" Kruppin said.

I said, "Hand Pil the knife."

"Gah! No, I don't want to cut off your ear!" Pil said.

"I trust you."

"Bleh. You'll pay for this. Something rare and shiny."

I managed not to scream as she sliced off my right ear.

"Here." Kruppin must have either scavenged a quill and inkpot in the past few minutes or he always carried them with him in an inexplicable monster fashion. He handed me the quill and held out the inkpot.

By starlight, I managed to write "Bib" on the right ear and "Asa" on the left. "If they fade, come find me. We'll burn them in."

Kruppin didn't answer, and when I looked around, he was gone.

Pil grabbed my hand. "This is a story I'll tell over and over back home. Everyone there will be horrified. Krak! You're freezing to death! And I mean that literally, not the way my mother meant it when I forgot my coat. Put on this ring. We'll swap back and forth."

I objected but not too hard. "That solves the least of our problems."

"Bib, I have a magic rope I can call once. It's just about unbreakable, but it only lasts a short time, which wouldn't be so bad except 'short time' is poorly defined and could be anything from an hour to ten minutes. Then it evaporates. I'd have done better, but all I have to work with are sticks, dirt, and goat dung."

"We'll just have to find some solid place no more than ten minutes down the slope. What else do you have?"

"I also have a twig that will cut any non-magical object into seven pieces."

"That one's probably not useful right now." I peered over the side again. "How long is the rope?"

"One hundred one feet."

We scanned the side of the mountain as well as we could on a clear but moonless night. The waning moon would rise before long, and everybody on the dragon's rectangular outer lair would be able to spot us just by looking around for the privy.

Pil pointed. "I think that's a ledge."

"I think it's a rock."

"Hmm. All right, I trust your eyes. What about that ledge?"

"Tiny, but the best I see," I said.

Pil grabbed my arm. "Wait! Let's think about other options. Would Kruppin come back? Can he carry us down the mountain?"

"Maybe. What do you want to cut off me this time?"

"All right, can we trade with the gods for help?"

"Not Baby Harik, but maybe somebody else."

"Baby Harik?"

"I'll tell you later. If we want a god to pluck us off a mountainside, we'd better be willing to make a deal that could ruin the rest of our lives. Death might be better."

Pil grabbed my arm. "All right, let's climb down to that ledge that's tinier than your ass, and if things don't work out there, we still have Kruppin and the gods as options."

"One question. Can we cut your rope to make more than one rope?"

Pil cocked her head. She pulled a stick from her hair and snapped it in her left hand. Then she began gathering rope that had appeared at her feet. I thought the rope might resist being cut, but the sword passed right through, giving me ten feet to rig a harness for the sharp sword and its scabbard.

It seemed fair for Pil to climb down first. If she had made a terrible rope that fell apart, she took the risk of falling.

Pil climbed down to the ledge and shouted, "Come on! This place is really, really small!"

I climbed down the rope fast, but not in too big a rush. A few seconds before my feet would have touched the stone, the rope disappeared. I dropped down and slipped but caught my balance before I plunged down the mountain.

"That was not ten minutes!" I yelled.

Pil grabbed me in a gigantic embrace. "Sorcery is imprecise," she shouted in my ear. "You know that. Unfair and murderous. Damn, I'm glad you're not dead!"

I patted her hair. "You're right, this spot is tiny." The snowy, semi-flat space of frigid rock ran about eight feet long and stuck four feet out from the mountainside.

Pil said, "At least we can rest, although we're still in the wind."

The sword was still rigged on my back, and the harness was fine. I asked, "Why didn't this rope disappear?"

"Are you complaining? Question not my ways of sorcery! Really, I have no idea why."

I crouched to brush snow off the rock closest to the mountainside. An astounding gust of wind hit us, and Pil screamed. She grabbed the sword harness on my back as she fell and slid toward the snowy edge of the rock. I fell on my side as the harness dragged me toward the edge too. My foot went over, but with both hands, I grabbed a small but sharp ridge of rock on top of the ledge.

I lay flat on the ledge, clinging to the small stone ridge by both hands with my back to the drop-off and half of one leg hanging over. Pil was dangling as far below the ledge as the harness allowed. The harness happened to be made from a rope that might disappear at any moment. Both of us were naked.

Pil called out in the most matter-of-fact way possible, "We should ride your monster next time."

THIRTY-FIVE

Sorcerers like to appear unconcerned in the face of danger. The worse the danger, the more unconcerned they want to seem. A group of sorcerers facing a horrific threat might all strive to be the most unconcerned, right up to the point where their lack of concern kills them all.

Nobody said sorcerers are smart. At least, I didn't say it.

I didn't care about looking unconcerned while clinging to a mountain with Pil dangling from my back. I babbled in panic, "Kruppin, I want you."

Kruppin didn't answer.

"Kruppin!"

The monster was most likely being lauded by Gek and maybe choosing which lady monsters he wanted to spawn with. He wouldn't be helping us.

"Fingit, I wish to trade!" I lifted myself up through the top of my head, seeking the gods' trading place. Something stopped me while I was still folded in blackness.

Baby Harik's voice said, "I guess you want me to save you, huh? I don't see any incentive for me."

"Make me an offer," I said.

"Make me an offer, what?" Baby Harik said with a grin in his voice.

I imagined drawing myself up like an orator. "Make me an offer, you dripping vat of impure fluids wrung from your mother's corpse!"

"You've done worse, but as your last insult of all time, it's a little weak. Go and die, Murderer. I get the sword as soon as you expire, you nit!"

Baby Harik dropped me back into my body, not so hard that he could be accused of killing me.

"No success with the gods," I yelled. "Kruppin—"

Pil shouted, "Stop, that's not going to save us, and you know it! Listen, Bib! If I hear one word that sounds like you're about to kill yourself somehow in order to save me, I will let go of this rope."

"What do you want me to do, then?" I yelled.

"I don't know!" she screamed.

My fingers slipped a little more.

Pil yelled, "I love you! I'm letting go now!"

"Wait! Give me two more minutes."

"To do what?"

"I don't know, just give them to me!"

The only thing I had to work with was weather. I spun seven white bands and wove them into the wind, which was already astoundingly strong on the mountaintop.

Then I had a dumb idea. "Swing back and forth on the rope like you intend to swing yourself up and grab the rock."

"I can't reach that far! I'll be killed!" she shouted.

"Damn it, thirty seconds ago you were about to let go and die! Swing back and forth, but don't try to swing yourself up until I tell you!"

I imagined the words she was saying under her breath. "I'm swinging now!" she shouted. I could tell. She almost dragged me off the mountain.

I twisted the bands and sent the wind straight up the side of the mountain at near hurricane force. "Now!"

Some of the strain came off the harness. I scrambled to pull as much of the harness away from the ledge as I could.

Pil roared, and for a second, I thought she'd fallen. When I looked back, she was climbing up over the edge. I scrambled to squat and pull her up by the wrists.

We pressed ourselves against the mountainside as far away from the edge as we could. I put the ring on her hand, which was shaking so hard I had to hold it between one hand and my knee. Then we huddled, sharing as much warmth as we could.

"We're alive and we're free," I said to Pil. "I count that a victory."

"Alive and free? You could say the same thing about a lizard. Or a mushroom. The soldiers will spot us down here once the sun rises."

We held each other and shivered our way down the path of freezing to death.

When my teeth began chattering, she handed me the ring. "While we rest for a moment, you can tell me," I said. "How did you come to be captured by a dragon?"

"I was traveling by horse across the Spine from Gallin on the Mere to Popping Knot, and let me say that Teeb, the headmaster of Popping Knot, is a whirling idiot and deeply offensive. I had gone there to search through the library, but he demanded that I teach a class on evil spirits since nobody else there had ever seen one, and he also assumed he could force favors of a prurient nature from me, the rotting bastard."

I chuckled. "He really is an idiot."

"He woke up the next morning cradled high in a tree, and my horse and I were far down the road toward Gallin."

"And the dragon?"

Pil said, "I was foolishly riding in the dark, trying to reach the next town, when One dropped down and snatched me off my horse. Then he held me in one claw while he ate my horse. I have to say, it was disturbing. Then he brought me to his lair. And you?"

"Red yanked the longboat I was in out of the ocean and flew away with it."

"Krak and Casserak!" she said.

"I wonder why the dragons grabbed both you and me? It can't be a coincidence."

She turned her head to stare at me. "Of course it's not a coincidence, and it shocks me that those words came out of your mouth. Give me that ring. You're too foolish to be warm."

She was smiling and slapped my hand when I reached to take off the ring. She held me tighter and spoke in my ear over the wind. "The dragons have been capturing sorcerers to fight in their little battles, I suppose because they thought sorcerers would be more successful, and I suppose they were correct, so there has been a competition among them to field the best sorcerers possible. I'm not being arrogant when I say that you and I have vastly more experience than any other sorcerers on this island, so it was inevitable that we would both be captured."

I took a deep breath, and the cold air hurt my lungs as I thought about how to say the next thing. "Pil, your granddaughter Pala came to the Dark Lands with Vargo."

Pil stiffened.

"She was killed there."

At first, Pil didn't ask how or why Pala died, and those things probably didn't matter. She cried, but not much. She sounded grim and sad as she sat against the mountain talking about how much she loved the young woman, who was brave, generous, and as stubborn as a boulder in a muddy stream. At last, Pil asked, "How?"

"A tall, skinny ass who says he's a hero stabbed her. His name is Alamore."

Pil stared at me. "You let him live?"

"I'm hunting him."

She nodded. "When you find him, stand out of the way."

The moon rose after midnight, waning away from a half-moon. I peered over the edge looking for ridges or paths, something we could navigate down. I didn't spot any, but maybe they'd be more evident in the first light of dawn.

We spent the rest of the night pinching each other to stay awake. When the sky began shading to gray in the east, I scanned below us for any place we could climb down from and escape. Before the total lack of possibilities had time to discourage me, a dragon rose and blocked out most of the world in front of us.

We pushed ourselves against the mountainside and curled up as tiny as possible. That wasn't as effective as I had hoped. Red hovered fifty feet away, wings flapping slowly and staring right at us.

"You're mine," growled Red.

"I'm not going to object at this point," I said.

Red shifted to gaze at Pil. "You're not mine, so you shall remain here."

I grabbed Pil as tightly as I was able, and after a moment, she grabbed on to me.

"You two release each other," the dragon said.

I said, "Sorry, you have to take us both."

"I do not appreciate this willful behavior, Chartreuse."

"Chartreuse?" Pil asked.

I said, "I'll tell you later."

"Stop mumbling between yourselves! I hate that."

I said, "Unless your claws and tail could pluck a goose, I don't think you can separate us without killing us."

"Then I'll just have to kill you both!"

Pil and I waited.

Red reached out and grabbed both Pil and me with one set of claws. "I will remember this disobedience."

After two minutes of shocking flight, Red landed with a bump in front of his caves. He dropped us and flapped once to shift and stare at us from fifteen feet away. "There, I have allowed you to be together. Chartreuse, I have tasks for you. Woman, you are Food."

"Red, I must be honest with you now," I said. "If you eat, kill, or otherwise harm Pil, I will climb that wall and throw myself over."

"You will not. That's foolishness."

"But if you let her stay unharmed, she can be useful, and better than that, the fact that you have her will aggravate One to holy hell. It will drive him crazy with frustration. He won't be able to think about anything else. Doesn't keeping her here unhurt sound better now?"

Red growled and whipped his tail. "Chartreuse, you're saying words that are a tiny bit clever. Remember this later and ask yourself how clever you really were." The dragon walked away but said, "Your skin is repulsive, soft, and pale. Helline, cover them with something from the hoards."

Helline stepped out of a cave and beckoned us. We followed her and her lantern fifty paces down the tunnel before stopping at an opening to the right.

"Find yourself something in here," Helline said. "It's the Hoard of Clothing Worn by Important People Who Were Executed." She stood inside the opening holding the light as Pil and I dug through piles of silk doublets and jeweled skirts looking for the absolute warmest things to wear. The clothing wasn't organized in any way that I could understand. Everything was just piled together.

I came out wearing a padded green doublet with two silk shirts underneath, yellow velvet trousers, tall cowhide boots, and a red leather hat lined with fur. Pil chose four linen shirts under a padded black leather jerkin, gray leather trousers with silk trousers underneath, shiny black half boots, and a broad black hat made of felt. Neither of us commented on the variety of bloodstains and even a few punctures in the clothes.

I gazed up and down at Pil. "You look like an assassin."

"You look like a juggler."

Back outside, Acton and Kenzie wanted to know everything I had seen and done since I left. Pil and Vargo embraced before discussing where the family might have gone and whether they were safe. Jon claimed he had figured out where the invaders were coming from. He had done it by combining Shura's comments with prisoner statements, making close observation of Red's appearances, and whispering with birds. His eyes were bright but sunken, and his face was drawn. I listened to him and nodded a lot.

As far as energy went, Pil and I were entirely destroyed. We lay down together to sleep.

A few minutes later, Red landed with a whoosh and a thump. He said, "Chartreuse, come here."

I stood, and Red grabbed me. We hurtled to the small clearing at the mountaintop.

"You haven't entirely failed at everything today, Chartreuse, although you were unforgivably willful. Still, I will allow you to ask me one question."

I hadn't given this a bit of thought today. I spit out, "How does this island compare to the realm you came from?"

Red blinked three times before staring out over the shorter mountains and hills. "When did you leave your mother behind?"

It wasn't a question I expected. "I was ten years old."

"Did she give you what you needed?" Red asked.

"Yes, I imagine so."

"You see it, then."

I didn't see a single flipping thing, so I scrambled for something to say. "When I left her to study my trade, I almost killed myself. Three times. It was very satisfying."

"Yes." Red's black forehead bits swept back and lay relaxed. "I will ask you a question. Answer or don't. Why did you kill your child?"

It was my turn to stare out over the lower mountains as I wondered how Red would answer this. Manon had been foolish, but no more than any child. She invited a malevolent god to take over her, and she was killing people across the city. I thought I had to kill her, but later I realized I shouldn't have given up on her.

I said, "People thought I should kill her, but I shouldn't have."

Red blinked and whipped his tail. "Yes, I see it." He grabbed me so fast I lost my breath, and he flew me back down to his lair. I curled up with Pil and we slept, paying no attention when the sun rose above the walls.

I woke before midday and looked up to see Red's maw four feet above me.

"Stand up and follow me."

I squeezed Pil's hand and followed Red into a side cave I had only visited a couple of times. Red walked, crawled, and slithered all the way down the tunnel, maybe four hundred feet, where a dark opening lay.

"Go inside," the dragon said.

I walked inside a large space that was faintly lit from above.

The ceiling behind me rumbled and clattered, throwing dust into the air and tossing rocks across the floor. I didn't run back for fear of being crushed. The little avalanche continued until I was shut off from the main tunnel.

"Red!" I bellowed. "Let me out!" It was possibly the stupidest statement I could have made since the dragon had just put me in.

I shouted for Red again and again for about a minute. Then I turned to scan the big space, starting with the ceiling. It was domed, and a shaft ran upward to show the morning sky, letting some light in. This place would be dark at night, then.

I gazed around at the floor and froze.

"I guess Red is a girl dragon."

THIRTY-SIX

My father told the stories in my family. On most nights, my mother played the harp while we sang—a clash of voices that must have offended our neighbors and the gods alike. But now and then, my father told us the tales of our people.

Normally, my father's face was as hard as the deck of his fishing boat and as expressive as an anchor, yet by the tenth word of "Jagen and the Wolf" or "Folly of Autumn," he was as lively and as rhythmic as the surf.

My father's favorite story was "The Milkmaid and the Dragon." Because he loved it so much, we all came to love it too.

The milkmaid, a virtuous, brave, and clever girl, is taken prisoner by a horrible dragon and held in a cave, along with six other girls from her village. The dragon intends to eat the girls, but the milkmaid overcomes a different challenge each day to stay alive while another girl is killed.

While all this is going on, she falls in love with a sorcerer in the form of a bluebird who has come to help the girls.

When the milkmaid is the last girl remaining and the dragon comes to eat her, she and the sorcerer sing a duet for the dragon. The dragon is moved and offers her a choice. She may go free with a cask full of treasure if the sorcerer is eaten in her place, or they may both go free if they never see each other again. She chooses that they both go free.

This story burned through my mind as I stared at two smooth, round, barrel-size objects before me in the dragon's cave. My father had told in painfully etched detail how one of the seven girls was sealed in a room with dragon eggs and how the baby dragons hatched, stalked her, and devoured her as their first meal.

I scrambled around the big room, examining walls and floors for concealed passages or for a trap door under a rug. There were none, and there wasn't any furniture to stack and climb to the hole in the ceiling. A small pool of clear water lay in one corner of the room, but I could touch the bottom without getting my shoulder wet. Sticks and slivers of wood lay scattered, but the room was bare of lumber or rocks to make a defensive position, which might only delay my death by seconds, anyway.

Sorcery would prove difficult or even useless here. We were sheltered from the weather. There were no plants or roots nearby and just a few rodents. Maybe I could call one hundred geese to come fly me out of the room, but I had never been able to convince more than fifteen geese to do the same thing at the same time, other than fly in formation.

I cursed the room for its arrogance. It was too commonplace to exist in a dragon's lair.

When I looked over at the eggs, one of them quivered.

Baby Harik grabbed my spirit and yanked it up into the trading place. Thick fog surrounded me. I could hardly see the patch of dirt I was standing on. Distant laughter sounded from somewhere out in the fog.

"Hi, Murderer," Baby Harik said. He sounded like he was holding in a laugh. "Got off that mountain, I see. Relying on the dragon to save you was disappointing. I expect my sorcerers to handle their own problems."

"Baby Harik, it's always a pleasure to talk to you, on the order of having nails driven into my ears and being ridden like a horse by rich children. Why are you calling for me?"

"You are aware that baby dragons are about to eat you, right? Their teeth are unbelievably sharp."

"Maybe they'll like me."

"Maybe they'll like how you taste. Every baby dragon in history has eaten a man, or a manlike creature. Don't plan to be the exception."

"I can defend myself," I said.

"With the Death God's sword? Maybe."

"What do you propose, then, Baby Harik?"

"Give me the sword now," Baby Harik said. "I'll give you a way to defend yourself."

"A way that's certain?"

"Come on. Nothing's certain."

"No, I'd rather count on using the sword," I said. "It's infused with the power of a god. I bet a dragon wouldn't want to be stabbed in the eyeball with this sword."

"Fine, I can work with you on this. I'll give you a way to defend yourself if you receive knowledge from me."

Most deals involved doing something bad or not doing something good, or maybe having something bad done to you, such as being convicted of a crime, or even losing memories of people or events. But the most perilous payment was agreeing to receive knowledge. The gods would always tell you things you wish you didn't know.

"No, Baby Harik, I'm not interested in that. I'll rely on the sword."

"I hope the sword doesn't fail you, then. I'm the most considerate of the gods, you know, so I'll give you this knowledge anyway, and for free. You don't need to bargain. You can just have it."

"I don't want it!"

"You'll take it, and you'll like it. Although you probably won't like it."

I tried to jump back out of the trading place, but Baby Harik retrieved me.

"Very impolite," Baby Harik said. "You hurt my feelings when you do that. You remember seeing the Knife drown, right? And then later your memory changed, and you saw that she didn't drown. She paddled away just fine."

I nodded.

"Did you ask yourself how this *see it now, don't see it anymore, see something else* business happened to you?"

I had asked myself that a number of times and hadn't come up with a good answer. "It's all in the past now, so I don't care. I'll be going!"

"No, you won't. It takes a sorcerer to make a deal like changing memories. How many sorcerers did you know back when the Knife left?"

"Two," I said.

"Two including you. Did you wiggle around in your own mind and change things? Don't answer. Trust me, you didn't. And that leaves . . ." He raised his eyebrows.

"Pil did it," I whispered. "She did want me to think she was dead. Why?"

"That would be a fine thing to ask her, eh? It will give you two so much to talk about. If you don't die today, that is." Baby Harik flung me back into my body, where I stumbled.

Now both eggs were quivering. I backed away and pulled the Death God's sword from its tiny realm. I found myself holding a big smoked ham by the bone. I cursed for ten seconds before sending the ham away so I could try again and get the sword.

The ham wouldn't leave. I dropped it and called the sword. Nothing happened.

One of the eggs cracked down the side, and a baby dragon pushed its way out. It was the size of a big hound, with a stubby neck and tail. The baby looked green, but the room was dim. Its head was shaped like its mother's, and its mouth was full of finger-length teeth. Its eyes looked enormous.

The creature tripped coming out of the egg, fell flat, and scrambled back up, nosing the air. By now, the other dragon was halfway out of its egg but stuck. It struggled and made mewling sounds like a fifty-pound cat. This baby seemed to be bronze or rust in color.

I tried Harik's sword again, but nothing happened. I drew my sharp sword and backed away.

The green one ran toward me, unsteady and its tail high. Ten feet from me it skidded, overshot the ham, and rolled back toward the ham to get a bite. The bronze one had kicked free and reached the ham a few seconds later. This one seemed a lot steadier on its feet, and it sunk its teeth deep into the ham. The two clawed and bit at each other as they ate.

Within a minute, the baby dragons had devoured the ham, including the bone. I figured that they'd be able to eat my whole body within five minutes. The green one spotted me, and they both charged toward me. I backed away some more and swung at the green one's neck. The sharp sword didn't even leave a mark on the baby dragon.

I backed myself against the wall and lifted my spirit toward the trading place. "Baby Harik, I might want that weapon, after all!" Some god slapped me back down.

Baby Harik was not answering.

The green dragon leaped on me and knocked me down against the wall. I raised my arms to protect my head and told myself that it wouldn't be much better for the baby dragons to chew off my arms.

The green one threw its body onto my legs and snaked up to slam its head into my armpit. The bronze one leaped on my other side, clamped onto my arm with its claws, and slapped its open mouth onto my neck. I could feel its teeth push against me.

I waited to die, but nothing else happened. I was too terrified to move one finger, much less get up and run for safety that didn't exist.

A few seconds later, both baby dragons started buzzing. They were asleep.

THIRTY-SEVEN

Baby dragons wiggle around in their sleep. Sometimes they flop around. Baby dragons may not be as hard as grown ones, but they're hard enough to leave big bruises when they roll over, stretch, and smack you on the side of the chin.

They are not cuddly like puppies. They are cuddly like big puppies made of granite that like to kick you with their iron boots.

The babies woke up after a few hours of putting my legs to sleep, and they awoke ready to run at full speed. Since their hustle was a lot better than their control, they bounced off stone walls quite a bit. Running full tilt into rock didn't seem to upset them or even slow them down much.

As I watched them play, I named the green one Bounder and the bronze one Slash. I wondered what would happen when feeding time came around again. And what would have happened yesterday if I hadn't conjured a ham.

Hell, I hadn't eaten for most of a day, and I wouldn't mind conjuring a ham for myself. However, it had been a random object delivered in place of the death sword, and I didn't know how to repeat that ham-producing event. I settled for hoping that Red would bring me something to eat when she came back.

Before daylight had faded, I heard grinding and crashing from the collapsed wall where the door had been. Soon, Red dug a hole big enough for her head and neck to push through.

The babies squealed and rushed to bounce around her. They had never seen her before, but they treated her like their favorite being in all existence. She murmured something too low for me to make out.

Red looked up, saw me, and stopped moving.

I waved at her.

She glanced at the babies and back at me. So, she had intended for the baby dragons to eat me.

"Chartreuse!" she said in a voice loud enough to make me cringe. "Come out here!" She backed out of the hole and beckoned me through it using her tail. "Stay here!" Then she shoved her head back into the room.

The baby dragon nursery was lit by a lantern on the floor, and three unlit lanterns sat next to it. Two freshly dead goats tied with lengthy ropes lay beside them. After more than an hour with her babies, Red backed out of the doorway.

Red waved her tail over the lanterns. "Take those lanterns inside and come right back here."

When that was done, Red stared at me as we stood in the tunnel. The lantern light reflected on her head and her huge eye.

I said, "Well, this was all a surprise."

After a slight pause, she said, "I hope it was. Surprise defends us against the others knowing."

"It sure defended against me knowing. What's happening here, Red?"

"The others would not be pleased to find that I have children. They would feel it gives me an advantage when it comes time to claim territory in this new land."

"Will it give you an advantage?" I asked.

"Of course it will." Red laughed. "Because of this, the others would have destroyed my eggs, and now they will destroy my children if they can."

"I doubt I can defend them if it comes to that."

"It's ridiculous that you even think about such a thing! But I am relying upon deception, not force. You and I both are relying on it."

Then Red lifted her head up to the ceiling and lied to me as masterfully as any sorcerer. "You have done as well as I had hoped with my children. Now I require that you keep attending them so that I will not be suddenly absent. If I disappeared, it would cause suspicion. If you do a good job, you'll receive treasure."

"That makes sense." I nodded, not believing a single word.

"One and A would tear down this mountain to discover how I am plotting against them. Then my children would die."

I blinked a few times and felt uncertain about whether that last part was also a lie. The idea of One tearing apart the babies nauseated me. I took a deep breath. "Red, I will care for your children in exchange for some consideration. When they no longer need my care, my companions and I will be released. Is that acceptable?"

Red lowered her head for a moment. "Perhaps I would agree to that, with a slight modification. You will care for them until they no longer need you. In exchange, I will not kill you or any of your companions, unless you misbehave and deserve to be killed."

I cursed silently. Dragons evidently didn't enjoy bargaining. "That is a fair arrangement, and I accept. What will your babies need in the way of care?"

"They require very little. They need food, a warm place to sleep, and constant attention. Tell them stories, even stories in your language. Play with them. Think up games. Give them unwavering love. You needn't worry about teaching them to fly or other things that dragons do. Oh, prevent them from killing one another."

"Is that a real possibility?"

"It does happen," she said. "Fairly often."

I stared at her.

"I suppose you should know. More dragon infants die by the teeth of their siblings than by any other cause."

I nodded. "What if one of the other dragons finds us and attacks?"

"You needn't worry about that. You will die within the first few seconds."

"Of course. Have you named them?"

"I have, but you may not know their names."

I said, "I've given them names in my language. Bounder and Slash. They don't really mean anything."

Red paused. "Those sound like the names one would give a pet, and that is certainly inappropriate. You mustn't forget that they are more intelligent than you. If you wish, you may call them Praxsis and Chexis."

"Both males?"

Red gave me two slow blinks. "Why do you say that?"

I couldn't damn myself out loud, but I wished I could. I had spent a fair amount of time listening to the dragon language. Praxsis and Chexis sounded like the kind of words that referred to males.

I scrambled for a good lie to disguise the fact that I had been eavesdropping. "They both seem active and aggressive when they play. They just remind me of boys. Also . . . I've never had any boys of my own." I looked at the floor and slumped a little to sell it.

The dragon chuffed once, and in an instant, the air got so hot I began sweating. Then she grunted and turned away from me. I strolled off, glancing back. Once Red had pushed all the way into the room with her babies, I ran toward the tunnel mouth.

The tunnel mouth leading outside was blocked by fallen dirt and rock. That was disappointing but made sense. Red didn't want me running out to tell the world about baby dragons.

I called out as loudly as I dared, "Hello! Pil! Acton! Pil! I'm in here!"

Pil's faint voice came through the fallen dirt. "I thought you were dead! No, I really didn't think that, but I thought something bad was happening."

I said, "Red laid eggs, which hatched. I've been minding the babies."

Pil didn't answer.

"Don't tell anybody else. It might put them in danger."

"All right. How will you use this to escape? Can you hold one hostage or threaten it?"

"I guess we can, but I'm not too sure we should."

Pil came back fast. "What should we do, then?"

Swallowing, I said, "If we threatened one, Red might kill us all."

"Red might kill us all if we try to escape, or for standing around looking at goats. Death from kidnapping a baby dragon is no worse than death from trying to climb out of here. Anything we do with the baby dragon will at least be unique."

I didn't want to think about threatening the kids. My hands started sweating. "Let's each consider it. Come up with ideas. I'll come back tomorrow, and we can talk about it some more."

"Bib, between now and tomorrow, Red may kill one or all of us."

I said, "No, as long as I'm taking care of the babies, Red promised not to kill us unless we deserve it."

A long silence followed. "Bib! Pay attention to me! Red has confused you. You shouldn't do nice things for the dragons. Your job is to help us escape, and that's your only job!"

"I am helping. Everything I'm doing is for us." I glanced around at the darkness, listening for a dragon who could be quite silent when she wanted. "I have to get back now. Just . . . nothing's wrong. If I do a good job, Red will owe me a favor. I'll be here tomorrow."

I jogged back into the tunnel and waited outside it until Red crawled out of the room.

I said, "Since another day has passed, may I ask you another question?"

Red's tail whipped, but she said, "You may."

I prepared myself to be whisked to the top of the mountain.

"Why are you waiting?" Red asked. "Do you have a question or not?"

"I'm sorry, I thought you had to fly us to the top of the world before I was allowed to ask."

"How outlandish you are, even for a man. Ask."

"What does a dragon do when he stops being a dragon?"

Red stood with just her bellows of a chest moving. After a while,

I thought she wasn't going to answer. Later still, I thought she had forgotten me.

At last, she said, "That's a difficult question. Wouldn't you rather know why we like to keep yaks?"

"No." I laughed, and she did too.

Red drew a great breath. "He decides who he tries to fool and where."

I chewed the inside of my mouth as I watched Red. "Anything else?"

"What else could there be?"

I felt like I was on the edge of understanding what might be the least important part of that. I dared to expose my ignorance. "Try to fool everybody or try to fool himself."

I paused, and Red didn't slither away or kill me.

"Or . . . try to tell himself the truth. Did you say where?"

Red growled "Yes!" and turned to nudge at the soil above the doorway.

"And, um, where. Go where they know the truth! Where they write down truth! Go where the truth is!"

Red glanced at me without stopping. "You see parts of it. Not the important parts." Red snorted.

I said, "All right, I see parts of it. I'll keep thinking about it."

"Good. Now, go and care for my children. Carry the goats inside. You should drag the goats around so they may chase them."

"Red, what about food for me?"

"Oh." The short, black tentacles on her head fell forward. "I'll bring you something soon. Just take care of my children."

I pulled the goat carcasses into the room by the ropes, and Red collapsed the doorway again. The babies tripped over each other, growled, and whimpered until they put some goat between their teeth.

When the goats were half-eaten, I invented a game I called Goat Drag. I trotted around the room pulling both dead goats by ropes. The babies chased me, running and slamming into walls between bites while mewling with hunger.

After a minute, the ropes got harder to pull. I looked back and saw Chexis clamped on to a goat to slow me down, giving Praxsis more time to eat. Then they switched so Chexis could eat.

Later, the ropes became even harder to pull. I looked and found that each baby was crouched atop a mostly devoured goat carcass, riding as I pulled them around the room.

Red was right. They were smarter than me.

I sat, and they crawled on top of me to sleep. I may have slept a bit too.

I considered what was happening outside this room. Alamore was somewhere in the world breathing air and murdering girls. Pil's family was running from the war, or maybe they were about to be killed. I needed to kill Jon for Princess Bannice, and because it would be a good thing for mankind.

And Lossil would die when I found him, no matter how many soldiers or magic curtains he had around him.

I preferred not to chase my enemies all over the kingdom, though. If I gathered them in one place, I could destroy them with great efficiency. I had heard a lot of them say they wanted to go home. The thing that could take them home would be damned important to them.

I didn't know where that thing was, but it was definitely not in this room. I'd have to go find it.

"Just as soon as the babies don't need me anymore," I said. That almost sounded odd when I heard myself say it, but I shook that concern off as crazy thinking.

I slept some more when the baby dragons weren't kicking me in the stomach and nipping me on the butt.

Red came back with four goats the next evening. I was too beaten up to ask her a question. I hadn't mastered the art of reading dragon moods, but she seemed distracted.

"Did you bring me food?" I asked.

"Not this time. I will soon. If you're that hungry, do something about it. You're a sorcerer."

After she crawled inside the room, I ran back to the tunnel mouth, which had been blocked again. "Pil!"

Pil called back, "What are you going to do about the baby dragons?"

"When they get bigger, I'll ask Red to release us." I couldn't imagine why I had said that. Red had already said no to that idea. The thought had come out and filled up the conversation, and there was no room left for me to correct it.

"Bib!" Kenzie yelled, "Bib, are you lying to us?"

"Pil! I told you not to tell the others!"

Kenzie said, "So it's more important to help the dragons than us? Do you love that dragon more than us now?"

"No!"

"He's lying," Vargo said. "We're without him now. The dragon has him charmed in some way."

"Vargo, you know that's not true," I said. "I'm not charmed."

Kenzie raised her voice. "Then you've chosen to abandon us. You want something from the dragons, and you'll let us die to get it."

"That's crazy. Pil, tell her that's crazy."

Pil didn't answer for a few seconds, which told me a lot. "Bib wouldn't do something to hurt us," she said at last.

"That's crap!" Acton said. "He won't hurt you, Pil. However, he would throw the rest of us off this mountain for a few secrets and a sack of wine!"

"Trust me!" I said. "I've earned your trust."

Vargo said, "How many times have your plans included killing one of us? Or all of us?"

"How many times have I saved you?" I asked.

"You saved yourself," Kenzie shouted. "We merely were by chance standing around close by. I, not you, have saved our folk from dying, over and over."

"This will all be clearer tomorrow, I promise." Part of me believed that. Another part thought this situation was already as clear as it could get and that they'd see it soon. "I have to go before Red catches me. Meet me here tomorrow." They were still talking when I turned away, but I ignored them.

I trotted back up the tunnel and waited until Red came out of the room. Before I could ask a question, Red snapped, "Inside now!"

I stepped inside with Chexis and Praxsis, then Red collapsed the doorway.

The babies played like they would die if they stopped. Twice they bit each other hard enough to draw blood. They bit me that hard once. The only thing I found that distracted them from such murderous behavior was singing. They didn't mind that I was off-key. They sang worse than I did.

My stomach growled like a big, hungry dragon, and I wondered whether Red intended me to starve to death. I gathered a large pile of sticks and wood splinters, then used the blade of my sword to shave some splinters into kindling. The babies watched every move, mewling to me and to each other.

Then I did something that I regretted but was necessary. I tossed a yellow band into the sky, then another, and finally two more until I found a flock of geese. I try to never harm a creature when I call it, although sometimes it happens. I had no choice now.

I called five geese in through the hole in the ceiling. The babies started chasing the terrified, honking geese. I grabbed one and killed it while the little dragons scrambled after the others. The room wasn't big enough for the geese to take flight, but the clumsy babies had never seen prey before. The hunt lasted quite a while.

By the time Chexis and Praxsis had caught and devoured their four geese, I had cleaned my goose, used the lantern and the sticks to build a nice fire, and set it to roasting on a spit. The babies watched the fire as if it might jump up and give them a present, even pushing their faces into the flames. I distracted them by singing the loudest and nastiest drinking songs I could remember. They bounced around and joined in with squeals and snorts.

Praxsis and Chexis got the drumsticks. I ate the rest.

By the time their mother returned the next day, the babies had grown to the size of a small pony. Sessions of Goat Drag had to end when they tried to ride the goats. They spoke their first words, the chorus of a song in my language: *Punch him in the gut, his sister is a slut.*

They sang it for Red, who was not pleased, but I couldn't go back and do something else.

"Go outside the tunnel," Red growled to me when she pushed into the room. "When you didn't fight today, One wanted to know where you were. You should be out there when he flies over tonight." Red shoved one eye up close to my face. "Do not tell anyone about my children! No one!"

I nodded. "All right. Who fought in my place today?"

"Not-Food."

"Which one?" I asked with more impatience than was wise.

Red flipped her tail and whacked it against the tunnel wall. "Who can tell? Go."

"Is the Not-Food still alive?"

She had already slithered into the room with her babies.

I trotted outside and found it was sunset. In a glance, I saw Pil and Vargo standing away from the others in conversation. Kenzie and Acton sat on the ground holding each other, although it wasn't really that cold today.

Evonne shocked me. She was kneeling beside Jon and pushing a bowl of nasty-looking stew into his hands and scolding him to eat. He was staring at the sky and ignoring her.

A dozen dazed new people had arrived.

"All right . . ." I muttered.

Everybody seemed to see me at once. Pil, Evonne, Acton, Kenzie, and Vargo ran and crowded around me. Jon sat watching the sky. The new prisoners stood huddled or lay on the ground.

Pil said, "What is your plan, Bib?"

"Any plan will fail unless we create an incredible distraction for Red."

"Like taking her babies hostage," Acton said. "Threaten to kill them unless she flies us all to Ebring."

I stared at him. "I may be a bit confused about a few tiny things, but such overblown ignorance as that has never plopped out of my mouth."

Acton stepped toward me, but Vargo held him back.

I said, "My plan is to do as Red asks while I explore until I find an opportunity to escape and live through it."

"And that leaves the little dragons alive," Acton sneered.

"No matter our plan, we must kill them for the safety of the kingdom," Kenzie said. "We all agree on that."

"Oh? Does everybody agree?" I asked.

Kenzie, Acton, and Vargo nodded. Evonne gave a little nod after hesitating. Vargo and Acton began edging toward me. Pil didn't nod, but she looked down.

I took a breath and relaxed until I had just enough tension left to stand.

"Back! Get back!" Pil shouted, dragging Vargo and Acton away from me. "All of you, go over there by Jon!"

They questioned and complained, but they went. I saw that in just a couple of days they were all following Pil's lead. It didn't surprise me. She had led everything from armies in battle to families at the supper table.

Pil stepped close. "I know you weren't going to kill us all, but I wanted to stay extra safe."

"I wasn't going to kill you all," I said. "I was going to kill everyone but you. That sounds odd, doesn't it? Why did you ask Harik to change my memories so that I'd think you were dead?"

"I didn't do that!" she barked. She waved Vargo away when he tried to join us. "Did Harik say that? You know he's a liar!"

"And I know you're not." I sighed. "Pil, you understand that I want to escape as much as anybody does, but we have to be smart. Do you trust me?"

"Do you mean as much as you trusted Harik when he told lies about me?"

Nothing I could say would help me answer that and come out looking good, so I changed the subject. "What happened here today?"

Pil crossed her arms. "Acton fought as Red's champion and won, but it was brutal and I think it weighs on him. He's not as hard as he thinks he is. But Kenzie saw the fight and decided she loves him. How many years have they pretended she doesn't?"

I shrugged, not caring much. "What about Evonne and Jon?"

"I think he may have lost his mind, or he's a marvelous actor, but Evonne seems to have been overtaken by a maternal instinct. I hope she doesn't regret it someday."

"You and Vargo?"

"We're looking for a way to escape. One that makes sense." She glared at me.

"Have you shoveled the dragon crap yet?"

She made a face.

Pil and I discussed escape, the people we needed to kill, and the ones we needed to save, as well as the wisdom of doing each. We solved nothing and at last moved apart from the others for a shred of privacy and then sleep.

Deep in the night, I kissed Pil, got up, and walked into the tunnel where Jon and I had polished buckets and barrels. Helline, lying beside a fire, nodded at me as I walked past.

The day Pink had taken me to the room of buckets and barrels, one of the darkened rooms along the way had bothered me. I hadn't been able to stop and explore it, though. Now as I padded down the tunnel and found it, I realized that something inside glinted in the torchlight. This had to be Red's hoard of treasure. I entered with great caution, in case Red had set traps.

I found the gold, but it was far less extravagant than I expected. It consisted of three golden frameworks against the far wall, each wide enough for two people and eight feet tall. A cloth, such as the one I had used to fetch Lossil, hung from one of them. I stared around, perplexed.

When I turned to the other wall, I found three large wooden chests banded with gold. Each was packed with nondescript cloths like curtains.

I wanted to cheer since this might be an escape. Then guilt slammed me when I thought about leaving Chexis and Praxsis. Well, the others could escape this way even if I stayed behind.

My urge to cheer crumbled. I didn't know where any of these curtains would take us, and I didn't know how to find out.

Well, that wasn't true. I did know how to find out.

I grabbed the curtain that was already hanging. I would take it with me, hoping that it would bring me back here even if something went wrong. By lantern light, I examined the other curtains. I didn't see any labels saying THE WAY HOME or LOSSIL'S CAMP or THE BOTTOM OF THE OCEAN.

I pulled out a curtain at random, hung it on the framework, and drew my sharp sword. I was already stepping through the thing when I wondered whether taking a curtain through another curtain would blow the top off the mountain.

THIRTY-EIGHT

I stepped out of the curtain, and my boots squished. The thick crescent moon hung like an empty fishing net in the night sky, and the stars told me I was still on the island. The smells of cold mud and rotting vegetation filled my nose. Light flashed behind me, and I turned to see lightning and fire blaze around a long, low set of buildings.

Even though I couldn't see the buildings well, I recognized Gallin on the Mere, the school where I had learned sorcery. Gallin backed up to a wide marsh, which had always protected it from attack on that side. Tonight, Lossil's soldiers were attacking it, and it looked like they needed only three sides to overrun the place.

I splashed fifty feet toward the school before the frigid marsh mud began sucking hard at my boots. No road seemed to be nearby when I scanned around.

As sorcerous attacks spewed from the school, I watched soldiers, backlit against the fires, pushing in among the buildings. Everybody at the school might be dead or captured by morning, and I couldn't do a damn thing about it.

I turned around but couldn't find the return curtain waiting for me. Panic closed my throat for a moment before I saw it hanging

320

from the nearest tree branch, one hundred feet away. So, the traveler might not arrive at quite the same place as the curtain, then. Whoever designed that should be poked in the eye.

I slogged over to the curtain and stepped through, which put me right back in Red's curtain room. After laying the Gallin cloth by itself in a corner, I reached into a chest and pulled out another as if I were pulling an apple out of a barrel at the village fair. I hung this curtain on the framework and walked through it.

"This damn thing is broken," I muttered, when the curtain put me in the marsh again. However, I couldn't see Gallin on the Mere being destroyed, and here the ground's surface was frozen. The water around Gallin had been cold as hell but not frozen, so I was not in the same southern marsh.

I examined how the stars had shifted, and it put me on the north end of the island. Some quick calculation showed I was likely in the large Klipid Swamp, just east of Ebring along the coast. When I was young, Klipid had been a fallback refuge for Ebring in case something truly horrible happened at the capital.

I crept around for a few minutes, keeping the curtain back to the lair in sight. I didn't see or hear any people, nor anything made by people, so at last, I walked back to the curtain and passed through into Red's lair again.

It seemed odd that I had arrived in two different swamps one after the other. Pausing to consider that, I realized I had been thinking about the swamp at Gallin when I pulled out the curtain that took me to Klipid.

I pictured King Elgus's war room in Ebring while fishing for a curtain elbow-deep in a chest, trusting my hand to grab the proper cloth to get me there. Instead, it dropped me on a dark, windy beach pocked with driftwood. Eight reks had clumped around a fire, warming their hands and ignoring the rest of the world, including me.

I probably could have killed them all in a few minutes. Instead, I turned around and walked right back through the curtain. These soldiers were just standing around, and if they could stand around long enough, maybe they would live to reach home. Besides, I should hurry. I expected Red to come looking for me at sunrise, which was just a couple of hours away.

Before I chose the next curtain, I pictured King Elgus's war room again but in as much detail as I could manage. I did leave out the enormous wolf in the floor. I felt around inside one of the chests for the proper curtain, although I couldn't describe or even imagine how I would know the right one.

The curtain I selected did not send me to the war room, but it put me fairly close. I stood on the big hill south of Ebring, where I could see both the main gate and the side gate. The city was burning, and it looked as if the palace was burning too. Some reks and difar charged into the city through the main gate. Others dragged residents out through that gate to kill them.

Both Gallin and Ebring were being overrun on the same night. It was a horrible thing, but I did have to admire Lossil's efficiency.

I spotted people running out the side gate into a shallow defile leading southeast, and plenty of Lossil's troops were chasing them. A few of Elgus's soldiers led the way, and a bigger detachment fought at the rear to protect seventy or eighty fleeing people.

I could've left them on their own, and maybe I should have. Elgus hadn't protected his people too well, and they didn't think much of me, anyway. I had no time to shepherd the sad creatures that the people of Ir had become.

"Shit!" I muttered, forcing myself not to think about this too carefully. I ran down to the leading soldiers, waving my arms, and I managed not to get killed by mistake. After pointing the vanguard uphill toward the curtain, I ran to engage Lossil's soldiers. The rear guard and I killed more than half within a few minutes, and the rest ran.

People had begun to gather in the vicinity of the curtain. However, some had begun wandering away while others had kept running. Despite that, the soldiers did a reasonable job of keeping most of the scared residents close.

I shouted, "I'm sending you to a safe place. Well, safer than this. When you step through this curtain, you'll be partway there. Do not go exploring! Stay put! I will personally impale anybody who wanders away."

About ninety people crossed into Red's lair, and I hoped by Krak's ferocious nose that I'd have time to get them back out.

Nobody seemed to have toddled off for a holiday in the dragon's lair. Those who weren't crying were shouting about witchcraft and the end of the world. I grabbed the curtain that led to Klipid Swamp just as King Elgus clutched my arm.

"You have saved us, sir!" He didn't seem terrified, but he spoke with great fervor for a man about to collapse.

"I haven't saved you yet."

The king patted my shoulder, and I thought he might try to hug me next. "You may have any reward you choose, sir." He glanced at his daughter.

Princess Bannice jerked and lifted her eyebrows as she examined me. Some inner cruelty made me smile at her. She fell back as if punched and then stared at the floor.

I had to agree with her that I would make a lousy king.

Elgus almost babbled, "What do you want? Tell me now!" His face was sooty and his eyes wide.

"Your Majesty, with the greatest respect and deference, I want you to let go of my damn arm. Is Klipid Swamp still your refuge?"

Elgus looked confused but nodded.

"All right. Shut up and follow your soldiers through here."

The soldiers hesitated before stepping through, followed by the king, his daughter, a number of nobles whom I'm sure were essential, and fifty terrified subjects. I crossed into the swamp after them.

"Your Majesty, this swamp is your planned refuge?"

"It is," Elgus said. "Perhaps we should have updated the plans more frequently."

I gazed around for several seconds before shaking my head. "Good luck, then."

I saw Shura hiding behind Elgus, so I grabbed her wrist. "You said you know where Lossil's forces are coming from."

She nodded, no less filthy and exhausted as the king.

I said, "That must be the way home for them too, right?"

Shura sighed. "That probably makes sense."

I dragged her through into the dragon's curtain room without asking or commenting. Then I yanked down the curtain to the swamp and laid it against the wall where I could find it later.

"Shura, look at me! Tell me about the place Lossil uses to go back and forth. Concentrate! I won't kill you or even hurt you if you fail. Lossil's bloodletting murderers will take care of that for me."

Shura asked, "Is it time to destroy them?"

"It will be soon."

The woman clenched her jaw and stood straight. In a few seconds, she seemed four inches taller. "I think it's a marker, or monument, or something. Maybe a bush, or a statue. It could be a fountain, but I don't think so."

"Not that! Tell me what the place around it is like. What does the area look like?"

She jerked her head back. "I don't know."

I shook her by the arms. "Really? You don't know anything? Even a tiny thing?"

When her head stopped flopping back and forth, Shura said, "I don't know what it looks like, but it should be south of Lossil's camp at Krak Hill. I have never been there, but that region is said to be full of hills and canyons."

"How big are these canyons?" I asked.

"The stories say they are great, enormous things that the gods dug. They are bigger than anything in the world, except mountains, which are probably bigger, and you have to not count the ocean."

I asked, "How deep are they? What color is the ground? Are there trees? Do rivers run at the bottom of them? What do the sides look like? I need every detail you can think of!"

Shura's enormous eyes turned up to me. "They're deep. You don't want to fall in because you can't survive it. Apart from that?" She shrugged.

I hung the curtain to the swamp again. "All right, Shura, step through here and go back to your king."

"No. If you are fighting to end the war soon, I will stay with you and fight too."

I shook my head. "That's brave, but you'll die in the first five minutes. That won't help anybody."

Shura jutted her jaw. "I have the right—"

I shoved her through the curtain to the Klipid Swamp and yanked down the curtain.

That might have been abrupt, and I realized it. I hadn't thanked Shura, even though she had been braver than a lot of soldiers. I hadn't needed to be so harsh with her. I didn't know why I had treated her like crap, but I had and couldn't change it, so I put it out of my mind.

I imagined a canyon, deep enough that falling to your death would take a few seconds. I tried not to throw in other details, assuming that no details were better than wrong details. Then I calmed myself and concentrated before digging out another curtain and hanging it.

When I walked through, I almost doubted I was still on the Island of Ir. I stood in darkness near the edge of a cliff. When I blinked hard, I saw by moonlight a matching cliff eighty paces away, so I truly was standing at the top of a wide canyon.

I had never seen terrain like this on the Island, but far to the south, Ir's three highest peaks stood unmistakable. After some calculations, estimates, and guesses, I decided I was in a remote area someplace south of Krak Hill.

If Lossil's troops had built any fires down in the canyon, they were too small or too far off to see. The moon wasn't full, but it was bright enough for my fine eyesight to make out quite a bit on the canyon floor. Ten difar trudged north carrying torches. Two small groups with torches did the same but farther away from me. Two large, tight formations headed south past me at a quick march, moving toward roads that could take them inland.

Part of me concluded that Lossil's means of going home must be someplace to the north, in or near this canyon. Little groups of soldiers were straggling that direction, maybe wounded and going home. Big, well-organized groups were moving south, away from it at a near run.

Only part of me thought that, however. The other part imagined ten more explanations for what I was seeing. There might be a kitchen up there serving hot meals from home. It could be a place for healing. Maybe it was the place where Lossil handed out medals, or rewards, or pet lizards. Those were far from the most fanciful ideas. I needed to see this place for myself.

Looking east, I saw no trace of sunrise yet. Maybe I should return to Red's lair to make sure I wasn't caught. However, Red might not allow me outside tomorrow, or for the next week, or until the babies were grown.

If I could find the place Lossil's men used to come and go, I could tell Pil everything I knew about it the next time we talked, even if it was through two feet of dirt. Then Pil and the others could take action.

Continuing to explore seemed worth the risk.

I mentally marked the curtain's location and loped north along the lip of the canyon. I came upon regular but widely spaced sentries and dealt with them as I reached them. I did it brutally since I wasn't stealthy enough to surprise a butter churn. One fire down in the canyon became visible.

A dozen or so figures crowded around the big campfire, or small bonfire, some sitting and some standing. Most were reks. Two were difar. One was a man, and I found myself looking down on Alamore the repugnant, wicked, pissant hero who had murdered Pala as casually as he'd pick his teeth.

I didn't consider killing him with magic. Wiping out a single man at that range was an uncertain endeavor.

That was a lie. I could drop a lightning bolt on him without much strain. But I didn't just want Alamore dead. I wanted him to suffer and be afraid. I wanted to watch his face while he knew he was dying. I would love killing him as much as I had adored killing when I was young, and I didn't care.

Ten feet away, a rope ladder hung to the canyon floor so the sentries could climb up and down. I sheathed my sword and swung down onto the ladder.

THIRTY-NINE

I surprised a rek at the bottom of the rope ladder, pulled a knife I had stolen from a sentry up above, and killed him before he could cry out. Then I loped away into the darkness that smelled like dust and woodsmoke. I wouldn't be able to stay hidden all the way to the big campfire, so before long, I crouched and considered the problem.

After examining the relatively dry, warm area, I cast five yellow bands around the fire to grab the attention of some creatures. It got them moving and prepared in case I should call them later.

I couldn't creep up to Alamore unseen, but screaming and assaulting him and his allies would be a ridiculous risk. I decided to confuse and unsettle him before I closed in to kill him.

Standing, I bellowed, "Alamore! The Bridge Guardian has come for you!"

Still in darkness, I sprinted to my right while the reks and difar peered at the place I had been moments before. Alamore stepped away from the fire, drew his sword, and began turning his head to listen.

"Alamore!" I shouted again. "Come here and die for your

cruelty, you sack of fat and ashes!" I ran farther around the camp-fire, keeping to the darkness.

Somebody at my feet said something I didn't understand. I looked around and realized I had stumbled into a mass of soldiers trying to sleep on the ground. I wasn't just surrounded. The troops surrounding me were themselves surrounded by a larger circle of their friends.

I sighed, too disgusted to curse. That's when I noticed that the sky was beginning to lighten in the east. Red would come looking for me soon.

My enterprise was not going well. The only thing I could think to do was make sure that it didn't fail entirely. Whether I walked away or was carried, Alamore should be lying dead behind me at the end of this.

I charged toward the fire, cutting soldiers on both sides with my utterly sharp sword as they tried to rise. At the same time, I cast two white bands into the air. Some reks in front of me were hopping to their feet and raising their weapons. I shifted toward a gap between two of them. I left one of them stunned on his ass and the other dead from a horrible head wound.

Ten more reks and difar were blocking my way to Alamore and the fire. I charged into them, using all the tricks I had learned in the Dark Lands. I pushed through in less than a minute, leaving eight dead behind me. I squeezed the white bands, and a gale rose all around us. Sand choked the air and the fire billowed. Just as the sand had blinded everybody, a difar appeared and slashed me, leaving a big, ragged cut across my left leg.

I dealt with the difar before limping toward the faint, jumping firelight. I yelled again, "Alamore! Come here, you baby-murdering piece of horseshit!" I didn't know whether he really murdered babies, but he killed Pala, and that was enough. Then the wind surprised me by dying off, but only a small circle around me. I blinked away sand in time to see a smirking Alamore thrust his sword at my throat.

I parried and dodged, even though my wounded leg shook. I thrust at Alamore's heart, followed it with another thrust, and then lunged toward his eye when my leg held. He leaned away, so I just caught the side of his head, but even that produced a satisfying stream of blood.

My windstorm was still blowing all around us, but somehow Alamore had countered it in this small space. A rek stumbled into our clearing, and I whipped my sword aside to kill him as I withdrew. Alamore glanced at my bleeding leg and circled toward it, stalking instead of rushing me.

I doubted that people called Alamore a hero because his heart was pure. They probably called him one because his sword arm was mighty damn strong. He slashed toward my neck and grazed my shoulder. To throw him off, I withdrew into the sandstorm. Right away, our empty little circle of bloodletting became just a bit bigger and exposed me. That bastard Alamore winked at me to show that he could manage the wind too, although I couldn't feel him using sorcery.

I staggered on my wounded leg and parried just in time when Alamore rushed me. He hooked around to attack me from that side again and force me to rely even more on my wounded leg. I staggered when I sidestepped and almost missed the block.

Then Alamore did a stupid thing. He assumed that I wasn't lying. My leg wasn't good, but it wasn't so bad, either. When he made his third attack on that side, I twisted, raised my utterly sharp blade, and allowed him to cut off his own sword arm at the elbow. He shouted a curse and then groaned, but he didn't retreat. I kicked his knee with my wounded leg and then smashed his jaw with the hilt of my sword.

All that abuse sent Alamore staggering backward, but I wanted to be sure he hit the ground. I seized his collar with my free hand. Just then, another rek rushed into the clearing.

Alamore shouted, "Kill him!"

The rek glanced at each of us, turned, and rushed into the sandstorm again.

Shoving Alamore down, I knelt with my knee on his throat. His eyes bugged out at me. "You didn't have to kill her," I said, leaning over his face. "She couldn't have hurt you in a thousand years, and you threw away her life like trash. You're dying now, but you could have lived if you hadn't been such a royal asshole."

I watched the cruel bastard's face and ignored how many people must have called *me* a cruel bastard. "Don't bother struggling, and you can't beg. You're a cavern of a man—hollow, cold, and worthless. I'm glad you'll die, but I'm no prouder of killing you than I am of killing a bug. You're not worth my pride." I examined his eyes, but by then, he was dead.

The sandstorm couldn't protect me all the way back to the curtain. It would take too much power to keep it blowing on the soldiers as they chased me. I figured most of the reks and difar in the area were gathering near the fire, blinded but looking for the right place to be. I squeezed the yellow bands I had spun earlier and called the gathered creatures to listen as I suggested that the soldiers were about to destroy the creatures' nests, food, children, and anything else their tiny minds cherished.

I dropped the wind, and all the soldiers looked at me. Then everything in the area that could sting or bite swarmed the poor difar and reks, who shouted and sometimes screamed while running in random directions. I returned to the rope ladder at a limping run, grumbled and cursed my way up it, and ran back to the curtain.

Back in the lair's curtain room, I snatched the cloth I had just used and stuffed it behind a chest, where I knew I could recognize it later. Breathing hard, I ran out of the room and turned left toward the outside, Pil, and my other companions. The sun hadn't fully risen, and I began to relax.

Something slammed me to the ground from behind, and I tasted blood. Red's voice snarled from above my head. "What are you doing in here?"

I could hardly breathe with Red's flexing, clawed foot mashing down on me. Not breathing wasn't so bad. If I could breathe, I'd have to talk, and I couldn't think of anything to say that wouldn't get me squished deeper into the floor.

Red growled like a great cat that can knock down stone walls and carry away boats. "And what happened to your leg? Answer me, Chartreuse!"

Then Red roared three feet from my head. I could imagine that roar making men and beasts hurl themselves to the ground to wait for death. I was already on the ground waiting for death, so I was ahead of the game. I could spare a few seconds to think while my bladder opened.

Red was vastly more powerful than me, and also smarter. No lie could save me. I reached for anything that might be no more than half a lie. "I was scouting," I squeaked. "Someday I may need to escape, and I was looking for a way."

"Escape?" Red breathed. Hot ashes fell on my neck.

I nodded. "To save your children. If One attacks and drives you away, he'll want to kill them and me. I would need to escape with Praxsis and Chexis. Or, if the other people here get jealous and try to murder me and the babies while you're gone, we'll need some way to escape. One of these new people has already swung at me and cut my leg." *Or, if the yaks stampede and start goring everybody to death, I'll have to flee from the fury of the yaks.* I didn't say that last one, but it seemed as likely as the others to me.

Red stood silently on me for a long while, breathing ash and whipping her tail. "If any of these things happen, you won't get away. I order you to let yourself be killed."

"I will!"

Stepping back, Red prodded me with one claw. "Go outside. I may kill you, but maybe not. I could kill all your nasty human allies instead."

I hurried outside ahead of the dragon, who snapped at Helline, "Bring the chain and follow me." Red pointed with her tail at Vargo and Kenzie. "You come too. Bring that ladder."

Vargo lifted a ladder from inside the tunnel mouth, a bent and flimsy thing. "Hell, this thing may have killed more people than the dragon."

We all trudged around to the room that held Red's babies, and Red knocked down part of the wall.

The squealing babies jumped into the opening but then bounded away from the strange people, murmuring and glancing sideways. I realized they were talking to each other, although I couldn't make out the words.

Helline directed that I be chained by the ankle to a great ring set into the ceiling. It would allow me to go anywhere in the room. That didn't concern me. When I was ready to leave, I'd just slice the chain with my sharp sword.

While chaining my ankle, Kenzie whispered, "We're ready to act. Be prepared."

"Act? How are you going to act?"

Kenzie hissed and dragged the chain against my anklebone. "Don't you go being obtuse!"

"I'm not," I whispered. "What can you possibly do at this point? No, just stay healthy and pay attention. I'll come rescue you soon."

Kenzie raised an eyebrow as she looked at the length of chain, then glanced at the dragon.

I whispered, "Ask Pil. She'll tell you. She trusts me."

Kenzie sniffed. "She's the one who said to tell you to be ready. Because you've lost your mind."

After Red drove out Vargo and Kenzie, Evonne and Jon brought in eight goat carcasses. The dragon said, "Chartreuse, you shall be imprisoned here until you behave more properly. I may not be back tomorrow."

That meant Red would definitely be back tomorrow to catch me if I was misbehaving.

Before I could answer, Red began collapsing the wall. Soon, I was alone with the babies.

"Goat Drag, Chartreus!" Praxsis shouted. Chexis grabbed a goat carcass and carried it to me without straining.

I set six of the goats aside for later, and I agreed to play Goat Drag if they promised not to ride the carcasses. I towed goats until I had sweated through my clothes.

When the babies had worn out and piled on top of me, Chexis told us a story. It was the first time he had done that. The day before, I had told them one of the stories from my village, "The Shark and Paedla's Nets." It was one of those dead-simple stories that are easy to tell when you're drunk or have two crying babies in the room.

In the story, a wicked shark steals the child of the virtuous fisherman Paedla because he caught too many fish. Paedla and his family sail to the shark's underwater cave with a tribute of fish to get the child released. Once the shark gets the fish, he refuses to let the child go. But Paedla had filled the fish with tiny thorns, which kill the shark. Everybody except the shark goes home and has a nice supper.

By the next day, Chexis had changed the story. Two shark brothers live in their enchanted cave, but arrogant fishermen come to catch them. They trap the sharks in their cave for many weeks, until the sharks are starving. The foolish fishermen then sail too close, trying to kill the shark brothers, but they soon experience the horrible fury of sharks that are hungry. The sharks eat all the fishermen and their families, and they live happily in their cave.

I exclaimed over how wonderful Chexis's story was and asked him to tell it again. Not many sorcerers are allowed to appreciate the raw workings of the dragon mind, especially when the dragon is hungry and has had only one goat today.

The babies ate again and then slept while I pondered ways to escape. I wouldn't escape yet, of course, but I had promised to rescue Pil and the others. When Praxsis and Chexis woke up, they raced around the room for a while, battering the stone walls and each other. I supposed they understood how fragile I was because they didn't try to batter me nearly so hard as they battered one another.

The bit of sky I could see through the hole far up in the ceiling was lightening toward midday when I heard Red begin digging at the blocked door. I smiled at my prediction that the dragon would come back early, trying to catch me doing something wrong. The babies and I stood waiting in the center of the room while Red collapsed the wall and made an opening to the tunnel.

The visitor wasn't Red. The gray dragon, A, pushed his head and forelegs through the hole he had just made. "Oh, I thought it was something like this! Well, not something like this, but something inappropriate."

The dragon's arrogance kept us alive those first few seconds. While he talked to himself, I rushed Praxsis and Chexis to the corner of the room, out of the dragon's sight. He would have to slither around the edge of the door if he wanted to turn and cook us all in that corner.

The babies cowered as deeply into that corner as they could, screaming in fear. I crept along the wall toward Dragon A and the opening.

The dragon chuffed and blew a ten-foot blast of flame toward the center of the room where we had been a few moments earlier. The heat slammed me like a blazing iron door, but he had attacked where we had been, I guess to scare us and show how powerful he was. It was a lazy, smug attack that gained us a few more seconds of life.

I called for the God of Death's sword, hoping I wouldn't get something like a dead snake or a sack of turnips. The white sword appeared in my hand. Without pausing, I lunged around the edge of the door and thrust the sword into the dragon's left foreleg. I withdrew as fast as possible, since I feared that dragons might be impervious to this weapon too.

The dragon screamed and then roared. Rocks and dust plunged from the ceiling. I heard a great thump and let myself hope that the dragon was dead. However, the roaring went on.

Nothing good was going to happen if I stayed against that wall. I darted around the door again and saw that Dragon A's leg had withered. I lunged toward his neck, but he whipped his wing over me and drove me into the floor. Something in my left shoulder crunched, and pain screamed up my left leg, which was still cut and already thinking about giving up.

If only the dragon had knocked me toward the center of the room, he could have breathed fire at me or heaved himself fully into the room to bite me in two. Maybe he instinctively kept me down and under control to avoid any more pain. As it was, Dragon A's left wing was less than a hand's width from my sword, so I couldn't very well miss. I thrust into the wing and its swirling colors. It withered in just a moment.

The dragon roared even louder and dragged itself backward out of the room. I staggered after Dragon A as he turned into the main tunnel with a sound like *slither-thump, slither-thump*. My chain jerked me to a stop in the tunnel, with A moving off at what was probably a respectable speed for a crippled dragon.

Without hesitating, I threw the death sword. With two arms, I could throw it well and even hit my target sometimes. The blade poked into the dragon's behind. He shuddered, bounced off the side of the tunnel, and slammed face-first into the floor. He didn't move. The damn thing looked dead to me.

I called the sword safely back into its tiny space and staggered back into the room. Panting, I slid to the floor and wiped blood off my face with one hand. "Are you all right?" I asked the babies.

Chexis and Praxsis were chittering, a sound I hadn't heard from them before, and they bounced around me. They both licked me several times and thanked me for saving them.

Praxsis squealed, "We love you, Chartreuse, we love you!"

I smiled and patted him on the neck.

Chexis said, "I'll feel sad when we eat you."

FORTY

When Chexis revealed that he and his brother planned to devour me, all of my childhood nightmares about being trapped with hungry young dragons were reborn. Although it seemed insane, I began wondering whether caring for the babies was really the most important thing I had ever done.

"Why do you want to eat me?" I asked Chexis, trying to sound casual about the whole thing.

"We don't want to, not exactly. It's tradition. Mother says you can't defy tradition," Praxsis said.

"You're right, we can't do that." I drew my sharp sword and cut at the chain that was lying at an angle against the floor. One tiny spark flew, but nothing else happened. I tried from a different spot, which left a link of the chain smoking but unharmed. I drew the Death God's sword and hurled a ferocious cut at the chain. It must not have been vulnerable to having its life withered out of it.

"Gorlana's conquering bosom!" I put away the death sword and sheathed my other blade. The babies jumped around and shouted to encourage me. I stared at the chain with no ideas, not even foolish ones.

"It's enchanted, eh?" Pil asked from the opening to the tunnel. "That's a challenge . . ."

I smiled. "Why did you come in here?"

"We heard the horrible sounds of you trying to rescue us, so we thought we should come save your life," Pil said.

Evonne followed right behind Pil, and the babies scampered to huddle and murmur on the other side of the room. Evonne said, "Bib, did you kill this dragon?"

"I suppose I did. I didn't mean to. I stabbed it in the butt, and it just died."

Evonne nodded. "Yes, I am certain it happened in just that way."

Pil said, "We should wait to throw any parties because Red may be on his . . . her way here right now."

I staggered toward Pil and almost fell. Drops of blood hit the floor, and I realized they were coming from my head.

Kenzie marched over to me and grabbed my head to examine it. "Oh, this won't kill you. The raging mother dragon probably will."

Vargo said, "Wait, I'll help you walk if you promise not to bleed or pee on me." When he came to take possession of me from Kenzie, they clasped hands for a length of time that I considered more than just friendly.

"Do you like Vargo or Acton better?" I asked her. "Would you describe the merits and weaknesses of each for us?"

Kenzie kicked my leg, and it collapsed under me.

"I'm sorry!" she breathed with huge eyes and one hand over her mouth.

"Stop." Jon was leaning against the doorway. In an almost distracted way, he said, "Stop. It's time to obliterate our foes or give our lives. The kingdom needs us, so let's stop fighting each other."

Acton was helping me stand when Pil called out, "Everybody, look away!"

I stared at the tunnel. An intense light flared behind me, and a crack sounded. When I glanced back, I saw that the chain was melted in two.

"Now we must descend from this mountain without being smashed," Evonne said. "I do not know how that can happen."

I said, "Don't worry, I have prepared our escape. It involves a desperate assault on Lossil and his armies within his own stronghold."

Nobody spoke for a moment. Then Vargo said, "I think we ought find something easier to start with."

"No, this is the right thing," Jon said. His eyes were too bright, but his voice was steady. "This is the right time. We should escape this captivity and then prepare to destroy the enemies of Ir. How far away are these enemies?"

"About five minutes."

Again, nobody spoke.

I laughed. "Follow me. I found a room full of magic windows that could probably take us anyplace. I know for sure that one of them will take us to Lossil's camp or close to it, because I was there this morning. Oh, Pil and Vargo, Alamore is dead. I'm sorry I didn't save him for you, Pil. I hope you'll feel better knowing it was an ugly death. Now, Vargo, help me walk out of here. Let's see if we can run."

Chexis and Praxsis called my name as I left, but they didn't follow me, and I didn't look back.

Vargo and I moved down the tunnel at a snappy limp. Before we reached the outdoors, somebody pulled my spirit up through the top of my head, stretching me toward the trading place in the Gods' Realm. I felt Acton, Kenzie, and Pil, all three, grab on and get pulled up with me.

I couldn't think of any good thing I might get from Baby Harik, so I tried to struggle free. When that didn't work, I said, "Baby Harik, I've been feeling poorly and need to vomit, which would be a far more productive thing than speaking to you. Goodbye."

I tried to leave, but I had not persuaded the god.

Arriving in the trading place, I stood on what I assumed was the customary dirt patch. I couldn't be sure because water was standing up above my knees. Clouds filled the sky, sullen gray with a purple cast.

Rain wasn't falling, but a stiff wind blew. Water poured like a waterfall out of the sagging green forest, pooled around the gazebo, and drained off through the great field, washing away swathes of flowers.

"Baby Harik, you pinch-butt, groaning molester of innocent animals everywhere, I have nothing to say to you!"

"I shall pass on the compliment, Murderer," said a plain but resonant man's voice.

"Mighty Fingit!" I shouted. "It's been a long time! How have you been?"

"I have been perfect, as I always am," beardless Fingit said while pushing back his red hair with one of his great hands. The Blacksmith of the Gods' hands were truly massive, even for an immortal being. "Looking back, I now regret helping you become the guardian of the Dark Lands. Not a single good thing came of it, as far as I can see."

"I can't think of anything good, either, Mighty Fingit. Thank you for snatching me away from Baby Harik."

"Do you really call him Baby Harik?" Fingit turned his head a fraction to achieve a more divine profile.

"I do. I think he likes it."

Fingit laughed, and his godlike posture cracked. "He's a buffoon. Krak must have chosen him to elevate because he would never seriously challenge FOG."

"FOG?"

"Damn it all!" Fingit shouted, rippling the water all around us. "Father of the Gods. The new Harik is crass, overconfident, and foolish, but he is also insidious. These abbreviations of his have flown all around the realm until they have infected the speech of the gods themselves!"

"What abbreviations, Mighty——"

Fingit raised his voice louder. "FOG. MuH. EOG. SSaP. NAP! For the sake of Krak's early poetry!"

"NAP?"

Fingit waved a hand. "Naked Ambrosia Party. Harik is insignificant to us, but he is a god, so watch yourself."

"Mighty Fingit, do you really make the Feather here abase herself and pray to you?"

"No."

Kenzie stammered, "B-But you're my patron god!"

"Do you have a patron pair of shoes too? Do you pray to them?" Fingit asked. When Kenzie didn't answer, Fingit said, "I never asked her to go around abasing and praying. But I wasn't going to make her stop when it was her idea."

Kenzie blinked, and then her chin quivered.

"Mighty Fingit, you called for us. What would you like to talk about?" I asked.

"Several things. First, I have an interest in the Feather here." He nodded at Kenzie. "She and the Anvil must kill you for Harik, and normally you would slaughter them during the attempt. I want you to agree that you will not, under any circumstances, kill them."

"That sort of leaves me with my butt hanging out here," I said.

"Not at all. I imagine a future in which they attempt to end your life now and then, a good-faith effort to kill you every time. When they try, you pound them black and blue without killing them. Then they will lick their wounds and begin planning their next attempt. This could go on for years, keeping their bargain with Harik satisfied and the three of you alive."

I said, "Kenzie? Acton? What do you think?"

"You'd agree to never, ever kill us?" Kenzie asked. "Acton, what do you think?"

"Oh, that would be all right, I guess." He choked back a laugh.

I said, "I will agree to this deal in exchange for seven squares of power and specific instructions on how to find and destroy this 'wicket' Lossil is using to reach other realms."

Fingit shook his head. "No extra power for you if I tell you how to destroy the link. But why do you want to destroy it? There's some carnage associated with it, sure, but the Dark Lands were a sewer of maiming and blood, and you didn't seem to mind."

I thought about that for a few seconds. "The people here can't live with things the way they're going."

"Do you care that much about them?"

"No. Maybe a little."

"Ah. Destroying the link will be a singular and final act for whomever does it. And the indications are that you must be the one. Do you care enough about these island rats to die for them?"

I thought for a moment. I had already risked death over and over, both here and in the Dark Lands. I did it to kill my enemies, not really to help people. I supposed that doing both at the same time wasn't to be despised.

I glanced at Pil and said, "Fingit, I want to talk to you privately."

"The others cannot hear us now," Fingit said a moment later.

"Baby Harik said that Pil wanted me to think she was dead, and she asked him to change my memories. Pil denied it, said that was crazy all the way around. Can you tell me which is true? I can't make a decision on the deal until I know this."

Fingit said, "Harik lied. The Knife didn't ask him to change your memories. But the Knife lied too. In her heart, she wanted you to believe she was dead."

I blinked at Fingit, but he seemed to think he had said enough. "Why did she want that?"

"She was leaving. I didn't read her mind or anything else so shoddy, but I am certain she understood that if she was alive, you would never stop searching for her."

Fingit looked down and tapped his leg with his finger while he waited for me to catch up.

I said the thought as it came to me. "If I never stop searching for her, then she'll never be free."

Fingit nodded. "It's not a thing she'd admit, even to herself, but that doesn't make it untrue."

I tried to grasp that, but it was too big and too strange.

Fingit went on: "Harik saw these things in her, and he took action without her asking. He changed your perception and memories."

As Fingit said the words, I knew it was true. In the past days, Pil and I had been working too damn hard trying to make things seem right and normal when they weren't that way at all. "Damn it! What was Baby Harik trying to gain? If he'd just opened his mouth and asked me for whatever he wanted, I might have given it to him to avoid all this!"

Fingit lowered his voice. "He just wanted to hurt you. He is a meager god."

I sighed. "If he did all that to hurt me, why are you telling me about it?"

"To hurt him."

I considered it all. I could help people and grind my enemies to powder at the same time. That didn't seem so bad. I might not survive, but as things stood, I couldn't think of anything I particularly wanted. "Fingit, give me the specific instructions on closing the wicket as well as five squares."

"One square."

"Let's settle on three squares," I said.

"Done. The wicket, as you call it, is a small tree. You'll find it beneath a great overhang in the canyon you visited. The person whose actions opened the link must be the one to close it."

"How do you know I opened it?"

"Hm." Fingit put a finger to his chin and examined the sky. "Let me consider that. You, the Dark Lands Guardian, a quasi-mystical being when you're in that role, abandon your pledge and prepare to desert that realm." He gave me a flat look. "That ripped something somewhere, I'll bet."

"The war is weeks old," I said with a scowl. "I left just a few days ago!"

"When did you begin preparing to leave the Dark Lands?" Fingit asked. "Never mind. You don't have to admit it out loud."

That was fortunate. I had started preparing to leave, one way or another, when Pil left. I shut my eyes for a moment before saying, "Oh, screw all that. Let's go kill somebody. I mean, somebody who deserves it. How do I destroy this link?"

"You must embrace the tree. Give it a big hug and don't let go. The tree will begin to wilt, and when it is dead, the wicket will be destroyed. You will be too, almost certainly."

I bowed my head. "Thank you, Mighty Fingit. It has been nice knowing a god with a streak of humanity."

"How dare you?" Fingit roared, and everybody flinched. "Leave this holy place!" I saw him smiling as he flung us back into the world of man.

Fingit didn't slam us back into our bodies, but he threw us with respectable force. The others stumbled, but my leg collapsed and I crashed to the stone floor.

Kenzie felt my leg and then my hip. "Broken. The bone is more than cracked. Some ligaments are torn too. You won't walk far."

I waved her away. "Get us to the curtain room and out of Red's lair, then we can worry about how fast I can run."

Vargo supported me on the wounded side until we reached the outdoors. Pain screamed from my heel to my shoulder, and at times, my leg just gave way with no warning.

"Helline!" I shouted when I saw her trot out of another tunnel. "We're escaping!" Before I could form another word, she threw down her stick and sprinted toward us.

On the other side of me, Jon was urging the twelve new prisoners to join us. All of them came except one, who covered his face with his arms and turned away.

By the time we reached the curtain room, Vargo and Evonne were carrying me while my leg dangled limp. I directed Acton and Kenzie to hang the curtains I pointed out.

I raised my voice. "All right, it's time for an important decision. On this side, we're going to save the kingdom and fight monsters. Most of us will die, but if we live, it'll be free beer and adoring women for the rest of our lives. On the other side, you'll go to the swamp east of Ebring where the king is waiting. If you go there, you'll bow a lot, eat swamp grass, and be forgotten by history. We're leaving in fifteen seconds, so decide fast."

Seven men and Helline chose to go to the swamp. I sent them through and then buried the curtain in a chest so it wouldn't be obvious where they went. Four men went with us, two soldiers, an older fisherman, and a scraggly, bristle-faced man who looked as big as a draft horse to me. The soldiers were Kip and Skally, the fisherman was Terdire, and the big man, who fought in bars for a living, was Jo.

We found ourselves at the top of the canyon in late morning, close to where I'd been the night before. We scrambled into a stand of brush to organize ourselves. Jon and the soldiers stood guard.

The night before, I couldn't appreciate how beautiful the canyon was. The walls stood one hundred feet high and showed a narrow tan layer at the top, a thicker black layer beneath that, and stripes of dark brown, white, red, and greenish brown all the way down to the canyon floor.

Her voice tight, Kenzie said, "I need to heal you up before the fighting, Bib. I must heal everybody, but especially you. If you're not at your deadliest, we'll all be killed down there."

"I'm ready," I said.

"Of course you're ready, you raw bastard!" she snapped. "I'm not. But we'll do this without regard."

Kenzie healed me before handling anybody else's hurts. When she had finished, I lay on the ground while she panted above me. "There, you're well. I even gave you ears again. If you're nice to me and we live, I'll fix your teeth sometime." She bent down and kissed my forehead. "Although I should leave you snaggle-toothed as a warning to nice people you may meet."

"Why the kiss?" I sat up. "Don't you still hate me? Or do you like me right now? I can't keep it clear."

"I like you all right. You're not going to kill me, and that goes a long distance toward me tolerating you."

By the time Kenzie had healed everybody of their wounds, the sun had passed midday. She groaned as she sat on the ground, leaning back in Acton's arms, while he sat behind her.

I said, "I'm sorry, Acton, but you need to come with us."

"We cannot leave Kenzie alone!" he said. "By herself she may be killed!"

"No, he's right, dear," Kenzie said. "You'll need sorcerers, but I can't keep up. Someone who's not a sorcerer will stay and help me. We'll catch up when we may."

Acton stood and stared at Vargo.

Vargo nodded.

Evonne said, "Jo, the mammoth one, he can stay with Kenzie."

Vargo shook his head while Acton said, "No. I do not trust him with this. I don't mean to insult you, sir."

Jo said in a voice so low I thought my teeth would shiver, "No blood drawn. Most of the people I know don't trust me."

"Then you belong among us," I said. "Let's hurry along this rim for a bit. We should find a rope ladder before long."

We had hardly reached the rim of the canyon when the sound of a landing dragon's wings screamed like a high wind. Red sat down on the canyon floor below us, close to the spot where I killed Alamore. The dragon stretched and folded her wings while craning her neck as if looking for somebody. I hoped it wasn't me.

"What do we do now?" Acton whispered.

"That's a fine question," I said. "I probably should have thought up an answer before something like this happened."

<h1 style="text-align:center">FORTY-ONE</h1>

I watched Red on the canyon floor surrounded by Lossil's soldiers, beating her wings and whipping her tail. I couldn't make out the words she was shouting. The reks and difar backed away but froze when the dragon popped her wings with a boom worthy of a volcano spitting boulders. She roared, spun, and knocked half a dozen big difar tumbling with her tail.

"Hide behind those boulders!" I said over my shoulder.

Jon said, "If the dragon flies this direction, those boulders will not conceal us."

"All right, lay on the dirt and hope she thinks you're a dead pony," I said.

After a few more minutes of terrorizing the soldiers, some of whom just fell to the ground as she roared, Red took flight. She traveled straight down the canyon and never looked toward us.

I signaled for the others to follow me. We trotted along far enough back from the rim to be unseen from the canyon floor. When we reached a rope ladder leading down, I paused at the top.

Pil said, "Anything could be facing us, so we sorcerers need to conserve our power. If we can defeat it with steel, don't waste magic."

I nodded to her and then glanced up at the clouds that were collecting. Kenzie may not be able to keep up on foot, but she could still manage the weather for us. She had begun that task when we trotted away from her and Vargo.

I climbed down the ladder first. Three sentries stood around near the bottom, staring up at me like dogs that have treed a squirrel. More sentries were running toward us. If this was the way our luck was going to run today, I might as well surrender now and offer to groom Lossil's dog and his monster.

Ten feet above the ground, I drew my sword and dropped off the ladder, slicing a man's weapon, arm, and shoulder on the way down. I rolled as he collapsed, then I spun to drive the other sentries back so Evonne and Jon could reach the ground. The three of us advanced in different directions, attacking four sentries and clearing a space around the ladder.

We decided on a rough formation for moving through the canyon. Evonne, Jon, and I would travel side by side in the front rank. Acton and Pil would follow us, ready to fight or use magic. The two soldiers and the sailor would make up the back rank. Finally, we would put Jo in the center of it all so he could run to help anybody who was struggling.

We pushed north along the broad canyon for a couple of minutes, killing or driving away sentries as they reached us. The canyon walls gradually closed in, which squeezed our formation. Just when it looked as if we might have routed these reks and difar, we reached a side canyon on the right. A wave of sentries charged out of it, slamming into Jon and Pil.

The sentries pressed us hard, almost collapsing our formation, until Jo and I wheeled to push them back. Evonne kept them from surrounding us on the left. Acton tossed lead balls over our heads, then detonated them farther back in the mass of sentries. I absently wondered how many of these little lead balls he had brought with him from Drup and how he was able to stagger along under the weight.

Within a few minutes, we had killed or driven away all the sentries near us. Pil had taken an annoying, shallow cut most of the way down her arm, but nobody else had suffered more than minor wounds.

We regrouped and pushed north again before more reks and difar could arrive. The canyon opened up again to almost two hundred feet wide, but none of our enemies pestered us for a bit.

Beyond the open space, the canyon narrowed quickly to about fifty feet wide. I saw ahead that it curved hard to the right. We pushed around that curve and saw a great mass of soldiers, one hundred or more, and they appeared well organized for defense.

Rather than charge us, the soldiers waited for us to attack their strong position. That is what undid them.

Acton and Pil moved forward into our front rank right away. Acton created half a dozen explosions among the soldiers. The ones who didn't die cried out, fell back, or just ran the hell away. Then Pil drew two sticks of modest length from her belt and snapped one of them. She didn't warn us, and the flash of light blinded me for a moment. After rubbing my eyes, I saw a ten-foot swath in which every soldier as far as I could see had simply been burned away from the waist up.

Lossil's soldiers fell back, but forty of them regrouped not far ahead where the canyon had begun to open up again. We charged, and even outnumbered, I felt confident that the shock would rout them. Evonne, Jon, and I assaulted them, and the others held back to help if any of us got into trouble.

The soldiers wavered when we hit them, and I killed three in the first ten seconds. A man in a fanciful cloak with a tastelessly long sword shouted orders, whacked a fleeing soldier on the butt, and took a noble pose. Evonne had seen him first and was cutting her way through the soldiers to reach him. I followed to support her and protect her back.

That's when the next sixty soldiers arrived from around a bend in the canyon. It taught me that in this canyon we could expect enemies to arrive from anywhere at any time. Evonne refused to retreat. While she dueled the leader, who must have been one of the five heroes, I protected her with a storm of swordsmanship. Pil cut her way forward to help me. By the time

Evonne swept off the hero's head, I had killed or wounded at least twenty soldiers.

Evonne, Pil, and I fell back to rejoin the others. Evonne had been stabbed deep in the shoulder, which was bleeding. Two reks jumped forward as we regrouped, grabbed Pil, and dragged her down before I could rush to help her. Within seconds, Jo hurled both soldiers off her, picked her up unharmed, and set her on her feet as if she were made of glass.

A wave of difar pushed to surround me, knocking aside a couple of reks who were in their way. Acton ran to me, swinging the green fire sword, and the difar hesitated. Acton put his back to mine, and we fought that way for a couple of minutes. When I at last could look around, the entire fight was over. Every enemy soldier in sight was on the ground either dead or wounded.

When I turned to Acton, the front of his body was soaked with blood. A good amount of it came from a deep scalp wound above his left eye. He kept trying to push the blood out of his eye using the heel of his hand. More blood came from several small wounds that shouldn't interfere with his fighting. The rest must have been the blood of his enemies.

"Thank you, son," I said as I examined his scalp. "You are a tolerable ally in a fight, for a mainlander." He nodded and winced as he held his scalp wound closed. I wrapped his head wound with strips from my shirt and gave him my hat to help hold the wound in place.

Jon had made a stand with his two soldiers. He had survived with a few ragged cuts. The soldiers had both died defending him. A rek had stabbed Jo in the chest, but the blade had just scraped up his breastbone, bounced over his throat, and stabbed him in the bottom of the chin. Although blood was dripping from his chin, he waved the sailor, Terdire, away when the man tried to help him.

Terdire was the only one of us unwounded. He snorted. "It's all due to my sweet face and my bitter marriage."

Evonne said, "I do not see more of them, but that might mean nothing. I wonder if we should send forward a scout or two to find the enemy?"

Pil shook her head. "We're so few, I believe we should stay together, because one of us or even two would be easy to surround and kill without the rest of us to protect them. It won't be good to blunder into the enemy's positions, but that's how we discover everything else in this world, and it's worked so far." She grinned around at everybody.

We crossed a great area of canyon, over half a mile long and up to three hundred feet wide, without seeing any of Lossil's soldiers. When the canyon had narrowed again to two hundred feet, I held up a hand to stop everybody.

I pointed ahead. "Way up there, where the canyon gets as narrow as a snake's ass, I see fortifications."

"I don't see that," Jon said. "I don't see anything like that. I know you're not a coward, so why are you telling this lie? Are you a traitor?"

I sighed. "Yes, I'm a traitor. You have discovered me. I've been planning treason every night before I go to sleep and while I'm at the privy. I got us captured by a dragon as part of my mysterious, traitorous plan to betray the kingdom by treason." I glared at Jon. "By Lutigan's devastating manhood, Jon, you make me tired."

Jon stared up the canyon for a few seconds. "Well, perhaps there is something odd there."

Pil shook her head. "What do you see, Bib?"

"It looks like some kind of low fortification, maybe wooden. That's all I can tell."

Pil wrinkled her forehead. "We should attack before we get close to them, I can tell that, because if I created that position, I would back it with an archer for every bow I could find. Will Limnad help us?"

"I don't think so. Not yet, anyway. She's grieving," I said.

"What about Kruppin?" Acton asked.

I shook my head. "He's busy waving my ears around in the monster town square. I think we have to rely on ourselves."

The tingle of lightning built up under me.

"Don't move! Close your eyes!" I shouted.

A sorcerer behind the fortifications had a fine sense of location, and he would have brought the lightning right through us if I hadn't whipped out a white band and shoved the bolt's strike point sixty feet. I felt battered when it struck but not stunned.

"Charge them! Get out of this!" Jon yelled.

"No!" I said, grabbing the man's arm. "Don't get closer! I can't protect you from lightning and arrows at the same time."

"Protect us? I don't see you doing *anything* to protect us!" Jon said.

Pil took a step toward Jon. "Shut up and do what you're told."

Jo stepped in front of Jon to protect him from Pil.

Evonne said, "I see you have another bodyguard, Earl of Soppingham—"

"Close your eyes again!" I shouted.

I pushed the lightning strike eighty feet toward the canyon wall. Rocks cracked, and a few tumbled into the canyon. I had learned what I needed to learn, though. This sorcerer was inexperienced, and I could push her or him around easily as long as my power held out. I was carrying a reasonable amount, even for an extended fight.

Shifting lightning was a complex business. I could engage in a lightning duel with this sorcerer, but all I knew about his location was that he was "over there someplace." The bastard knew exactly where I was.

The complexity of dismantling arrows made shifting lightning look like dusting off a chair. Our main problem now was that Lossil's troops could see us, but we couldn't see them, or at least not well. I yelled, "When I give you the word, run toward the enemy!"

I whipped five white bands up into the storm. Kenzie had done a fine job, and the clouds were full of water and potential energy. A few seconds later, a heavy rain began falling on the fortifications, making it impossible for anybody manning them to see us down the canyon.

"Run now!"

The enemy sorcerer threw lightning again, but it landed where we had been, two hundred feet behind us. He or she didn't know where we were anymore. But I knew exactly where the enemy's rampart was.

I shouted, "Slow down!" Over the next two minutes, I dropped eight strokes of lightning on or behind the enemy's fortifications. I could feel the other sorcerer pushing against them without success.

All of us had drifted back into our formation. "Rush them!" I yelled.

We ran forward, and when we were fifty feet from the enemy, I lifted the rain. The wooden fortifications were pulverized, and survivors were struggling to stand or stagger away. I felt lightning build under me again, and I saw a woman behind the wreckage, swinging her arms side to side as she stared at the sky.

As the woman's charge built, I shoved the strike point right under her. She should have run. Instead, she fought to push it back toward me but failed. I had probably dealt with lightning a hundred times more often than she had. The bolt struck and obliterated her.

I called down one more bolt of lightning on the running survivors. Then we charged again. I watched for arrows as we ran.

Evonne, Jon, Acton, Pil, and I jumped over the charred remnants of the fortifications and cut down the few soldiers still there. Jo fought beside Jon, who must have bribed the man to serve him. Terdire stayed back and watched for trouble behind us.

As we pursued the survivors, a thirty-man counterattack closed on us from ahead along with twenty more men from each side. I reached for the Death God's sword and came out with a handful of soaked weeds. "Shit!" I shouted. I almost tried to create a small sandstorm but realized I didn't have time.

I faced forward with Pil beside me. Evonne and Acton turned left, while Jon, Jo, and Terdire spun right. Acton threw lead balls and ignited them among the enemy, who screamed and pointed at him. I ran straight through the enemy formation, killing as I went, then turned and ran back through to rejoin Pil where I started. The reks began backing away, and one threw down his sword.

Pil broke another twig. An enormous cloud of steam appeared in front of us, engulfing a dozen soldiers who screamed, ran, and fell. Any qualms Pil had about killing must have faded, or at least been set aside for now.

Glancing around, I saw Evonne surrounded by difar as she

stood over Acton, who lay facedown in the sand. I crashed into the difar, then Evonne and I killed three of them in less than three breaths. The remaining two ran.

I was panting, and my sword felt heavy. I figured at least one-third of the enemy soldiers we'd fought had survived unhurt and simply ran away. That didn't please me as much as it might have, since they would reinforce whomever we fought next.

Hell, Lossil might be sacrificing a great many soldiers to suck us into an ambush that nobody could survive. I shook that thought aside because I couldn't do much about it right then.

Acton screamed for a second when we rolled him over, then he bit his lip hard enough to draw blood. He had taken a belly wound. He howled and shoved my hand away when I tried to examine the wound.

"Stop it! I can walk," he panted. He tried to sit up and let loose a full scream this time. I saw blood in his mouth.

"Sure. See if you can walk over to those rocks and hide until this is all over," I said. "I can help you."

"Wait, I'm sorry."

"Hell, you've got nothing to be sorry over," I said.

"I'll be dead soon. That won't help you much." Lying on his back, he blinked hard, and one tear ran down the side of his head.

I said, "Maybe you won't die. Kenzie might come along. Or you could make some sort of deal with Lutigan."

Acton made a face. Under all the blood, he didn't look like a boy at all anymore. "Bib, we're sorcerers. We know that we will end up like this. I knew it was possible, yet I came along anyway, so I'm the one at fault. Thus, I can be as sorry as I care to be, you superior bastard." He laughed for a second and then bit back a scream.

I glanced around but didn't see any more of Lossil's troops approaching yet. Pil was putting Jon's left arm in a sling. Evonne knelt, pushing a cloth into her shirt against her bleeding shoulder.

Acton said, "Kenzie tells me that the Bib stories are true. Literally true. If that's so, Bib . . ." He paused to gasp. "Doesn't all your murder and fury go back to one thing? Your daughter was dying, and you killed many, many people to save her. Why did you do that?"

"Misplaced heroism."

"Crap. I'm dying. You can be honest and not fear I'll tell anybody."

I grinned at him. "Selfishness. Her life wasn't worth more than the lives of anybody I killed. But it was worth more to me." I shrugged.

"Just selfishness? Nothing more?"

"It's plenty. As destructive as a crossbow bolt to the forehead."

"That's interesting. I don't know whether I'd do the same." Acton sat up without groaning. "Maybe I'm not dying yet. I suspect I misjudged my wound."

I stared at him. He reached up, but I didn't help him to his feet. "You pretended to be dying?"

"It was educational. I used your guilt against you, Bib. You should be careful of that." Acton clambered to his feet. "Guilt may be worse than selfishness, at least for you."

I walked away from the young man, careful not to shake my head or give any sliver of information away now that I knew he was watching me so closely. I had sworn not to kill him, but he hadn't sworn not to kill me. And now he possessed one of the great keys to sorcery. He was a sneaky son of a bitch.

Pil and Jon came over to me, and she asked, "How much farther?"

"Pretty far, I guess."

Jon said, "We will never get there. We'll be killed first."

"That's not a very sunshiny attitude, Jon," I said. "Go home if you want to. I won't even talk mean about you. You can wait around in the swamp for Lossil to come kill you, because he's coming to kill everybody."

Jon frowned at the dirt.

"Hell, Jon, fate has given you a chance to save your entire people. That's a gift you oughtn't throw on the ground. You and I will never be heroes because we're too cruel and devious. Today may be the closest we can ever come."

Jon didn't agree before he walked away, but he didn't tell me I was full of crap.

Pil leaned toward me and murmured, "I think you're wrong. You're a hero."

I snorted. "I'd rather be a blind, three-legged dog."

Pil, Evonne, Acton, Jon, Jo, and I jogged across the open canyon until we reached another sharp curve. There we halted.

I said, "I'll take a peek. Stay close, but not too close."

I crept around the corner and eased out my head. After examining things, I walked back. "Forty men and two monsters."

Evonne straightened. "That is not so bad."

"That's between here and the next curve, maybe one hundred fifty feet. Just past that is another section that must be about like it. Possibly more than one," I said. "Hell, maybe ten, or fifty."

Jon grunted. "Who's not being sunshiny now?"

Pil shook her head at me. "You can't be sure there are more of these sections."

"Oh, I can be sure there's at least one. Lossil's not in this section, but his monster is. I've never seen Lossil without the nasty, glittery beast."

Jon took a deep breath. "Good!"

I raised an eyebrow at him.

Jon added, "If Lossil is ahead, that means we're close to ending this war. We should be celebrating!"

FORTY-TWO

Before we rushed up to round the corner and charge Lossil's troops, I reached again for the Death God's sword. It plopped into my hand. I glanced at Pil and saw a knife in her hand, the one that years ago she had enchanted to be hard to see and deadly. But she had been young and done it the hard way, spending a sinful amount of power.

"Pil, are you out of magic?"

"Almost, but if our enemies can be killed by magic rope ladders or campfires that light themselves, you're about to witness a great slaughter."

I kissed her and turned to everybody else. Holding up the death sword, I said, "I'll go first and kill all I can. Stay back to defend our flanks. If I see a good place to pause and regroup, I'll signal like this. If I don't, we'll drive forward until Lossil and Burrud are dead, and the survivors are running."

Nobody told me I was crazy, so I ran toward the next corner with Evonne and Jon flanking me. Jo kept close to Jon, and Pil followed Evonne. Acton trotted along in the middle of us all, and Terdire followed at the rear. The sailor was the only one of us who hadn't even been scratched, and I had started to wonder whether he was Lutigan, or maybe one of the other gods, in disguise.

A furnace-like blast of air overwhelmed me, along with the resounding bang of a dragon's wings slapping the air above us. Red had come to a halt fifty feet in the air ahead of me, hovering with a slow flap of wings.

"Chartreuse!" she bellowed, and my ears rang. "You left my children unattended!"

I waved the others back with my left hand while dangling the Death God's sword as casually as possible in my right. After I had killed A with the sword, I realized I should never have worried whether it could harm dragons. The old God of Death had slain half the dragons in existence, and this sword's power came from him.

I yelled, "But Red, I also saved your children's lives!"

"And you abandoned your position as my servant without permission!"

I walked toward Red, which might seem insane. However, the farthest I had seen a dragon breathe fire was about thirty feet. I could hurl the death sword that far. With a modest amount of luck, I could hit what I aimed at. It helped that the dragon was a big target.

"Red, I was happy to care for the little critters. They're lovable. But I chose not to dawdle around in that cave until they ate me. Can you blame me for that?"

"Of course I can blame you!" Red lifted her head and roared. Behind me, I heard Jo groan and hit the ground. "Being eaten by a baby dragon is an honor!"

I had closed the distance to forty feet. "Well, why didn't you explain it to me that way?"

"It was supposed to be a surprise."

"And why was that?"

Thirty-five feet.

"Your mind is too primitive to understand the honor that you were being given!" Red shouted it, but then she glanced away. She knew that she was full of crap.

"I hadn't thought about it that way, Red. You make an interesting argument."

Thirty feet. I grasped the sword's hilt tighter.

Red growled. "You're behaving insolently at my expense. Stop it."

"It hurts me to think that if I could strike you dead right now, Praxsis and Chexis would be left alone to die," I said.

"That's impossible!"

"I imagine A thought it was impossible too."

Red's voice dropped, and she said evenly, "Are you daring to threaten me, you pasty rodent?"

"I certainly am not! I'm offering you a gift. I intend to secure life and freedom for you and your sons."

Red paused, flapping a few feet closer to me. "That is the most moronic thing I have ever heard you say."

"The magnificent dragon One is a wise and kind leader, as well as a gentle lover," I said. "That is certainly the most moronic thing you've ever heard me say. My gift comes in two parts. First, I won't destroy you now, so you and your children will live. Second, I'll destroy the path back to your realm, so you'll be free."

Red lifted her head again, roared, and shot a great tongue of flame in the air. "I should never have answered your slime-crawling questions!"

I pressed on. "Your effort in this realm has gone poorly, Red, I can see that. Soon, more dragons will come to find you, question you, and crush your life until you're small and safe. While they're looking for you, you'll never be free, so let me go on and shut down the path to your realm."

"You'll die before you close the wicket. You'll die before you even get there."

"Then you won't have lost a thing."

Red hovered for a few seconds, and the only sound was the beat of her wings. "I see it."

"You see it."

Red soared up out of the canyon and toward the mountains.

Acton was slapping Jo awake. Pil put her forehead on my

shoulder and sagged. Evonne, Jon, and Terdire had backed away and were staring at me as if I might breathe fire and fly away too.

"Dammit!" I whispered to myself. I walked toward Acton, pretended to trip on nothing, and fell on my face. When I climbed to my feet like a clumsy fool, people seemed far less scared of me.

I beckoned to the others and lifted the Death God's sword without saying anything. Then we ran down the canyon and around the next corner.

I charged toward the closest monster, a tall and willowy blue thing with four arms and a bite like a shark's. My sword performed in its supernaturally horrible manner. I cut down soldiers ahead of me and to the sides, all aged to death in a moment. I heard cries from behind me, but I couldn't spare even a second to look back.

Some other type of monster was following the willowy one. I wasn't able to see it clearly because the willowy one picked up two soldiers and hurled them at me.

I yelled, "Watch out!" which was possibly the most useless warning I could have given. I threw myself flat, and the screaming reks hurtled above me. A shout from behind me cut off as though the shouter had been stomped flat.

Eight or ten soldiers jumped toward me while I was on the ground. Several fell back moaning or crying with withered arms. I killed two more before I gained my feet, but I didn't go after the wounded ones. Today, a disabled enemy was as helpful to us as a dead one. Also, I felt a little bad that if we destroyed their way home, they would be trapped in this cold place.

The willowy monster was within stomping distance of me when I got to my feet. He made an error, then. He tried to smack me with all four hands, which normally would have been a devastating attack. I stuck my sword in the air, and he petrified all his arms by hitting the sword one hand after another. He stared at his hands with what I believed was a monster look of amazement just before I thrust into his body to wither it.

I ran right between the willowy monster's petrified legs to surprise the second monster. He was a wolf much like the one that had attacked us in Ebring. I caught him peering with his head cocked at the willowy monster as it sagged. I lunged, scratched him on the chin, and ran around him as he withered.

I looked around for Lossil's gem-necked monster, but he seemed to have run off. Now only a few soldiers stood between me and the next bend in the canyon, and they were running away. Some threw down gear and weapons. I turned back to my allies, who were busy killing a dozen troops, although three escaped back the direction we'd come from.

Our only casualty was Terdire. One of the hurled soldiers had crashed into him. Acton knelt beside him and shook his head at us a moment later.

Acton kicked the ground. "He shouldn't have come. I tried to make him stay behind. I should have made him. He didn't deserve to get killed after coming this far."

I cocked my head at him. "Probably not, son, but when we're done, you can build him a monument a hundred feet tall. Wipe your eyes." I motioned for everybody to follow me and then ran around the next corner.

This section of canyon was truly narrow, no more than thirty feet wide, and it seemed to be bursting with angry soldiers. Maybe Lossil had inflamed them with rage against we cruel and evil criminals who were committing unclean acts to avoid being wiped out as a people.

I charged into the packed soldiers, slaughtering the ones in front of me and trusting Evonne and Jon to protect me from behind. We pushed down the canyon one rank of enemy soldiers at a time. In five minutes, we traveled just 150 feet.

To my left, a soldier shrieked as his weapon grew white hot. He spun around in agony, hitting two other soldiers with the blade. To my right, a rek's fur coat immolated, then exploded.

I chanced a look back. Pil had moved up to replace Evonne, who was stumbling along holding her shoulder. Jo had pushed ahead of Jon, who was limping with his trousers leg covered in blood. Acton was craning his neck, looking for targets to take some of the strain off Pil and Jo.

I was moving too fast. The others were taking wounds as they tried to keep up and protect me. I began dealing with soldiers to my left and right, as well as ahead, before I moved up. It helped my allies behind me, but I took more wounds, including a slice on my neck that was spectacular but not particularly dangerous. None of my wounds were serious, but I had taken more than a dozen, and I was starting to slow.

When about thirty soldiers remained, one of them turned to run. A couple more followed, and within half a minute, they were all running toward the narrower place at the end of this section.

I gave the signal to regroup. Pil bound Jon's leg while Jo watched, and Acton rebandaged Evonne's shoulder. I stood facing the next section with my sword ready in case something should rush us from there.

Pil walked up behind me. "Take off your shirt."

"I'm fine."

She whacked my shoulder lightly. "You aren't going to ask me whether I can wait until we're alone?"

"Never mind my neck—it looks worse than it is."

"Of course. What about all this blood running down your back?"

She stretched a bandage around me to handle the cut somebody had made across my back, right below my shoulder blades.

"It wasn't fatal," I grumbled.

"Not until you bled to death in about twenty minutes. And if it had been a tiny bit deeper, you'd never have walked again." Pil tied off the bandage.

When I was reclothed, I said, "I'll look ahead again."

I padded down a narrow area, only twenty feet wide and almost entirely closed to the sky. The narrow space ended after several hundred feet, and it opened on a great, near circular section of canyon over a quarter mile across.

Six monsters were stomping around in this space, each one like Lossil's hornless rhino monster. These also sported gems on ridges over the neck, and each one's gems were a different color.

As I walked back to my companions, I glanced at the sky. Kenzie must still be burning power to pull more and more energy into the storm above us.

I said to my comrades, "Anybody who can't run fast should wait here. Six charging monsters are waiting for us, and fleetness is our only hope to destroy them."

Jon, Acton, and Evonne were hindered by leg wounds. Jo wasn't, but Jon ordered him to remain behind, and Jo didn't argue. Only Pil was hearty enough to join me. The two of us walked back to the open area and stopped to listen.

Pil had insisted I keep the onyx ring for now since I was more likely than she was to overhear dragons. Therefore, I understood what these monsters were saying. One of them shouted, "Where might they be? They have been given no permission to delay us. I wish to crush them to death!"

Another called out, "Steady, be steady now. We must coordinate our efforts."

"Oh, sit upon your own efforts and coordinate them, Yellow."

Another said, "Coordinate your face into your buttocks, you slithering pile!"

Yellow shouted, "I have been put in command, and I demand that you adhere to my commands!"

"Chew a granite phallus!" yet another shouted.

Pil poked my shoulder. "What are you listening to?"

"The monsters. If we could wait here for two hours, I think they might kill each other for us."

Pil said, "If we wait two hours, Lossil will reinforce his soldiers, and then we could stab each other in the heart to avoid torture when they capture us."

I nodded and stepped out into the open area.

"There they are!" yelled Green, White, and Purple at the same time.

"Wait!" Yellow shouted.

Blue said, "Oh, allow them this. There is little glory to be found here."

"I shall mock them from a distance," Orange said, "and harm their feelings with criticism when they are done."

Green, White, and Purple charged us fast enough to make my mouth dry.

"Go left against the wall, but not too far," I said.

Pil ran left, and I ran right.

"Which one?" Green yelled.

Purple shouted, "The one with the odd magic sword!"

All three monsters veered toward me. Even though they could run fast, they couldn't turn fast. I got out of the way and wasn't crushed when they reached the wall. All three slammed into the stone with bone-shivering force.

I darted to the closest monster, Purple, and sliced its rear leg, which withered at once. As I ran from the wall and a possible avalanche above me, Purple spun my direction, tripped over its own dead leg, and flopped onto its back with its other three legs running in the air. Green launched itself over Purple's belly to crush me. I swung and nicked Green's jaw before rolling out of the way. Green's entire body shriveled.

White stared at the carnage for a moment before charging back to its allies, who jeered and criticized White. Purple struggled back upright, but I slashed its nose before it could sneeze acid on me or some other monstrous trick.

The ancient husks of Purple and Green lay near the entrance we had used. I rejoined Pil at that entrance. All four surviving monsters were bellowing, slamming their bodies into each other, and whipping the enormous gems on their tail tips.

Orange's voice rose above the shouting. "Shame! Shame!"

Pil and I watched the monsters for a few minutes until their shouts and slamming died away. When the monsters had quieted, Yellow said, "We must try a different strategy."

Blue said, "Our leader chose the previous strategy. I propose we select a new leader."

Yellow wheeled and charged Blue, smashing its ribs. Blue heeled over and landed on its side.

"Maybe they'll destroy themselves in a lot less than two hours," Pil said.

"Orange!" the leader yelled. "Charge the one carrying the

bizarre sword! We shall follow and annihilate him no matter what his path of escape may be."

Orange said, "I should not care to be slain in the manner of Purple and Green. It seems distressing."

Yellow shouted, "Of course it does! I should not consider it to be a holiday with berries and available females, either. But it must be done."

Blue said to Orange, "I suggest you step in a particularly lively fashion."

Orange slammed Blue with its shoulder and yelled some foul curses. All four monsters began bellowing and stomping at the same time.

"I wish I could let them live," I said. "They remind me of my sisters."

The monsters organized themselves with surprising speed. Almost as soon as I compared them to my sisters, they ran toward me. Orange led the way.

I sprinted to the left this time, motioning for Pil to run right. Orange slammed into the wall just behind me. I skidded to a stop and ran back in front of Orange, evading Blue, who had smashed the wall next.

I sliced Orange's cheek as he shook his head, then spun and slashed Blue's neck. Both of them withered as Yellow climbed over Orange's body to jump on me. Yellow smacked me with its shoulder and hurled me to the dirt, knocking the air out of me. My hand banged against the ground, and the sword tumbled away under Yellow's body.

Yellow reared about three feet high, I suppose to plant me in the ground like a carrot. I rolled, and Yellow's crusty foot pinned my shirt to the ground instead of my flesh. Yellow held me in place and lifted the other foreleg while I rolled from side to side, trying to draw my sharp sword. Yellow said, "Remain in place, you vile wiggler!"

Then the monster stiffened and sagged as its eyes closed.

I sat up just as Pil pulled her knife from the back of Yellow's head. "You're a decent distraction, Bib. I think I'll dangle you in front of every monster I want to kill."

I jumped up and looked for the remaining monster, White. Pil pointed at White's body twenty feet away and smiled. "That's all six. I'll run back and tell the others."

"Thank you, darling. I was uncommonly near to death," I said, reaching for the death sword's hilt poking out from under Yellow's chest.

Before she could answer, a dog barked from someplace ahead. Even with my poor hearing and the odd canyon echoes, I felt sure the dog was no more than half a mile away. I also felt sure it was Lossil's dog, although I couldn't point to any real evidence. But hell, I was a sorcerer. I could just say I knew because of my mystical powers, and anybody who wanted to challenge me about it could eat a bug.

Pil brought everybody up to join me. I said, "We'll face Lossil next, along with his guards, soldiers, monsters, and dogs. Be ready."

Acton squinted toward the next bend in the canyon. "How the heck can you tell that from here?"

"Eat a bug."

FORTY-THREE

I led us around the next three corners. We didn't bother sneaking because we sure weren't going to surprise Lossil now. We marched at a sharp pace, but we didn't run. I wanted to display confidence. Lossil would know it was false confidence, but the fact that we showed it was a kind of confidence in itself.

The next part of the canyon was long and narrow. Reks and difar stood motionless along the canyon walls, about sixty of them. At the far end stood Lossil, taller than everybody else, with six of his guards flanking him. In front of Lossil, twenty difar guarded three dozen people—men, women, and also children.

Pil stiffened. "That's my family," she whispered.

Lossil shouted in a deep, carrying voice, "I guess you recognize these people. If you wonder why I have them, stop and think. You walked all over the northern end of this island asking men and kids and dogs about them. If you wanted me to notice them, you could only have done it better if you stood them in front of me and set them on fire."

I hadn't anticipated this, but Lossil was right—it was entirely predictable. I drew a breath to say something that I hoped wouldn't be foolish, but Pil seized my arm.

Lossil said, "Do you really care as little about the people of this land as you claim? I think you lied about that, or maybe you exaggerated a whole lot. Here's my offer. This family and your allies there can go free, as long as they never come back to these islands. But you, Bib, have to give yourself up in exchange. I can't have you tromping around destroying things and killing your betters."

I glanced at Pil, who was still clamped onto my arm, shaking her head.

"And I want the weapon," Lossil said. "You know which weapon I mean."

Pil shouted, "Bib will surrender! And I will bring the weapon if you let these people go free when we begin walking toward you!"

I didn't believe that Pil was really handing me over to Lossil, especially since she had promised to come along for my ignoble surrender. "What are you doing?" I muttered.

"I'm saving my family."

"You've made a fine job of it, then. And after that?"

"You and I will kill Lossil. In the confusion, we'll rush on to this wicket-y thing."

I cursed quietly.

Lossil called out, "What did you say?"

"I said since you only want me, Pil will stay here to help these folks. I'll hand the sword to one of your soldiers here. He can carry it to you."

"No!" Pil snarled.

I glared at her. "You want to take care of your family, so stay the hell here and take care of them the right way. In the Dark Lands, you wanted me to think you were dead—Fingit said so. Let's work it the other way. Pretend that I'm dead. I'll be the biggest pain Baby Harik will ever have in his tender parts."

She stared at me as I squeezed her hand and then walked on toward Lossil, beckoning to the closest rek. I held out the sword to the soldier and said, "Hold it only by the hilt, son, never the blade. You might nick yourself."

I was pissed off at Pil, of course. She had thrown out the idea of giving me up to Lossil as a prisoner, but worse than that, she had intended to go with me. She wouldn't have been a prisoner, of course. She'd have been a hostage that Lossil could use to force me to do as he pleased. It was unlike her to be so foolish.

I began considering ways to use this prisoner exchange to find and destroy Lossil's wicket, or gate, or dingus, or whatever the hell it was. That was still the main goal. I didn't know whether I could do that and save all of Pil's family. I might not be able to save any of them. Better that they all die than see everybody on the island slaughtered. That was a choice Pil probably couldn't make, so I'd have to make it.

Pala's definition of serious help flitted through my head—when you don't mind if the person helping you destroys everything else in sight. I almost laughed.

I realized how tired I felt, which was an awkward realization to have in the midst of dire conflict. I passed the first of Pil's family, a limping, dirty older man supported by two gaunt teenagers, a boy and a girl. They didn't look much like people I would claim as mine.

I focused on Lossil. He stood solid and calm in his fur coat, with his chin up and a curved sword in his hand. I couldn't see his dog, but I heard it barking someplace far behind him. His gemmed horn-less-rhino monster stomped around in the back, managing to express great boredom.

I prepared to fling white bands and call lightning down on every enemy I could reach. I'd have to send them one at a time, but I could deliver them surprisingly fast.

While I was still walking, I shouted, "Lossil, why do you even want a weapon, anyway? You're going to retire to your estate and grow hyacinths soon."

Lossil gritted his teeth but said, "That's a hell of a story. Nothing's been settled. Maybe I'll plant you in my garden."

Lossil's guards stood in front of him in a line. I stopped when I reached them, and Lossil said, "Is this the weapon?"

"Maybe," I said, holding up a hand as I watched Pil herding her family back the way we came. When they had all disappeared and Pil was waving, I said to Lossil without looking at him, "Sure, that's the weapon. It killed your army at Sandell. It killed the shit out of the dragon A. It's the sword that was carried by the God of Death."

"How did you get it?"

"I killed him," I said.

"Who?"

"Harik," I said. When Lossil kept squinting at me, I said slowly, "I killed Harik, the God of Death, in the Dark Lands. I stabbed him in the heart and then took his fancy sword for myself."

"No, seriously."

I held up both hands. "You found me out. I didn't kill Harik, this isn't his sword, and I slew all your soldiers using a bent stick painted white. And the dragon laughed himself to death when I told him a joke about whales and mermaids. I guess that clears things up."

Lossil shook his head and pointed at the rek who was carrying the death sword. "Bring that to me."

I said, "Until you get accustomed to it, it's safest if you handle it by the blade."

Lossil frowned at me and grasped the hilt. He practiced a couple of easy cuts. "It doesn't feel special."

"You have to sing the song," I said. "'The Ballad of Death.' The sword doesn't do much without singing the song."

Lossil blinked at me.

"There's a dance too."

After a few seconds, Lossil grinned. "A dance. I'm sure it's enchanting. Tell me all about this sword."

"There's a lot to tell," I said. "It doesn't have a name, and it's not too good at cutting things like iron and wood. You have to sharpen it like any other sword. You have to kill at least five people with it every day, or else your teeth will start falling out. Of course, Harik's spirit is trapped inside the blade, and you can only use it in battle if you're worthy."

Lossil was shaking his head at the ground as he smiled. "I can't help it, I have to ask. What makes you worthy?"

"It's a complex thing," I said. "You need to have killed at least a thousand enemies in combat, and of course, you must have killed one person you love, although more than one is better. At least two immortal beings must have tried to kill you and failed. You must have lost your humanity at some point or come damn near to it. You have to be able to tell a joke, of course."

Lossil smiled, stepping forward so that his line of guards separated. "I'm not sure what to say."

"You can say whether you think you're worthy."

He held up the sword. "I'm worthy enough." He raised the sword and swung it in a mighty cut that would slice me from my left shoulder to my right hip.

I drew the sword back into its tiny realm. It disappeared from Lossil's hand before it hit me, and he stumbled.

"Worthy enough?" I asked. "Are you sure about that?"

Lossil stood staring at his empty hand.

I squeezed one of the white bands I had tossed into the sky. Lightning jumped from cloud to cloud, and thunder slammed down on everybody in the canyon. Rocks and boulders split off the canyon walls.

Everybody except me stared up at the clouds.

I stepped back from Lossil as I called four lightning strikes a little way out from the canyon walls, two on each side. A few soldiers were hit, but most retreated toward the walls. I had been watching Lossil, and when he recovered from his shock, I called the Death God's sword. My hand grasped a child's doll made of straw and twine.

"Dammit, Baby Harik, this is a lot more often than one time in five!" I drew my utterly sharp sword.

None of Lossil's soldiers or guards paid attention to me until I drew my sword. Then I was the most fascinating thing in the canyon to them. Twenty soldiers rushed toward me from the walls, while the six guards hung back with Lossil. I backed farther away toward the middle of the canyon. If I could gain enough distance from Lossil and his guards, I could drop three or four lightning bolts on them in a hurry.

The soldiers pressed me, so I disabled one with a cut across the leg and killed another with a compact slice to the throat. I had just disarmed the third one when screams rose from the canyon walls.

The rocks and boulders dislodged by my thunder clattered and smashed to the ground. Most soldiers either ran or were injured, but a few were killed on the spot. Some of the soldiers near me looked away to see what was happening to their comrades. I killed three of them with quick thrusts.

As I retreated, I threw four more white bands into the sky. It used up a lot of my remaining power, but there'd be nothing later to save power for if I died in the next few minutes.

At last, I had backed away far enough to throw lightning at Lossil without cooking myself. I squeezed the band just as Lossil and his guards charged me. All of them were thrown to the ground, and only some of them were moving.

Lossil's monster said "You repugnant purveyor of filth and misery!" before it ran in an arc around the soldiers to reach me. I aimed the next bolt of lightning to hit that arc at its farthest distance from me. The lightning shot straight through the monster's body, leaving a blackened corpse and an unforgettable stench. I fortunately caught a few soldiers in the blast at the same time.

I withdrew again so I could chance a quick scan of the battle-field. I still faced ten determined soldiers. About three dozen soldiers were running or staggering away from the canyon walls. Lossil and three of his guards were struggling to their feet.

I threw two lightning bolts at the biggest groups of soldiers behind me. Then I assaulted the soldiers in front of me and disabled four.

Lossil charged me then, right through the middle of his soldiers and guards. I ran in a half circle around them, putting the soldiers between Lossil and me and slashing a guard as I ran.

When I entered this part of the canyon, I had seen a small gap in the wall at the far end, just behind Lossil. Now I sprinted to that opening and found that it led into a long channel, hardly wide enough for two people to fight side by side.

With Lossil and his troops behind me, I threw another white band up, but this time, I released intense rain on the area behind me. When a soldier ran through the rain chasing me, he ran right onto my sword. The same thing happened to a guard and then another soldier right afterward.

Lossil emerged from the rain. I thrust at his big chest, but he managed to squirm aside, although he suffered a long, deep scratch from my sharp sword. Lossil countered at my head, and I jerked aside. His sword wasn't as sharp as mine, but it was sharp enough to leave a big gash above my ear.

A guard rushed up beside Lossil and slashed at me. I stepped inside the swing and sliced him hard, then shoved him at Lossil. With one powerful hand, Lossil knocked the staggering guard back toward me. I retreated fast and reassessed the wisdom of pushing or throwing things at Lossil.

Lossil's weapon must have been enchanted, because mine couldn't cut or even scratch it. He was stronger than me and faster too. My only advantage was having faced far more opponents than he could possibly have fought.

We traded thrusts and slashes until a soldier ran up to join Lossil. The rek glanced behind me, and I threw myself against the canyon wall. A difar swung from behind me and destroyed the air I had just been standing in. I sprinted past the difar before he recovered, killing him as I went by.

The difar who attacked me from behind me had friends some distance away, charging to help Lossil attack me from both sides. I whipped a white band into the clouds, silently thanked Kenzie, and threw a bolt of lightning on top of the newcomers while I kept sprinting away from Lossil. All of the arriving soldiers fell to the ground, and at least some must have been killed.

I spun to face Lossil and kill him, mounting a series of thrusts to pull him off his center line and over against the wall. That earned me a mangled little finger on my off hand. He left himself open to a bizarre thrust that forty years ago a poetry-spouting demigod had almost killed me with. It surprised Lossil too, and he retreated with blood running down his trousers.

Then Lossil attacked me with raw, furious thrusts and cuts. They left no room for his soldiers to fight beside him. None of his attacks were masterful, but they came so fast and with such power that I couldn't do anything but defend. I searched for an opening, but Lossil didn't seem to repeat himself or fall into a pattern. The son of a bitch wasn't slowing down, either, but I was tiring fast.

My hopes of beating Lossil with the sword were fading. I could pull my knife and fight two-handed, but that would only help him kill me faster, since my two-handed fencing was unexceptional.

I brought the rainstorm closer so that the line of rain overtook Lossil from behind. His eyes widened when he realized I was about to blind him in the rain. He withdrew, and I pushed forward to kill him with a thrust while he couldn't see me. I missed and was reminded that blindness works in both directions. He thrust out of the rainstorm and almost caught me above the belly button.

Lossil reemerged from the rain, and I stopped trying to dink around with the rainstorm. He resumed his ferocious attacks, but I caught his off hand unprotected. A moment later, he had two fingers on his left hand instead of five.

I didn't celebrate. I was growing weaker by the second, and I could hear soldiers shouting someplace behind me. Lossil didn't seem to have gotten weaker since we started. I threw another white band, reassessed, readjusted, and called lightning as close behind me as I dared. It blinded me, and it must have blinded Lossil too. Instead of attacking with my sword, I threw another bolt of lightning just fifty feet behind him. It wasn't close enough to kill him, but he was thrown to the ground. I knew that was true because the lightning was less than sixty feet from me, and I slammed against the ground too.

The entire fight then became a race to see which of us could get to our knees first. Lossil dragged himself up, but he was tall and massive. He had also been closer to the lightning. I hauled myself to my knees first, and when he lifted his sword, I struck his hand off at the wrist. Lossil roared and threw himself forward like a crocodile. I twisted and thrust my weapon through his chest. He spit blood at me, fell, and lay still.

Shouting sounded from someplace ahead of me in the rain. I stood, slipped, and pushed myself upright against the wall. A few seconds later, Pil crept out of the rain drenched, with her hair soaked and straggling.

She yelled, "Krak's hairy goats! Bib! Stop the damn rain!"

I laughed and let the rainstorm ease away. She held my mangled hand but didn't have anything to bandage it with.

I asked, "Where are the others?"

"They're moving up to the place where Lossil was waiting," she said. "Where is the wicket thing?"

I shrugged, breathing hard. "Someplace ahead of us, I guess."

"We should hurry. We don't want a thousand difar to stroll past in the middle of your heroic attempt to close it."

The two of us gripped our weapons and walked fast down the canyon. At that point, running or even trotting was out of the question.

FORTY-FOUR

Pil and I strode down the lovely canyon, saving our breath and strength to fight whatever was ahead. We met tiny groups of soldiers, as well as individual fighters. Word of Lossil's defeat must be spreading, because most of them fled from us. A group of six tried to stop us, and we let four of them live to run away.

"Why didn't you kill them?" Pil asked me. "Is something wrong?"

"I've been converted," I said in a flat voice. "The Bib stories convinced me that killing is bad, along with drinking, lying, laziness, and riding horses on Thursdays."

Pil's pale skin turned red under the dirt. "I'm sorry, I didn't think you'd ever know how people reacted to the stories, so I didn't say anything. It just would have frustrated you."

"What if I had said yes one of those times you begged me to come back?"

"I would have kept you drunk for a month and then eased you into the idea."

"Well . . . as long as you had a plan."

After a few minutes, the canyon narrowed and divided into two branches.

"Right, left, or split up?" Pil asked.

"Let's stay together. We're headed off into the unknown, and I may get scared. Let's go right."

One hundred paces down the right-hand branch, it split in two again. The canyon had narrowed some more, giving us just enough room to walk side by side.

"Go right," Pil said. "We'll go right every time it divides so we can get back out if we need to."

An hour later, the canyon had divided seven more times, and we had taken the right-hand side every time. The seventh right-hand branch led to a dead end.

I cursed a little. "We started off heading north, and now we're facing west. If this is a maze, and I guess it is, we're walking around the outside edge of it. If we were on a path straight through it, we'd probably have come out the other side by now."

"We can turn to go inside the maze. Or back to the beginning," Pil said. "I think those are our only choices."

We walked back to the previous split, and I swung my sharp sword three times to cut an arrow into the rock. "We're going this way."

Over the next two hours, we passed forty splits in the canyon, reached three dead ends, and crossed our own path twice.

"The sun will go down in a few hours," I said. "If it gets dark out here, we won't be able to see our marks."

"Hm. I wonder what kind of predators wander this maze at night."

I gave her a light whack on the shoulder. "You're scaring the troops."

Four branches met at the next intersection. The stone canyon wall between two of the branches had been dug out to make a large, ten-foot-high empty space. It left a great overhang to protect that space.

Fifteen reks and ten difar were shouting at each other in the middle of the intersection. Each race was blaming the other for Lossil's death and the expedition's failure.

I considered trying to scare them away. Kenzie's storm had drifted apart more than an hour ago, so I'd have to do it using ferocity and guile. As I considered the problem, one of the difar pointed at us, and they all began stalking toward us with their weapons ready.

A campfire appeared in front of them and *whooshed* into flame. Pil muttered to me without looking, "Go be scary."

I raised my sword and stomped toward Lossil's soldiers, roaring and making myself as big as possible. They stopped. Three more campfires appeared and lit themselves in front of the soldiers while I shouted insults and shook my sword.

The soldiers fell back and then straggled away, in some cases looking over their shoulders.

"It wasn't a rout, but it was enough," I said.

Pil lifted her chin. "Never doubt the power of a fire that can start itself." She tossed a handful of broken sticks on the closest fire and pointed at an object standing below the overhang. "I suppose that's it."

The object turned out to be a short tree with a barrel-shaped trunk. It had five branches at the top, and dark green leaves hung from each. The tree looked healthy, even though it couldn't get much sunlight in this dim space. The trunk was studded with spines that were broad and sharp, but only half an inch long.

"Pil, here's what Fingit told me about this tree. Since my realm-hopping shenanigans made this tree possible, I need to hug the thing. It will wilt and die, destroying its usefulness for moving folks between realms. Easy."

"The timing is off—you arrived just a few days ago."

"That's what I said! But since time between realms flops like a trout in a stream . . ." I shrugged.

"And that means it's your fault? Why would you accept an idea like that? I sure as hell don't!"

I held up a hand. "Maybe I got here just a shake or two ago, but it's been pointed out to me that in my heart, I left the Dark Lands a long time ago. Right about when you left. I was just waiting around for the party to end."

Pil sighed. "More than a year. That must be far enough ahead of time. If you do this, what happens to you?"

"Fingit did not say that I'd be hurt."

"You're lying. More than usual. I think I deserve a little truth."

"All right. He did not say that he was certain I'd die."

Pil crossed her arms.

"He said he was almost certain."

I felt Pil lift herself toward the gods' trading place, calling for Fingit. I grabbed on for the ride. We jerked to a stop while everything was still black and formless.

Fingit's voice said, "What do you want, Knife? And you'd better be quick. Krak is laughing about something and expects us all to laugh as well."

"I want something to keep Bib alive when he destroys that wicket tree."

"I can't help you."

"Why not?" Pil sounded a little more aggressive and insistent than I usually heard her be with gods.

Fingit said, "Harik created that tree. Sort of." Fingit's voice then took on the tone of somebody gossiping over the back fence. "All right, it seems that Harik paid Krak to create it for him, since Harik hasn't quite mastered putting on his big-god boots yet. That's funny but not important."

"Please go on," Pil said.

"Only Harik can change the terms of the tree's destruction. Murderer, do you plan to offer him the sword in exchange for your life? Why would he agree to that? When the tree kills you, which will be your own doing, not Harik's, the sword will become his, anyway. Plus, he'll have the pleasure of watching you suffer and die. I hate to say this, but nicely done, Harik."

Pil said, "I want to bargain for Bib's life."

Fingit's voice might have softened, but it couldn't have been much. "Harik wants three things. He wants the sword, he wants Bib to suffer, and he wants Bib to die. He's about to get all three, and there is nothing you can offer him that's better than that, Knife."

"He could take my life instead!" Pil yelled.

"He doesn't want your life. He pays no attention to you. He hardly knows you exist. Now, go home."

Fingit dropped us, and we drifted back into our bodies.

"Thank you for trying, darling," I said.

Pil clenched her fists and teeth, and her brows pulled together. She was ready to fight, but every wicked thing she hated was beyond her touch. She had offered her life for me without a blink, but she hadn't offered her family's life, or the lives of the Ir people, to save me. I didn't expect her to, either.

Pil held my hand until I wrapped my arms around the tree. She kissed me and then stepped away in case she might set the magic awry by standing so close. The tree's sharp spines hurt some, but they were short. I watched the dark green leaves above me, waiting for them to wilt or turn yellow.

A couple of minutes passed. I said, "Maybe I'm in the process of being killed here, but it doesn't hurt as much as my ma's scrub brush at bath time. Pil, does it look to you like this tree is withering?"

She shook her head and turned away so that I might not see her wipe her cheeks. "I think it looks healthier than when you started."

"Do you think I ought to stab it with Old Harik's sword?"

"I say try it."

I stepped back and called the sword, which arrived in my hand. Then I thrust the blade into the tree. Nothing happened, so I thrust again. I leaned in and stared at the tree but didn't notice any change. I made four quick thrusts into the trunk, but that made no difference. I released the sword back into its tiny realm.

"Perplexing, ain't it?" Hurd said from behind me.

Pil charged toward Hurd, summoning her knife into her hand. Hurd backed away, his eyes bigger than pot lids. Pil grabbed him around the neck and kissed him. "Thank you for hauling Bib out of the Dark Lands. I'm too tired to kill you just now, so I'll do it tomorrow."

Hurd mumbled something, the only time I remembered seeing him embarrassed. Then he straightened. "I am bringing you a message of importance that you'll want to listen to. Bib, you can hug that vegetable until it falls in love with you, and it won't do a speck of good." He glanced at Pil.

"Why not?" Pil and I said at the same time.

"Bib, you ain't the one to blame for this tree business. Not your fault at all. It's kind of ridiculous that anybody ever thought it was, especially Harik since he's a god and ought to have divine sight. And maybe smell."

I cleared my throat. "Hurd, I don't know what that means. What should we do about this tree?" I was so tired that every word I said was like lifting a weight.

"I can't be certain of this," Hurd drawled. He blinked at Pil and then glared at me. "I'm not in the minds of the gods, you know!"

"I understand. Just say what you think."

Pil was ahead of me, though, and maybe ahead of Hurd too. Before I could stop her, Pil walked over and embraced the little tree.

"Pil! Let go! Stop!" I yelled.

She answered me by screaming.

Every spine on the tree, each a sharp, barbed blade, had pushed outward by two finger-widths. By the time I reached her, Pil was writhing and hanging from the spines wherever her body touched the tree. She screamed without stopping.

I shouted in her ear, "Pil! Come with me!"

I lifted myself up toward the trading place, and I felt Pil grab me. When I arrived at the brown dirt spot reserved for sorcerers, I found it was nothing but grayish-brown dust. A searing wind brushed the forest, and leaves by the barrelful blew away amid the smell of sulfur. Some of them burst into flame as they flew. The sun slammed my head and neck like a molten stone, while the endless field of flowers sprouted wave after wave of flames.

Baby Harik paced on the lowest level of the gazebo. "That was supposed to be you, Murderer, not her! Who do you think you are, Knife, to stir crap into my plans?"

Pil said, "I was—"

"Quiet!" Baby Harik shouted. The wind hesitated.

Pil said, "It's done, Harik, and even you can't change it."

Baby Harik hissed. "If Krak wasn't such a . . . if he were more . . . if he . . . oh, hell, he's Krak, and there's nothing we can do about him." He smiled a little too broadly and said a little too loudly, "The grand old father of us all, right?" Baby Harik glanced around.

I pushed myself to smile. "Baby Harik, you are the tender, lost place in the hearts of all you abandoned to become a god."

Baby Harik flinched.

I went on: "I want to discuss helping the Knife."

"Maybe. It's worth trying to salvage something. What do you want?"

"I want her to live. I want her not to suffer," I said.

Pil said, "Bib, stop. Anything you can get in trade here will cost far more than it's worth."

"Hush! How do you know how much you're worth?"

"Oh, that's as charming as a baby snake," Baby Harik said. "Worthy of any adolescent. Let's start with this staying alive business. I refuse to just say, 'Let her live!' and *poof*, she'll live. You've got to do these things in a certain way. Well organized."

I squinted at him. "Well organized? You have never reminded me more of Old Harik than you do right now. Would you like to tell us how many crocodiles have eaten wildebeests since the beginning of time? How many erections tortoises have had?"

Baby Harik scowled.

"How about this?" I pointed at Pil. "You will extend Pil's life by a day from the time she is done with the tree. Or it's done with her, I guess."

"A day? Maybe five minutes."

I shook my head. "It has to be long enough for Kenzie to get here and save her."

"And you think a day is enough?" Baby Harik asked.

"A week would be better."

"Two hours."

"Five," I said.

"Fine." Baby Harik waved a hand.

"All right," I said. I had been hoping for three hours, so I felt good about five.

"But since I'm being so generous," Baby Harik said, "she'll suffer the whole time."

I decided not to push that. "Now for the other side. I will offer the Death God's sword to you right now. No waiting."

"No." Baby Harik gave a snide grin.

My shoulders dropped. "Isn't that what you wanted?"

"I admit it is," Baby Harik said. "But I'll get it as soon as you're killed, and I see that you're doing stupid things to save other people. I won't have to wait long for your death. In the meantime, I can strike a great deal to make you suffer too. Hey, do you have any suggestions for that? Sorcerers usually suggest the most awful, painful things for themselves."

"Well, I could go back to the Dark Lands for some length of time."

"Seriously? Would you like some cake and a puppy with that?" Baby Harik asked.

"Lose my left arm?"

"The Feather would pop it right back on."

"Have a headache that never goes away?"

Baby Harik squinted. "Maybe . . . for the sake of symmetry, you could take an open-ended debt. You'll have to kill a certain number of people, and only I will know that number."

I laughed. "Baby Harik, you're more amusing than I suspected. I've done this bargain to kill people before, and you've got to know it. For the right incentive, I might agree to kill flies instead of people. Or wildflowers. Or mugs of beer. Otherwise, put that out of your mind."

He shrugged and then glanced back and forth between Pil and me. "There's sure a lot of 'kill me to save her, kill me to save him' stuff going on between you two. How about the two of you never see each other again?"

"No," Pil said.

"I don't think much of it," I added.

"You're right, it's not too creative. Let's go the other way.

Neither of you will remember anything about the other one. It would be like you never met."

"No!" Pil yelled.

I shook my head.

"You two are tough. Let's see . . . Knife, you won't remember anything about the Murderer, but the Murderer will remember everything about you."

I must not have kept my face still.

"I saw that, Murderer!" Baby Harik said. "Yes, that's the one. If you want her to live, that's the price."

"Bib, if you do this, I'll strangle you to death!" Pil shouted.

Baby Harik said, "You won't do that, because you won't remember anything about it."

"Bib . . ." Pil growled.

I'd rather her be alive and forget me than simply dead. "Baby Harik, what about this? Pil will remember everything about me up until the time I went to the Dark Lands. Between then and the time she embraced that horrible tree, she won't remember me."

"Ah. She won't remember anything that happened while she was with you, she won't remember hearing about you, and she won't remember thinking about you, from the point where you went to the Dark Lands. And, no one can try to help her remember, including you."

Pil was crying, but she sounded as fierce as a bear. "If you do this, I will cut your throat! I'll never forgive you. Do you want to bet that I won't know something strange is happening no matter what? That I won't find some way around this memory bullshit?"

"Baby Harik." I took a breath. "I agree to your terms."

"Done. It's a little sad, right? You have all your memories, but she's gone. It's like I killed her without killing her. Let's see Krak do that."

I turned to Pil. "Darling, I—"

Baby Harik flung us back into our bodies. I stumbled and fell on my knees, then muttered, "The petty son of a bitch didn't even give us a minute to say goodbye."

Pil was still hanging from the tree and screaming. Hurd was

hovering like a butterfly and doing just as much good. I grabbed Pil's hand and held it, which didn't do a damn bit of good, either.

From behind me, a deep and harsh voice said, "Conspirators. Tomorrow it will be as if you lot were never here. As if you never lived even, and this tree will survive."

I spun and saw Dragon One standing outside the overhang, pushing his head in toward us beneath the stony ceiling.

FORTY-FIVE

The dragon's first concern had to be Pil. She was the one destroying the wicket tree. I sprinted straight toward him, calling the Death God's sword to me. Instead of delivering an old broom handle or a worn-out boot, the sword appeared in my hand.

One pushed his bulk toward Pil, and I imagined how he would tear her body off that tree. I veered left while brandishing the sword and shouting, "I killed Dragon A by stabbing him in the ass with this blade!" Maybe One didn't know exactly what the sword was, but I doubted he would ignore it after that.

The dragon swung away from Pil to follow me with his head as I ran. He chuffed. A wall that I could shelter behind against his fire stood forty feet away, but I only had two seconds before One breathed fire at me. The wall may as well have been forty miles away.

Being engulfed by dragon's breath was far louder than I would have imagined, and it smelled like the privy of a tavern that served old, dubious meat. I found myself lying in the dirt on my side. My body was burned red all over and blackened with soot. My skin smoked where all my clothes and my boots had burned away, and pain screamed across my skin. My utterly sharp sword had melted.

Only two of my possessions still existed. One was the death sword. The other was Pil's onyx ring, the one she had enchanted to keep you cool in the heat and warm in the cold. That ring had kept me just cool enough to survive. But now I felt it melting on my finger, which hurt like hell but couldn't compete with having a dragon breathe fire on me.

One had turned away from me, probably figuring I was dead. It would have been a fine assumption most of the time. Now he slithered toward Pil with his claws clacking against the stony ground.

I leaped up and flung myself toward One, and the only thing I could reach was his right wing. I nicked it with the sword, and it withered in a second. The shimmer and glowing colors disappeared as the wing shrank to dried crust.

The dragon screamed, which was a lot louder than being caught inside dragon's breath. He whirled my direction while backing away. I ran toward his face, dodging and trying to be a difficult target for fiery breath, which was a narrow stream of fire when it first shot out of the mouth. At the same time, I wanted to stay back so I couldn't be snapped up and swallowed.

This went on for several seconds until One snatched at me with his right foot. That turned out to be a feint, as I realized when his left foot bashed me instead. I tumbled away, feeling my knee wrench and my left arm break.

I could throw the sword as I had done with Dragon A, but Dragon One would be a more difficult target. Although he was huge and missing a wing, he was also shifting and twisting, while dragon A had been crippled and slithering straight away from me. If I threw at Dragon One and missed, I would have to send the sword away before I could call it back. I might end up with a moldy onion instead.

Limping fast despite the pain, I kept close enough to One's face to make him swing his head side to side while aiming at me. I had never seen Red breathe fire while turning her head at the same time.

That was a damn thin observation to hang my life on, but I didn't have many options.

At last, Dragon One caught me in the right place to snort flame at me. I hurled the sword at him, and he dodged instead of breathing fire. He swooped to the side and twisted almost as if he had no bones, and the sword sailed past his neck.

Before I could call the sword back, Dragon One shot his head forward and grabbed me with his mouth. He bit down, crushing my right arm and lacerating my legs.

The clever dragon had seized me so that my left arm stuck out away from his face. I called the sword successfully to my left hand, hoping I could flop the sword around somehow and nick the dragon even though that arm was broken.

While I waited to be crushed and eaten, Dragon One raised up on his rear legs to roar and I suppose to call me bad dragon names. In that moment, his tongue flicked out of his mouth. With my left hand, I made an awkward swing that sliced off the end of the dragon's tongue. Then the sword spun away because my broken arm couldn't hold it.

Dragon One's entire body withered and desiccated.

Pil was now screaming, crying, and panting. I wriggled out of the dragon's dry and leathery jaws, then I staggered over to her. It appeared that the spines had pushed deeper into her body, and blood was pooling at her feet. Except for my deal with Baby Harik, she might be dead already.

Pil looked at me but didn't recognize me or anything else except pain. However, the leaves at the top of the tree were all yellow now, and half of them had dropped off.

I could feel my burned skin tightening all over my body.

"Thank you for helping me kill that dragon, Hurd, you asshole," I said when he walked around from behind me.

"You did fine, son. Impressive. I'll write a poem about it."

"At least bandage me up a little."

"You'll regret it if I do." He ran his palms over my body without touching me. "I doubt you'll die. It'll sting for a bit." Hurd shrugged. "I can patch up a few of the holes he bit into you."

I plopped to the ground to sit beside Pil, unable to do a single useful thing, and I let Hurd bandage me with a few grimy rags. Pil had stopped screaming but was panting and mumbling too softly for me to understand. Before I fought One, she had been crying, but now that had stopped. She probably didn't have enough water left in her to make tears. I glanced at the blood around her feet and looked away.

At sunset, the last yellow leaf dropped off the tree. Pil fell off the tree too, landing on her back. At first, I feared she was dead, no matter what Baby Harik had said, but I saw slow, shallow breaths. Her wounds were raw and horrible, but they didn't bleed. Hurd dribbled water into her mouth.

"They have five hours to find us in the darkness," I told Hurd as I held Pil's hand despite the pain in my palm and fingers. "I doubt they can do it. I hope they have entered the maze at least. I need to go get them."

Hurd stared at me for a few seconds and then laughed.

"Don't leave her alone."

"I wouldn't do that. You may get lost in this place and starve, you know."

"That's helpful. You wouldn't go in my place, would you?"

Hurd shook his head.

I stumped off into the maze. My knee threatened to give way at every step. The moon hadn't risen, but the stars shone just enough for me to see the signs I had made to mark our path. My memory and my strong sense of direction took me the right way. I even felt a little optimism until I realized I was walking slower and slower. Somebody started pouring lemon juice all over my raw skin.

I began calling out for Acton and Kenzie, hoping I didn't attract a pride of lions instead. I cleared my head enough to realize I'd have to be riding a lion for him to hear me, since what I thought was yelling had hardly been whispering.

When I saw Acton and Vargo, I told them, "Pil doesn't have much time. Hey! Listen!" They walked past me, and the next time I looked around, I didn't see them. Maybe I was hallucinating. It's hard to be sure when you think you might be hallucinating.

After a while, I stopped walking. I dropped to my knees, groaned a little, and for the sake of thoroughness fell to the ground on my side. I had rarely regretted losing my skill at healing so much. Every inch of my body hurt except for my eyeballs, and they can't hurt, anyway. I kept the writhing under control but let loose with as much groaning as I wanted. I wished I could fly so that no part of me would touch the ground.

At some point, Vargo knelt over me and lay his hand on my forehead. I screamed, and he jumped back.

"Bib, what happened to your clothes?" Evonne asked. "Are you burned?"

I said, "Pil doesn't have much time. I already told you once. Don't you pay attention?"

Hurd rumbled in the distance, "Here! We're here!"

"That rhymes," I muttered.

Kenzie stood over me, staring with cold eyes. This would be the perfect time to kill me.

As she fingered her knife, I said, "Go on and help Pil! Hurry, or she'll die!"

Kenzie drew her knife.

"I'll probably die out here by myself. Hurd said so," I lied. "Just go!"

I watched Kenzie lower one eyebrow. "I don't know."

Evonne drew her knife and stood on the other side of me from Kenzie.

Hurd called out again.

"Go on! You're wasting time!" I croaked.

Kenzie put away her knife and stepped back.

"I will stay beside him," Evonne said.

Jo stood guard while Acton, Kenzie, and Vargo discussed things. Evonne spoke up to comment now and then. I contributed by moaning.

I closed my eyes. When I opened them, Evonne was standing over me with her sword bared. I heard nobody else.

"I'm not making any jokes about putting me out of my misery," I said. Evonne said something and laughed, but I didn't pay attention. That was the last thing I remembered until I woke up in the sunlight. I went right back to sleep.

When I woke up later, it was dark again. I was shivering, but I screamed when Evonne laid her coat over me. She gave me more water instead. I laid awake until the moon rose. I didn't make any jokes, but Evonne later said I talked a lot. I didn't remember anything I said. Sometimes, men I've killed have called out for their mothers. I may have done some of that.

Sometime before dawn, I realized Kenzie was touching my arm. It wasn't painful enough to make me wish I'd be destroyed on the spot. My pain gradually eased, and her breathing turned into panting.

It wasn't until then that I realized Kenzie should be plunging a knife in and out of me. I sure as hell didn't want to question that she wasn't. "Stop," I grunted. "I bet I can walk now. Somebody else may need you."

"I shan't argue against you," Kenzie said.

"Why did you heal me?"

Kenzie blew out a breath. "Hurd told me how you and Pil saved us all. In that light, it seems rude to kill you today." She sat back, but a moment later Evonne and Acton helped us both stand.

As Kenzie and I stumbled through the canyon, I reached and gripped her hand.

"Oh, hell, not this again!" she said, but she didn't shake off my hand.

I grinned. "No, this is one part of thanking you for not killing me."

"One part? What other thank-you parts do you have for me?"

"First, I will never kill you, even if my deal with Fingit is voided. Second, I will try never to hurt you, but remember I'm a dumb bastard and may hurt you by mistake. Third, I will teach you anything I know. We can talk about what I know and what you want to learn."

We walked on for most of a minute before she said, "That's all? I thought you'd be really grateful, but I guess this is all right." She squeezed my hand and dropped it. "You know, we wouldn't have found Pil if you hadn't been out here bellowing like a very happy moose. You got us close enough for Hurd's shouts to reach us."

The trek back to Pil lasted until after sunrise. On the way, I asked, "Where's Jon? Not that I care too much, but he was a decent ally in a fight."

"Dead," Evonne said in a flat voice.

"Killed by a trap," Acton explained.

"We didn't see it happen," Kenzie said, nodding at Vargo.

Jo stood beside Acton and didn't comment.

"What kind of trap? We might run across one," I said.

"A fire trap," Acton said. "Nasty." I couldn't read his face, especially by starlight. Kenzie glanced at him with drawn eyes and a tight mouth.

I felt no doubt then that Acton had murdered Jon and had probably bribed Jo to leave Jon unguarded.

When we reached Pil, she was laying on the ground with her eyes closed. That didn't surprise me. Healing all Pil's wounds might have crippled Kenzie for a time, or even killed her. Pil would be exhausted too.

Kenzie knelt beside Pil and touched her chest. "I don't know why she was alive! She shouldn't have been."

"She'd be dead but for a deal with Baby Harik."

Acton walked past and assessed Pil, Kenzie, and me as if determining how much we weighed. I figured he must have traded something important away to the gods since I last saw him. That was the greatest danger to a sorcerer: giving away so much you become something different. Acton had been a sharp young man before. Now he was like a razor.

I lay beside Pil until midday, when she woke up and said, "Bib! Where did you come from? I thought you must be dead by now. It's been such a long time since I saw you. Years upon years." She sighed, and her eyes wandered. "Help me find my . . . something, I don't know. It was here . . . am I lying on it?" She reached to feel under her legs while her eyes shifted as if something she couldn't hear was following her.

When somebody's memories are taken away, they often feel

they've lost something but don't know what. The feeling passes after a couple of days. I said, "Get some rest, Pil. We can look for it when you feel better."

Pil nodded but kept looking around. "Where have you been, Bib? What trouble have you gotten into?" She hesitated when she spoke, something I had never heard Pil do before. "You look well. Did you get married again?"

I nodded. "Sure, you know me. I've been breaking things and pissing people off."

She laughed. "I've been—" Her whole body seized, and the blood drained from her face.

"Kenzie!" I shouted.

Pil said, "No! Leave her alone, she's worked hard enough." She lowered her voice. "I just remembered . . . Bib, I went back to the Dark Lands. It was, well . . . I don't know how to tell you what it was. It was horrible. I wanted to leave, but I couldn't. I don't know why I couldn't. Say, look behind you for my . . . oh, you'll recognize it probably. Just check."

She looked so confused I went ahead and checked behind me. "Nothing here."

"Maybe by my feet." Pil lifted her head and saw the tree. She jerked her eyes away and started panting.

I touched her shoulder. "It's all right—that thing's dead."

She shook me off and rolled to face away from me. For the rest of the day, she didn't answer me when I spoke.

FORTY-SIX

After Kenzie saved Pil, we all required three days of intense rest and dawdling preparation before we set out for Ebring. Acton, Jo, and Vargo scavenged for supplies. Pil enjoyed the company of her family, whom she had feared were dead. Once Kenzie tended my wounds, I watched for stragglers from Lossil's army and sent them on their way. None appeared eager to fight, anyhow.

I also watched for Red, Praxsis, and Chexis, but they never appeared.

The day after I killed One, Lossil's shaggy brown dog came trotting down the canyon and stopped near us, growling. Kenzie walked out to make friends with it since she was a Caller and able to charm animals. Lossil's dog must have been uncharmable, and Kenzie barely escaped being mauled.

The dog would have presented no problem if it had continued down the canyon and left us alone. Instead, it lay in the intersection watching us, barking, and threatening anybody who came close.

Evonne and Vargo took responsibility for dealing with "Lossil's damn dog." After the creature chased Vargo for a quarter of a mile, their favored solution involved swords and spears.

Before the animal was condemned, I said, "Acton, why don't you try?"

"I don't like dogs," he said.

"How can you not like dogs? It's unnatural," Vargo said.

Acton shrugged.

I said, "Go ahead and try, Acton."

Acton sighed, drew his sword of green fire, and approached Lossil's dog. The dog stood, stretched, and padded over to Acton. Then it sat on the road in front of him. Acton glanced at me.

"Go on, make friends!" I yelled.

Five minutes later, Acton was sitting on the ground with the dog, who was wagging its tail and making a life's work out of licking Acton's face. There were some tight sphincters when Acton brought his dog over to us, but it didn't tear out any throats. From then on, it walked, sat, and slept beside Acton while watching everybody else with great suspicion.

Acton asked me, "Bib, how did you know?"

I shrugged. "Sorcery. Not really. I knew Lossil tolerably well, and I know you. I guessed that a dog that loved Lossil might love you too. That's not an insult. Lossil was our enemy, but he had a great number of fine qualities."

Once we started the journey to Ebring, we walked for over three weeks to reach the city. The distance wasn't that great, but the terrain was challenging. Much of the road traversed canyons, hills, and mountainous foothills. Pil's family included small children, so we traveled gently to keep us all safe and moving forward.

The remains of Lossil's army couldn't go back to their own realms, so I supposed they scattered across the island. After the first week on the road, we no longer met any of them.

Pil and I rarely spoke. She had her entire family to chat with. Apart from us both being sorcerers, we had little to speak about. When good friends have been apart ten or fifteen years, their friendship can seem a distant thing. Pil and I had been close friends when she was young, but now in her mind, she hadn't seen me for seventy years. I was far less familiar to her than Kenzie, who had saved her life within the past week.

Harik had been exaggerating when he claimed he was killing Pil without killing her, but he had spoken a certain kind of truth. The person I lived with for so long had gone, but I remembered everything about our life.

I noticed that now Pil seemed less sharp and carefree than before she lost those memories. She even seemed less happy now than she had been in the awful Dark Lands, although that might have been my resentful imagination.

When Pil and I had been together in the Dark Lands, things sometimes didn't seem real until I told her about them. Now my life sometimes felt unreal, the way it had when I thought she had drowned.

The king's court and many of his surviving subjects had returned to Ebring, even though nearly half of it had burned. King Elgus had caught a chill in the swamp and then died, so now Princess Bannice had become Queen Bannice.

Nobody in Ebring knew quite what had happened to the invaders. The enemy had just fled one day and not returned. We arrived to tell the story. Acton ended up telling most of it, and he did not lie, but he slanted the tale to his advantage. Within a week of arriving at Ebring, Acton and his bodyguard, Jo, could often be seen in the queen's company.

Our rewards included clothing, weapons, nice horses, and purses of gold that didn't weigh too much. Pil and her family returned to their home in Sandell, and she said goodbye to me politely and even a bit warmly.

I stayed in one of the surviving inns, rode my horse during the harsh, snowy days, and drank more than was wise at night. Frankly, I was a mean bastard and didn't mind thrashing people who I thought needed it.

Winter came to an end and found me considering what I might do next. I had not been offered any titles or secure positions in Her Majesty's kingdom. Vargo had been made a baron, and Kenzie was offered the position of Queen's First Sorcerer. Acton had no titles, but everybody assumed he would become the next king.

Evonne was given the title Bearer of the Daylight Blade, and she traveled the kingdom to find the queen's enemies and deal with them before they became a problem. She also received four extra silver pieces per month.

Even Jo had been awarded the title Bearer of the Stronghold Blade, which came with an extra four silver pieces per month. He didn't even like using a blade and preferred to bash his enemies with his fists.

As for me, there at the cull end of winter, I caught more and more hints that the queen would love me a lot better if I lived elsewhere, such as someplace across the sea.

Evonne shared her opinion about the queen's thinking. "When you face a terrible enemy, you rejoice to have a vicious hound you may set upon them. When the enemy has been killed, the vicious hound must go somewhere, and you may not rejoice as much to find it in your home."

The idea of leaving Ir for a while didn't bother me much. I have always been easier to love from a distance.

Shura found herself unwelcome at court and moved to a small village to work as a seamstress. When I visited her, she laughed and told stories. The monsters had been defeated, and that was the only thing that mattered to her.

Vargo had greater insight than me into the queen's plans, possibly because he gave a damn what she was planning. He found me out riding on the first pretty afternoon of spring. "Bib, I have some horrible news."

"I probably don't care, son. I'll be gone by summer. I know this place is your home, but it has some stiff memories for me."

"Sure, I know. But throw that in the ditch for a minute. Do you know how many of Lossil's soldiers are still on the island?"

I reined in my horse. "More than fifty. Less than a thousand. Which is a way of saying I have no idea."

"I don't either. But the queen has proclaimed they are a lot of cruel, baby-murdering villainous monsters, and she plans to solve that problem right quick with a lot of spears."

I said, "Technically, a lot of them truly are baby-murdering villains. They slaughtered whole villages to pour blood and make those holes or whatever they were." The glowing holes in the ground had disappeared over the winter.

Vargo nodded. "I guess they are. But I think their baby-murdering days have passed. The island won't be any safer if we hunt them down and slaughter them."

I thought about that for a bit. "Here's what I bet is really happening. Bannice has some nobles who hate being ruled by a girl and might do something violent about it. She's sending the army, the nobles, and their troops out on this crusade to save the island while she quietly murders the most annoying nobles. Well, she's thinking like a monarch. Good for her."

"Acton may be giving her advice about all this. I'm not sure, but it sounds like the little turd. Bib, do you want to see dozens or hundreds wiped out for no real reason? Lots of them didn't want to be here, you know."

I grunted. "You sound almost kind and understanding. Has Kenzie changed you that much?"

"Bullshit. Shut your damn mouth," he said, smiling.

"Vargo, thank you for telling me. You can put it out of your thoughts now."

"No, if you're going to do something, I'm going to help."

I shook my head. "Go back to Kenzie. I'd like to hear about your babies one of these days, or maybe even see one."

Vargo slumped a little. "Kenzie says her life may be short, and she has a lot to do besides having babies. I already had children, and I'll settle for being happy I had them, I guess."

I didn't go back to Ebring in case somebody knew that Vargo had talked to me. I rode away that moment, west across the fields. I knew where I would hide if I were Lossil's soldiers.

Two days of hard riding brought me back to the foothills of Ir's tallest mountains. It was another gentle afternoon, and I tied my horse before walking into the uneven, uphill ground. I shouted, "Red! I know something you need to hear!" Then I waited.

I saw her diving at me. Maybe I should have already called the death sword, but I didn't want to fight. She halted fifty feet above me in a crash of wind and sound, and she hovered there, flapping her wings slowly. "Well? What do you have to say, you murderer?"

I almost laughed when she called me murderer, but I swallowed it. She was probably touchy about a man killing any dragon, even the ones she didn't like. "The queen of this island wants to hunt and kill all your surviving soldiers. I want to save them. Will you help me if it costs you almost nothing?"

Red stared at me. "I know why you want to save them. But do you think I want them to live more than I want you to die?"

"I do think that, but it's not the point."

Red paused. Instead of asking me what the point was, she said, "If you had arrived much later, you would not have found us here."

"I won't presume to ask where you're going. I hope it's a good home for you. Say farewell to your sons for me."

Red laughed. "They only saw you for a few days after their birth. They don't remember you."

"That's probably for the best."

"They still sing your horrible songs, though."

I grinned. "You're welcome. What about helping your stranded soldiers?"

Red hovered and didn't answer.

"Not to be obvious, but I did you a favor. You don't see dozens of dragons flying around, creating a land of rules, demands, and self-important, fat-ass dragons, do you? You wanted freedom, and you wanted freedom for your sons."

Red grunted. "You see it."

"I damn well see it. I solved that problem for you. The wicket is gone. Now I want to save your troops, whom you can't save by yourself. I need one small thing from you. It will take you no more than five minutes. Will you listen to what it is?"

Red agreed, and I told her. She brought me the small thing and flew away.

I rode straight to the closest port town and bought a seaworthy boat I could sail by myself.

I had never been a good student, but I managed to learn things now and then. I needed a remote place to bring Lossil's men. The coast of the western kingdoms lay three days to the east of Ir. The Bending Sea was eight days north from there, and the northern kindgoms' far shore lay seven days beyond that.

The common thinking in the west was that the sea beyond the northern kingdoms was empty of land. Various events had led me to doubt that. For example, in the Dark Lands, I had met some people who claimed to hail from that region.

Contrary weather slowed me on my voyage, so I didn't reach the northern kingdoms for nearly four weeks. The farther north I sailed, the warmer the weather became, and I explored the northern ocean for another two weeks.

I at last found a likely island with good water, food, and materials. The place was small, but I doubted that Lossil's survivors numbered more than a few hundred.

After tying up my boat, I hung one of Red's curtains from a tree and stepped through. It put me at the top of the canyon where we had fought our last battle with Lossil.

I shouted, "Hello! This is Bib! I want to talk!" The echo was magnificent. I called out like this every few minutes until some figures arrived on the canyon floor. They didn't answer me, though.

I continued shouting until I saw the feline form of Burrud appear. I yelled, "It's nice to see you're alive! The war is over for us! But others are hunting you! Talk to me!"

Burrud shouted, "Come down, then."

Once I had climbed down to the canyon floor, the reks and difar stayed well back from me. Burrud said, "You are indeed the one from another realm, then."

"Sort of. I was born here, I went there, I came back here, so what does that really mean?"

"Dammit, I knew it from the start. One foresaw that you would either cause problems or ensure victory."

"It's nice to be wanted."

Burrud flicked his tail. "We didn't suspect how big the problems would be."

"The important thing is that the queen has put her mark on you lot," I said. "She intends to see you all dead before the harvest."

"I know. We have been fleeing from them. I doubt that we can run much farther."

"You can't go home, and I'm sorry for that, but you know why we had to strand you here, don't you?"

"Of course, we understand. It was war. Nobody understands better than us."

I nodded. "Because I respect you as adversaries, I want to give you a way out. It would be a shame if you were hunted and killed here." I pointed at the top of the canyon. "I just arrived up there using one of the dragons' curtains, or cloths, or rags, or whatever you call them. Anyway, on the other end is an island with everything you need to live. And there's a boat tied up there so you won't be stranded. Best of all, it's warm, and it should stay warm year-round."

Everybody in earshot stared at me.

"All you have to do is walk through," I said. "Send a couple of men to scout and report back. Hold me hostage until they return. I am not trying to fool you."

Burrud said, "I do not think I can trust you. Why are you doing this?"

I squinted at the sky. "Let's just say that I fought for the people I was born to, but philosophically, I'm one of you. Not one of your masters, but you."

Some of the soldiers around us nodded.

Burrud's whiskers quivered. "If you're trying to atone for something, you'll be disappointed. Helping us won't help you."

"Then it's good that I don't believe in atonement. I've come to believe in just doing things, and this is a thing I want to do."

"Doing things?" Burrud's ears came forward, and he blinked. "Even bad things?"

I smiled. "Sometimes."

Burrud's men required a day to prepare. I was pleased to see that they had brought tools from their realms and could take them to the island. None of them thanked me or spoke to me before they walked through to their new home, and it was right that they didn't.

FORTY-SEVEN

My march back to Ebring went much faster now that Pil's great-grandchildren were at home causing trouble instead of with me throwing rocks and chasing lizards. I had spent most of my coins, so in Ebring, I took a room at the cheapest and nastiest inn the city could offer.

I sent word to Kenzie that although I didn't feel secure going to the palace, she could visit me at the inn if she wanted. She brought Vargo, and we shared a simple dinner that tasted good if you didn't look at the food too hard. They had gotten married and were happy with their lives, at least for the moment. Acton sent his regrets for not coming.

I told them I intended to travel to Sandell, say goodbye to Pil, and then sail to the mainland to raise hell and break hearts. They laughed but looked me over in detail, I guess for signs that I had gone insane.

My departure from Ebring the next day didn't happen until past noon because the night before involved drinking on a heroic scale. My hangover and I walked out of town since I didn't own a horse, and I didn't own much of anything else, either. I carried the fine but non-magical sword Bannice had rewarded me with, a knife, some clothes, a pack with more clothes, and a thin, unloved purse. When sunset came, I moved far off the road to sleep. Although I had left the Dark Lands months ago, sleep still felt like a sinful luxury.

The *whoosh* and *crackle* of flames jabbed me awake. I rolled to the side and came up on my knees before I saw the blade of green flame slash the ground where I had just been lying. The green fire from Acton's sword threw sinister light on both his and Kenzie's faces. Kenzie rushed me and thrust her spear at my throat.

I grabbed the spear with my left hand, yanked, and punched Kenzie on the side of her face. She staggered into Acton's path as he charged me with his sword upraised. I slipped aside to keep her between us, kicked her knee, and shoved her into Acton when she started hopping on one leg and cursing.

Grabbing Kenzie's arm, I threw her to the ground. Acton had recovered and was charging me again. I stepped inside his swing and bashed him with my shoulder. He hit the ground not far from Kenzie. As they lay there, each of them got a punch to the stomach to knock the air out of them, followed by a punch in the jaw.

By the time they dragged themselves to their feet, I was sitting twenty feet away with their weapons on the ground behind me.

Kenzie stepped toward me. "It was our last chance to kill you unless we chase you to the mainland."

"I understand," I said.

Acton stayed back. "Thank you for not killing us, although you did promise Fingit you wouldn't."

"That's true, I did. Sit here with me." Once they had sat, I said, "What did you learn?"

Kenzie said, "Don't try this when you're asleep. Wait until you're drunk."

Acton leaned forward. "Don't use the flaming sword. It gives me away. Use some other weapon."

"Hire some men to help us," Kenzie said.

Acton nodded. "Learn to use the bow so we can kill you from a distance."

Kenzie sat up straight. "Why are you teaching us? We're trying to kill you."

"I'm not teaching you. You're telling me all your ideas so I can be better prepared next time."

Acton laughed. "That's a lesson in itself."

Kenzie laughed too. "I brought some wine. It's in here some-place." She dug in a big bag.

I said, "No, thank you. I don't feel like being poisoned tonight."

Kenzie frowned. "Fine!" She tossed the bag on the grass.

"This may be the last time we ever meet," I said, "but I don't have any advice for you. You're doing well on your own. You two are friends, but you may have to betray each other or kill each other someday." I shrugged. "Gods fight among themselves, and sorcerers get caught in the middle."

Neither of them said anything.

"It's the way of sorcery, so don't pout over it. Let those be my last words to you. Pick up your weapons and go home."

They took their weapons and walked away. Acton looked over his shoulder. "I guess I could have just burned you and your clothes up with no warning from three hundred feet away. For some reason, it never occurs to me to do that when the time has arrived to kill you." He smiled, and they walked away.

I walked on toward Sandell the next morning. Rain held itself heavy in the still spring air, and the season's last wildflowers had just passed their full bloom.

"I can't think of any more destruction you can make happen around here," Hurd said from behind me as I walked.

"What do you mean? I haven't even started setting things afire yet."

Hurd chuckled and caught up to walk beside me. "Maybe I mean there ain't nothing around here worth the two seconds it would take you to destroy it. This place is pudgy and boring now. You might fall asleep while you're fighting and drown on your own spit."

"You know how I hate to be bored. That's why I plan to head to the mainland and drink my way across from west to east."

Hurd chuckled. "That ought to be fun for a day or two, but after that? You need some challenge and violence in your life. You could go back to the Dark Lands."

I stopped and closed my eyes.

"Just listen! Since you left, things ain't gone as smoothly as some figured they would."

I smiled at him. "Tell me. Describe every screwed-up thing they tried."

"With you gone, nobody needed to come and kill you anymore. All the immortals took their oaths again to stay out of the Dark Lands and to keep everybody else out. That very same week, hundreds of demigods and Void Walkers showed up hunting for magic weapons, the skulls of their ancestors, and so on."

I said, "Oh, hell, let me guess. Within another week, there were skirmishes. Then both sides sent forces in to punish the other. The first major battle happened when? Within the first month? Less?"

"Close enough," Hurd said. "I ain't been given leave to share details, but soon immortals on both sides were being killed. Guarding the Dark Lands didn't seem quite such a foolish idea anymore."

"Who did they find to guard it?"

"First off, they assigned a few heroes, ten from each side, to protect the place. The heroism got a little out of hand, and soon they had one thousand warriors from each side. And neither heroes nor warriors have the word *guardian* anyplace in their names. That all led to the biggest battle yet."

I laughed. "Did they look for single guardians, then? Pulled from other realms?"

Hurd nodded. "They've gone through fourteen of those slick dogs. The last one was killed this morning. So, you see, you'd be welcomed back."

"That's an interesting offer. Do you want me to slam my dick in a door too?"

"It wouldn't be like that. You'd get some real rewards," Hurd said. "Magic weapons, creature comforts, a mount so that you wouldn't have to run all the heck over the place."

I walked away.

"Of course, they'd send Pil there with you."

"She doesn't even remember me! That would be nothing but cruel."

"She might start remembering!"

Without turning back, I asked, "Will the gods restore her memories?"

"That's a little complicated. The gods who can do that don't like you too much. Or at all. But Krak has promised to figure out something."

I spun and knocked Hurd to the road, at the same time summoning the Death God's sword. When the weapon was in my hand, I held the point a finger's width away from Hurd's throat. "Don't talk, Hurd. Just be quiet if you can."

Hurd held his top half still, although his legs and feet writhed.

I said, "You worked for Baby Harik this whole damn time, didn't you?"

"Yes," he said.

"For all the pain you helped him cause, I should kill you now."

"No, Pil wouldn't want you to do that."

I sneered. "Pil once promised she would erase you from existence, and I should do it on her behalf."

"I'm not working for Harik anymore!" Hurd's deep, profound voice jerked noticeably higher. "I'm working for Krak now. I bet he'll be mad if you murder me!"

"He's been mad at me before."

"Don't kill me!" Hurd said. "Haven't you had enough death lately?"

"Wait. Aren't you telling me to go back to the Dark Lands where, face it, there's nothing to do but kill?"

Hurd's face darkened, and his eyes shifted side to side. "I just said it as part of my job! I don't have to mean it!"

I sighed. "Maybe I have had enough. I'm going to say goodbye to Pil and then leave this island. Hurd, you should stay away from me for a while." I lifted my sword from his neck, and he faded before disappearing.

I tried to put Hurd out of my mind as I walked on to Sandell.

That afternoon, I found the main Pierce home in the nicer part of the city. They were prosperous and ran several establishments, including the smithy, the chandler's shop, and the brewery.

I knocked on the front door and felt surprised when Pil answered. She furrowed her brow. "Bib. What are you doing here?"

"I came to say goodbye."

"Oh? Well. I hope you have a prosperous trip."

"I plan to drink a great deal. It may take years, so I'm leaving today."

Her eyebrows raised, and she grinned. "Oh? Well, I'll get you started. Would you like some beer?"

"That's very kind. I would."

She turned to go inside, and I stepped in to follow. Without looking back, she said, "Just a minute, I'll bring you a mugful right here."

I stood on the threshold and watched her walk away. I didn't know what I had expected, but this wasn't it.

While Pil fetched my beer, I contemplated an act that would be an excellent way to get myself killed. When she returned and handed me the mug, I touched her hand, reminding myself that if I was killed now, I had sought it out and damn well deserved it.

I lifted myself up to the gods' trading place. "Trutch, I call on you to trade!"

I found myself standing on the sorcerers' patch of dirt, but instead of brown, it was almost gray. Everything looked washed out or leaden. Storm clouds hung in layers. The marble gazebo looked stark and shaded instead of aggressive white. The flowers in the field were closed, showing the flat, silvery backs of the petals, and the forest leaves had flown, leaving cracked, gray trunks.

The wind carried the smells of chalk, ash, and old wood, and it kept changing direction as if it were circling around me.

The Goddess of Life stepped forward from the shadows within the gazebo. She brought luminous color and light with her, the only vibrant thing in sight. Her gown clung to her perfect form and shone the color of the early morning sun. Trutch's soft, tranquil face with poppy-red lips and ocean-blue eyes stared down at me, and I stopped breathing. Her honey-blond hair dangled across one bare shoulder.

Trutch walked toward me with a thrilling sway of her hips and frowned. "Murderer, you are insane to call on me after what you have done."

I still couldn't breathe. I knew that it wasn't possible for me to suffocate here, but I felt a twinge of panic anyway.

Trutch knelt at the edge of the gazebo. I would have argued for hours that I had just seen the most graceful movement made by any being at any time in all existence. I still couldn't breathe.

"You killed my husband, Murderer. Whatever his faults, and they were many, when you killed him, you disparaged me!"

I pointed at my throat.

"Very well."

All at once, I could breathe. "I apologize, Your Magnificence. There is no possible excuse. I do wish to offer a fragment of perspective. I killed Mighty Harik in self-defense."

Trutch stood and glared down at me from what seemed like a height of fifty feet.

I rushed to speak before she killed me. "And at that time, he was betraying all the gods, including you, Mighty Trutch." Then I waited.

Trutch looked into the distance as if she were posing. I almost turned that direction to see what she was looking at. She said, "It is not impossible to understand how you could do something so wicked and perverse. But what made you come here when you must know that I'll obliterate you for all time?"

I nearly asked whether somebody could be obliterated for less than all time, but she might find that distracting. I said, "Your new husband recently removed a significant number of memories from the Knife. I'd like those restored."

Trutch laughed, and it wasn't one of her pretty laughs that makes flowers grow. "You have lost your mind, Murderer. If there is something you want, I have great incentive to prevent you from having it."

"In exchange, Mighty Trutch, I will give you Mighty Harik's sword."

She sighed. "I know that sword is part of a contract between you and the new Harik."

I nodded and dared to look into her eyes. "I have learned a thing from dealing with the gods, Your Magnificence. Contracts and obligations don't mean shit compared to possession. I will sell you my side of the contract with Baby Harik."

A grin flickered on her face when I said "Baby Harik," but she replaced it with the most severe scowl yet.

I pushed on. "All of my rights and responsibilities regarding the sword will become yours. You will take actual possession. And you will have the sword for more than a year and a half before, contractually, it should go to Baby Harik."

"A year and a half?" Trutch's lips turned as if she were biting something sour.

"But once you have possession, I am sure there are deficiencies in the contract that you can contest. In an argument like that, an immensely intelligent god of great experience could crush Baby Harik like a crippled bug and keep the sword for hundreds of years. Or thousands."

Trutch paced two steps deeper into the gazebo and then back toward me. "This is mildly interesting. I would require more than the sword, however. I perceive that you wish to make this bargain in order to regain the Knife's affection. I will require you to leave your homeland this very day and never return. Unless you can convince her to come with you before the sun sets, you shall never see her again."

"It's a wonderful, generous offer, but I think I ought to have a week to convince her." I smiled without thinking.

"In this place, your teeth are unbroken, Murderer."

I couldn't help touching my mouth. She was right.

"The improvement to your beauty is miniscule. A week is ridiculous. You have until the sun sets." She held up a hand before I could answer and then said in a deep, oily voice, "You may strive, however uselessly, until the setting of the sun. Failing that, you shall be plunged into misery without surcease." She gave the tiniest of nods. "That's how Old Harik might have phrased it, don't you think, Murderer?"

"It's a remarkable impersonation, Your Magnificence."

Trutch went on: "It is right that we hear from that tedious, self-aggrandizing walrus on this topic. Do you know why, Murderer?" She offered a smile of pensive but soul-shredding beauty.

All I could manage to do was shake my head.

"Because he was my husband." Trutch clenched both fists. "And you killed him!" Her bellow knocked me on my butt. The bare trees in the forest whipped. Dust drifted from all three gazebo ceilings.

The Goddess of Life smoothed her gown and seated herself as if sitting down were part of a dance. "Do you care to accept my terms, Murderer?"

I glanced down. "Yes, I do, Mighty Trutch."

She smiled and flicked two fingers of her left hand, throwing me back into my body.

I staggered against the doorframe of the Pierce home, dropping the mug of beer.

"What's wrong?" Pil asked, still in the doorway. "Are you trading with the gods? I felt you leave."

I nodded but didn't say anything.

A few seconds later, her eyes snapped open. She went pale, and her jaw sagged.

"Pil, what is it?"

She slapped my face, and she did it pretty dang hard.

"That's all right," I said.

"Oh?" She kicked my shin, and I yelped. "Is that all right too? What did you do? You screwed around with my memories before, and I warned you what would happen if you did it again!" She punched me in the stomach. I stood there and took it. Then her enchanted knife appeared in her hand. I backed away so fast I tripped and fell on the dirt.

I heard people inside the house running toward us.

From the ground, I said, "I made that deal to save your life."

"What a thin excuse! I bet you can do anything to anybody and then claim you were saving their life."

"I've watched you die too many times," I said.

Pil raised her knife and cursed, holding the blade above me. Then she pulled back a leg to kick me, but she dragged her leg to a stop as she roared. She looked up and cursed Krak along with all the other gods and their flying horses too.

At last, Pil plopped onto the ground and sat facing me. Her knife had disappeared. Her shoulders were squared, and her eyes were full of light. "Died too many times? What does that mean? I'm not dead, I'm just . . . what the hell happened, Bib?"

As soon as she asked that question, her eyes squeezed shut. She pushed hard against the sides of her head. "I feel like I'm seeing two of some things and others are gone. Or maybe they never happened. What is this?"

For a moment, Pil looked uncertain, as much as she ever had when she was a girl. She hid that uncertainty fast, though.

Losing memories was tricky, and sometimes getting them back was too. Pil had lost fifty years' worth, and we couldn't expect them to all slide back into place like a dresser drawer.

"Pil, don't stab me for the stupid-sounding thing I'm about to say, because it's a true thing." I cleared my throat. "It's a complicated situation. And the story has dragons, which always complicates things more. There was this ledge—"

"Yes, I remember an awful, cold ledge just a few months ago, but you weren't there. I think I'd have seen you on that tiny ledge that couldn't have hidden a mouse's whisker. And a dragon would have been hard to overlook!"

"Pil, I'm about to ask you something odd."

She nodded but crossed her arms.

"Do you remember offering to stay in the Dark Lands for me?"

Her crossed arms dropped. "I remember that! Why would I do that, I wonder? You said no, didn't you?"

"If you remember offering, that means I must have been in the Dark Lands with you sometime, right?"

She blinked, saying, "Oh, Krak's knobs, Bib! What happened to your teeth?"

It was the first time I had smiled since Pil lost her memories. I stopped doing it right away. "It's not important." Keeping my face calm, I asked, "Do you remember us getting married?"

Pil's mouth dropped open. "You're kidding. Right?" Then she laughed. "I'll admit it. When I was young, I was a bit smitten with you, but it wasn't serious. It's been far too long to think about something like that. Wedding?" Pil shook her head.

I glanced away and wondered what to do. "Do I look about the same age as I was the last time you saw me?"

Pil frowned. "It's hard to say. You're . . . you've been hurt a lot, especially your teeth, but all those scars too. I guess you're about the same."

"People don't age in the Dark Lands, right? So, I haven't aged. I must have spent all this time, all of it, in the Dark Lands."

"Oh, that's crazy! I've been in the Dark Lands for years and years, and I never—" Pil slapped both hands over her mouth. "You were there! Sometimes!" She shouted, "Bib, you did steal some of my memories! Damn you!"

I wanted to say I was innocent, but in truth, it was my fault. I had put her in this spot by dealing with Baby Harik and Trutch. Out of instinct, I said, "Pil, when we first met, you almost died, but I saved you, and for a while, we were bound. Do you remember it?"

"Of course I do!" She grabbed my hand with both of hers but never stopped scowling. Then she squinted at my hand as if it were something strange that came out of the ocean.

"Do you trust me?" I asked.

She hesitated as her scowl fell away. "It's hard to say yes. Bib, you're a horrible liar. I mean you're a liar to a very horrible degree."

I leaned toward her. "I admit that I have lied to you many times."

"Huh. That sounds like something that would put me in a bad mood." She sat up straight. "You must know a lot about me, but you lied about things, so I don't know those things about you. It's not exactly the same, but you know what I mean. I don't like the idea."

I ignored most of that. "Yes, Pil, I know a lot, and I'll help get your memories straight."

She yelled, "You're the one who screwed them up!"

"Who better to fix things? But you need to come with me right now, this minute. We'll sail away from Ir before sunset."

"That's crazy, even for you." Despite what she said, she was still holding my hand.

"If we don't go now, we will never meet again."

Pil quirked her mouth and lowered one eyebrow. "Really? That sounds like a lie. Why should I trust you?"

Pil stared at me with her jaw hard, full of confidence, power, and suspicion, a true sorcerer. She was probably the greatest sorcerer in the world, unless somebody else had fifty years of sorcery experience in a forty-year-old body. When it came to sorcery, she had me beat all to hell.

That didn't answer her question, though, and she was still staring.

"I could say a lot of things that I think are good answers, Pil. We have each saved the other from harm or death. I loved you for—"

Pil rolled her eyes the way she had as a young woman. It was so dramatic you could almost hear it.

"I loved you for most of the time you spent in the Dark Lands. That means a lot to me. But I'll violate my nature and be truthful now. I can't give you a good reason to trust me. I did all I could think of for a lot of years to make you well and happy, but you still left me. I don't know why, so I can't promise I'd do any better tomorrow."

Pil nodded. "That sounds honest. And I guess because you're being honest, you expect me to grab a pair of boots and follow you across the ocean." She dropped my hand. "It won't be that way, Bib, so you go on and sail away from here. I'll come find you when I can stand the idea. I can almost promise it, so have some hope."

"If I go, this is the last time we'll speak. Trutch said it."

"No, I can't believe you. What you're telling me is so unlikely, and it so much gives you precisely what you want, and you stole my memories, you asshole! And stop looking so hopeless!"

I rubbed my face and stood up. She stood but turned away, and I couldn't stop seeing her drowning in that lake, even though I damn well knew it never happened. "Goodbye, Pil. I look this way because I don't have much hope." I made an effort to grin. "I'll try not to be a miserable no-hope bastard, though."

Pil gasped as if a donkey had kicked her in the belly. Spinning around, she whispered, "You said that before, when you were chained to a wall, a wall that belonged to a dragon! There were three dragons!"

I nodded along as words flooded out of her like the Pil I remembered. I hadn't seen her grin this way in years.

Pil grabbed me by both arms. "I remember all of that, everything from the dragon snatching me off my horse and eating the poor thing until we escaped by jumping through that strange cloth —well, really, I walked through, but jumping sounds better!"

I embraced her, but she wiggled away. "And there were dragon babies! Bib, we should make a study of dragons, no one has had this chance for a thousand years, so let's go find them!"

Pil did not need to know that two of the dragons were shriveled up and beyond study, or that the third had probably taken her children away to some unknown place. Pil didn't need to know that she herself had made sure no more dragons would come to this world. She sure as hell didn't need to know that she sounded crazy for dragons in an unhealthy way. None of those things would get her aboard ship with me.

So, I said, "That's a great idea! Let's go right now. Don't wait. Red told me she was leaving the island, so we'll have to go find them on the mainland!" That might not be a lie. Red could be on the mainland as easy as anyplace else. "Grab some money and follow me!"

Astounded members of the Pierce family had gathered between us and the doorway. I grabbed Pil's hand as she jostled through them into the house. If somebody wanted to take her away, they'd have to cut off my arm again.

Pil grabbed a heavy leather purse out of a small chest made of dark wood. An old woman by the fire scowled but went pale when

Pil raised her hand to show her enchanted knife. Pil put the weapon away and grabbed a sword off the wall, then she pulled me by the hand back outside.

As Pil dragged me along, I checked the sky to see how much time we had until sunset. I couldn't see the sun itself through the high clouds, of course. I did see something dip below the clouds. It was probably one of those great seabirds, or maybe a flock of smaller birds. But part of me knew it wasn't any sad, old bird. By now, I damn well recognized a dragon when I saw one.

I snapped my head around. If Pil looked back and saw what I was watching, she might recognize that a dragon was up there and demand we study it right away. I'd never get her off the island.

A few seconds later, Pil shouted "Wait!" and stopped.

I closed my eyes and waited, sure that everything was about to go to hell. "What?"

"We're not going back to those horrible Dark Lands, are we?"

I dared a glance at the sky. The dragon had disappeared, so I smiled at Pil. "No, we won't, and I swear I'm not lying about that."

Pil gripped my hand harder. "Well, that's good, it's fine. I don't want to have kissed Hurd for no reason."

THE END

HOW DID BIB'S ADVENTURES START?

Find out in *Death's Collector:* Book 1 in the Death's Collector series!

A wizard compelled to kill. A slaughter he vowed to prevent. A murderer who pissed off the wrong guy...

Bib the sorcerer hates how much he loves his job. Cursed by the God of Death to collect lives, he focuses his thirst on snuffing out only lowlife losers and contemptible ass-clowns. But when innocents under his protection are brutally murdered, Bib flips the switch on the ultimate revenge spree.

Bent on obliterating the bum responsible, Bib is more than a little miffed when he discovers the shocking truth about his own degenerate nature. But knowing the type of killer he is inside, the reluctant hero won't be stopped until he mows down every evil dude in his path.

Can Bib fight his way to redemption before he loses his soul to bloodlust?

Death's Collector is the first book in the darkly humorous The Death-Cursed Wizard fantasy series. If you like snarky heroes, top-notch magic systems, and epic sword and sorcery, then you'll love Bill McCurry's addictive tale.

Buy *Death's Collector* to flirt with darkness today! On sale at:
    tinyurl.com/2kzbnyjt

Readers are saying:

"Oozing with sarcasm and humor."
    —Quella Reviews

"We loved this book from start to finish."
    —OnePageToAnother

"I just finished Book 1 of *Death's Collector*. I read constantly and usually start skimming within a chapter. I savored every word of your writing. The carefully correct grammar, the deviously dark psychology, the Nobel Prize–winning curses—I cannot thank you enough for capturing my imagination."
    —Jean L. H., direct sale reader

"*Death's Collector*, the intro to the saga of Bib, the death-cursed wizard, leads you gently by the hand into the life of a good man who became obligated to kill people for the god of death. And then it trips you and dumps you into the muck and the blood and the guts and laughs at you. This irreverent book is the memoir of a man who kills people and likes it for beings that he neither loves nor respects, a truth he tells to their powerful faces every time he meets them. But underneath the deadly sardonic exterior is a gold-leafed heart that wouldn't mind loving again if the opportunity presented itself."
    —Ted S., Amazon reader

Death's Collector is on sale at:
tinyurl.com/2kzbnyjt

ABOUT THE AUTHOR

Bill McCurry blends action, humor, and vivid characters in his dark fantasy novels. They are largely about the ridiculousness of being human, but with swords because swords are cool. Before being published, he wrote three novels that sucked like black holes, and he suggests that anyone who wants to write novels should write and finish some bad novels first. You learn a lot.

Bill was born in Fort Worth, Texas, where the West begins, the stockyards stink, and the old money families run everything. He later moved to Dallas, where Democrats can get elected, Tom Landry is still loved, and the fourth leading cause of death is starvation while sitting on LBJ Freeway.

Although Dallas is a city that smells like credit cards and despair, Bill and his wife still live there with their five cats. He maintains that the maximum number of cats should actually be three, because if you have four, then one of them can always get behind you.

CONNECT WITH THE AUTHOR

Bill-McCurry.com
Facebook.com/Bill.McCurry3
Twitter.com/BillMcCurry
Instagram.com/bfmccurry

Sign Up for Bill's Newsletter!

Keep up to date on new books and on exclusive offers. No spam!

https://www.bmccurrybooks.com/contact-us-2/

PLEASE LEAVE A REVIEW

Please leave a review on the platform of your choice!
https://linktr.ee/reviewdragonsman